HOTEL
Las Flores

HOTEL
Las Flores

KATE McCABE

POOLBEG

Published 2005
by Poolbeg Press Ltd.
123 Grange Hill, Baldoyle,
Dublin 13, Ireland
Email: poolbeg@poolbeg.com

1 3 5 7 9 10 8 6 4 2

A catalogue record for this book is available from the British Library.

ISBN 1-84223-219-3

Typeset by Patricia Hope in Bembo 11.3/14
Printed by Cox & Wyman, Reading, Berkshire.

www.poolbeg.com

About the Author

Kate McCabe lives in Howth, Co Dublin where she enjoys walking along the beach. Her hobbies include travel, cooking, reading and dreaming up plots for her stories. This is her first novel.

Acknowledgements

I would like to thank the staff at Poolbeg Press particularly Paula Campbell and my editor Gaye Shortland. I would also like to thank Helen Carey, Anna Doherty, Anne Marie Brennan and the staff at the Centre Culturel Irlandais in Paris where part of this novel was written.

For Maura, Caroline, Gavin and Marc
In grateful thanks for all your help

Chapter 1

Any girl who has ever been dumped by a man would have sympathised at once with Trish Blake. Just this morning, her lover of ten months, Henry Doran, had rung to tell her he was ending the relationship. The phrase he used was "announce closure" which was typical of Henry Doran who rarely spoke English when he could use jargon he had picked up on a training course somewhere. It was all part of his carefully cultivated image: the flash suits, the casually slicked-back hair, the Armani aftershave, the briefcase, the Diners cards, the arrogant self-confidence and the spouting of sales talk on every available occasion.

Being dumped by Henry Doran wasn't entirely unexpected and it wasn't the worst thing that had ever happened to Trish. Which doesn't mean it wasn't painful and didn't dent her morale. He had called her at exactly two minutes to twelve, knowing she had her weekly sales conference at noon. He began by telling her how much he appreciated the relationship, that the sex was wonderful, that he would never forget her as long as he lived but sadly his wife was getting suspicious and, well, he had the kids to think about and anyway hadn't they both agreed at the outset that it was only a fling?

Trish listened with sinking heart as he galloped to the inevitable conclusion. She realised with dismay that she was hurt by the brutality and coldness of the conversation. What a way to end a relationship! He hadn't even the decency to buy her a nice dinner and tell her to her face. Why hadn't he been really brave and broken it off by text message? A rubber duck would have shown more backbone.

But she hadn't interrupted or argued. She had read somewhere that the best course in these situations is to let the other person sweat. And she had experienced a certain sadistic pleasure in imagining Henry Doran perspire as he wriggled and twisted and finally slithered away like the miserable worm that he was.

'Good riddance to bad rubbish,' she muttered under her breath as she grabbed her files and rushed off to her meeting, feeling downcast and flustered and a good ten minutes late.

Why hadn't she told him about the other news she had received this morning? That she was pregnant? She hadn't told him because she knew in her heart that it wouldn't have mattered. If anything, it would have made him panic and run even faster. She was going to have to deal with the baby problem on her own. She would have to devise some explanation. And this was going to present a major problem. For Trish hadn't slept with her husband for almost a year.

She recalled the thrill she felt at the first hint that she might be pregnant. She was thirty-seven years old and had recently become aware that time was running out. She had been married for fifteen years and, despite irregular hurried sessions of mechanical sex with her husband Adrian, nothing had happened. Not even a late period. Indeed, she had been on the verge of asking Adrian to go for a sperm test when she bumped into Henry Doran.

Henry was a rep for a computer company that did business with the auctioneering firm where she worked. They met at a lunch after a sales deal, in a smart restaurant in Temple Bar where the portions would have left a gerbil feeling hungry but everybody raved about the decor. He was seated next to her, dominating the company with talk of his sales conquests while the wine waiter kept pouring the chilled Chardonnay.

He was tall, with broad shoulders and smouldering brown eyes and a cute dimple in the centre of his chin. Mid-thirties, Trish calculated. For some reason, her eyes were drawn to the gold wedding band on the third finger of his left hand. She knew it instinctively. It was like the Law of Gravity. Good-looking men like Henry Doran were *always* married.

By half past three everybody had drifted back to work and only Trish and Henry remained. He poured the last of the wine and they tipped glasses together in a toast.

"Nice lunch," Henry said, stretching his long legs and loosening his tie. "Been here before?"

"Once or twice," Trish confessed. She didn't want to tell him that she hated the place with its snooty waiters and overpriced menu and dainty portions that made you want to grab a hamburger on the way home.

"Well, my boss will be happy. That's the second contract this week."

"I take it you work on commission," Trish said.

"Oh, it's not just about commission," Henry said dismissively. "It's reputation. When word gets around that I'm shifting product, the competition will set the hunters on me."

"Hunters?" Trish asked, thinking maybe he meant bloodhounds.

"Yes. The head-hunters. They'll be lining up to offer me jobs. That's what business is all about, nowadays. Reputation."

"I see," Trish said.

Henry grinned like a happy schoolboy and drained his glass. "Aren't you going back to work?"

Trish looked at her watch. She was feeling happy after all the wine. "Not much point now. I'll catch up in the morning."

Henry's eyes twinkled. "So how about cutting this place and getting a proper drink somewhere?" He leaned closer and smiled seductively. "Just you and me."

Why not? Trish thought. He's better company than waits for me at home. A lonely night watching TV soaps while Adrian remains locked in his study revising his bloody novel that has already been rejected by twenty publishers.

"Okay," she said. "Where will we go?"

They went to the Octagon Bar in the Clarence Hotel where Henry Doran ordered vodka and tonics.

"You're a very attractive woman," he said after the waiter had delivered their drinks.

"Thank you. You're not bad-looking yourself."

"Well, I try to keep trim," Henry said, taking the compliment in his stride. "I pump iron. Hit the bricks a couple of times a week. I used to play rugby, you know."

"Really?" Trish said, pretending to be interested.

"Old Belvedere. Friends say I could have made the national squad. But I was just too busy with other things."

"That's life for you," Trish said, realising how inane she sounded.

She swallowed a mouthful of vodka and felt it warm her stomach. Now that she knew what was going to happen, she felt amazingly relaxed. She just wished he would make his move quickly so that she could get home in time to make supper for Adrian.

"What does your husband do?" Henry inquired.

"He's a teacher. But he really wants to be a writer. He's working on a novel."

"That sounds very interesting."

"He hasn't got a publisher yet. What about you? What does your wife do?"

Henry suddenly lowered his eyes and looked grave. "She's dying. The Big C."

Trish almost spilt her drink. She felt her heart jolt. Surely he wasn't serious? "That's terrible. Poor woman. Is there nothing can be done?"

"Afraid not. She's seen all the top specialists. They say her case is hopeless. It's only a matter of time."

"And do you have children?"

"A boy and a girl."

"That's awful. I didn't realise."

"It is hard," Henry conceded. "We have absolutely no sex life." He turned his smouldering eyes on her. "Which is why you'd be doing me a major favour if you came to bed with me. You could look on it as an act of mercy."

They took a room in the hotel. Henry paid by credit card and ordered a bottle of Veuve Clicquot to be sent up with Room Service.

Trish had a shower and, when she emerged from the bathroom, Henry had stripped down to his Hugo Boss underpants. Her first impressions had been correct. He had a beautiful body: strong muscles, hard stomach, tight ass. And hair! My God, it was everywhere. It covered his arms and legs and curled like barbed wire along his chest. Trish felt her knees go weak at the sight.

He handed her a glass of champagne, then bent his handsome face and whispered, "You don't know what this means to me."

Trish felt a delicious shiver run along her spine as he wrapped his manly arms around her and led her to the bed.

The sex was marvellous. Henry was a practised lover. There was none of the mad urgency she had expected. Instead, he was careful and patient. He took his time. And the stamina! When he got going, Henry performed like a racehorse. At last, when they had finished and lay side by side in the twisted sheets, Trish felt a lovely warm glow envelop her whole body.

Henry ran a wet finger along her breast and gently squeezed a brown nipple. "Thank you," he said. "You were marvellous. You just absolutely light up my dials."

What the hell is he talking about? Trish thought and closed her eyes.

He called her at work a week later and asked her to go for a drink. Trish had been expecting this and every morning she had packed fresh underwear in her bag for just such an eventuality. They met in a little pub off Grafton Street.

Henry presented her with a single red rose and kissed her softly on the cheek.

"I've missed you terribly," he said. "I've been thinking about you all the time."

"I've thought about you too," Trish said. She wondered if she should ask about his dying wife but decided against it. It would only break the mood.

Henry ordered the drinks and casually took her hand and placed it on his crotch. Frantically, she pulled away.

"For God's sake," she hissed, "not here in full public view!"

But it had excited her. She could feel the blood pounding in her brain.

"I want you so much, I could eat you," Henry said.

"Can't you at least let me finish my drink?" She gulped at her glass.

This time, he took her to an apartment at Charlotte Quay which belonged to a friend. There were stunning views across Dublin Bay and in the distance they could see the green nose of Howth Head shining in the evening sun. Henry suggested they have a bath together.

Trish thought it a wonderful idea. He ran the taps and they got in, sipping vodkas while the room filled up with steam. Afterwards, he got her to put on some black stockings and a little white basque he had bought. Trish found it terribly exciting. She thought of the dull sex she had with Adrian and wondered if she had married the wrong man.

The relationship developed into an affair. Each morning when she logged on at work, an e-mail awaited her. Sometimes they were witty, other times passionate. Frequently, they were downright obscene and she hurriedly deleted them. He phoned every day. They had lunch together in quiet out-of-the-way bistros. They went shopping. They went to the cinema, driving over to the north-side where no one would recognise them.

And, once a week, they went to the apartment at Charlotte Quay and made wild, sensuous love. Trish couldn't believe what was happening to her. She felt rejuvenated. She giggled like a giddy schoolgirl. She blushed whenever his name came up in conversation. She woke every morning as if she was seeing the world with fresh eyes for the very first time.

Even Adrian, engrossed in his novel, noticed the change in her. One morning as they had breakfast together in the kitchen of their terraced house in Sandymount, he stared across the table and said: "My God, Trish. You look resplendent. What's come over you?"

She smiled intriguingly and said: "I've just realised how lucky I am."

And then they heard the thud in the hallway as the

postman delivered the mail. Adrian came back carrying a battered jiffy-bag and a face like a gravedigger's shovel.

"Bad news, darling?"

Adrian sat down mournfully and poured a cup of tea. "They've rejected it again. They say the dialogue's all wrong."

And the moment of intimacy – or potential intimacy – passed.

Love was the one word that was never mentioned between Trish and her new lover. Early on, Henry had said to her: "You know I can never leave Louise? Not with the condition she's in."

"Of course," Trish laughed, light-heartedly.

"It wouldn't be fair. Not with all she's going through."

"No. It wouldn't."

"There's no reason why two people can't simply enjoy each other's company and give each other mutual pleasure from time to time. We're sophisticated people. And this is the 21st century, for God's sake."

"That's right."

Her acquiescence seemed to cheer him up. He cuddled close. "I'm so sorry we didn't meet sooner. You're ideal for me. Did I tell you I sold another package today? That's six this month so far."

His remark got her thinking. What would have happened if she had met Henry Doran instead of Adrian? Would they have married? Would they have had children? She longed for a child. And, as she approached the Big Four O, as Henry called it, she felt a little ball of fear tighten in her chest.

Because she had no children, people assumed she was too busy with her career. But it wasn't true. She desperately wanted a baby. Once she had even written under an assumed name to an agony aunt in one of the Sunday papers asking for advice. The agony aunt replied that thirty-seven wasn't too old to have a child. Lots of women were doing it. She gave the address of a pregnancy clinic. Trish went and had a series of tests. The doctor told her she was perfectly fertile and there was no reason why she shouldn't get pregnant. Which meant the problem had to lie with Adrian. She thought sadly of her husband. What was happening to him? Why had the dashing man she had married turned into a bad-tempered middle-aged recluse whose only interest in life was his bloody novel?

They had met twenty years before in college where Adrian had been auditor of the Debating Society. He had looked so handsome in his flared trousers and Zapata moustache that he swept her completely off her feet and when they graduated she couldn't wait to get married. Adrian got a job teaching English in St Ignatius's Comprehensive College. He explained to friends that it was only a temporary measure till he decided what he *really* wanted to do. She found a position as a trainee agent with a major auctioneering company.

In the beginning, everything was bliss. There was the excitement of the new house with its distant views of the sea from the bathroom window and the gay round of dinner parties with other young married couples from college. They had enough money for a foreign holiday every year and a car which Adrian quickly commandeered, leaving Trish to get the bus into her job at the auctioneering firm.

But she soon discovered that the glamour of the debating hall had cloaked Adrian's innate dullness. He had no style or dress sense. He took to dressing in baggy corduroy trousers and check shirts. He wore hush puppies and polka-dot cravats. She had to tell him when to get his hair cut. Worse, he was awful in bed. He had absolutely no imagination and the sex was often over before she was even aware it had begun. She endured him but got no pleasure. Adrian seemed to regard sex as just another bedtime chore like putting the cat out and locking the doors securely.

And school quickly got him down. He would sit at the kitchen table marking essays and groaning loudly as he scored and scratched with his red biro.

"Can't spell. Wouldn't know an iambic pentameter if it stood up and bit them. Why am I wasting my time like this?"

Trish would attempt to soothe him. "We all have difficult moments at work, darling."

"Moments? Who said anything about moments? This is all the bloody time! From when I arrive in the morning till the last bell goes at four o'clock. It can't be done. How can I instil an appreciation of English Literature into a bunch of gurriers who think Lord Byron is the guy who runs the rock concerts at Slane Castle?"

The idea of writing had come about by accident although Adrian later claimed it had always been a lifetime ambition. A famous American novelist called Sheldon O'Neill had arrived in Dublin to research a book and track down his ancestral roots. Trish was given the task of finding suitable accommodation for the great man while he stayed in Ireland. She eventually discovered a renovated farmhouse in County Wicklow with views over Glendalough. Sheldon O'Neill was delighted. As a reward, he invited Trish and Adrian to dinner at Patrick Guilbaud's restaurant in Merrion Street to celebrate.

Here, while they dined on lobster and wild salmon, Sheldon O'Neill regaled them with stories of the wonderful life of an internationally renowned writer – the interviews, the travel, the publishers' lunches. And of course, the money. Adrian's eyes stood out on stalks.

He joined a writers' group. They met once a week in a pub in Ranelagh. Each participant had to prepare a piece of work and then the others would read it and give their comments. It was like a refuge for battered wives. Everybody was eager to support everybody else. Adrian would come home afterwards beaming with pleasure.

"I read them my short story tonight. Must say it went down a treat. Reggie Arbuthnot said it reminded him of early Hemingway. Same sort of rugged, descriptive prose."

Trish encouraged him. It gave him something to look forward to and took his mind off school. He spent more and more time in the spare bedroom which he had fitted up as a study. He bought a word processor and installed a desk and easy chair and a jam-pot filled with sharpened pencils. Most evenings, he sat in there happily typing his short stories.

Then he decided he was going to write a novel.

He announced it solemnly one Saturday evening after dinner when he had poured himself a large glass of brandy.

"Of course, it's a massive undertaking. I envisage something on the scale of Dickens. Or Pasternak. A groundbreaking work that will shatter the cosy consensus of modern Irish writing. We're looking at a big book here, Trish. Two hundred thousand words. I've even got the title. I'm calling it *The Green Gannet*."

It didn't sound like a very good title to Trish. "What will it be about?"

"The Famine."

She felt her heart sink. There had been so many books about the Famine.

"Are you sure? It's such a painful period in Irish history. It would require a really sensitive approach."

He raised an eyebrow. "Are you suggesting that I can't write sensitive prose?"

11

"Not at all," Trish rushed to mollify him. "It's just such a big task you're taking on."

"I'm ready for that. That's where the challenge lies."

"And it *has* been done before."

Adrian had a gleam in his eye as he swirled the brandy in his glass. "Not the way I plan to do it. I'm going to deconstruct the myths. It will be narrated through the eyes of a 160-year-old man who has lived through the events and is discovered alive in a bog in Connemara. He will report on the Famine at first hand. This novel is going to cause a sensation. Irish writing will never be the same after it hits the bookshops."

He was so clearly carried away with the idea that Trish hadn't got the heart to argue.

"And don't you see? This is my ticket out of that goddamned school. When *The Green Gannet* is published to world acclaim, I will never again have to stand in front of that mob of ungrateful gobshites and explain that *The Ancient Mariner* is *not* a pub in Ringsend."

He set about it with gusto. He drew up a draft outline of the novel and sent it off to Sheldon O'Neill for his comments. Mr O'Neill duly replied. He said the idea struck him as sound and he thought it had potential. But he gave Adrian an important piece of advice. "*Take it slowly. This is an ambitious novel in its scope and theme. There is no necessity to rush.*"

It was exactly the encouragement Adrian required. He went out and bought several large boxes of paper and each night and every weekend he barricaded himself into his study and Trish could hear the sound of the keyboard tap-tap-tapping away inside.

Adrian read the early chapters to the writers' group and their response was overwhelming. One member compared it to Dostoevsky. Another said it had echoes of Proust.

"They're going to give me a big head, if I'm not careful," Adrian laughed modestly over breakfast the next day. "These are only early drafts. They require revision. But they all like it and that suggests that I'm certainly on the right track."

He worked like a maniac through the winter and into the summer. After fourteen months, the novel was completed. The word counter on Adrian's computer showed it came to 333,872 words. He wore out three ink cartridges printing it and spent a fortune having copies made and bound at a stationer's shop in Nassau Street. Then he started looking for a literary agent to represent him.

"That's the way it works nowadays," he said knowledgebly. "No serious publisher will even look at your work unless it's been submitted by an agent."

He bought a copy of *The Writers & Artists Yearbook* which contained a list of all the agents in the UK and Ireland.

"Should I go for a big agency or a smaller, more personal one?" he asked Trish.

"I know absolutely nothing about it," she confessed.

"A big agency carries more clout but then a smaller firm would be able to give me more personal attention."

He fretted about it for a week and in the end selected the first agency in the book. It had an address in London. He carefully packaged the manuscript and enclosed a covering letter.

It cost €20 for postage. Adrian waited confidently for the response he knew would launch his literary career.

Nothing happened. After six weeks, he could contain himself no longer. He got on the phone to inquire if the package had arrived safely. A secretary informed him that they had indeed received Adrian's work but they had a policy of not accepting unsolicited manuscripts and if he wanted it returned would he please send them a cheque to cover postage. Adrian was outraged.

He tried another agency. This time, he sent an advance letter explaining who he was and giving a brief synopsis of *The Green Gannet.* He got a reply saying they were very sorry but they were oversubscribed and were not taking on any new clients. Adrian opened a bottle of Beaune that they had been saving for a dinner party and proceeded to get drunk.

A few days later, he picked himself up and started again. This time, he chose a small agency. He calculated that they would have fewer clients and would therefore be eager to sign him up. From the description in *The Writers & Artists Yearbook,* it seemed to Trish that it was a one-man band working out of a backroom. But they replied, asking to see the work. Adrian was overjoyed. He packaged it neatly and enclosed what he considered to be a witty covering letter. Then he settled down to wait.

A month went by and there was no response. Adrian grew impatient. He consoled himself with the thought that the novel was probably being considered by the board of the agency who were devising a strategy for placing it with a major publisher. But when the time stretched into two months, he decided to ring. A man with a superior accent left him hanging on while he went away to make inquiries.

He came back after five minutes and said that the manuscript seemed to have gone astray and would Adrian mind awfully submitting it again.

Adrian groaned and sank into a deep depression.

His behaviour grew increasingly bizarre. Some nights he would sit up till the early hours working on his manuscript. There were mornings when he was late for school or went into work unshaven and unwashed.

He decided to dispense with the service of an agent altogether and deal directly with the publishers.

"Why give these buggers 15 per cent of my money?" he said haughtily. "I'm the one doing all the work."

The manuscripts went off in large jiffy bags and came back regularly unopened. Various publishers read the novel and rejected it. Sometimes they offered advice. More often they didn't even bother to do that. Adrian grew obsessive. Each rejection letter sent him into a fury.

"Just wait till *The Green Gannet* is published to rave reviews. Wait till I win the Booker! There'll be blood all over the carpets when the directors discover that these bastards have rejected my novel without even reading it. Oh, they'll be a sorry bunch then!"

His confidence, once adamantine, began to crack. He took to revising and rewriting, hacking out whole chapters and then changing his mind and inserting them again. He stopped going out to visit their friends. He ate his meals at odd hours and left Trish to dine alone in the kitchen. Finally, he moved a camp bed into his study and forsook the marital bedroom altogether.

Trish watched helplessly. She didn't know what to do or who to turn to for advice. She still maintained a strong affection for the man she had married when she was twenty-two. But he had changed beyond all recognition. She busied herself with her work. And she sought solace in occasional affairs.

It was in this mood that she had fallen in with Henry Doran and now he had thrown her over. No point fretting about it, she decided. It was bound to come to an end sooner or later. At least she had achieved something she had longed for. She was pregnant! There was no doubt about it. She had bought herself a pregnancy-testing kit and the positive result had sent her rushing off to her doctor who confirmed it. She was six weeks pregnant.

Trish wanted this baby. She wanted it more than anything else in the world. But how was she going to explain it to Adrian? He was crazy already. If she told him the truth, it would probably send him over the edge completely.

She had a hurried lunch in a sandwich bar while she pondered her options. Could she seduce Adrian into bed and then pass the child off as his? It would be difficult but not impossible. But it couldn't be done while he remained at home, obsessed with his damned novel. And then the solution came to her like a flash of blinding light. She gave a little squeal of delight and then quickly suppressed it when the couple at the next table turned round and stared.

She quickly finished her meal, collected her bag and headed out to the street. Five minutes later she was in a travel agency.

"I'd like to book a holiday," she said to the eager young woman behind the desk. "For two people."

"When would you prefer to travel, madam?"

"Next week," Trish said.

Adrian's school was breaking up for the Easter holidays on Friday. The timing was ideal.

But the woman didn't appear too encouraging. "You've left it rather late."

"You must have something," Trish said, desperately. "I don't mind where it is."

The woman scrolled through the computer for a few minutes and then seemed to brighten up.

"I've just the place. Tenerife. The weather will be ideal at this time of year."

"I'll take it," Trish said quickly, in case the woman changed her mind.

"It's a one-bedroom self-catering apartment."

"Single or double beds?"

The woman checked the computer again. "Double. Is that all right?"

"Perfect," Trish said. "What's it called?"

"Hotel Las Flores," the young woman replied. "The Flowers Hotel."

Chapter 2

Mollie McGinty was a firm believer in Fate. She watched for signs, she read tea-leaves, she consulted palmists. Every time she visited Dublin, she went to see a woman in Moore Street who read the tarot cards. Her name was Madam Zora and she told Mollie lots of wonderful things like how the weather was going to change and who was going to win the elections and even the sex of a neighbour's child before it was born. Mollie trusted in these portents because she believed in a divine plan. She was convinced that somewhere in the vast Universe, God kept a book and in it was written down all the things that would ever happen to each single person in the whole of their lifetime. Which was why, when she won the National Lottery, she didn't even blink an eyelid. For just the day before in the *Dunmuckridge Clarion*, Mollie's horoscope had plainly stated: *Your financial situation is about to improve.*

Mollie sat in her favourite armchair in front of the television as she did every Saturday night after dinner. It was the highlight of her week. Her husband, Ned, dozed in a chair beside her.

Mollie ticked off the lottery numbers, one by one, as they came out of the big coloured drum. When she had finished, she checked her ticket again against the list that flashed along the bottom of the television screen. Then she shook her husband awake.

He sat up and blinked.

"What is it?"

"We've got a full house," Mollie said, calmly.

It was Fate that had brought Mollie and Ned together thirty years before, when she was sixteen and he was twenty-three. Her parents farmed a couple of acres of boggy land in the hills above the town and Mollie was their only child. It was hard work, tilling the land and planting the crops and tending the cattle. There were so many jobs to be done that Mollie was glad to escape from the drudgery of the farm to the warmth of the schoolroom in Dunmuckridge, even though the town girls sneered at her because her stockings were darned and her clothes were shabby and she didn't get nice birthday presents like they did.

But Mollie didn't mind because she knew she was clever. She was far cleverer than all the town girls put together. Whenever the teacher, Miss Sweeney, asked the class a question, Mollie's hand was the first to shoot up with the answer. Knowledge just seemed to come naturally to her. She had only to hear a thing once to remember it.

Miss Sweeney used to tell her that she should go on to secondary school and get a good job; maybe become a nurse or a teacher like herself. Mollie would have liked that. She would have loved to teach children. But she knew it would never happen. Her father didn't have the money to send her to secondary school. And anyway, she was needed around the farm.

She liked it best at the end of the day, when Miss Sweeney took down the big Bible and read stories to the class. She loved to hear how God had looked after the Israelites, sending plagues to the Pharaoh and having Moses strike water from the rock. She loved the story of little Moses in the bulrushes. It was listening to Miss Sweeney reading the Bible that convinced Mollie that nothing ever happened by chance. God had a plan and everything was preordained. It was the only way to make sense of her life.

Eventually, when she was fourteen, she left school for good. She was sad to leave. She had been happy there, despite the taunts and jealousy of the town girls. But Mollie didn't complain. She knew this was the way it was meant to be. She had her health and her family and she could read and write and do arithmetic. What was there to complain about?

She helped her father with the planting and the milking. She cleaned out the byre and fed the cattle. She helped her mother with the household chores: cooking and cleaning and washing. It was a battle to make ends meet and Mollie feared to think what would happen when eventually her parents grew too old to work. But she knew that something would turn up. And she was right. One day, she went into Dunmuckridge Fair and met Ned McGinty.

The fair was held on the first Monday in May and farmers came from all over the county to trade livestock. Mollie's mother always insisted that she accompany her father because he had a tendency to go into Murphy's public house when the fair was over and spend his hard-earned money drinking porter with his friends.

It was a sunny day and the hedgerows were ablaze with

colour and there was a clean, fresh smell from the fields. Her father had a bullock to trade and they had eggs and butter to sell and scones and cakes that her mother had baked.

When they got to the town square, Mollie's father unyoked the bullock while she began to set out their wares. He was a frisky animal and the journey into town, tethered to the back of the cart, had made him nervous. Mollie was just laying out her butter and eggs when she heard a yell. She turned to see her father lying on his back and the bullock breaking free. Next minute, the animal was charging down the street.

Immediately, she dropped what she was doing and gave chase. A loose bullock could smash a shop window, or worse still, break his leg and then he would be useless. Mollie ran down the street shouting out warnings to the startled onlookers. People scattered out of the way as the bullock charged hither and thither. She ran as fast as she could but the bullock ran faster and Mollie feared it would all end in disaster.

And then, a young man stepped out from the crowd. He leaped on the animal, threw his arms around its neck and brought it struggling to a halt. The onlookers cheered and clapped their hands. Mollie drew up, panting and out of breath. The man took a rope and tied the bullock in a leash and gave it to her.

"I think he's all right," the man said, "but you need to keep a tight rein on him. A beast like that could do an awful lot of damage."

"He knocked my father over. I'm very grateful," Mollie said.

The man took off his cap and wiped his forehead. Mollie saw that he had a mass of curly black hair and keen, bright eyes.

He smiled and his eyes twinkled. "What's your name?" he said.

"Mollie Kane."

"I'm Ned McGinty."

The following Sunday afternoon, as Mollie was helping her mother clear up after the Sunday lunch, she saw Ned McGinty come walking up the lane towards their farmhouse. He had got his hair cut and had put on a shirt and tie. She saw that his boots were polished till they shone.

She listened from the scullery as he knocked on the door and asked to see the man of the house. Her mother called for her father. Ned McGinty took off his cap and said he would like a word with him.

"What's it about?" her father asked.

"Your daughter."

"Come in," her father said.

The two men disappeared into the kitchen and after half an hour Mollie was called in. Her father and Ned McGinty were drinking whiskey from a bottle that Ned had brought.

"This young buck says he would like to walk out with you. What do you say to that?"

Mollie averted her eyes. She had never walked out before. Indeed, she had only been kissed once, by a town boy in the schoolyard. And Ned was a grown man and very handsome.

"I don't mind," she said.

Ned McGinty clapped his hands and poured out more whiskey. "So it's all agreed, then."

Mollie knew that walking out was only the beginning. When a girl started to walk out, it meant she was pledged to one man. Mollie had never been to a dance and never had the opportunity to meet other boys. But none of this mattered. Mollie thought she was very lucky. There were plenty of girls who never got asked out at all. And anyway, it was her Fate. Ned McGinty was what God had decided for her.

He began by taking her to the cinema in Dunmuckridge where they saw films with Elizabeth Taylor and John Wayne and afterwards had tea and cakes in Morelli's café. They travelled by bicycle with Mollie sitting on the crossbar while Ned steered along the bumpy country lanes. He took her to the dance in the parochial hall once a month and every Sunday afternoon they went walking along the road as far as Kilmurray crossroads.

On the walks, Ned would kiss her. Mollie liked that. She loved his big strong arms wrapped around her and the tender touch of his lips. When he kissed her, he would tell her he loved her. For Mollie, it was all so romantic. It was just like the films. She would gaze into Ned's strong handsome face and wonder what it would be like when they were married.

Mollie had absolutely no doubt that this was going to happen. However, a problem had arisen with Ned and it was a big one. He had no land. Ned was a casual labourer who hired himself out to work for the farmers in the area. In return, he got a small wage and bed and board. It was a difficulty that Mollie's father must have foreseen when he agreed to Ned walking out with her in the first place but now, as the courtship developed, it assumed greater significance. Tucked up in bed at night, Mollie would hear her father and mother discussing it in the kitchen.

"I'm worried that she might be throwing herself away on that buck," her father would say. "He hasn't got two halfpennies to rub together."

"He's got his health and strength," her mother would say.

"How do I know he's not just after her for the bit of land?"

"Would you get some sense? Sure if it was land he was after why would he be bothering with us?"

"She could do better. There's young Delaney. He's a fine young fella and he'll get the family farm when his parents die."

"She's very fond of Ned," her mother said.

"Yerrah, what's fondness got to do with it? It's money and land that make a good match, Maggie. Any fool could tell you that."

Her mother, who knew better, said nothing.

Upstairs in bed, Mollie felt miffed at the way they talked about her as if she was just a child with no mind of her own. But she didn't worry. She had already consulted a fortune-teller over by Carrickbeg who told her she would marry a tall, dark, handsome man who worked with his hands. And if that wasn't Ned McGinty in a nutshell, then what was?

And it came to pass. Mollie's father hadn't reckoned on her mother's cunning. She had a trump card and eventually she played it.

"We can't live for ever," she said, "and there's too much work around this farm for one pair of hands. Either she marries Ned McGinty or the farm will have to be sold. And you know this land has been in your family for five generations."

"Oh, give over, woman," her father said, annoyed. "The land will never leave this family so long as I have anything to do with it."

"So is she to marry Ned McGinty or not?"

Her father let out a loud sigh. "I suppose I have no say in the matter?"

"No," Mollie's mother said, "you haven't."

The wedding was a modest affair. A dressmaker in the town

was prevailed on to run up a lovely wedding dress for Mollie and Ned borrowed a suit from one of his friends. After the ceremony, everybody retired to the house for a party. There was porter and whiskey and a fiddler, and at the end of the night, when everybody had gone home drunk or tired, Ned took Mollie's hand and led her into the spare bedroom that had been given to them by her parents.

They undressed in the dark and got into the big bed with its thick goose-down mattress. Ned put his arms around her and held her close.

"I love you, Mollie, and I always will. And I swear I'll be a good husband to you and I'll work hard so that you'll never want for anything."

"Sshhh," Mollie said and cuddled closer to him. "Money doesn't mean a thing to me. It's you I want."

And she meant it too. She closed her eyes and thanked God for the Fate that had sent her Ned McGinty.

Ned kept his word. He rose early in the morning before it was light and was out feeding the cattle and tending to the jobs that needed to be done around the farm. He worked till the daylight had faded. He was young and strong and well versed in farm work.

With Ned's help, the farm began to prosper. Whereas before it had barely sustained the three of them, now it began to show a modest profit. Ned suggested to her father that he borrow some money from the bank and buy more land so that they could raise extra cattle.

Her father was doubtful at first but gradually he came round. Ned had a good eye for an animal and went to the marts and fairs and invested wisely in calves that he fattened up and sold on to the meat factory. Soon he had the bank loan paid off. The bank manager was delighted to lend him more money and the farm grew even bigger. Neighbours began to comment enviously on the way the Kanes' little two-bit holding had now become a substantial spread.

One night, Mollie overheard her father say to her mother. "There's no doubting it, Maggie. That buck has his head screwed on. The best thing that ever happened to us was the day he came courting Mollie."

At the door where she was listening, Mollie smiled quietly to herself.

Ned's next project was to modernise the farmhouse. It consisted of two bedrooms and a kitchen and the privy was out in the yard. Mollie knew that when the children began to come along, they would need more space.

One evening after dinner, Ned spoke to her father. "I was wondering if you ever thought of building an extra bedroom."

"Yerrah, why would we do that?"

"Because we might need it. And anyway, it would add value to the house."

"It would just mean more housework."

"I wouldn't mind that," Mollie said, quickly.

"How much would it cost?" her father wanted to know.

"Not too much," Ned replied. "I could do a lot of the work myself. You're really only looking at the cost of materials and the hire of tradesmen to do the speciality jobs like plumbing and wiring."

"Let me think about it," her father said.

They got him to agree. By now, her father had come to rely on Ned 's judgement. But Ned didn't plan to stop at just an extra bedroom. He went into town one day and talked to an architect and came back with plans for a whole new house with two extra bedrooms, a bathroom, a modern kitchen and oil-fired central heating. When he saw what was planned, her father almost had a heart attack.

"You'll have me in the poorhouse at this rate! How are we going to pay for all this?"

"I've taken out a mortgage," Ned said.

"I'd love a new kitchen," her mother said.

"And central heating would mean the house would be nice and warm in the winter," Mollie said.

"Why don't you put in a swimming-pool when you're at it?" her father replied testily and stormed out of the room. Ned and Mollie smiled at each other. The following day, Ned lodged the planning application with the County Council.

The new house was finished in time for Mollie's first pregnancy. Everyone was excited. Her mother fussed and her father looked proud as punch at the idea of a grandchild.

"My God, it'll be great to have a child in the house again," he said.

"I hope you spend more time with it than you did with the last one," her mother said.

"What are you talking about, woman? Sure, wasn't I out in the fields in all weather trying to make sure there was enough food on the table?"

"Well, you don't have that excuse now," her mother replied.

It was true. Her father had practically retired and left the entire running of the farm to Ned. And the farm was flourishing. Ned had bought new machinery to do the heavy work. He had built a new milking parlour for the cows and put up new byres. He was now hiring men to work for him. Instead of spending backbreaking days in the fields, Ned now spent long hours at a desk in the bedroom poring over accounts and bills.

The child was a girl and they called her Mary. Ned said very little. He let the women do all the fussing, but privately he was delighted. At night, he would lie awake listening to the rise and fall of the child's breath where she lay in the crib beside the bed. Ned McGinty thought he was the happiest man in the world. Or at least in Dunmuckridge, which was all the world he knew.

Almost a year later, Mollie got pregnant again, and this time, she had a little boy. They called him Edward after his father. Ned believed they would go on having children like this. And he didn't mind. He enjoyed children. And now that the farm was doing well, they had the money to support them. But the months grew into years and no more children came along.

Eventually, Mollie consulted a gypsy woman at Dunmuckridge fair. The woman held her palm and studied it in the dim light of the booth. And then she violently pushed the hand away.

"What's wrong?" Mollie cried, alarmed.

"I don't want to read it," the woman said.

"Why not?"

"Because I see blood."

"Blood?"

"Blood and pain. And disputation. Here, Missus." The woman took the pound note that Mollie had paid her and gave it back. "Take your money and go. Sometimes it's best not to know what the future holds."

Another person would have laughed at this, but not Mollie. She knew that the gypsy woman had seen something in her hand that frightened her. She knew it was only a matter of time before she would see it too.

She didn't have long to wait. One afternoon, a few months later, she was in the kitchen with her mother baking bread. Her father had decided to stroll down the field to inspect a new tractor that Ned had just bought. As the two women chatted and the children played at the kitchen table, they became aware of a commotion. Mollie went out to the yard. Ned and one of the labourers were carrying a third man between them. Another labourer was running ahead of them and shouting out her name.

"In the name of God, what is it?" Mollie screamed.

"There's been an accident, ma'am. Ned says you're to ring for the doctor."

The men were drawing closer. Mollie saw that the person they were carrying was her father. And he was covered in blood.

Her face went pale. She ran back to the house and called the doctor. By this time, they had brought her father into the house and laid him on the kitchen table. Ned was bending over him and listening to his chest. Her mother was sitting in the corner silently weeping into a handkerchief.

"What happened?" Mollie asked. She was amazed that her voice sounded so calm. Inside, she could feel her heart thumping like a piston.

Ned took her in his arms. "He slipped and fell under the tractor. There was nothing we could do."

"Oh, no!"

"I stopped the machine at once. But by then it was too late."

"Is he going to live?"

Ned shrugged. "He's still breathing, but only just. And where there's breath, there's hope, I suppose."

The doctor came and examined him. His face was grim. When he was finished, he stood up and said: "We'll have to get him to the hospital."

"I'll go with you," Ned said.

They drove away. Mollie busied herself about the house.

She tried not to think about what had happened. She tried not to raise her hopes. She put the children to bed and then she came and sat with her mother in the kitchen. Neither woman spoke. They just sat together holding hands while, outside the window, the sun began to go down and the shadows lengthened across the yard. Shortly after ten, the phone rang. Mollie answered it. It was Ned.

"He didn't make it," he said.

There was a big turnout for the funeral and that pleased Mollie. She wanted a good attendance for her mother's sake. A big turnout was a mark of esteem in the community. The parish priest shook hands with them all and said her father was now in heaven with God and all his choirs of angels. After they had buried him, everyone went back to the hotel and had tea and sandwiches.

About a week later, there was the reading of the will. They gathered in the solicitor's office and waited while he took the document out of the safe and spread it on his desk. There were some small bequests to the children and various charities and then came the main item. The farm and land were to be shared between Mollie and Ned on condition that they gave a home to Mrs Kane for the rest of her life.

The solicitor raised his head from the document and looked at them over the top of his thick-framed glasses.

"There is one condition here but, quite honestly, I don't believe it's enforceable. Nevertheless, when he was drawing up his will, Mr Kane insisted that it go in."

"What is it?" Mollie asked.

"He has stipulated that no matter what happens, the farm is never to pass out of the family."

After her husband's death, Mollie's mother seemed to slip

into decline. It was as if she no longer had any will to live. Soon after Christmas, she took to bed with a bad flu. It quickly settled into her chest and turned to pneumonia. By March, she too was dead.

Mollie thought back on all that had happened to her in the last twelve months since she had consulted the gypsy at the fair. She had been warned of blood and it had come to pass. And she had endured more than her share of pain. But the gypsy had been wrong about one thing. There were no disputes or arguments in this house. It was the most peaceful household for miles around.

With the two old people gone, Mollie and Ned concentrated on the farm and the family. The farm consumed a lot of Ned's time but it brought in a good income and they were able to live comfortably. The children grew up. Mary was dark, like her father, and very good-looking. She had a constant stream of young men calling to the house. Mollie wistfully remembered the day, all those years ago, when Ned had come up that very same lane to ask her father's permission to court her.

Mary was clever, like her mother. She did well at school and always got good reports. Even when she wasn't studying, she had her head stuck in a book. But when the time came to take her Leaving Cert exam, she began to get restless and unsettled. One day, Mollie sat down with her at the kitchen table and poured two cups of tea.

"There's something bothering you," she said. "What is it?"

Mary sank her head in her hands. "I don't know what is best. My teacher says if I put my mind to it, I could get the points to study Law or Medicine at college."

"Is that what you want to do?"

Mary shook her head. "I don't think so."

"What, then?"

"Tell you the truth, Mum, I'd really like to be a librarian. You know I love books."

Mollie smiled to herself. "Well, then, a librarian is what you will be. I'd much prefer my daughter to be a contented librarian than an unhappy doctor. But remember, it's entirely up to you. You've got to get the points and no one can sit that examination but you."

Mary sat the exam and gained the necessary grades. The following October, she left for college in Dublin. She got a flat with some other students in Clontarf and travelled home at weekends. Mollie was happy for her. She knew that Mary would be fine. She was a popular young woman and made friends easily. And Mollie was proved right. In due course, Mary got her degree and secured a library post in a town just ten miles away. She bought a second-hand car and moved back into her old bedroom. Now she was walking out with a young vet called Peter Reilly who lived over by Carrickbeg and they all expected to hear wedding bells any day soon.

But it was with Edward that all their hopes lay. He grew up tall and strong, like a young bull. From when he was a child he was out in the fields helping his father with the work. Nothing was ever said publicly but everyone understood that Edward would take possession of the farm when the time came for Ned to retire.

But Edward's easy nature gradually gave way to stubbornness. And as he grew into manhood, the obstinacy increased. It was as if he was trying to create a space for himself and grow out from under his father's shadow. At first, the stubbornness manifested itself in small things: a disagreement over a calf or the type of fertiliser to be used on the fields.

Ned understood what was happening and graciously gave ground. But the differences only increased until it seemed that the two men couldn't even agree on the day of the week.

One evening, Ned confessed to Mollie: "I can't understand him. It seems he's determined to cross me no matter what I do. If I say a thing is white, he'll say it's black just to be different."

"It's only a phase," Mollie said. "He'll grow out of it."

"Will he? I'm not so sure."

Edward was studying Agricultural Science at a nearby college and working on the farm in his free time. As he approached his final year, the tension between the two men got so bad that they could hardly bear to be in the same room together. Mollie came to dread mealtimes. And it was on just such an occasion that Edward dropped his bombshell.

It was Sunday lunch. When the meal was finished, and the dishes were being cleared away, he spoke.

"I've something to tell you."

The room fell silent.

"Yes?" Mollie asked, cautiously.

"You know I'm due to finish college in four months' time?"

"Sure."

"Well, I'll be leaving. I'm going to New Zealand."

Mollie felt faint. She glanced at Ned and saw that his face had turned grey.

"We thought you would stay," she said weakly.

"I can't. I have to get away. New Zealand is a good place. And with an agricultural qualification, I'll easily find work."

Ned cleared his throat. "If you want to go, Edward, I can't stop you. You and me have had our differences. I won't deny that. But this farm belongs to you and you're needed to work it. Your grandfather stipulated that the land should remain in the family. That's where it's been for a hundred and fifty years."

Edward stared at his empty plate. "It doesn't matter," he said. "I'm going to New Zealand."

Mollie tried to remain calm. But her emotions were in turmoil. Two of the people she loved most in all the world, her husband and her son, were in conflict and it broke her heart. She knew it was Fate but that didn't give her much comfort. She took to praying. If God had everything written down in the big book, maybe he could be persuaded to change it. It was with trembling hands that she lit candles in Dunmuckridge church and said a prayer to St Jude, the patron of hopeless cases.

And then she won the Lotto. Most people would have been overjoyed, especially when Ned checked on Monday morning and discovered that the prize money was €600,000. But Molly took it all in her stride.

They had to go up to Dublin to collect their cheque and get their photographs taken holding it up for the newspapers. When Ned had given the cheque to an astonished bank clerk to be lodged into their account and they had eaten a celebratory lunch and were free of all the razzmatazz, Mollie led him into a quiet little pub along the quays.

"I'm going to deposit you here. Just get yourself a pint and wait for me. I won't be long."

She slipped out of the pub and headed for Moore Street. Madam Zora's business had gone downhill since the last time Mollie had been here and she was now reading the tarot cards from the backroom of a boarded-up butcher's shop. She spread out the cards and looked pensive.

"I see much conflict," she said.

Mollie nodded her head.

"But I also see joy. And money."

34

Mollie nodded her head again, vigorously this time.

"I see water. A large expanse of water and you are crossing it."

"What does that mean?" Mollie asked.

Madam Zora frowned. "I can't tell you that. I can only tell you what I see in the cards."

The whole way home on the train, Mollie pondered what the cards meant. She wished Madam Zora had told her something about Edward. Instead she had mentioned water. And she was crossing it. They were getting off the train at the station, when it came to her. She was going to travel! She was crossing the ocean!

She rushed home and excitedly gathered the family together. She knew that Mary would pose no problem. It was Edward she was worried about.

"I want you all to do something for me. I have never asked for much."

"What is it?" asked Mary.

"I want you to come on a week's holiday with me. It will be a celebration. Do you realise that in all the years your father and me have been married, we've never had a holiday?"

"Oh, Mum, that would be marvellous," Mary said. "Make it Easter, when I get my break."

But Edward looked doubtful. "Who's going to look after the farm?"

Mollie turned to him, a beseeching look in her eyes. "Tom Mooney can do it. He's been foreman now for the past four years. He'll be well able to manage."

"All right," he said, reluctantly. "But make it somewhere with a bit of sunshine."

The following morning Mollie was on the phone to the travel agent.

"Can you advise me?" she said. "I want somewhere nice and sunny."

"What about Tenerife? It's got everything. Sunshine, sea, restaurants, bars, shops. You can't go wrong in Tenerife."

"Are you sure? It's very important that it's sunny."

"I'm only back from there myself," the travel agent said, "and the sun was splitting the stones."

"Ok. I'll need three rooms. A double and two singles."

"I've got the very thing," the travel agent said. "Nice complex. Right beside the beach. Place called Hotel Las Flores."

"Book it for us," Mollie said.

Chapter 3

When Charlie Dobbins was fifteen, he developed a crush on a girl who worked at the checkout in the local supermarket. Her name was Jacinta Brennan and she was seventeen. Charlie packed shelves in the supermarket after school. As he went up and down the aisles, he had plenty of opportunities to study Jacinta Brennan and admire her from afar.

Jacinta was short and plump and wore tons of mascara and pale, corpse-like make-up. She wore tight skirts and had purple hair and a large silver ring in her nose. To Charlie, she was the most exotic creature he had ever seen. When he had finished packing shelves, he would hang around Jacinta's checkout desk, hoping she might ask him to carry out some task for her. But Jacinta just ignored him and this only inflamed his passion more.

The job that Charlie craved was stuffing customers' groceries into bags at Jacinta's checkout. He would have done the work for nothing, just to be close to her. But Mr O'Leary, the manager, gave this job to a pimply youth called

Anto Duffy, who was eighteen and worked full-time and therefore had seniority over Charlie.

In the run-up to Christmas, the ring in Jacinta's nose led to an incident which almost closed the store. It started when Mr O'Leary brought Jacinta into his office and told her he had received a number of complaints from customers who found the ring offensive and unhygienic, especially for someone who was handling items of food.

He said that he, personally, had no problem whatsoever with body jewellery and people could have rings wherever they liked, but since the customers were the people who paid their wages at the end of the week, he had to take account of what they said. Regrettably, he had to ask Jacinta to remove the ring while she worked on the checkout.

Jacinta was outraged. She said there were baldy ould fellas coming into the store every day with a smell off them like they hadn't washed for a month and she had even seen one of them take out his false teeth and wipe them with a handkerchief at the vegetable counter and she had never complained. Mr O'Leary said this might well be true but they had a motto in their store that the customer was always right.

"And why can't I be right?"

"Because you're an employee."

Jacinta shifted her chewing gum from one cheek to the other. She pointedly stared at Mr O'Leary's fingers which were grubby from handling invoices. "I don't see what difference it makes. At least my ring is *clean*."

Mr O'Leary sighed and thought of his wife and five children and how he would willingly give up this job tomorrow if he could find some alternative means of feeding them.

"I'm sorry, Jacinta. But my mind is made up. The ring

will have to go and that's all there is to it." Jacinta left the office in tears and went immediately to Tommy Thunder who worked at the fish counter and was the union shop steward.

Tommy said: "Right. This is a clear case of discrimination contrary to paragraph 6, subsection 2a of the house agreement."

He told everybody to stop work immediately and assemble in the carpark outside, where he addressed them for twenty minutes about the way the company was persecuting Jacinta Brennan because she was a young woman who was simply trying to do her job and this was unacceptable in this modern age of equality. He said that women had been put down long enough and they were not prepared to stand for it any more.

The staff, who were 90 per cent young women, cheered every word. Jacinta stood beside him with her head bowed, looking like Joan of Arc before they tied her to the stake. Eventually, Mr O'Leary came out and said he would like to discuss the matter further and he and Tommy Thunder huddled together in his office for another half hour.

In the end, the company agreed to pay Jacinta Brennan £50 compensation for emotional pain and distress and she was allowed to wear the ring. But while she worked at the checkout, she was obliged to cover her nose with a sticking-plaster which made her look gruesome. Tommy Thunder claimed it was a victory for the union and Mr O'Leary said it was an honourable compromise and everybody went back to work.

This incident raised Jacinta Brennan even further in Charlie Dobbins's eyes. Now, he regarded her as a martyr who had suffered for her principles. Charlie had been prepared to go on strike if necessary and picket the store to ensure that justice was done. He saw her as a heroine and any time she looked at him, he blushed and had to turn away.

He had fantasies about her. He dreamed about walking hand in hand with her along Dollymount Strand in the moonlight like he had seen in a film. He thought of asking her to go out with him but he knew he didn't have the nerve. He feared the humiliation of rejection. And then he hit upon a wonderful idea.

Jacinta's younger sister, Teresa, was in the class next to him at school. He decided to write a letter to Jacinta and get Teresa to deliver it. He spent hours composing the letter in the bedroom he shared with his brother, Darren.

"Dear Jacinta", he wrote,

"I wonder if you would like to go to the Multiplex with me next Saturday to see the new James Bond film? I hear it's extremely brilliant. Afterwards, we could go to McDonald's for a hamburger.

Your admiring colleague, Charles Dobbins Esq.

P.S. I'll be paying for everything."

He signed himself Charles because it sounded more formal than Charlie which might strike Jacinta as too familiar seeing as they had never actually spoken to each other. He checked his school dictionary to make sure he had spelt all the words correctly and, when he was satisfied, he sealed the letter and next day, at break, he gave it to Teresa and asked her to pass it on to her sister.

He could scarcely contain himself while he waited for her response. This was the first time Charlie had ever asked a girl out. And Jacinta was older and much more sophisticated and so glamorous it made his knees go weak just to look at her. He counted the money he had saved in a tin box he kept in a drawer in his room. There was nearly £80. He was prepared to spend it all on Jacinta so that they could have a good time and she would see that he wasn't mean.

The next few days were torture. Charlie spent his time keeping an eye out for Teresa and waiting for Jacinta's reply. The suspense was killing him. But every time he saw Teresa, she was with her friends and Charlie was terrified they would make a laugh of him. By Friday afternoon, he was so desperate he decided to confront Teresa after school.

He hung around the gates till he saw her shuffling out, a smaller, plumper version of her sister, her socks round her ankles and her trainers scuffed and worn.

"Hello, Teresa," he said. He realised he was almost as afraid of Teresa as he was of Jacinta.

She turned to look at him. "What you want?"

"I was wondering . . ."

"Yeah?"

"Did you give my letter to Jacinta?"

"Oh that? Yeah, I did."

Charlie could feel his heart hammering in his breast. "And what did she say?"

"Nuthin."

"Did she not say *something?*"

Teresa observed him with small, sly eyes. "No."

"Did she read it, even?"

"Yeah."

"And?"

Charlie couldn't bear to hear the answer.

"She just laughed and threw it in the bin."

Charlie was devastated. He called in sick and didn't go back to the supermarket for a week and when he did, he made sure to keep well away from Jacinta's checkout. He avoided Teresa and any time he saw her in the school corridors, he ducked into an empty classroom till she passed.

He had never felt so humiliated in his whole life. He felt people were sneering at him behind his back. And all the time, his heart burned with passion for Jacinta Brennan. The more she rejected him, the more infatuated he became. He couldn't sleep at night for thinking about her. Over and over in his head, he tried to figure out what he was doing wrong.

And then it came to him. He had been too timid. Girls liked boys who were strong and decisive and knew what they wanted and weren't afraid to ask. Charlie had been too meek. No wonder Jacinta had thrown his letter in the bin.

He got the bus into town and spent his £80 on Levi jeans and a denim jacket and a pair of Converse runners. He got his hair cut. He locked himself in the bathroom and spent an hour in front of the mirror squeezing out his blackheads. He scrubbed his teeth till his gums felt sore. At last, he stood back and examined himself. He thought he looked great. When he walked up to Jacinta Brennan's front door and asked her to come out with him, how could she possibly refuse? All he had to do was pray that he didn't blush or stammer when she appeared on the doorstep.

Friday night, when the supermarket closed, Charlie rushed home and put on his new clothes. Friday night was the big night out. People got paid and headed for the pub or the disco.

He found the Brennan's house easily enough. No 44, Snakepit Lane. It was the one with the abandoned car resting precariously on six breeze blocks in the front garden.

But just as Charlie approached the house, he saw the front door open and Jacinta stepped out. She was wearing her tight skirt and high heels and a little leather jacket. Immediately, he hurried towards her, shouting out her name. He was astonished at his own boldness. It was the first time he had ever spoken to her. But she didn't seem to hear him.

He ran after her but it was amazing how fast she could

travel in those high heels. She had reached the corner where the Chinese takeaway was when Charlie beheld a sight that made his blood chill. Waiting for her was the pimpled figure of Anto Duffy. He kissed Jacinta's cheek and, without once looking back, she took Anto's arm and walked up the road and out of Charlie's life.

Poor Charlie! He eventually got away from the supermarket, but he never got away from Jacinta Brennan. She cast a blight that was to follow him like a shadow down all his days.

He left school the following year, when he was sixteen, and got a job as a messenger boy in a bookshop. And here, a minor miracle occurred. Charlie discovered that he liked reading.

The shop regularly got uncorrected proof copies of upcoming books from the distributors and Charlie would take them home and devour them in the privacy of his bedroom, while downstairs the rest of the family watched Gay Byrne on the *Late Late Show.*

He consumed crime novels and romances and travel books and biographies. This was amazing, because at school Charlie had rarely opened a book unless the English teacher, Mr O'Rourke, was standing over him breathing down his neck.

And not only did Charlie read the books but he also began to develop a critical sense. When a customer came in looking to buy something for a present, Charlie was able to advise on what would be suitable. This ability quickly came to the attention of the owner, Mr Gregg, and before long Charlie was promoted to sales assistant.

He had to buy a new suit and wear a shirt and tie and appear neat and tidy at all times. But his wages doubled. Charlie loved his new job. He never complained about working extra hours or staying through his lunch break. He was the first person to arrive in the morning and the last to leave at night.

Mr Gregg appreciated this. Charlie was single, unlike the rest of the assistants who were married and had other demands on their time. As he grew more experienced, his responsibilities expanded. Soon, Charlie was dealing with the distributors and publishers, ordering books and negotiating over prices. And he turned out to be very sharp. Charlie took personal satisfaction in shaving margins and haggling over returns. And the strange thing was: nobody resented this. Charlie was such a likeable guy that nobody had a bad word to say about him. When the manager, Miss Price, resigned to take up another position elsewhere, Charlie was given her job.

Here he was at twenty-two, managing a busy bookshop in the centre of Dublin. He was the only man in his street who went to work in a suit. People began to reassess their opinion of Charlie Dobbins. His parents were proud of him. His mother would tell anyone who would listen that the reading came from her side of the family, since her own dear father, Tosser Doyle, was never known to have a book out of his hand while her husband, Christie, never looked at anything except the racing pages of the *Daily Bugle*.

But Charlie had further surprises in store. When he had learned everything there was to know about the book trade, he announced that he was going to open a shop of his own.

He found it in a side street at the back of Christ Church Cathedral, a dilapidated cobbler's premises that had been abandoned when the trend for heel bars stole the business away. Charlie had been careful with his wages and had £6,345 tucked away in a special savings account in the Allied Irish Bank.

He made an appointment to see the manager, and after a meeting lasting forty-five minutes, came away with a mortgage for £30,000 repayable at £300 a month over twenty-five years. It was enough to enable Charlie to buy the shop, fit it out and purchase stock. He hired his brother Darren and a couple of his pals to rip out the old fittings and put up new shelves and racks, paint the inside and put up a sign. He called the shop *Dublinia,* because it was in the centre of the old Viking city.

On the opening night, Charlie gave a party with chilled wine and canapes. He invited his former colleagues and representatives from the book trade. He even cajoled a photographer from one of the glossy magazines to take pictures which were splashed all over the next issue. Charlie's bookshop quickly gained a social cachet. He organised poetry readings and book launches and this got him more publicity. The shop became known as *the* place to buy your books. When Temple Bar began to develop, Charlie captured the trendy young crowd who frequented the area.

His bookshop thrived. In five years, he had paid off his mortgage and taken out a new one and opened two more shops in quick succession. He brought the same business flair to these. He worked long hours, squeezed margins, gave discounts. He had an eye for design and innovation. Charlie's bookshops were the first to open cafés and introduce browsers' sections where people could sit and read and nobody put pressure on them to buy.

Charlie Dobbins had arrived. He was the owner of three thriving bookshops and was already receiving offers from the big stores to buy him out. He drove a 2005-registered Mercedes and had long ago moved out of the family home into a four-bedroom townhouse at Sutton which backed onto the beach. He dressed well, ate in good restaurants and had a healthy bank account. But despite all this, Charlie was not a happy man.

He was thirty-four and still a virgin.

The truth was, Charlie was terrified of women. He had never got over his rejection at the hands of Jacinta Brennan. Once, he ran into her on the street and barely recognised her. She was pushing a buggy and had two screaming kids in tow. She looked old and raddled, her hair hanging in untidy knots down the sides of her small, pinched face. She was nothing like the exotic creature that had once broken his heart. Charlie had already passed her by before he realised who she was.

It wasn't that he didn't have opportunities with women, for Charlie was widely regarded as a *very* eligible bachelor. He was almost six feet tall, with dark hair and a warm friendly face. At parties and receptions, women would corner him and engage him in conversation but if the situation turned serious, Charlie would break out in a sweat. His mouth would dry up and he would get nervous and embarrassed. Charlie was then like a claustrophobic trapped in a lift. He just had to escape.

He watched with envy as his friends moved easily in the company of women. He listened to stories of their conquests. In restaurants, he would see men huddled in corners with beautiful companions, holding hands and smiling into their eyes and he wished that he too had the confidence to behave like that.

In desperation, he decided to seek professional help. He consulted the Golden Pages under *Psychiatrists* and found a man called Dr Spitzer who operated out of rooms in Donnybrook. Charlie made an appointment to see him, using an assumed name.

Dr Spitzer looked like something out of a horror movie.

He was small and fat, with a huge head of black, curling hair and dark, menacing eyebrows. His piercing eyes stared out from behind thick glasses. He reminded Charlie of a giant tarantula spider. Dr Spitzer told Charlie to sit down and asked him what the problem was.

Charlie began nervously to explain. Dr Spitzer closed his eyes and folded his hands on his ample belly and seemed to go to sleep.

"I can't relate to women," Charlie said.

"Are you a homosexual?" Dr Spitzer said, suddenly coming awake again.

"Oh, no. It's nothing like that. It's just that I get nervous if I find myself in a close situation with a woman. I don't know what to do."

"What is there to know? Women are like men. They have the same desires, the same wish for physical and emotional fulfilment."

"But that's just the point. I've never been with a woman, you see. Not like that." Charlie felt his face glow red with shame. "I've never had . . . er . . . sexual intimacy."

"You're repulsed by their bodies?"

"No. The complete opposite. I'm very attracted to them. But I'm terrified of doing the wrong thing and making a fool of myself."

Dr Spitzer scratched his head. "But how can you do the wrong thing? It's simple. Do you want me to show you diagrams?"

Charlie almost curled up with embarrassment. "Oh God no! I know what to do. It's just that I'm afraid they'll laugh at me. I'm afraid of *failing*."

Dr Spitzer examined Charlie intently from behind his thick glasses. "I think I know what the problem is. You're fixated on your mother."

Charlie thought of his mother in her house out in Artane: her pendulous breasts, her legs like giant sausages encased in gargantuan stockings, the cigarette never out of the corner of her mouth. This Dr Spitzer had more problems than he had.

He stood up.

"How much do I owe you?" he asked.

He enrolled with a dating agency. It was called Executive Nights. The literature said the agency aimed to match young professional singles. Charlie filled in a questionnaire and paid his fee and a week later, the postman delivered a list of potential dates.

Charlie read it eagerly. There was Charlotte who worked in banking, Eimear in technology, Rosemary in advertising, Clodagh who was in media. They all sounded eminently suitable. In the end, Charlie stuck a pin in the list and came up with Davina who was an accountant. He rang Davina and they chatted for a few minutes and agreed to have dinner. Charlie booked a discreet table in the Trocadero in St Andrew's Street.

Davina turned out to be a bubbly brunette about five six with small breasts and nice legs. She had given her age as twenty-seven on the list that Charlie had received, but he reckoned that, for an accountant, she was lousy with figures. He calculated that thirty-five might be closer to the mark.

The dinner went very well. Davina talked about her job, her friends, her holidays. She had a high-pitched voice that seemed to echo round the room and an embarrassing way of punching Charlie's shoulder whenever she wanted to make a point. He told her about the bookshops and how he had built them up from nothing and she seemed very impressed.

Davina had roast flank of prime veal with a *jus de maison*. She left the vegetables untouched on the side of the plate. Charlie had a steak. They drank a bottle of Burgundy. After the coffees were finished and the bill paid, Charlie offered to drive her home. She lived in Malahide which was handy as it was only a couple of miles away from Sutton.

Charlie felt relaxed as they settled into the Mercedes. He turned on the stereo and played Paul Simon. Davina admired the car and Charlie felt good. Here was a woman who seemed like excellent fun. She hadn't pushed too hard. And she had listened. Davina seemed to *understand* him. Charlie felt sure that, given time, he and Davina could have a bright future.

He dropped her at her apartment and she invited him in for a nightcap. Charlie locked the car and bounced up the steps to the front door. The apartment was a nice two-bed, tastefully decorated and beautifully furnished. Davina took off her coat and asked Charlie if he would like a drink.

"I'm not sure that I should. You know what the cops are like."

"Oh, c'mon, Charlie! Be a devil."

"Okay, then. I'll have a brandy."

"I'll join you."

Davina poured two large shots. She put a cassette in the sound system. Cleo Laine. She took Charlie's hand.

"Care to dance?"

Mysteriously, the lights began to fade. Charlie couldn't figure it out. She must have hit a switch somewhere when he wasn't looking. She laid her head on his shoulder and he could smell the heady scent of her perfume.

Davina leaned close to him as they swayed around the room. She closed her eyes and Charlie wondered if she had gone to sleep. And then he began to feel a tingling sensation in his groin. It was as if . . .

He looked down and sure enough, there was Davina's little white hand moving stealthily up his thigh.

He felt his heart jump into his mouth and panic rise in his breast. This was incredible. He had only known this woman a few hours and here she was attempting to get into his underpants.

He looked around desperately for a means of escape.

"Got to use the loo," he croaked.

Davina smiled languorously.

"No problemo. First door on the right."

"Thank you," Charlie whispered.

He went out to the hall, through the front door, quickly down the steps and into the Mercedes. He didn't take his foot off the accelerator till he reached Portmarnock.

He buried himself in his work. For the next few weeks, Charlie Dobbins practically lived in his bookshops. He turned down dinner invitations. He didn't go out. On Sundays, he brought in carry-outs and watched old movies on television.

But the shameful problem remained. And Charlie knew, deep in his heart, it would never go away till he found the courage to confront it. If only he could succeed with *one* woman, it would give him the confidence for others. But where was he to start?

He had an old friend called Tommy Brick. They had been to school together. Tommy had been a bit of a ladies' man in his time, but now he was happily married with three kids and a house in Killester. If anybody could advise him, it would be Tommy. Charlie gave him a call and arranged to have a drink.

Tommy listened patiently while Charlie outlined his

dilemma. When he was finished, Tommy said: "It seems to me, you've got to get away."

"Away?" Charlie said.

"Yeah. Somewhere like Ibiza. I saw a programme on the telly the other night. They were going at it like rabbits."

"Rabbits?"

"Yeah. You know what rabbits are supposed to be like, shacked up in their burrows all winter long with nothing else to do."

"But . . ." Charlie started.

"Don't you see? It would be perfect. If you got to first base with some young one, it wouldn't matter how you performed. It's only a one-night stand. You're not going to see her again."

Tommy made it all appear so simple.

"You know, I think you're right," Charlie said.

"Of course, I am. You've been working too hard, Charlie. You need to take a break, man."

The following morning, Charlie went down to the travel shop.

"I'd like to book a holiday in Ibiza," he bashfully asked the young – and fortunately male – travel agent.

"Ibiza's all gone," the travel agent said. "You have to book early."

Charlie felt his spirits sink. "Is there somewhere else? Somewhere the same as Ibiza?"

"There's Tenerife. It's beautiful this time of year."

"Does it have night-life?"

The travel agent laughed. "Is the Pope a Catholic?"

"Is there plenty of . . ."

"Women? There's loads of them. Believe me, you'll be fighting them off."

Charlie's spirits rose again. "OK."

The travel agent consulted his computer. "I can give you an apartment in a nice complex near the beach. Week after Easter."

"What's it called?" Charlie asked.

"Hotel Las Flores."

"I'll take it," he said.

Chapter 4

When Bobby Bannon met Alex Piper, she knew within five minutes he was the man she was going to marry. He was witty, he was charming, he had excellent manners and he liked animals. Liking animals was very important to Bobby. She had two cats and a dog and they meant everything to her. The cats were called Romeo and Juliet and the dog was called Cleo. She was a mongrel bitch, part collie and part sheepdog, that Bobby had rescued from the animal shelter. Bobby loved her pets. They were her only family since her parents were both dead and she lived alone. And she had vowed she would never marry a man who didn't love them too.

But most of all, she fell for Alex Piper because he was drop-dead gorgeous. He was five feet ten inches tall in his stockinged feet and had blond hair and smooth, delicate skin. He had the most sensual eyes that Bobby had ever seen. She just had to look into them to feel her heart go pitter-pat.

Bobby had always wanted to get married. Ever since she was twelve years old and began to regard boys as something more than bothersome pests, she had been in love with the idea of marriage. Those who knew her well said it had something to do with security and in reflective moments she was inclined to agree with them. Bobby longed for stability. She longed for the routine and the responsibility and of course the love, which she was sure she would find in a good marriage. While her friends were happy to extract all the excitement they could from their single lives, flitting from partner to partner and scene to scene, Bobby dreamt of commitment. It had nothing to do with loneliness and everything to do with peace of mind. Bobby just wanted to settle down and be happy.

For although she was only twenty-three, she had led a very disruptive life. Her father, Robert Bannon, had been a diplomat. When she told people, they immediately assumed that he must have had a wonderful career, travelling to exotic foreign countries, living in style, eating in fine restaurants and meeting lots of interesting people. There was a certain element of truth in this, of course, but for Bobby the reality had been very different. For her, it had meant shuffling from place to place and only staying long enough to start making friends before she was uprooted and moved on again.

In one three-year period when Bobby was in her early teens, her father had been posted to five different locations. For her, it meant five different houses, five different schools, five different groups of friends. And some of the locations were far from exotic. There was the nine months they spent in Luxembourg where everyone was very polite but there was nothing very much for a young girl to do in her free time. And the winter in Ottawa when it snowed all the time so that Bobby was rarely able to leave the house except to go to school and visit the homes of her friends.

Her father did eventually get posted to some exciting

places like Paris and Madrid but by then her parents' marriage was in trouble and the tension and worry that this brought meant that Bobby was unable to enjoy them. The chief memories she had of these cities were the arguments and the slamming doors and the nights when she lay in bed and listened for the sound of raised voices from the sitting-room below.

Sometimes Bobby believed it was the constant disruption to their lives that had driven the wedge between her parents. In later years, her father claimed it was her mother's adultery with a junior diplomat who worked in the embassy that had done for the marriage. But Bobby often wondered if this would have happened if they had led a more settled life, if her father had held down a nine-to-five job somewhere, if they had a home where everyone could sit down together like a family and just be together for a while.

Instead, her mother had been forced to endure long separations while her father was travelling on diplomatic business. And when he was at home, there were boring lunches for visiting dignitaries, visits to neighbouring embassies for their national days and a constant round of drinks parties where everybody tended to overindulge. It was at one of these parties that the fatal affair had begun.

According to her mother it was short-lived, a bare couple of months before the couple were discovered by another embassy person having a private lunch together in a restaurant they thought was discreet. Her mother insisted she had been about to terminate the affair when the discovery was made. But it was too late. The embassy spy reported the sighting to Bobby's father and the damage was done.

Bobby didn't entirely blame her mother. She could understand why she got lonely. The life of an embassy wife wasn't easy. She was always on call; she always had to look her best; she always had to be available to act as hostess at parties and functions. She got little time to relax and hardly any time at all to spend with her husband. Was it any wonder she got bored? Was it any wonder she gave in to temptation? If there had been less disruption in their lives, would the affair ever have occurred at all?

While the marriage was breaking up, Bobby was packed off again to a boarding school in Dublin. She was now sixteen and an only child (another result of her parents' unsettled life style) and the prospect appeared daunting. But amazingly, it turned out to be one of the happiest periods in her life. For at school, she met Angie Clarke. Angie was a day-girl and the same age as Bobby. Her father owned a clothing business and the family lived in a big rambling Victorian house in Howth. At school breaks, Angie took Bobby home to stay with her and it was here that she discovered the warmth and intimacy of close family relationships.

The Clarkes were a large family – Angie had five brothers and sisters – and the house was a constant buzz of activity. There was little privacy and hardly any peace and there were always squabbles and arguments going on among the kids but Bobby loved it. Mr Clarke worked hard at his business and was often away for long hours at his office in the city but he always made sure to be home for dinner in the evening when they would all gather round the big table in the kitchen and discuss the affairs of the day. When the holidays eventually came to an end and Bobby had to go back to school, she missed the Clarkes' house in Howth with its rough and tumble and its noise and laughter and swore that one day she too would have a house just like it.

Eventually, the two friends left school. Bobby got a job as an advertising sales executive with a major national newspaper. Her father had given her a small legacy which she used as a deposit for a house near the bay at Ringsend and she spent three months painting and decorating it and installing a new kitchen and bathroom. When she had finished, she threw a housewarming party and everybody admired the house and said how lucky she was to have a place of her own.

Angie did a business course and started working for a firm of accountants in South George's Street. She continued to live in the family home. But the two young women remained firm friends, chatting daily on the phone, eating lunch together once a week, going on holidays together and partying at weekends. They were so close that some people said they were psychic and could read each other's minds.

It was at a 21st birthday party for Angie's sister Claire, that Bobby met Alex Piper. It was a Saturday night and Mr and Mrs Clarke had wisely decamped with the younger children to Mrs Clarke's sister in Dundalk, leaving the house to the older siblings. Bobby had gone into the kitchen to get glasses and came upon Alex drinking beer with some of his friends. As she turned to leave she bumped into him and he accidentally spilt beer down the front of her dress.

Immediately, he began to apologise. "Oh my God, I'm terribly sorry. It's all my fault. I shouldn't have been waving my arms around like a lunatic." He grabbed some paper napkins and began to dab at the stain.

Bobby stepped out of his range, looking down at the dark stain on her pale lilac dress. It would now stink of stale beer for the rest of the night. Who invited these louts, she thought? She would have to mention it to Angie.

"It's nothing," she said, coldly. "It has to go to the cleaner's anyway."

"Well then, let me pay. Here, take my phone number. Send me the bill."

"It really doesn't matter," Bobby protested.

But Alex had produced a card and was pressing it into her hand. "I insist."

She took the card and glanced at it. Then she looked into his face and saw those liquid blue eyes and something inside her began to stir.

"I'm Bobby Bannon," she said, her voice softening.

He stuck out his hand. "Alex Piper. Delighted to meet you, Bobby."

They spent the rest of the evening together.

"Do you live, here? In Howth?" he asked after he got her a glass of wine.

"No. I live in Ringsend."

"In the family home?"

"No." She wondered if she should tell him about her parents and decided not to. "It's my own house."

"Wise woman," he said. "Getting a foot on the property ladder. Way to go."

"It's only a small place," Bobby said, modestly. "A couple of bedrooms, a kitchen, living-room and bathroom. But it's perfect for me and my pets. I've got two cats and a dog."

Alex beamed. "So you like animals?"

"I should think so."

"Well, we have something in common. We've got two Springer Spaniels at home. And a cat. His name is Houghton."

Bobby laughed. "What an odd name."

"He was called after Ray Houghton. You know the footballer? He scored the winning goal against Italy in the 1994 World Cup. But I suppose you're not interested in football."

She shook her head and smiled. "Not really." Although I suppose I could get interested for the right man, she thought.

They huddled together in a corner of the sitting-room

while the party swirled all around them. They talked about pets and work and films they had seen and books they had read. Bobby was only vaguely aware of the envious glances from the other women.

And Alex turned out to be a perfect gentleman. He kept on getting her refills of the corky wine that Mr Clarke had bought at a discount from the local off-licence. He made sure to get her a plate of cold chicken and salad and a paper napkin and cutlery when the buffet was served. And when the DJ started playing music, he asked her to dance.

At one o'clock, Alex inquired if he could see her home. He organised a taxi and insisted on walking with her to the front door. And then he asked if he could kiss her goodnight. Bobby was bowled over. No man had ever asked permission to kiss her before. Most of them just grabbed you before you had a chance to resist. She leaned her face towards him and felt his warm lips on hers.

He thanked her and returned to the taxi. Bobby went inside and closed the front door. She let the cat in and went upstairs and got undressed. Cleo jumped up on the bed and wagged her tail.

"You'll never guess who I met tonight," Bobby said.

The dog licked her face.

"That's right. The man I'm going to spend the rest of my life with."

Alex rang her at five past nine the following morning, as she was just setting up her desk preparing for work. I was right, she thought. This guy is keen.

"Can you talk?"

"For a few minutes."

"How are you this morning?"

"I'm fine, thank you."

"Sleep all right?"

"Like a baby."

"You must have a clear conscience."

"You bet I do."

She heard him laugh. She liked his easy line of conversation. The more she listened to Alex Piper, the more she approved of him.

"I was wondering if we could meet for lunch. I work in Parliament Street. It's not far from you."

"I know where you work. You gave me your card, remember?"

"So what do you think?"

Bobby pretended to check her diary. She had nothing planned but she wasn't going to tell him that. "I could squeeze you in at one o'clock."

"Perfect! What about Chez Pierre? It's in Crow Street."

"I know it."

"So I'll meet you there?"

"OK."

"Look forward to seeing you, again."

"Me too."

"Bingo!" Alex Piper said and put down the phone.

Chez Pierre was an expensive French place. Bobby had eaten there only once before when a client had brought her to lunch. The fact that Alex had chosen it showed he had taste and wanted to impress her. It was another good sign.

The lunch was a huge success. In anticipation, that morning Bobby had put on one of her best outfits: a natty little suit and a white blouse with dark stockings that showed off her legs. At ten minutes to one, she went off to the ladies' and applied some bright-red lipstick, a little foundation and a spray of perfume and arrived at the restaurant ten minutes late which wasn't too late to be rude and not early enough to appear eager.

Alex was waiting at a table beside the window where they could see out onto the street. He looked relieved to see her. He immediately ordered two Kir Royales and handed her a menu in a smart leather folder.

"You look stunning," he said.

"Thank you."

"Even better in daylight."

Bobby smiled. "I take it that's meant to be a compliment?"

"Of course. Now, what do you want to eat? The sole is very good."

She flicked through the menu, then handed it back. "I'll take your advice. I'll have the sole."

Alex waved for the waiter and gave their order like a man comfortable about eating in expensive restaurants. He asked for a bottle of Sauvignon Blanc, nicely chilled.

Bobby sipped her wine and listened attentively while he told her more about himself. He had two brothers and a sister, lived with his family in Castleknock, played rugby at weekends and was a trainee solicitor with the firm of Humphrey and Partners.

"Do you like your job?" she asked.

"Love it. It's what I always wanted to do."

"You don't find it boring? All those musty old law books?"

"But it's not like that at all. I'm dealing with people all the time. And I'm getting great training. I cover everything from conveyancing to inheritance tax. In a few years, I plan to set up my own practice. I'm going to specialise in family law. That's a growing area."

Bobby probed gently about salary and prospects. "I'm told that mergers and acquisitions is where the real action is."

"That's the glamour area. But it's only for a handful of people and most of them get burnt out very quickly. It's extremely volatile and the competition is cut-throat."

"But it's where the big money is."

Alex patted his lip with his napkin. "Believe me, Bobby, I've thought about this. Family law is the coming thing. I reckon in five years' time I could be earning 200K a year."

"Really?" she said, calmly.

"Oh yes. Maybe more."

Bobby almost spilt her wine. "Of course, money isn't everything." She smiled and felt the words stick like treacle in her throat.

The romance blossomed. Alex rang again the following day and asked if she would like to come to the theatre. They went to the Abbey to see *Dancing at Lughnasa*. There were dinner dates and parties and trips out to Fairyhouse to the races. Bobby's life became a wonderful round of social engagements and she enjoyed every thrilling moment. Eventually she decided it was time to tell him about her parents.

It was at the end of an intimate little supper in a quiet bistro in Ballsbridge.

"You wanted to know about my family," she said.

"Sure. What's the big mystery? Every time I ask, you evade the question."

"They're dead," Bobby said.

His expression immediately changed. "Oh, I'm sorry. I had no idea."

"It's OK. They didn't have a very happy life. They separated when I was sixteen and a few years later, my father was killed in a car crash in France. Two years ago, my mother died of cancer."

"My God. That's terrible."

Bobby shrugged.

"And you have no other family?"

"No immediate family. My grandmother is still alive. She lives in Kilkenny."

He put his arms around her shoulders and pulled her close. "I'll be your family," he said as his lips pressed gently on her forehead.

Naturally, Angie was keen to know how the friendship was developing.

"I don't think I've ever seen you get so close to a guy before. Is this it?"

"Could be," Bobby confessed. Even though Angie was her best friend, she wasn't going to tell her the truth till she was absolutely sure.

"So maybe I'll be getting measured for a bridesmaid's dress any day now?"

"He has to ask me first. And I have to accept."

"But you *will* accept, won't you?"

"I'll certainly think about it," Bobby said.

But Bobby was already laying plans to nudge events along. For Alex's twenty-sixth birthday, a few weeks later, she arranged an intimate little dinner party at her house. She went to the local delicatessen and bought smoked salmon with capers and Beef Wellington and green figs in syrup for dessert. She chilled a bottle of Moet and Chandon champagne and set out the brandy on the sideboard. She put Ella Fitzgerald on the sound system, turned the lights down low and lit candles to enhance the atmosphere. She surveyed her handiwork. It was a perfect seduction scene.

The dinner went exactly as planned. Bobby made sure that Alex was well fed and his glass topped up. She wore a clinging black dress that hugged her figure. She had put on a subtle scent. Underneath, like wisps of gossamer, she could feel the scanty little bikini briefs she had bought at a lingerie shop in Essex Street.

When they had finished eating, he asked her to dance. She melted in his arms. She felt his breath hot on her cheek and his strong arms pulling her closer.

"I want you," he whispered. "I've never wanted a woman so much in all my life."

Bobby waited for him to speak the magic words.

"I love you, Bobby, I'm absolutely crazy about you."

"I love you too," she said.

"I want you to marry me."

She gently disengaged herself. "Are you absolutely sure?"

"Yes."

"You know what you're asking?"

"Sure I do. I'm mad about you. Absolutely besotted."

She hesitated.

"Please say yes," he pleaded.

"You promise to love honour and obey me?"

"I'll promise anything. Just say you'll marry me."

"Of course I will, you fool!"

She flung her arms around his neck and kissed him hard.

As they mounted the stairs to the bedroom, she could hear the haunting strains of Ella Fitzgerald crooning "If This be Love" from out of the sound system.

The engagement was formally announced in the social columns of *The Irish Times*. Some of Bobby's friends said it looked a bit sad because it just stated: *Mr and Mrs David Piper are pleased to announce the engagement of their son, Alexander, to Ms Roberta Bannon,* and didn't mention her parents.

"Who's going to give you away?" Angie wanted to know.

"No one. I'll give myself away."

"You mean, you'll walk up the aisle all on your own?"

"Why not? Anyway, this whole business of giving the

bride away is just a load of male chauvinist nonsense. It's *so* old-fashioned."

"It'll cause a stir," Angie said.

Causing a stir was exactly what Bobby had in mind. She wanted to create a dramatic effect. She wanted her wedding to be remembered for years as the one where the beautiful bride walked up the aisle alone because her parents were dead.

Alex bought her a solitaire diamond engagement ring and Bobby took great delight in showing it shyly to her friends and colleagues and anyone else who asked. She hadn't inquired how much it cost because that wasn't good manners. But privately, she had it valued in a jeweller's in Capel Street and was amazed to discover he had spent €5,000 on it. That pleased her mightily. After much consultation, the wedding date was fixed for the following Easter. Since her parents were dead, Mr and Mrs Piper said they would pay for everything. They said this was only fair since the couple would be going to live in Bobby's house and that would save Alex a lot of money. Bobby didn't argue and immediately set about planning.

She asked Angie and Alex's sister, Orla, to be bridesmaids. Alex's best friend, Freddie Dunne, was to be best man and his brother, Stephen, was to be groomsman. Bobby hadn't fully understood the amount of planning that went into a wedding. The church had to be booked plus an organist and a singer. A woman had to be engaged to bake the wedding cake. A photographer had to be contracted to take the official photographs. The hotel had to be booked and limousines ordered to take the guests to the hotel and a band booked to play at the reception afterwards. Menus had to be prepared, flowers arranged and invitation cards printed.

She threw herself into the organisation and delighted in the buzz. She was the first of her friends to be married and it caused great excitement. She was the centre of attention and enjoyed every moment of it. She spent weeks with Alex's mother, poring over the guest list. Bobby wanted a big wedding with lots of friends but after some gentle nudging from Mrs Piper, she agreed to pare the number of guests back to three hundred. It was still big. Bigger than anybody could ever remember.

Alex's uncle James knew a man who collected antique cars and owned a pink Cadillac which had been imported from the United States. It had even featured in a movie with Clint Eastwood. After some persuasion, the man agreed to loan it to them to bring the bride to the church.

Next was the honeymoon. Alex suggested New Orleans because he liked jazz and had always wanted to visit Bourbon Street. Bobby wanted Brazil because she had read in a fashion magazine about a well-known model who had honeymooned in Rio de Janeiro and it sounded blissful. In the end, they compromised on the Caribbean.

Finally, there was the wedding dress. Bobby was determined that she was going to look spectacular. When she walked down the aisle on her own, she wanted people to gasp in admiration. After much deliberation, she decided on a white silk dress with a corsetted bodice and a full skirt made from layers of tulle. Topping it off was a full-length veil and tiara. It was known as the Fairy Princess look. Yes, Bobby said to herself. That's definitely me.

They held a party in her house to celebrate the engagement and all their friends came and brought presents. People commented on what a lovely couple they made and how well matched they were and how they would be just wonderful for each other. Bobby smiled demurely and clung to Alex's arm as they welcomed everyone into the house and directed them to the dining-room where the drinks and food were laid out.

"I hope you realise how lucky you are," Angie said to her. "You've hooked a dreamboat *and* you've got this lovely house all ready to move into. With the price of houses in Dublin today, I'll be lucky to get a shoebox in Portlaoise if I ever get married."

With Bobby so busy with all the preparations, the months seemed to fly past. She opened a wedding account in Brown Thomas's store and sent a list of wedding gifts to all the guests. There was no item on the list under €200.

Once all the big things had been taken care of, there were still lots of small details to be arranged, like disposable cameras so that the guests could take pictures of each other and little cans of bubbles to blow instead of confetti because the priest said confetti only littered up the church. There was the printing of the wedding service and the seating arrangements for the lunch and a piper to be hired to pipe the couple from the church.

At last, everything seemed to be in order. The rehearsals were over, the cake was baked, the lunch menu chosen, the dresses made, the flowers ordered, the organist paid, the deposits given for the hotel and the honeymoon. All that remained was Bobby's hen party and Alex's stag.

About a dozen of her closest friends took her by train to Kilkenny for the weekend at the end of March. They booked into a bed and breakfast and went out on the town, ending up at a disco in the local hotel were they got drunk and flirted outrageously with some English soccer supporters over for a match.

Alex's friends had something more exotic in store. He announced that they were going to Barcelona. Freddie Dunne had organised a package.

"Barcelona?" Bobby said when he told her. She thought of her own trip to Kilkenny. "That sounds a bit extravagant."

"Not really. It's costing €300 all in. Plus spending money, of course. I'm told it's a wonderful city. And it should be beautiful this time of year."

Bobby was miffed. But there was nothing she could do. She had already come to the conclusion that Freddie Dunne was a bad influence on Alex. She consoled herself with the thought that this was his last fling as a single man. When they were married, she would quickly ensure he was removed from the sway of creatures like Freddie Dunne.

Alex set off on the weekend before Easter. Bobby drove him to the airport and kissed him goodbye.

"Make sure to call. I want to hear everything you get up to. I don't trust you on your own in a big city like that."

Alex laughed and squeezed her tight. "Don't worry, I'll call," he said, as he strolled off to join his friends.

Bobby returned home and took Cleo out for a walk in the park, then picked up an Indian takeaway and a bottle of Piat D'Or and settled down to a night in front of the box.

He rang at ten the next morning.

"Just to let you know we arrived safely. Hotel is fine – weather is marvellous – we're heading off now to the Ramblas – I'm told there are some great little tapas bars down there – love you," he said before she could get a word in.

Bobby looked out the window and saw the rain coming down. It was so unfair. *She* should have been in Barcelona with Alex, strolling under the cherry trees, instead of that mob of drunken no-goods he called his friends.

The following morning she waited patiently for his call but it didn't come. She knew instinctively what had happened. They had got him drunk in some Spanish nightclub and he was sleeping it off. By the afternoon, when he still hadn't called, she decided to ring his mobile. He had the damned thing switched off. She got put through to his message minder.

She rang several times more and when she still didn't get through, she thought, 'Hump this for a game of soldiers!". In a fit of pique, she rang Angie and arranged to go out on the town with some friends.

It was Monday evening before Alex finally made contact. Bobby had already decided she was going to give him the freeze treatment. If they were to be man and wife, then he had to learn how to behave. And not returning phone messages was a big no-no in her book. But the minute she heard his voice on the line, she knew something was wrong.

He sounded slow and hesitant, not the usual bubbly Alex she had come to know and love.

"I'm afraid I have some bad news," he said.

She felt her heart flutter. Had he been involved in an accident? Had he fallen for some sultry *senorita*?

"What?"

"I've been thinking. I went for a stroll on my own on Saturday afternoon and, well, I came to a decision."

"Tell me!" she shrieked.

"I want to postpone the wedding. I don't think I'm ready for it yet. I need more time."

Bobby felt her knees go weak. "Are you mad? You can't do this," she yelled.

"Why not?"

"Because everything's been arranged!"

"Then it will just have to be *un*arranged," he said and the line went dead.

Angie came to the rescue. She came round to the house immediately and began making the phone calls. Bobby lay on the settee, alternately wailing and sobbing, while Cleo nuzzled her face with her cold snout.

"What am I going to do?" she wailed. "How am I going to face everybody? That bastard has made me the laughing-stock of Dublin."

Angie pressed a large gin into her hand. "Everything will seem different in the morning."

She rang the priest and the hotel and the caterers and the photographer and cancelled everything. She even managed to get back the deposit that had been paid to the photographer although the hotel refused point blank to return any money on the grounds that they had turned down other weddings and were going to be out of pocket as a result.

She recruited Orla and, between them, they managed to contact as many guests as possible and told them that the wedding had been postponed indefinitely. They didn't give any reason. When it was all over, everybody was exhausted.

The three women sat together and finished the bottle of gin.

"Why are men such unreconstructed bollixes?" Angie asked.

"Because their mothers spoil them," Orla said.

"But that means us. We're the mothers of the future."

"Yeah, I suppose it does. You could say we're the authors of our own misfortune."

Bobby started weeping again. "What am I going to do? I can't go to work. I can't leave this house. Everybody will be talking about me. I'll be mortified."

"You'll disappear," Angie said. "That's what you'll do."

"What do you mean?"

"Just leave it to me. Now why don't you go to bed and try to get some sleep?"

She returned the following afternoon. Bobby was lying in bed with the curtains drawn and the phone off the hook so that no-one could contact her.

"It's all arranged," Angie said.

"What's all arranged?"

"Your escape. I got a last-minute cancellation. You and me are off tomorrow to the Canaries."

Bobby sat bolt upright.

"The *where*?"

"Tenerife. I've booked us into a nice little place called Hotel Las Flores. No one will ever find us."

Chapter 5

Monica Woodworth could have murdered her husband. She would have done it with a smile on her face and joy in her heart. And not just any kind of murder. For Woody Woodworth, only the most slow and painful death would have been good enough. Branding with hot irons, boiling in oil, hanging, drawing, quartering. She wanted to see him suffer. Nothing would have given her greater pleasure than to have torn out his fingernails, peeled the skin from his face and fed his entrails to her pet Border Terrier. But Monica couldn't murder him. She couldn't even touch him. For the miserable bastard was already dead and his ashes had been scattered from Killiney Hill to poison the environment wherever they happened to fall.

That, in a nutshell, was the cause of Monica's woes. That was the source of all her troubles. That was the reason she had pawned her jewellery, returned the sports car, put the house up for sale, the dog in the animal shelter and registered with a recruitment agency that specialised in temporary secretarial jobs. *She,* Monica Woodworth, who had once hired secretaries and fired them at a whim with one disdainful glance from her cold, dark eyes, had been reduced to seeking temporary clerical work.

Oh, the ignominy of it! Oh, the pretence and lies! Oh, the burning shame! And all because that miserable worm, that weak, spineless excuse for a human being, that philandering piece of dog-turd had up and died.

Monica glanced again at the letter that had just arrived with the morning's post. It was from the phone company. *FINAL NOTICE,* it read in gloomy type across the top.

The Occupant,

This is the third and final communication. Unless the sum outstanding is paid within seven days, we will have no option but to withdraw service. We would remind you that a reconnection charge of €100 applies.

If this bill has already been paid, please ignore this communication.

She tossed the letter with the others that already lay in a heap on the kitchen table. Why did she bother opening them?. There were similar demands from the electricity company, the gas company, the TV company, the building society, the credit-card company. She had never realised before, the number of people out there who were bent on extracting money from her. Woody had always dealt with the bills. Monica was reminded of a film she had once seen about a dying gazelle and how the vultures had circled the corpse before it was cold, waiting to tear chunks out of it.

That's what they're doing to me, she thought. Tearing chunks out of me. Scrambling to get a piece of me before I expire. They think if they don't get in fast, there'll be nothing left. But I have a surprise for them. I have no intention of expiring. I might be down. But it's only temporary. And, so help me God, I *will* bounce back.

She glanced scornfully at the solitary photograph that

remained on the mantelpiece. Destined for the rubbish bin along with everything else that reminded her of that scheming cockroach she had married. It showed Monica and Woody on a balcony, the sun going down, palm trees in the background, smiling for the camera while they clutched their frozen daiquiris. Montego Bay. Was it really only three months ago? Was that all the time it took for her world to fall apart?

Her thoughts went back to the first time they had met; a wet afternoon in late April, 1984. Grabbit and Leggit, Chartered Accountants, D'Olier St, Dublin 2. Monica was a twenty-two-year-old personal assistant to Mr Flynn, the junior partner. Woody was . . . what was he exactly? A man about town, a gay dog, what people used to call a dandy. He was thin with black hair and wore a white linen suit with a handkerchief flopping carelessly from the breast pocket. And his strong, handsome face was bronzed from the sun.

He made small talk as he folded his umbrella and followed her from the waiting-room to his appointment with Mr Flynn.

"Why do you stick this miserable weather?" he asked playfully, as outside the window the wind howled and the rain beat against the glass.

"Because I've no option."

"Rubbish. You should get away for a few weeks. Try Florida. Not a cloud in the sky. I've just been there. And I wouldn't have come back only business called."

"Sounds nice."

"Nice doesn't even begin to describe it. It's stupendous."

He was peering at her now, examining her closely. Monica didn't mind. She enjoyed the attention of handsome men.

"Pardon me for saying so, but you look a little peaky. You look like you could do with some sunshine." He rifled in his pocket and came out with a card. "Here. Give me a call. I might be able to fix you up with something reasonable."

Monica read the card. *Nigel Woodworth*, it said. *Investment Consultant. 215, North Anne St, Dublin 1.*

What age was Nigel Woodworth? That was the topic that consumed a good deal of the after-work conversation between Monica and her friend, Linda Matthews, as they sipped glasses of wine in the snug of Bowes public house in Fleet Street.

Linda ran the switchboard. She knew everybody who did business with Grabbit and Leggit, knew a good deal about their private lives as well. Working on the switchboard, you got to hear things.

"I'd say he's in his forties," Linda said, draining her glass. "He's got that look."

"What look?" Monica inquired.

"You know, like he's been around a while, seen a bit of action. He has a lived-in face."

"You mean mature?"

"No, it's more than mature. It's kind of *rakish*. I'd say he's the sort of man who lives on the edge."

"He gave me his card," Monica said.

"That's interesting."

"Says he might be able to get me a cheap deal for a holiday in Florida. Are you interested?"

"Could be. Depends on the price."

"You think he's married?"

Linda was shaking her head and simultaneously gesticulating to the barman for two refills.

"I wouldn't say so. I wouldn't say Nigel Woodworth is the sort of man who gets married."

Within a week, Monica was calling him Woody. Just like all

his friends. Only those people not in the golden circle called him Nigel. She rang the number he had given her and he arranged to meet her the following evening in the Horseshoe Bar of the Shelbourne Hotel. Monica wore her best outfit: a snugly fitting business suit that showed her to good advantage without appearing loud. She nipped into the ladies' room, fixed her hair and sprayed a little *Temptation* on each wrist before making her entrance to the bar.

He wasn't there. Monica looked around to make sure he wasn't sitting in some out-of-the-way corner. But there was no sign of him. She went to the counter and ordered a drink.

Ten minutes later, he still hadn't arrived. She was furious. Men did *not* stand Monica up. She debated whether to leave and reluctantly decided to wait for a while in case he'd been held up. So she sat it out at the counter, silently fuming as she tried to make the gin and tonic last, feeling that everybody in the bar was staring at her.

He came bustling in at last, half an hour late, wearing a black cashmere overcoat and scarf, waving and saying hello to acquaintances and friends.

Immediately, he began to apologise. "I'm dreadfully sorry. Detained at the office by a last-minute problem."

"You could have rung," she said coldly.

"But that would have held me up even longer." He put his hands together in supplication and Monica half expected him to go down on one knee. "Please forgive me."

The frown she had prepared melted away. "I forgive you."

At once he brightened up. "Well, now that's out of the way, what can I get you to drink?"

He ordered doubles, gin for her, Scotch for himself.

Monica couldn't help noticing that no money changed

hands. He led her to a corner table and threw off his overcoat.

"You didn't pay for our drinks," she said.

"Of course not. I have a tab."

"What's that?"

"It's an account. I settle with them at the end of each month. It saves going about with your pockets full of loose change."

"But how do you know they won't overcharge you?" Monica asked.

Woody smiled, indulgently. "My dear, it just doesn't arise. We're all gentlemen, here."

Afterwards, he took her to dinner in a smart restaurant off Baggot Street. Candles, waiters in dress suits, a pianist playing Cole Porter. The maitre d' met them at the door, fussed over them and led them to a discreet table at the back where they could see without being seen. Monica was *very* impressed.

Woody ordered a bottle of the best wine and advised her on the menu. The waiters grovelled and fawned but Woody took it all in his stride and tipped handsomely while Monica watched with open-mouthed wonder. This was a world she had never seen before. What did you have to do to get in?

When the meal was finished, he lit a cigar and smiled at her across the table. Monica thought he looked much younger than forty, but maybe it was the candlelight or all the wine she had drunk.

"Can we talk about Florida?" she said. "That's why I rang you in the first place."

"You don't want to go to Florida."

"But Florida was your idea. *You* told me it was marvellous there. *You* said I needed sunshine and there wasn't a cloud in the sky. *You* said you might be able to get me a deal."

He held her hand while he gazed into her eyes. There

was something about the way he looked at her that caused a pleasant flutter in Monica's breast.

"You're very beautiful," he said.

"Thank you."

"And you don't want to go to Florida."

"But I do," she insisted. "I've just told you."

"No, you don't. You want to come away with me. To Nice. I'm leaving in the morning. I'm spending two weeks cruising the Med."

It turned out to be the most exciting two weeks Monica had ever known. They picked up the boat in Nice harbour. It was a fifty-foot motor cruiser loaned to Woody by a client and came equipped with a crew of two men who did all the serious work. Their days were simple and blissful. They would rise around noon when the sun was already high in the azure sky and breakfast on coffee, croissants and fruit. Woody would then dress in white trousers and jacket and fuss around with charts and compasses in the saloon. He would take business calls and give instructions, while Monica stretched out on the deck and soaked up the glorious sunshine.

In the evenings, they partied. At each port they came to, Woody knew where the smart set was to be found. In Villefranche, it was the *Caprice*. In Monte Carlo, the *Lion D'Or*. In Cannes, Fat Johnnie's. Woody moved with ease in the company of bankers and film stars, fashion models and minor aristocrats. And everywhere they went, there were admiring glances for Monica and warm introductions. There was dinner and dancing, then a nightclub and finally they would all pile into sports cars and race off to a party in somebody's villa, only to leave when the sun was beginning to creep above the eastern horizon.

No wonder it turned Monica's head. No wonder she convinced herself she was in love with Woody Woodworth. She had never experienced anything like this before and enjoyed every golden moment.

But too soon, it was over and they were back again to the dreary skies and rainswept streets of Dublin. She gave up her bed-sit in Rathmines and moved into his townhouse in Leeson Street, close to St Stephen's Green. She left her job at Grabbit and Leggit. There had been a row anyway about the way she had taken off for Nice without getting permission from Mr Flynn.

Woody said she could work for him. But there really wasn't any work to do. There was just Woody and a secretary who filed documents and dealt with correspondence and took phone calls. Monica was installed as Office Manager. She spent most of her time shopping and chatting on the phone to her friends. In between, she harassed the secretary who quit after a week to be replaced by another who lasted a fortnight.

But she soon tired of terrorising secretaries. She needed something more exciting to occupy her time when she wasn't dining out or going to opening nights at the theatre or attending the races. She came up with a wonderful idea. With a couple of friends, she set about organising lunches for charity. All the stylish ladies about town would be invited and the proceeds would go to a worthy cause.

Monica soon discovered she had a talent for this sort of thing. She browbeat travel agents and dress designers to donate prizes for her raffles. She invited interesting speakers: fashionable actors and racing drivers and famous writers. The lunches were a great success and before long, ladies were scrambling for tickets. Not to be invited to Monica's lunches was the social equivalent of being cast adrift in the

Saragossa Sea on a life-raft. The events were written up in the gossip columns and the fashion magazines. *And* they made a lot of money for charities.

As well as the lunches and the shopping and the outings, Monica ran Woody's household. It wasn't a particularly arduous task. She ordered whatever was needed. The bills were sent to Woody and he paid. One of her responsibilities was organising parties, which required skills even greater than those needed for the lunches. It was vitally important to have the *right* people: this politician, that businessman, a certain actress, a particular barrister. And of course, someone who would leak the information to the press.

Monica's parties quickly became the talk of the town. She invited rock stars and television personalities. She hired jazz bands, which caused consternation among the neighbours and led to complaints which Monica put down to envy. She became known as the society hostess of her generation. She made reputations. To be seen at one of Monica's parties was to have arrived.

She also realised very quickly that the parties provided a potent weapon to strike fear into her enemies. If someone upset her for any reason, they were crossed off the guest list and consigned to outer darkness. If someone else was needed for a favour, they were invited and cultivated. And of course, if you invited the *right* people to your parties, they, in turn, invited you to theirs. And so the glittering life went on.

But the hectic social whirl took its toll and every few months Woody and Monica would fly off for a holiday to recuperate. In the winter, it was the Canaries or Florida; in the summer, Marbella or the South of France. And even from these distances, Monica managed to keep her profile before the public by faxing paragraphs to the social columns and ringing the gossip writers.

It was on one of these holidays at the Hotel Sol in Puerto Banus that Monica eventually persuaded Woody to marry her. She had been planning her strategy for months. It was a balmy evening, the air was heavy with the scent of orange blossom and Woody was half drunk. He had consumed a bottle and a half of wine at dinner and was now starting on his third brandy.

She gently ran her finger along his arm.

"If only this could last for ever," she sighed.

"Nothing lasts forever," Woody said, bluntly. "Surely, you've learnt that much by now?"

"My love for you does. It burns with the intensity of a flame that can never be extinguished."

It was straight from Barbara Cartland. Monica had been rehearsing all afternoon in the bathroom while Woody dozed in the garden.

He took off his sunglasses to get a better look at her. "Are you sure you're all right?"

"Of course I am."

"You don't sound all right. You sound like you've been drinking."

Monica laughed lightly. "Just because I tell you how much I care for you. My love is bigger than a mountain, deeper than the sea. It's like a star that lights up the darkness, a diamond that shines –"

"By God, I didn't realise you felt *that* strongly." Woody sat up straight.

"Of course, I do darling. You don't think I would have slept with you if I didn't love you. I've loved you from the very first moment I set eyes on you. You must have known that."

"I never gave it much thought, tell you the truth."

"But how could I *not* love a man who is so kind and generous and handsome. *And* so virile in bed."

"You're trying to flatter me, you little minx."

She leaned closer and put her lips to his ear. "Do *you* love *me*, darling?"

"Surely you don't have to ask."

"Then why don't you make an honest woman of me? You know people talk. They say cruel things."

Woody snorted. "Who the hell cares?"

"*I* do!" Monica said firmly. "There's no reason why you shouldn't marry me. It would simplify everything. You don't have a wife hidden away somewhere, do you?"

"What a silly question."

"Then *marry* me, Woody."

He lifted his glass and polished off the remains of the brandy.

"OK," he said. "When would suit?"

It was one of the biggest weddings Dublin had seen for years. It was held at the University Church in Stephen's Green. The bride arrived in a horse-drawn carriage and there were so many guests that most of them couldn't get in and they ended up blocking the traffic outside.

The reception was at Luttrelstown Castle, outside Dublin. Five hundred people sat down to dinner. They were the cream of society. Reporters and photographers fought to get quotes and pictures. Television cameras jostled for the best shots. And at the top table, looking radiant in her dress of white satin, Monica presided like an empress at her court. She closed her eyes and whispered to herself. *"I've done it. I've finally got where I want to be and nothing can dislodge me now."*

She was wrong of course, but she wouldn't know that for some time yet.

She never did manage to find out how Woody made his

money. If she asked, he simply replied that he advised people on how to get the best return from their capital. And some very important people came to him for advice. They were the type of people who Monica invited to her parties: politicians, judges, media personalities. But though she never discovered how it worked, there was never any shortage of cash. The money just seemed to keep pouring in, as if by magic. And as fast as it came, Monica and Woody spent it.

They decided that their townhouse wasn't really big enough for the sort of socialising they required. So, they sold it and bought a bigger one out in Dalkey with spectacular views across Dublin Bay. They were barely installed, when a rock star bought the house next door.

They had their own cars. Woody drove a top-of-the-range BMW. Monica had a little white Alfa Romeo sports number. She had an allowance that she rarely used. Most of the time, she just ordered whatever she wanted and charged it to Woody's account. It was marvellous. She never needed cash. It made her feel like a member of the royal family.

They never had any children. It just didn't occur to them to start a family. They were always too busy enjoying themselves. Monica didn't regret it and Woody didn't seem to care. And none of their friends made any comment, so it didn't matter.

And so they lived in a dizzy round of parties and holidays, shopping trips and lunches. Monica absolutely revelled in her position as first lady of the social scene. She loved the power it gave her and the tribute it brought. People envied her. She was flattered and admired. Nobody thought it would ever end.

It did. On a dreadful day in March 2004.

Monica would look back on it forever, as the day her world collapsed. But it began innocently enough. Woody had flown to London that morning for a business meeting.

She thought he looked a little bit tired. He was working too hard. She made a mental note to take him off soon for another holiday.

She had a lunch appointment at the Trevi, a little Italian restaurant she favoured, at the back of Grafton Street. Just a couple of her intimate friends to plan the next charity function. She was enjoying her meal when her mobile phone began to ring. She put it to her ear at once and heard a trembling voice on the other end.

"It's Noreen here, Mrs Woodworth. I hope I'm not disturbing you but I didn't know what to do."

She recognised the frightened voice of Woody's secretary. "What is it, Noreen? Speak up."

"I've just got a call from London. The manager of the hotel I booked for Mr Woodworth."

"Yes?"

"He says Mr Woodworth's after dropping dead."

"Whaaat?"

"I know. Isn't it terrible? I thought I should tell you."

Monica said: "Thank you, Noreen. You did the right thing."

She switched off the phone, felt the room begin to spin and collapsed face-first into her plate of *penne rusticana*.

But the nightmare was only beginning. Monica had to fly to London to identify the body. Then she had to wait for the autopsy. It turned out that Woody had died of a massive heart attack. Next came the transport arrangements to bring his body home and then the funeral. It had all happened so quickly that most of the time Monica went around in a daze.

The funeral was a grand affair. The great and the good turned out in force. Monica, in a black designer outfit complete with veil, got her picture in all the papers. Woody's obituaries appeared with glowing tributes to his patronage of the arts, of sport, of youth, of business and his generosity to numerous good causes including the annual taxi-drivers' pilgrimage to Knock shrine. Overall, Monica was pleased with the way it had gone. She had Woody cremated and his remains scattered over Killiney Hill.

She was still in shock when the following morning she was wakened by a loud knocking on her front door. She threw on her silk dressing-gown and went down to the hall. A heavily built man in a black overcoat and trilby hat stood on the doorstep. Beside him, was an even bigger man wearing dark glasses and a leather jacket. The first man took off his hat and made a little bow.

"Mrs Woodworth, I am sorry for your troubles."

"Thank you," Monica said. "That's very kind."

"My name is Zharkov. I've come about my money."

Monica blinked. "What money would that be, Mr Zharkov?"

"The money your husband was investing for me. Now that he is dead, I want it back."

"But I know nothing about his financial affairs," Monica stammered.

Mr Zharkov put his hat back on. He cracked his knuckles and looked at her with the frozen face of a gargoyle. "Then, I suggest you find out, Mrs Woodworth. Fast. I'll be back again in one week."

Mr Zharkov was only the first of numerous callers. At nine o'clock, the phone rang. This time it was a clapped-out writer turned restaurant critic in his declining years. He began by offering his condolences and then cut straight to the chase.

"Have you been into the office yet?"

"No."

"It's just that eh, Woody was looking after my affairs. I was wondering . . .?"

"I know nothing about it," Monica said and slammed down the phone.

By lunchtime, there had been a dozen inquiries from worried investors. Monica decided it was time to call in the professionals. She rang her old boss, Mr Flynn, at Grabbit and Leggit. He was now the senior partner.

"I need your help. I'm besieged by all these people demanding money and I don't even know where to start."

Mr Flynn listened patiently then said: "OK. I'll go in and have a look. But I'll have to charge a special rate."

"I don't care," Monica wailed. "Just get them off my back."

She poured herself a large glass of gin and watched the gentle heave of the sea beyond Dalkey Island. For the first time since Woody died, she felt the icy finger of fear run along her spine.

Mr Flynn returned a few days later. His face was grim. He sat down with Monica in the drawing-room and opened his brief-case.

"Prepare yourself for bad news."

"Yes?"

"There's no money left."

Monica laughed, nervously. "This is a joke, right?"

"No joke. Not only is there no money, there are considerable debts. It appears your late husband was diverting clients' funds for his own use. He was speculating on currencies."

"Is that good or bad?"

"In his case, bad. He was buying Russian roubles."

Monica thought immediately of Mr Zharkov. "So all these people who keep ringing me . . .?"

"There's nothing for them. Not a sausage."

Worse was to come. The banks appointed a liquidator to sell off the assets. That meant the house, the cars, the furniture, even the fax machine in the office. In the course of his investigations, the liquidator also discovered that Woody had been keeping a mistress and had set her up in a fashion boutique in Norfolk Street. Monica knew her. She was twenty-five. Her name was Julie Smyth. She had sold Monica the outfit she wore to Woody's funeral.

Monica went into shock and then depression. Practically overnight, she had gone from queen bee to social outcast. She moved out of the house while the banks arranged for an auctioneer to put it on the market. She rented a small apartment in Ringsend and tried to come to terms with the calamity that had overtaken her.

Luckily, she had a few thousand euro put away from the allowance that Woody had given her. That was her own money and the liquidator couldn't touch it. She pawned her jewellery and that brought in a few thousand more. She signed on with an agency that dealt in temporary secretarial placements and they promised to find her work. With a bit of luck, she would just about survive.

Monica was forced to survey the wreckage of her life. Not only had she lost her social position and discovered her husband's infidelity, she now faced the contempt of her enemies. Already, there had been a pointed paragraph in the *On the Piste* social column of the *Daily Bugle* by a harpy called Colleen McQueen who Monica had systematically snubbed and excluded from her parties. Now it was payback time. Monica shuddered at the thought of all those two-bit nonentities lining up to gloat and jeer at her downfall. The very thought sent a dagger through her heart.

She sat now at her dressing-table in the house that had witnessed so many of her social triumphs. It was the last time she would set foot under its roof. The auctioneer had found a buyer. Another rock star. Monica had arrived this morning to clear out the remainder of her clothes and erase every last memory of the despicable rodent who had brought this disaster upon her.

The face that stared back at her was that of a forty-two-year-old woman, still handsome, still vibrant, the eyes bright, the hair shining, the skin smooth and radiant. She sat up straight. No point feeling sorry for herself. No point moaning about her luck. She had suffered a reverse but it wasn't the end. She would rebuild her life. She would pick herself up and go forward. And in time, she would get her revenge on all those miserable reptiles who were now rejoicing in her downfall.

But first, she needed to get away. A short holiday. She deserved it after all she'd been through. She took her husband's picture from the mantelpiece and sent it crashing into the bin along with his shirts and ties. The suits she had already sold to a second-hand shop in Dorset Street.

She closed the door and dropped the key through the letterbox. She never looked back as she marched down the drive and out onto the main road. There was a travel shop at the end of Castle Street. She pushed open the door and a smiling young man came forward to greet her.

"I'd like to book a holiday."

"Certainly, madam. Where would you like to go?"

"Somewhere warm and sunny."

"How about Tenerife?"

She thought of the holidays she had spent in Tenerife in years gone by, always staying in the very best hotels: the Hotel Botanico or the Gran Hotel del Rey. Now, her budget wouldn't stretch to a gardener's shed in the hotel grounds.

"What do you recommend? I can't spend too much."

"I might have the very thing, Madam. I can let you have a studio apartment in a nice quiet complex."

"Is it expensive?"

"Just a few hundred euro."

"What's it called?"

"Hotel Las Flores."

"I'll take it," Monica said before she changed her mind.

Chapter 6

Adrian Blake shuddered as he listened to the captain's voice booming out over the intercom.

"Would passengers please ensure that safety belts are securely fastened? Landing shortly."

He felt his chest contract with fear. He clenched his teeth and began to mutter a silent prayer that the plane wouldn't shear off the top of the terminal building on the way in to land. With the type of luck he'd been having recently, this was precisely the sort of thing that could happen. Or else a wheel might drop off or an engine stall. Adrian screwed his eyes tight as his imagination began to conjure up even more grisly endings. He hated flying. He hated the cramped seating, the awful food, the noise. But most of all, he hated the fact that once the door was closed *you couldn't get off!*

Adrian had long ago concluded that flying was the only mode of transport, with the exception of space travel, where the passenger was a total prisoner. You could hop off a bus, a tram, a train. Or even a boat. But you couldn't get off a plane. Once the doors were closed, you were a captive and your fate was completely in the hands of the pilot. And what if he had been drinking? Or was on drugs? Or had just had a row with his wife? Adrian felt the fear come at him again like a wave and knew that he wouldn't relax till his feet were once more planted on solid ground.

He hadn't wanted to come to Tenerife. He had planned to spend the Easter break fixing his novel. After much soul-searching, he had come to the conclusion that the pace was the problem. He needed to jizz it up, give it a bit of sparkle before submitting it once again to a round of publishers. And this time he was convinced it would be greeted with the acclaim it so justly deserved. In fact, he was already rehearsing the speech he would give to the Booker reception excoriating the intellectual pygmies who had failed to recognise his talent when it was first presented to them.

And then, one day last week, Trish had delivered a *fait accompli*. Two tickets to Tenerife already paid for and no possibility of a refund. A last-minute bargain, she had claimed. Just had to snap it up! And she hadn't even consulted him, which caused him to sulk throughout dinner.

He had noticed recently that Trish was beginning to behave strangely. Coming home some evenings so flushed you would have sworn she'd spent a session in the gym. He wondered if she was going through that change-of-life thing women got. Made them behave oddly. Drove some of them completely bonkers, apparently. But Trish was only thirty-seven and surely that was much too young?

She had pooh-poohed his objections. "You can write just as well in Tenerife," she said firmly. "I'll borrow a laptop from the office and you can transfer the novel onto a disc. Think about it, Adrian. Sitting on your balcony, watching the golden sun sink into the indigo sea. Think of the inspiration. Think of Graham Greene and Somerset Maugham."

It sounded like something she had read in the travel brochure. But when she put it that way, the idea didn't seem quite so bad.

"I would remind you that Maugham and Greene had private villas," Adrian replied somewhat testily. "They didn't mix with the common herd. They didn't have to put up with spotty adolescents playing transistor radios and jumping into the swimming-pool at all hours of the day and night."

"Don't worry, darling," Trish cooed, soothingly. "We'll find you a nice quiet spot. Believe me, this is exactly what you need. You've been working too hard. Taking far too much out of yourself." She stroked his forehead. "You need to relax."

Adrian pictured himself in straw hat and sunglasses in the shade of a palm tree, a chilled glass of wine to hand. Were there any other writers in Tenerife? Maybe they could get together? Form a literary colony?

"All right," he said, grudgingly. "I'll give it a go."

And now, as they came in to land, he was reminded again why he hated to fly. He felt the plane bounce as the wheels hit the runway and the pilot applied the brakes. Adrian had read somewhere that this was the most dangerous time of all. Most accidents occurred at take-off and landing. Once you were in the air, nothing much could happen unless the pilot fell asleep at the controls and flew into a mountain. Or there was a crazed terrorist on board. Which was well within the bounds of possibility, he decided as he surveyed his fellow passengers with a scowl.

His fingers tightened like a vice round Trish's hand while the aircraft rattled and shook as it raced along the tarmac. It felt like he was strapped inside a washing machine. He opened his eyes and, from the window, saw the runway flashing past in a blur. He released Trish's hand, quickly unhooked his seatbelt and offered a silent prayer to God that, once more, his life had been spared.

There was a delay while passengers scrambled to unload their baggage from the overhead racks and then they were moving towards the exit doors. But the minute Adrian stepped outside the plane he was hit by a great wall of white heat. He looked up and saw the sun hanging like a giant ball of flame in the cloudless sky. He wished now that he hadn't worn the heavy sweater and scarf and the thermal underpants, but it had been cold when they left Dublin. He dragged himself down the steps and across the boiling tarmac, the perspiration streaming from every pore and his shirt clinging to his back like a clammy octopus.

It was like hiking through a sauna in hob-nailed boots. He desperately wanted a cold drink, but the priority was to get to the luggage ramp and reclaim their cases before some gouger made off with them. At last, they reached their destination, went through passport control and passed into the arrivals lounge, Adrian clutching the laptop computer he had insisted on carrying onto the plane and refused to let out of his sight.

A terrible scene awaited them. The lounge was a mass of steaming bodies. It reminded Adrian of a bazaar they had once visited in Tangiers. People were bumping into each other and jabbering in strange tongues. Children were screaming. Inert passengers lay stretched out on benches, apparently asleep. Adrian felt his heart sink as he fought his way to the luggage carousel and waited till their suitcases popped up on the conveyor belt. He grabbed the luggage, lowered his head like a rugby player and struggled back through the heaving crowd to the exit.

Here, a chirpy young woman from the travel company was waiting for them. She was dressed in a bright yellow blouse and skirt that made Adrian think of a pet canary his family kept when he was a child. The woman had a clipboard in her hand and was scoring off names.

"Blake," Adrian said, bad-temperedly.

The woman studied her board. "Patricia and Arthur?"

"Adrian."

"Oh, I see. They have you down as Arthur."

"Well, they have me down wrong," Adrian snapped.

"He doesn't look like an Arthur, does he?" the young woman said to Trish in a jolly voice. "Enjoying our holiday, are we?"

"We've just arrived," Adrian growled. "And so far, I am *not* impressed."

"Oh, you'll love it here. Everybody does. My name is Penny. I'm your rep." She quickly shook hands with them and glanced once more at her clipboard. "You're staying at Hotel Las Flores. You'll find your coach outside. Number 41. We're leaving in fifteen minutes so don't hang about. Don't want to leave you behind, now do we?"

"Thank you," Trish said.

"Ta ra," Penny said. "See you later."

Adrian groaned, lifted the cases and headed once more into the boiling sun.

Mercifully, the coach journey was short. The driver was a fat man with a thick moustache who introduced himself as Pedro. He immediately led the passengers in choruses of *Viva Espana* to get them into the holiday mood. Every time he negotiated a tricky bend in the road, Penny encouraged them to give him a cheer which he acknowledged by waving one hand and driving with the other till Adrian was convinced they were going to drive over a precipice and never be heard of again. In between, Penny gave them tips on where to eat and drink and warned about staying out too long in the sun. And when she wasn't doing this, she was reminding them of the wonderful sightseeing tours that absolutely shouldn't be missed and over which she appeared to hold the sole franchise.

Gradually, the coach dropped people at various hotels till only a handful were left for Hotel Las Flores. Adrian sneaked a glance at the remaining passengers. No children, thank God. That was a small relief. He'd spent the last three months locked up every day with the little bastards and he didn't want to see another one till the holiday was over.

In the back seat, a man sat alone, quietly reading a book. He was respectably dressed in blazer and slacks. Near him sat two young ladies dressed in light summer clothes. For people embarked on a holiday, Adrian thought they looked inappropriately downcast. In the seats in front was what looked like a family: mother and father and two grown-up children. The father was dressed in a heavy suit and had a strong weather-beaten face, while the mother had a solid country air about her. Farmers, Adrian decided, spending some of that money that flowed like a river from Brussels.

And finally, across the aisle, sat a striking woman. Adrian was certain he had seen her face before somewhere. She was approaching middle age and had dark hair, strong handsome features, and from what he could see, a fine, elegant figure. She looked sad. Maybe she's been unlucky in love, Adrian concluded, and is coming here to find romance and mend her broken heart. I wonder what her story is?

His reverie was interrupted by Penny who was babbling once more in her irritatingly cheerful voice.

"We're almost at the hotel so this is where I'll leave you. But I'll be back in the morning at ten o'clock for the Welcome Meeting when you'll be able to book some of those wonderful tours, I've been telling you about."

The coach came to a halt and the woman across the aisle

turned around. Her eyes met Adrian's and she smiled. Adrian found himself smiling back. And suddenly, something clicked inside his head. By God, he thought, I was right. She's hungry for romance. Poor, neglected, lonely woman. What sorrows is she hiding behind that tragic face? But before he could consider further, Trish was standing up and moving towards the exit.

Hotel Las Flores was true to its name. Outside the front door was a great profusion of flowering geraniums, climbing roses and trailing wisteria which presented a riot of bright colour against the stark white brickwork. Adrian carried the cases into the lobby and up to the Reception desk where a handsome young man was waiting. Adrian presented his reservation documents. The man immediately grasped his hand and shook it firmly.

"*Senor* Blake," he said in very good English, "we have been expecting you."

My God, Adrian thought, could word of my novel have reached Tenerife?

But the man was already turning to Trish. He gently pressed her hand and introduced himself. "My name is Carlos Hernandez. I am the manager of Hotel Las Flores. I hope you have a comfortable stay in our hotel. You are in Room 303. Here is your apartment key. And here is your safe key."

He offered the register for Adrian to sign and then he presented him with a chit of paper. "With our compliments, *Senor* Blake. For you and *Senora* Blake to have a drink in the bar."

Very civil, Adrian thought. Very civil indeed. He was beginning to like this place already. *"Muchas gracias,"* he said loudly, so the people queuing behind would know that he spoke some Spanish.

Senor Hernandez made a little bow. Adrian grabbed their

luggage and headed briskly across the lobby in search of the lift.

Their apartment was on the third floor close to the stairs. Adrian nudged open the door with his shoulder, put down the cases and placed the laptop carefully on the sideboard. "Let's see what we've got," he said, rubbing his hands together energetically.

There was a good-sized lounge with settee, television, coffee table and sliding doors leading to a large balcony, a kitchen with fridge and cooker, and a bathroom with toilet, shower and bidet. Adrian noted with approval the fresh white towels that had been laid out in readiness for them.

"And now for the bedroom," he declared. "What have they got us sleeping on?" He flung open the door. The room held a pine dressing-table, a bank of built-in wardrobes and, smack in the centre of the room, a king-sized double bed.

Trish held her breath.

"A double bed!" Adrian exclaimed.

"It was all I could get," Trish explained quickly. "And anyway, this is a holiday. Nobody sleeps in separate beds on their holidays."

But a change seemed to have come over Adrian. He was beaming from ear to ear. "Who's complaining? I think it's excellent."

"You do?"

He gave Trish a quick peck on the cheek. "Of course. You did well, my dear. I'm beginning to think I might get some good work done on my book, after all."

"I'm sure you will," Trish gushed. "Something tells me that before this holiday is over, our lives will have changed forever."

Adrian thought fleetingly of the mysterious woman he had seen on the coach and the way she had smiled at him.

"You know," he said. "I think you might be right."

Chapter 7

The bright sunlight woke Bobby. She was confused at first and didn't recognise her surroundings. She sat up with a start and stared at the unfamiliar room with its pine dressing-table and its built-in wardrobes and single beds. Where was she? How did she get here? But it took only a few seconds for the fog to lift and reality to descend. She was in Tenerife. In Hotel Las Flores and she was here because she had been jilted. It was such an old-fashioned word and she had always hated it. But it was the truth. She had been let down by the man she had dreamed of marrying and she couldn't face the shame and ignominy. She was here to escape.

Her mind went racing back to the events of the last forty-eight hours.

Angie had been an absolute rock. She had arranged everything: the accommodation, the tickets, the taxi to the airport, even the kennels for the animals. Not to mention the horror involved in cancelling the wedding plans. The only things that remained to be done were the return of the wedding presents and the engagement ring which Bobby had wanted to tie to the heaviest object she could find – preferably with Alex attached – and throw into the Liffey, until Angie persuaded her against it.

"Are you crazy? Didn't you tell me that ring cost €5,000?"

"But it's his. And I want nothing more to do with him."

"Well, let's not cut off our nose to spite our face. Five grand is five grand."

"I never want to see or hear or even be in the same space as Alex Piper again."

"I understand," Angie said. "The guy is beyond all human sympathy."

"Damned right, he is."

"He has to be taught a lesson."

"He has to be made to *suffer*," Bobby said.

"Yes! He has to learn that he can't treat marriage like it is one of his silly rugby games that he can just postpone whenever the weather changes. Marriage is a serious business and so is dallying with a person's affections."

"Anyway, what does it matter? It's all over."

Angie pursed her lips. "Well . . ."

"Yes?" Bobby said, suddenly suspicious.

"I wouldn't be entirely sure about that."

"What do you mean?"

"I think he'll be back."

"What?"

"Give him a week till he realises the prize he's let slip through his grasp and he'll be crawling on his hands and knees to get to you. And this is where you have to be cool. Remember, your self-respect is at stake."

Bobby forced herself to smile. "Now just hang on a

minute. This is the bastard who has just put me through the worst humiliation of my entire life!"

"I only said he'd be back. Let's not be rash. Let's see how things work out."

"You weren't listening," Bobby stressed. "He can crawl through barbed wire for all I care. Alex Piper is yesterday's news."

Now, from the kitchen, there emerged the sharp whine of a kettle coming to the boil. It was quickly followed by the emergence of Angie in her white hotel dressing-gown bearing two mugs of coffee. She sat down on the edge of the bed and gave Bobby one of the mugs.

"Strong, the way you like it. With two sugars. So how do you feel this morning?"

"Fine."

"You certainly slept well. You were snoring all night like the foghorn on the Baily Lighthouse."

"Excuse me," Bobby said indignantly. "I do *not* snore."

"Well, you give a pretty good imitation. If you recorded that noise you could use it as an insect repellent."

"I'll pretend I didn't hear that remark," Bobby said, "only because you're my best friend and have been so good to me during this recent little contretemps."

"Talking of which," Angie said. "We're here to relax, Right? There is to be absolutely no moping."

"No moping."

"No going around feeling sorry for ourselves."

"No."

"Bright face and sunny outlook at all times. Promise?"

"I promise."

"OK. Here's the schedule for today. I suggest we top up

the suntans till lunchtime. Then maybe we can do a spot of exploring. Then it will be time to consider the serious business of the evening. Which is: where to eat dinner?"

"Sounds good to me," Bobby said. "What about this Welcome Meeting?"

"We can look in for a few minutes. Might learn a few things."

Bobby had moved to the window and was staring down at the pool.

"My God!" she screamed. "It's the Germans!"

"What on earth are you talking about?"

"The Germans are taking over the sunbeds. They take it in turns to stay up all night just to snaffle the best ones."

"I don't think there are any Germans staying at this hotel."

"Well, somebody's doing it. Look!"

Angie joined her at the window where she could see the neat rows of towels draped carefully across the sunbeds. "My God! You're right. If we don't move fast we'll end up sunbathing out in the carpark."

Bobby quickly threw on a dressing-gown, grabbed two towels and headed for the lift. As she strode along the corridor, she couldn't help thinking of where she should be right now. Instead of fighting over sunbeds she should be stretched out on a golden beach in the Caribbean, drinking Pina Coladas with her brand-new husband while a reggae band played in the background. But Pig-face Piper had shattered that dream and now Angie had the nerve to hint that maybe she might consider taking him back. Well, he could freeze in hell till that day arrived!

Charlie Dobbins, meanwhile, was enjoying himself

immensely. Last night, after he had checked into his room and unpacked his luggage, he had gone for a few drinks in one of the local bars just to get acclimatised. It was a little *bodega* filled with olive-skinned *senoritas*, with flashing eyes and handsome good looks. They had laughed and smiled a lot but Charlie had been too shy to do or say anything. However, he had taken it as a good omen that Jimmy Brick's advice was sound. He had left the bar at one o'clock and gone straight to bed where he slept like a log till his alarm-clock woke him at eight. Now he had just finished breakfast and was looking forward to the Welcome Meeting where he hoped to pick up a few more tips.

As he approached the lift, he ran straight into a young blonde woman in a dressing-gown who was coming up from the swimming-pool area. Charlie immediately recognised her from the bus last night. He thought she looked quite attractive.

"Hello," he said breezily. "Having an early swim?"

The woman shook her head and looked a little guilty. "Booking a sunbed," she confessed.

"Really?" Charlie was intrigued. "I didn't realise you had to do that."

"Oh, you do," Bobby insisted. "If you want to get a decent one near the bar."

"Do you plan to spend a lot of time sunbathing?"

"Just enough to bring out my tan."

"I must give it a try," Charlie said, glancing self-consciously at his pale legs encased in khaki shorts.

"Make sure to use a sunscreen," Bobby said, "so you don't get burnt. It gets very hot out there."

The lift came and they got in together. Charlie gallantly pressed the floor button for her.

"Are you enjoying Tenerife?" she asked.

"So far, so good."

"Been here before?"

"No. This is my first time. You?"

"Same thing. I've come with my girlfriend. Just taking a little break."

"I'm going to the Welcome Meeting," Charlie said. "I might go on one of those tours the rep was talking about. See a bit of the island."

"Sounds like a good idea," Bobby said, determined to be bright and cheerful like she had promised Angie.

The lift arrived at her floor.

Bobby stuck out her hand. "I'm Bobby Bannon."

"Charlie Dobbins."

"Nice meeting you, Charlie."

"You too."

"Be sure to wear your sunscreen," Bobby said and stepped out of the lift.

What a very interesting young lady, Charlie thought as the doors closed and the lift carried him up to his room. And I was able to carry on a very civilised conversation without blushing or stammering once.

The Welcome Meeting was being held in the hotel bar and was beginning to fill up when Charlie arrived at five minutes to ten. Penny, in her canary uniform, was already up on the stage testing the microphone while a waiter circulated with complimentary glasses of sangria. Charlie took a seat at the back and let his eye travel around the room. He recognised several people from the bus last night: the country couple with the grown-up children, Bobby and her friend, that good-looking woman with the surly husband who had now donned a straw hat and dark glasses and gave a strong impression of being bored with the whole business.

And a tall, dark, handsome woman whose face was familiar. Charlie was convinced he had seen her before somewhere. But his reverie was interrupted by Penny's voice booming out of the sound system.

"Hello, everybody! Are we enjoying ourselves?"

A few people muttered: "Yes."

Penny wasn't satisfied.

"Oh, c'mon! You can do better than that."

This time they roared: *"Yes!"*

"Good. Are we happy with Hotel Las Flores?"

"Yes!"

"Are we happy with Carlos?"

"Yes!" everybody roared in unison.

A beaming Carlos came out from the bar and gave a little bow and Penny called for a round of applause.

Charlie stared in disbelief. He hadn't seen anything like this since he was a little boy at the Christmas pantomime. Any minute now, he expected to see the head waiter come out dressed as Mother Goose.

Now that she had broken the ice, Penny launched into a barrage of information about the transport system and car hire and shopping and the best way to deal with mosquitoes and cockroaches and other creatures that could make your holiday a misery. Finally, she got down to the real business of selling tours. She mentioned Mount Teide and the pearl factory and the cliffs of Los Gigantes and the parrot paradise of Loro Parque. She worked the crowd like a carpet salesman from the back of a lorry at a country fair.

"I have to warn you that these tours get booked out very fast. I'm only telling you so you won't be disappointed. I don't want people coming to me afterwards and saying they didn't know."

Eventually, the meeting broke up and people began to

drift away while others formed a queue at Penny's desk.

Charlie was moving through the throng towards the desk when he felt a tap on his shoulder. He turned to see Bobby Bannon again.

"So you're going on a tour?" she said.

"Yes. To Puerto de la Cruz. How about you?"

"I think I'll take a raincheck."

"You might regret it," Charlie said with a smile.

"Tell you what," Bobby said, "why don't you give me a report when you get back? And then if it's any good, maybe I'll go on one later."

"I'd be delighted," Charlie said. "Maybe we could have a drink?"

"Why not?" Bobby said, impishly. "I think I might enjoy that."

Charlie beamed with pleasure. This really was turning into a wonderful holiday. Why hadn't he done it before?

Chapter 8

Mollie was having a problem with the heat. It was the one thing she should have thought of. Indeed, she herself had stressed to the travel agent that she wanted somewhere sunny. But she had never thought it would be this hot. In fact, it had never crossed her mind in her anxiety to get everything organised and make sure that everybody was happy. Which hadn't been easy. Edward had grumbled about the disruption and Ned was uneasy about having to fly. Indeed the only member of the family who was entirely content was Mary who thought the holiday was a brilliant idea.

But in the end, it had all gone fine: the drive up to Dublin and the novelty of the flight, the first time any member of the family had been on a plane, and then the excitement of arriving in a strange new country.

But Mollie had only been on the ground two minutes when she knew she was in trouble. When she stepped off the plane, it was like opening an oven door. She was struck by an oppressive wave of heat that sucked the breath right out of her. And she hadn't got used to it yet.

She had come back from the Welcome Meeting and now she sat alone on the balcony of her apartment in the shade of a large umbrella while the others went about their business. She had taken off her shoes and stockings and immersed her feet in a basin of cold water. Mary had even put ice cubes in the basin to make the water cooler and had hired a fan from the nice girl at Reception. But none of this seemed to work. No matter what Mollie did, she still felt uncomfortable.

This morning, Mary had suggested that her mother buy a swimsuit and then she could sit by the swimming-pool. When she got too hot, she could just slip into the water and cool down. Mary had even offered to go with her to the shop and help her choose something nice. Everyone sat at the pool on holiday, Mary said, and as a bonus you got a nice suntan and when you came home, all the neighbours would be remarking on it. If you came home without a suntan, people would wonder if you had been on holiday at all.

Mollie listened patiently to what her daughter had to say. From the balcony, she surveyed the rows of bodies sizzling like lobsters on a grill and slowly shook her head. No one had ever seen her naked legs, except for Dr McCarthy and Ned. It was no behaviour for a lady. Besides, she was aware that her figure had long lost the youthful allure that once had men turning their heads to stare. Years of grubbing on a small farm and bearing two children had seen to that. She didn't care if everybody in Tenerife went about dressed in fig leaves. Mollie was keeping her clothes on!

So, she stayed on the balcony with her feet in the basin and prayed for a breeze.

The heat wasn't the only problem. There was also the business of the food. Ned had put his foot down early on and insisted there was no way he was eating anything strange. He had heard somewhere that foreigners ate all sorts of queer things like snails and frogs' legs. And horsemeat! How did you know when you ordered a sirloin steak in a restaurant that it hadn't been pulling a cart a few days before? The children had both told him he was mad, and pointed out that you could buy a good meal with a bottle of wine in any of the local restaurants for as little as €15. But Ned was adamant. He might be in Spain but foreign grub was out.

So, before leaving home, Mollie had carefully stuffed a suitcase with vacuum-sealed packs of rashers and ham and sausages so that Ned could eat good solid Irish fare. This morning, she had sweated over the stove to cook breakfast. It was hard work and it was made more difficult by the cramped space of the kitchen and the heat inside the apartment. But it was worth it to see the smile on Ned's face when he sat down to the nice crisp bacon and potato bread that she had brought specially and the Barry's Gold Blend Tea, all the way from Cork. This part of the holiday, at least, was going to be just like home.

The previous evening, a possible solution had presented itself – only for Ned to shoot it down. After arriving at the hotel and unpacking their belongings, the family had gathered again in the foyer. It was the one condition that Mollie had imposed. While she made it clear that the children were free to spend the holiday any way they pleased, she insisted that they all meet at least once a day, even if it was just to have a drink together. So at eight o'clock, after they had washed and changed their clothes, they congregated once more in the foyer.

"What will we do?" Mary wanted to know.

"We could go for a walk," Ned said. "Get a bit of exercise."

Mollie immediately thought of the heat. Would she be able for it? But she was surprised by the enthusiasm with which Edward took up his father's suggestion.

108

"That's a good idea. There's supposed to be a harbour nearby. Why don't we just wander off and explore the place?"

The young woman at the Reception desk gave them directions and they set off. Thankfully, the sun had gone down and it was much cooler now. Mollie gamely kept pace with the others and, after fifteen minutes, they reached their destination. The harbour was set in a natural inlet. It looked like a scene from a picture postcard with fishing boats moored along the stone wall and the sea shining like polished glass in the light of the moon. The only sound was the hush of the tide and the cry of the gulls.

"Isn't it beautiful?" Mary said. "I think it looks so romantic."

At the end of the harbour, they could see lights and hear music. As they approached, the music grew louder. And it sounded familiar. They rounded a corner and almost knocked over a large wooden board with a drawing of a little man in a green costume playing a fiddle. The board read: *The Lucky Leprechaun, Irish Bar and Grill*.

They exchanged amused glances.

"Well, I'll be damned," Ned said. "I thought we'd left all that behind."

Inside, the bar looked cool and inviting. They could see people laughing and drinking beer.

"Let's go in for a bit," Mollie said. "I need to sit down."

They found a vacant table and Ned went up to the counter to organise the drinks.

"Two pints of Guinness," he said to the curly-haired man behind the bar. "And two glasses of wine."

"Sorry, no Guinness," the man said in an Irish accent.

Ned was taken aback. "What? An Irish bar and no Guinness?"

"I know. But I'm right out of it. What about Spanish beer?"

Ned recoiled in horror. "Oh, no, I couldn't drink that."

"Why not?"

"Well, for a start, how do I know it's safe?"

The man smiled indulgently.

"It's perfectly safe. I sell gallons of it and nobody's got poisoned yet."

"But you don't know what they put in it."

"It's just water and wheat and hops, the same as any other beer. Here, try a drop."

He poured a glass of golden lager and slid it across the counter.

Ned took a tentative sip.

"Well," the man said, "what do you think?"

"It's not bad," Ned conceded, not wanting to be rude. "What's it called?"

"Dorada."

While he was organising the drinks, they got talking. The man said his name was Tom Casey and he came from Wexford. He had been living in Tenerife for five years and ran the pub with his brother, Brian.

"We do a good line in food too," he added. "I serve over a hundred meals every day."

"I'm not hungry," Ned said quickly and took the drinks back to the table.

They stayed till after midnight. Ned had several more pints of Dorada and Mollie noted with satisfaction that he spent much of the evening in conversation with Edward. When it was time to leave, Tom Casey accompanied them to the door.

"I hope you enjoyed yourselves," he said. "Maybe we'll see you again?"

"We'll be back," Ned said. "You can count on it."

"And the Spanish beer hasn't done you any harm?"

"I'm feeling no pain, anyway."

Back on the street, Mollie said tentatively, "Maybe next time you might try some of the food?"

"Oh no," Ned said emphatically. "Drinking their beer is one thing. Eating their grub's another thing entirely."

Mollie smiled ruefully at the memory. Still, things were coming along nicely. If only this damned heat would drop and a breeze come up from somewhere.

She thought of the €600,000 she had won on the lottery. It was a fortune. There were people who'd considered her the luckiest woman in Dunmuckridge when they heard about it. They'd expected her to go and splash out on new clothes and fancy furniture for the house. But Mollie cared nothing for these things.

She still hadn't decided what to do with her winnings. She had read stories about people who came into sudden wealth and it caused them nothing but grief. It broke up marriages. It tore families apart. It set friend against friend. Luckily, that hadn't happened to her. Neither of the children had shown the slightest interest in the money. She had promised them small gifts of cash but she had to browbeat them to accept even that.

Mollie realised she had all she ever wanted. Except for one thing – harmony between Edward and his father. If only she could mend the terrible rift between them. If only Edward would give up this crazy notion about going to New Zealand. She believed that Fate would play a hand in this too. Already, since coming to Tenerife, there was a bit of a thaw. Look how they had spent much of last night chatting amiably in the pub, something they hadn't done for a long time! The truth was that Mollie would happily give away all her money if only she could see the pair of them reconciled.

She reached for the newspaper that Mary had left this morning, one of those English tabloids that was filled with gossip about pop stars and football players. She quickly leafed through the pages till she came at last to the horoscopes.

Her eyes were drawn automatically to her star sign. Taurus, the Bull.

Time for change and new experiences. You will take it all in your stride. Prepare for a happy addition to the family.

Mollie put down the paper with a puzzled frown. *Addition to the family?* That usually meant only one thing. Surely it couldn't be?

Mary! Was Mary in the family way? With that young Peter Reilly?

Jesus, she thought as panic began to set in. I'll have to keep this a secret from Ned. If Mary's pregnant, he's going to hit the roof.

Chapter 9

If the heat was a problem for Mollie, it was none at all for Monica. Heat was what she craved. Heat and sunshine. It was what she had grown used to in all those splendid years she spent with Woody, before the bastard up and died and left a trail of destruction in his wake. And she needed heat and sunshine now more than ever, after the chilling experiences she had endured during the past few months.

Her day had begun at seven when the alarm-clock went off. Outside her bedroom window, she could see the sun rising like an orange beacon out of the azure sea. It was going to be a beautiful day. Monica showered and had a light breakfast of cereal and orange juice. She was on a tight budget since the Woody disaster and a light breakfast was all she could afford. But she consoled herself with the thought that it was a healthier option and much better for her weight. When she had finished eating, she pulled on her runners and set off for a brisk walk along the beach.

Exercise had become very important to Monica. Recently, she had been distressed to discover that dresses

KATE McCABE

and skirts that once fitted perfectly, now pinched a little. She could see the way her bust, which used to be so pert, had started to sag and the way the flesh around her hips had developed a tendency to spread.

But the biggest shock had come when she stepped on the weighing scales in the bathroom of her apartment back in Dublin and watched in horror as the arrow shot up to 9 stone 10lbs. That was a stone too far. Monica's weight had *never* gone over nine stone in her entire history. She put it down to the recent turmoil in her life. In the past, she would simply have signed into a good health farm for three weeks and then bought a new wardrobe. But those days were well gone. Now, she would just have to clench her teeth and go on hunger strike. This would mean cutting out pastries, chocolates and booze and surviving on rations of baked beans, porridge, cabbage-water and fruit. And this, in a providential way, actually suited her since she was practically broke.

She had done her sums. Her total wealth in this world stood at €6,435 and it was diminishing by the day. Of that, €2,500 was the money she had raised from pawning her jewellery. She knew the shyster, a crook called Sydney Sidestreet, had robbed her. The silver necklace alone was worth twice that. But what was she to do? She was in a corner and couldn't argue. If she was ever to make a comeback, she would have to find some way to repay Sydney Sidestreet and retrieve her pieces.

The rent on her apartment was €1,000 a month and it was only a one-bedroom in a block that looked like a barracks in a Nazi concentration camp. But the address sounded good: 32 The Gables, Ringsend. *And,* she kept reminding herself, Ringsend *was* in Dublin 4 which would look impressive on any letters she might have to write.

Her income at the moment was nil, which meant she

had just enough money to pay the rent for six months, provided she didn't eat in the meantime. On the credit side, Mr Flynn from Grabbit and Leggit had managed to extricate her completely from the Woody debacle so that none of his creditors had any claim against her. And she also had the prospect of employment as a temporary secretary. The charming man from the agency had told her she could earn between €15,000 and €23,000 a year depending on experience. But, she kept reminding herself, it was almost twenty years since she had worked as a secretary and she wasn't sure if she could adjust.

What *really* terrified her was the thought of word leaking out. She could imagine the glee with which that crone, Colleen McQueen, would seize on the information. She could see the headlines in her *On the Piste* column in the *Daily Bugle*: *FORMER SOCIALITE MANNING PHONES INSTEAD OF PHONING MEN.* And given the bitchy nature of Dublin society, Monica knew it wouldn't be long before it did leak out. Somebody somewhere would see to that!

She vaguely wondered if there was some way she could change her name. Or wear a disguise. Maybe put on a blonde wig and shades. But she knew it wouldn't matter. They would find her in the end. The bloodhounds would sniff her out. The prospect made her flesh creep. She kept reminding herself that she had been broke before. When she first met Woody, she had barely two pennies to rattle together. It hadn't stopped her rising to become queen of the social scene. She still had her good looks and her personality. Most of all, she had the driving ambition to pull herself out of this wreckage and build a new life. And Monica knew one thing for certain: the quickest way to do that, was to find a successful man and fasten herself to him like a limpet.

She was still attractive. She noticed the way men flirted

with her. She caught their admiring glances. She knew they were mentally undressing her and wondering what she would be like in bed. Monica could see the summit but she wasn't over the hill just yet.

After her walk, she had changed into her tightly-fitting bikini which showed off her figure to good effect, and gone for a swim. Then she had put in a spot of sunbathing. She timed herself. One hour in total (thirty minutes each, front and back). No point getting burnt and peeling like an orange. She decided she would structure it into her day. In the wake of her recent horrific experience she had concluded that she needed structures. They gave her a sense of security. When you had structures in your life, there was less chance of being ambushed by events.

Now she sat in the cool interior of the hotel lounge and tried to complete the crossword puzzle in the newspaper someone had left behind. The lounge was deserted and soft music filtered from the sound system. The quiet of the place appealed to her and it was also the perfect vantage point to observe what went on around the hotel.

"Stumped, are you?"

Monica was startled from her reverie by a loud voice booming in her ear. She looked up to see a fat, red face with dark glasses and straw hat grinning at her. The face sat atop a plump body and burly legs encased in navy shorts. She immediately recognised the man who had been sitting opposite her on the coach coming in from the airport.

She smiled pleasantly. "Eight across," she said. *"A wild man in his day.* Five letters beginning with O?"

"Oscar," Adrian Blake said, with satisfaction. "It's a reference to Oscar Wilde."

"Oh, right."

Monica pencilled in the word.

"What's the next one?"

"Five down. *Crustacean*. Seven letters."

"Lobster," Adrian announced. "Next?"

"*Man's best friend*. Three letters beginning with D."

"Has to be dog."

"Of course," Monica said. "D–O–G."

In three minutes flat, with Adrian's help, she had completed the entire crossword.

"That's the quickest I've ever done it," she said, tossing the paper aside. "Mind you, I suppose I cheated a bit. You *did* help me."

"Well, you had already completed most of it on your own," Adrian conceded gallantly.

Monica pulled a face. "You're just being kind. I don't know why I do crosswords. I'm not really very good at them."

"Nonsense," Adrian said, dismissively. "I only knew the Wilde question because I'm an English teacher."

Of course! Monica realised he had *teacher* written all over him.

"But I'm really a writer," he added quickly. "I only teach in my spare time."

"Oh," Monica said. A writer sounded much more interesting than a teacher.

"Yes. Adrian Blake's my name."

He held out his hand. It felt remarkably smooth and soft. Monica remembered reading somewhere that in the French Revolution, they could tell those who did no work by examining their hands. In the French Revolution, Adrian would have been carted straight off to the guillotine.

"Monica Woodworth. What do you write, Mr Blake?"

"Novels," Adrian said, proudly. "I'm completing one just now."

"You mean right this instant?"

"Yes. Up in my room. Just nipped down to get some refreshment." He held up a bottle of water he clutched in his plump paw. "I'm putting the finishing touches to it before submitting it to my publishers."

Monica looked impressed. "That must be very exciting. Has it got a title?"

"*The Green Gannet.*"

"What's it about?"

"The Famine."

"I must watch out for it," Monica said, without much enthusiasm. "When will it be in the shops?"

"About November. We aim to capitalise on the Christmas market. That's the busiest time in the book trade."

"Really?" Monica said. She tried to think of other writers she had known. Some of them were fabulously wealthy. And they did mix with all sorts of trendy showbiz-type people.

"Here on your own?" Adrian asked, casually.

Monica tried to look suitably mournful. Hopefully, he hadn't read anything about the Woody business in the papers. "Yes, my husband died."

"I'm dreadfully sorry. That must have been awful for you."

Monica raised a little finger to her eye. "It was very sudden. Heart attack. He didn't have a chance."

"My God. Do you have children?"

"No."

"So, you're all alone?"

"Yes," Monica sniffed.

"I knew it," Adrian said triumphantly. "I knew the moment I saw you that you were a widow. Call it my creative intuition, but something about the noble, yet tragic, way you carried yourself cried out to me."

"It's difficult," Monica said, "but one must get on with life."

"Yes, of course. And you seem to be bearing your burden gallantly. Tell me. Are you here every afternoon?"

"I plan to be."

"Well, then. Maybe I'll see you here tomorrow. We can complete the crossword together. Meanwhile, I must get back to my novel. *Au revoir* – it has been so stimulating meeting you."

Monica watched him go. What a strange man! But it just proved her point. They were still interested in her. And what was the phrase he had used? *Noble yet tragic.* She liked that. It had an artistic ring to it. Pity he had to rush away, she thought, as she sucked the end of her pencil, I would have enjoyed exploring his earning potential a little bit more.

She turned over in her mind a thought that had been slowly hatching. The last time she had been in Tenerife with Woody, they had stayed at the Gran Hotel del Rey. They had taken a deluxe suite in the five-star establishment with its eight restaurants, five swimming-pools (three outdoor, two indoor), three tennis courts, eight bars and extensive gardens. It was like holidaying in the palace of the Sultan of Brunei. The place was absolutely dripping with class and style. And, of course, money.

What if she was to go there some evening and have a casual drink in the bar? The staff would remember her. Woody had been a great man for tipping. Which was easy, now she thought about it, since it was other people's cash he was giving away. They would simply assume she was back again. She would wear her best evening clothes. She would sit quietly in a corner, looking noble yet tragic. (She really did like that phrase!) And she would let fate take its course.

In a way, it was like a fishing expedition. You baited your hook and cast it in the water and who knew what you might catch? One thing Monica was sure of. Any fish she might land in the Gran Hotel would be worth its weight in gold.

She checked her watch. Time for her session on the exercise bike in the gym and then maybe a nap. As she prepared to leave, she saw Carlos come into the lounge. Now *there* is a man I could fall for, Monica thought. Strong, charming and *very* attractive. Pity he's just the manager of the hotel and not the owner.

Carlos caught sight of her and came over at once. He made a little bow. "*Senora* Woodworth. It is so good to see you."

"I'm just resting from the sun," Monica said.

"And very wise too. You do not want to spoil your beautiful complexion." There was a playful twinkle in his eye. "I was just about to have a glass of sherry. I find it very relaxing. Would you care to join me?"

Monica didn't hesitate. The exercise bike could wait. Why let a good opportunity pass her by?

"I'd be delighted."

Carlos turned and signalled to the wine waiter to bring the decanter and glasses.

"Your wife doesn't mind if you drink with other women?" Monica asked, playfully.

"Wife?" Carlos said. "I have no wife. I am too busy working. Now, *Senora* Woodworth, tell me a little about yourself."

Monica crossed one leg over the other to reveal her nicely tanned thigh. She lowered her eyes and adopted her mournful pose.

"I'm a widow," she said.

Chapter 10

After Bobby had gone, Charlie made his way to Penny's desk. The queue had melted away and she was busy now counting her takings. She stopped and looked up as he approached.

"Hello," she said chirpily.

"I was thinking of going on a tour," Charlie said.

"Any one in particular?"

"Puerto de la Cruz."

"I can strongly recommend it," Penny said enthusiastically, reaching for a black metal box. "Puerto de la Cruz is one of the better ones. You get to see the banana plantations."

"That sounds interesting," Charlie said, doubtfully.

"And lunch is included. Typical Canarian cuisine."

"Sounds good," Charlie said.

"One ticket or two?"

"One."

"When would you like to go?"

"Tomorrow?"

She opened the box and took out a ticket while Charlie counted out the cash.

"There's ah, something else I'd like to ask you," he said cautiously, putting the ticket away safely in his pocket.

"Yes?"

"Where's the best place for night-life?"

"What sort of night-life?"

"You know? Discos. That sort of thing."

Penny stopped what she was doing and slowly let her eye travel over Charlie, taking in his tee shirt and shorts and his pale sun-starved legs. "You sure discos are what you want?"

"Definitely. They've been recommended."

"There's plenty of other entertainment. There are cabarets, for instance. And karaoke."

"I think I'd prefer a disco."

"You ever been to one before?"

Charlie thought briefly of the teenage dances he had attended at the church hall, sweaty youngsters gyrating wildly to records while the parish priest kept a wary eye on everything. "Years ago. When I was younger."

"Well, these discos are different. They're *very* loud."

"That's all right."

"And they go on late. Some of them go on till seven o'clock in the morning. Maybe you'd rather —"

"I don't care," Charlie interrupted. "I'm here to enjoy myself."

"People get out of their minds. They do weird things."

"That's *exactly* what I want," he said, eagerly.

Penny gave him a closer look. "You really *do* want to enjoy yourself, don't you?"

"Yes."

"Well, then. The Veronicas is the place for you. That's where all the big discos are. Places like The Ministry of Sound and Clockwork Orange."

122

"What do I have to do?"

"Just turn up and pay your dosh." She glanced once more at Charlie's shorts and sandals. "And maybe change your gear. Wear something . . . sharper."

"Like what?"

"Jeans, sports shirt, loafers."

"You think so?"

"No offence, mind. But you look a little bit . . ."

"Old-fashioned?"

"Yes. You've got to dress more casually. But still look stylish. When were you thinking of going?"

"Tonight."

"Can't wait, eh?" This time, she gave Charlie a knowing glance.

"Why waste time?"

"That's what I always say." She seemed to consider. "Tell you what. As it happens, *I'm* going partying tonight. Me and a couple of my friends. Why don't I meet you somewhere and you can come along? I'll show you the ropes. Then, next time, you'll know exactly what to do."

"That would be marvellous," Charlie said, excited, "but I wouldn't want to put you out."

Penny grinned. "All part of the service. *Anything* I can do to make your holiday a success. I'll see you in the Monaco Bar in Los Cristianos at nine."

Charlie went off, humming softly to himself. What a stroke of luck, Penny agreeing to take him partying tonight. And giving him advice about his clothes. This holiday really was getting off to a flying start. Good old Bricky. He had been dead right, as usual. Charlie passed through the foyer, past the fountain tinkling coolly into its marble basin and out to the street where he hailed a cab.

Fifteen minutes later, he was at a shopping mall. He wandered along till he found what he was seeking – an upmarket men's outfitters. As he came through the door, a smiling assistant came forward to greet him.

"I'd like to buy a pair of jeans, a couple of sports shirts and some loafers," Charlie said.

"Yes, sir."

The man took out a tape and measured Charlie, then opened a drawer and began to show him shirts and jeans. Charlie hadn't worn jeans since the time he worked in the supermarket and he was amazed at the kind of prices they were fetching. In the end, he bought a loose-fitting pair of Levis, which the shop assistant assured him were *very* fashionable, three navy blue sports shirts and a pair of white loafers. The assistant put them into bags. As he was about pay, Charlie spotted a bottle of Armani aftershave lotion.

"Is that stuff any good?"

"It's the best, sir. A very masculine scent. But unobtrusive."

"What does it do?"

"I'm not certain, sir. But the ladies seem to like it."

"I'll take it," Charlie said and gave the man his credit card. Then he left the store and went next door to a barber's shop where he got his hair cut. He finished up at a little outdoor restaurant where he had lunch of grilled sardines and salad under a eucalyptus tree and drank a half bottle of chilled white wine and felt very happy with himself.

After lunch, he decided to stroll back to the hotel. It wasn't far and the exercise would do him good. When he got back to his room he thought he would just stretch out on the bed and rest for a little while.

The next thing he knew, it was seven o'clock. He had slept for four hours which was amazing. He hadn't intended to sleep at all. Either he was more tired than he realised or the holiday was relaxing him. But it's no harm, he thought. If Penny is correct, I'm going to need all the energy I can muster for this disco business tonight.

He got up and went out to the balcony. It was getting dark and the lights of the town sparkled before him like a necklace of stars. A cool breeze brushed his cheek and ruffled his hair. He sniffed the night air filled with the scent of flowers and the salt tang of the sea. A perfect evening for romance! Charlie felt an excitement stirring in his blood. He left the balcony and went into the bathroom, stripped off and stood under the shower.

He luxuriated in the warm water as he soaped and scrubbed. He took out his razor and slowly shaved away the stubble of the day. When he was finished, he dried himself, went back into the bedroom and took out the new clothes he had bought. He felt good! Ready for whatever adventure the night might bring. He carefully dressed in his new shirt, jeans and loafers. He brushed his hair and examined himself in the wardrobe mirror. He liked what he saw. There was no doubt about it. He looked – what was that word that Penny had used? Sharp!

Satisfied, Charlie unscrewed the bottle of Armani aftershave and slapped some on his cheeks. Not too much! It was meant to be subtle. He counted out his money and put it in the back pocket of his jeans. He checked that he had his handkerchief, keys and comb. He gave the room a final look-over, then turned out the lights and locked the door. With a jaunty step, Charlie skipped down the corridor to the lift.

The Monaco Bar was in a maze of narrow streets behind the church. Charlie paid the cab driver and stood for a moment to appraise the place. It didn't look like a bar, at least not as he knew bars back in Dublin. It was a tiny building in a street of small white-washed structures that housed bakeries and shoemakers' shops and grocery stores. But for the fact that there was noise coming out and a battered sign above the door that clearly stated *Monaco Bar*, Charlie could easily have dismissed it. He tucked his shirt neatly into the waistband of his jeans, took a deep breath and pushed open the door.

It was dark inside and it took a moment to get used to the gloom. But gradually, he became aware of a cigarette machine in one corner, tourist posters and football pennants on the wall and a tiny wooden counter from where a couple of locals observed him with listless interest. But where were Penny and her friends?

A shrill voice caused him to turn round. There she was, frantically waving from a table at the back of the room. But this was a different Penny. She had been transformed. She had changed out of her canary uniform and was now wearing a short red skirt and a little white top with spaghetti straps. And her bleached-blonde hair was held together with a large clip-on bow in the shape of a butterfly.

Charlie felt a wave of relief. For an awful moment, he had thought he had come to the wrong place. Or worse still, that Penny had stood him up. He quickly made his way down to her table.

"Sorry I'm late," he said, slipping in beside her.

"You're not late. I'm early," she chirped.

Charlie could feel his earlier confidence return. "Well, anyway, we're both here. Where are your friends?"

"Oh them? They'll be joining us later."

"So why don't we have something while we're waiting? What's that you're drinking?" he said, pointing to the strange concoction in Penny's glass.

"Vodka and Red Bull."

Charlie had only a vague idea what Red Bull was. But he didn't want to appear ignorant, so he signalled for the barman and ordered two more. He gingerly took a sip and almost choked as the concoction set fire to his throat.

"I see you took my advice," Penny said.

"You mean this?" Charlie wiped his eyes and fingered his new sports shirt.

"And the jeans. You look cool."

"Thank you," Charlie said. "You look cool, yourself."

Now that he was getting accustomed to the dim light, he could see that Penny was wearing crimson lipstick. And the white top served to emphasise her nice dark tan. He realised she looked quite pretty in a brash sort of way.

"This is my night off," she said. "I'm letting my hair down."

"You mean you only have one?"

"Hair?"

"No. Night off."

"'Fraid so."

"That sounds a bit extreme."

"Well, we are here to work, you know. Being a holiday rep isn't a bed of violets."

"Roses," Charlie corrected her.

"It's bloody hard work. People think we have a wonderful time, lying round in the sun all day long. Well, I can tell you it's not a bit like that. You've no idea. In and out to the airport, finding lost luggage, dealing with complaints, looking after casualties."

"Casualties?" Charlie said, surprised.

"Sure. I've got a geezer in hospital right now with sunstroke."

"My God."

127

"Yes. Silly bugger fell asleep on the beach and got himself burnt. So what does he do when he wakes up? Goes straight into the sea to cool down. Came out in blisters as big as balloons, he did. He's in intensive care."

"That sounds dreadful. I didn't realise the sun could do that."

"Oh yes. And I've got another man had a row with his wife. Says he won't spend one more night under the same roof. He's insisting we find him another apartment."

"You certainly seem to have your hands full," Charlie said, venturing another sip at his vodka and Red Bull.

"You've no idea. Anyway, tell me about yourself. What do you do for a living?"

"I'm a bookseller," Charlie said, proudly.

"What kind of books do you sell?"

"Everything from Maeve Binchy to Charles Dickens."

"I like a good book myself," Penny said. "Whenever I get the chance to read. Here on your own, are you?"

"That's right."

"Not married? No wife back in Ireland?" Penny giggled and gave Charlie a naughty look.

"I've been too busy. Never got round to it."

"You're a dark horse," Penny said. "I had you figured as a dark horse, the minute I clapped eyes on you."

Charlie had a vague idea she was trying to pay him a compliment.

"You've got hidden depths," Penny went on. "Mysterious potential."

"You think so?"

"I certainly do. Has no one ever told you that before?"

"Not that I recall."

"Well, you have," Penny said, draining her glass.

Charlie ordered more. He was enjoying this conversation.

Mysterious potential? He had never considered himself in that light before.

"What I mean," Penny said, moving closer to Charlie, "is you're a mature man. You've got a more balanced outlook on life."

"In what way?"

"Well, you're experienced for one thing. I prefer experienced men. Some of these younger guys would make you sick. They haven't got a clue, whereas someone like you, Charlie . . ."

She tickled his chin with a long painted fingernail.

Charlie glanced at his watch. It was nine forty-five.

"You sure your friends are coming? They haven't got the wrong bar by any chance?"

"Forget about them," Penny said. "You know, you intrigue me. I think you're hiding something."

Charlie tried to laugh.

"Not at all. What you see is what you get."

"And I like what I see," Penny said, casually allowing one of her spaghetti straps to slip off her shoulder to display more breast.

By eleven thirty, Penny's friends still hadn't turned up. She had consumed six more vodka and Red Bulls and her mood had become decidedly amorous.

Charlie, who had tried gamely to keep up with her, was now feeling quite giddy. "Your friends haven't got losht? I mean lost?"

"Relax," Penny said. "The night is young. We'll have one more for the road."

As if reading her mind, the barman swooped with another round of drinks. Charlie tried to focus on the two glasses that still sat untouched before him. One thing I'll say for Penny, he thought, she sure can lower those vodkas. I wonder if they give them courses in it at rep training school?

He knocked back his glass and immediately got an attack of hiccoughs.

He stood up and felt his legs give way.

"Where's the little boys' room?" he slurred.

After that, everything seemed to pass in a blur. Charlie had barely a few moments of lucidity. He had a slight memory of getting into a taxi and Penny snuggling close beside him, then a packed dance floor with flashing lights and heaving bodies. In the men's toilets, someone passed him a cigarette that tasted funny and made him choke.

From then on, he only had a tenuous grip on reality. He could recall dancing madly to pumping music and then being outside in the fresh air and getting into another taxi. He had a vague recollection of being in a room with a large bed. His last memory was of a naked woman weaving unsteadily towards him across the floor. Charlie put out his arms to catch her and everything went blank.

Chapter 11

"You know, I'm sure I've seen that woman before somewhere," Angie said.

"Which one?" Bobby asked.

"The dark glamorous one. You must have seen her around. She sits in the lounge quite a lot."

"I know who you mean. Looks very striking? And she's here on her own?"

"That's her. Always chatting to Carlos. Flirting if you ask me. Mind you, I wouldn't mind flirting with him myself. I think he's very dishy."

"Don't waste your time," Bobby said. "He probably flirts with all the women. This is a holiday resort, after all. I'd say he could have any female he wants within reason."

They were in the lounge of the Lucky Leprechaun taking a break from the sun and sipping gin and tonics. They'd discovered the pub on their first day and had now made it their official headquarters.

"Does she work for television?" Bobby asked.

"Who?"

"The woman you were just talking about."

"I don't think so but her face is very familiar. I've definitely seen her before."

"Maybe she's an actress?"

"No. It's not that. But I have a strong suspicion that she gets her picture in the papers quite a bit."

"I wonder what she's doing here." Bobby said. "People don't usually come on holidays on their own."

"She's not the only one. There's that man you were talking to at the Welcome Meeting."

"Charlie Dobbins?"

"That's right. *He's* on his own. Maybe they've struck up a relationship?"

Bobby laughed. "I think your imagination has gone into overdrive. Mind you, I haven't seen Charlie for a couple of days. He told me he might pop down to the pool for a spot of sunbathing. But he never showed up."

"He could do with it," Angie said taking a sip of gin. "He looks like he's been locked away in a cupboard all his life. There's another person I haven't seen lately. You know the man with the straw hat and sunglasses?"

"He's a writer," Bobby announced.

"Really? How do you know that?"

"Somebody mentioned it. Adrian Blake is his name. I must say I never heard of him. And I don't think I've seen any of his books, anywhere. I suppose he spends his time writing. They're funny people, writers."

"And what about his wife?"

"She's around. I've seen her at the pool."

"She looks like a nice person. I'm not so sure about him, though. Looks a bit severe for my taste. Which reminds me, any news from Pig-face Piper?"

Bobby frowned. "I'd rather not discuss that particular individual, if you don't mind."

"Well, he *is* the reason we're here, after all."

"And the reason we're here is to forget about him. Right?"

"Only inquiring," Angie said with a hurt expression. "Sorry I mentioned it."

"If you must know, he's been messaging me."

"Hell, you never told me," Angie squealed, outraged.

"There's nothing *to* tell," Bobby said. "I haven't responded."

"But he must say something?"

"Of course he does. He says I may have misunderstood him and he would like an opportunity to talk things over."

"My God," Angie said. "The arrogance!"

"I know. As if anybody could possibly misunderstand being stood up at the altar. You'd need to be deaf and blind not to get that message."

"*Practically* at the altar," Angie corrected her. "It's not quite the same thing as actually standing there in your wedding dress."

"Well, it's as good as. There was only a week to go. The humiliation is the same."

"So what does he want you to do?"

"He wants to meet to discuss the situation. He says he still loves me and wants to marry me but he needs more time to prepare."

"I told you," Angie said, triumphant. "Didn't I say he'd be back?"

"You did," Bobby conceded.

"Make him beg," Angie said. "Make him grovel. If you give in too easily, he'll have no respect for you."

Bobby stared in astonishment. "What are you talking about? I haven't the least intention of giving in."

"Well, maybe you could at least agree to meet him. After

he's undergone a suitable period of chastisement. I don't think there'd be any harm in that. After all, a meeting is just a meeting. It doesn't mean you're taking him back."

"But what would be the point of meeting when there's nothing to discuss?"

Angie sniffed. "I'm your best friend, Bobby. I wouldn't like you to do anything you might regret. Alex Piper is quite a catch. There are plenty of girls would be delighted to sink their claws into him."

"So?"

"If you were clever, you would at least keep the lines of communication open."

Bobby's face darkened. "You seem to have a problem understanding. I want nothing more to do with Alex Bloody Piper. He had his chance and he blew it."

"We all make mistakes, Bobby."

"Some mistakes are bigger than others."

She finished her gin and tonic and put the empty glass down on the table. "Now, if you don't mind, I think it's your round."

While Angie tried to attract the barman's attention, Bobby glanced around the pub. It was the sort of place she would rarely go into at home with its fake traditional artefacts and its mock Irish atmosphere but it was comfortable and the food was quite good. They'd had dinner here last night and Bobby had been pleasantly surprised at the quality. Brian Casey, the owner's brother, was the chef and he had been trained at one of Dublin's top restaurants.

She considered what Angie had just said. If she let Alex Piper go, it wouldn't be long before some other girl captured him. Maybe she should take Angie's advice and relent a little? Maybe she should at least open a dialogue with him, listen to what he had to say? He was pestering her every day with messages so he plainly wanted to continue their relationship. Would there be any harm in allowing him to explain himself?

But Bobby's pride was too strong and the hurt too recent. She knew she couldn't sit in the same room with Alex Piper without wanting to strangle him with her bare hands for what he had done to her. If any reconciliation was to be possible, it was going to take a long time. At least long enough for her anger to cool. In the meantime, she would let him suffer.

The barman put the fresh drinks on the table. Four euros. Which was a ridiculous price when you considered that the same drinks would cost three times that amount back in Dublin.

"Now I remember where I saw that dark woman," Angie said. "She's a society hostess."

"A what?"

"You know, always throwing charity dinners and lunches. Mixing with the movers and shakers, getting her picture in the papers with rock stars and famous actors. That's why her face was familiar."

"What's her name?"

"Monica something or other."

"You're right," Bobby said. "But wasn't there some kind of scandal? Didn't her husband run off with another woman or something?"

Angie lowered her voice. "He dropped dead. That's what happened. And left her with a pile of debt. Turned out he was spending other people's money."

"My God!" Bobby exclaimed. "Can you imagine the shame?"

"I think I read in the paper that she had gone off to recuperate in a chateau in France. And now she turns up here. Very odd, isn't it?"

But Bobby's attention had been suddenly diverted. "Never mind the dark woman. Look at the hunk that's just walked in the door."

Angie put down her drink and turned to see.

Edward McGinty had just come into the pub with his father.

Chapter 12

Everything was going wonderfully for Trish. Indeed it had been so good she had to pinch herself several times to make sure it was really true. Adrian was behaving like a civilised human being and it was so long since she had seen him in this condition that she had forgotten what it was like. She was confident now that her scheme was going to work. It was only a matter of being patient and waiting for the right moment to pounce. Once she had seduced him, she would have her alibi.

On the first evening, after they had unpacked and washed and changed, they set off to get something to eat. Their expedition led them to the harbour where they found a lovely little restaurant right on the edge of the ocean within earshot of the waves rising and falling on the sand. Adrian was in expansive mood. He ordered a glass of sherry while he studied the menu and a bottle of chilled white wine to accompany his grilled squid. The bottle seemed to vanish as soon as it arrived so he ordered another one. After dessert, he had a large brandy and a cigar.

"I really must compliment you, Trish," he said, pulling

his straw hat down across his forehead and puffing on his cigar in imitation of Ernest Hemingway. "I had my doubts originally but you've really come up trumps. This place is perfect. I can feel inspiration in the very air."

"I'm delighted," Trish said, happily. "You've really been driving yourself much too hard."

Adrian shrugged. "That's the life of the artist. Only a fool believes that writing is an easy business. It can be a hard lonely road. And many of them never make it."

"Well, that's not going to happen to you," she said, hoping to keep him happy.

"Not if I have anything to do with it," Adrian declared and ordered another brandy.

By the time they got back to the hotel, he was in a very mellow mood and Trish began to wonder if she would have the good fortune to succeed with her plan on the very first night. She undressed and got between the sheets while Adrian finished his cigar on the balcony.

"Why don't you come to bed, darling?" she cooed. "I'm sure you must be exhausted after the journey. You'll feel much fresher in the morning."

Adrian came in and started taking off his trousers. Trish smiled provocatively.

"You know I'm feeling quite amorous," she said. "Must be the wine."

Adrian had a glint in his eye. "I'm feeling rather frisky myself," he said and let his trousers fall to the floor.

Trish reached out and took his hand, barely able to believe her luck, but then he started to pull his trousers back on again.

"Just had a thought," he said. "Must write it down or else I'll forget. Won't be a moment."

He disappeared into the lounge and Trish heard him

begin to tap at his word processor. I don't believe this, she moaned and fell back on the pillows. He was still tapping away an hour later when she fell asleep.

But, the following morning, she woke to hear him whistling in the shower. This was so unusual she had to sit up in bed to make sure she wasn't dreaming. She heard him leave the bathroom and pad out to the kitchen. Next thing she knew, the smell of fresh coffee was drifting through the apartment. By the time she was dressed, he had already cooked scrambled eggs and buttered rolls and poured glasses of chilled orange juice.

They ate breakfast on the balcony in the early morning sun. This was amazing. She couldn't remember the last time Adrian had made breakfast for her. Had he *ever* done it in all the years they were married? And his entire demeanour appeared to have changed. The angst-ridden Adrian had disappeared to be replaced by this jovial person who now beamed at her across the breakfast table.

"I got some excellent work done last night after you went to bed. I don't know what it is, but there's something about this place that stimulates the imagination."

"I'm very pleased," Trish said, wishing to keep him in this happy frame of mind.

"Oh yes. I'll have the novel finished in no time and ready for the publishers."

He took her hand and squeezed it. "Sorry to disappoint you last night."

"That's quite all right, darling. We have a whole week."

Adrian gave her a look that was meant to be seductive, but just made him appear silly. "I got a sudden creative urge and I just had to go with it."

"I understand. Of course I do! And you can make it up to me another night."

Alex smiled. "I'm glad you take it like that. You know,

I've been thinking. I wouldn't be surprised if some film director snapped up the rights to *Gannet*. That's where the big money is. Get your book turned into a movie and the next thing you know, the publishers are breaking down your door to sign you up. I might even have a go at writing the script if I can fit in the time."

"That would be absolutely marvellous," Trish beamed.

"*If* I can fit it in. I've no doubt I'm going to be extremely busy, what with publicity tours and television appearances. You know, our lives are going to change out of all recognition. Are you ready for that? You'll probably have to give up your job. And we'll have no privacy. I've watched that happen to others. Wherever we go, the scorpions will be waiting to pounce."

"Scorpions?" Trish said, puzzled.

"The press, dear. We'll be in all the gossip columns. Dinners, first nights. And all the time, they'll be snapping away. Look at that poor man, Salman Rushdie. Had to go into hiding to escape them."

"I thought that was because somebody was trying to kill him?"

"Yes, well, there was that too. But the press can be terrible bastards once they get on your case. You know, we might have to move here permanently?"

Trish almost spilled her coffee. "Move to Tenerife?"

"Why not? There's peace and quiet here. A person could be anonymous. Merge into the background."

"But what would we live on?"

Adrian smiled. "Why, the sales of my novel! We'll be rich. Never again will you have to bother your pretty little head about money."

This sounded crazy. "Wouldn't you miss home?"

Adrian gave her a disdainful look. "What's there to miss? Small-time begrudgers? Failures who are so envious of real talent that they can't be happy till they've dragged everyone down to their own miserable level? We'll be better off out of it. Believe me. When I hit the big-time, Trish, Dublin won't see my heels for the dust."

After the Welcome Meeting, Adrian switched on the laptop, donned his straw hat and dark glasses and sat down at the balcony table to write.

"What will we do about lunch?"

"I think I'll work through. But we'll have a nice dinner. We could go back to that place we were at last night."

She packed a shoulder bag and made for the door. As she was about to leave, Adrian called her back.

"Maybe you should take my photograph," he said.

"What for?"

"The jacket of my book."

"You think so?"

"Of course. They're going to require a photograph when they publish."

He pushed the sunglasses hard against his nose while Trish got the camera.

"You think I look sufficiently literary? Maybe I should tilt my hat a little. What do you think?"

Trish thought he looked ridiculous, but she was determined to humour him.

"I think it's perfect. You remind me of that famous photograph of James Joyce taken in Paris. You know the one where he's checking the proofs of *Ulysses*?"

Adrian smiled. "Yes," he said. "I do a little. Don't I?"

Trish stayed at the Welcome Meeting long enough to pick

up information about bus timetables, weather, taxi fares and restaurant prices, then left and went out to the pool. She swam a few lengths, than stretched out for a spot of tanning. She turned her face to the warm sun and gave a sigh of contentment.

Yes, things were turning out very well. But one thing disturbed her. She thought of their earlier conversation and Adrian's suggestion that they might come and live permanently in Tenerife. Surely he couldn't be serious? It was another pipe dream. Just like all the other wild stuff he talked about. She was beginning to doubt if Adrian's book was ever going to be published. But she hadn't the courage to tell him. He was mad enough already. Why drive him completely round the twist?

By one o'clock, she had tired of sunbathing and decided to venture as far as the harbour. She had a light lunch in a little beachside restaurant and spent a pleasant afternoon wandering around the shops and boutiques before returning to the hotel. When she got back, she found Adrian had moved into the kitchen and was typing furiously on the laptop.

"How did your day go, darling?"

He scowled. "Awful. I haven't been out of this damned apartment, except for one trip to the bar for a bottle of water."

"Oh, I'm sorry."

She ran her fingers through his hair, but he brushed her off.

"Really, Trish. I'm in no mood. This damned thing's not turning out as I had hoped."

She tried to console him. "I found a dinky little restaurant. Italian. Why don't we go there tonight?"

"I can't," he said. "I've got a really knotty problem here. Got to get it sorted."

"But you have to eat."

"I'm not hungry. I'll have a sandwich later."

"You can't expect me to eat dinner on my own," Trish protested. "What will people think?"

"I don't care what people think," he snapped. "I've got to get this book finished."

"We *are* on holiday, Adrian. I hardly see you when we're at home. I thought at least we could spend some time together while we're here."

"Oh God!" he groaned. "Did Charles Dickens have to put up with this? Did Scott Fitzgerald? Can't you see I'm *busy,* Trish? Can't you see I need some goddamned peace?"

"Suit yourself," she said testily.

She went into the bedroom and got dressed. She was feeling really angry. Only their second day in Tenerife and she had to eat alone. To cover her embarrassment, she took off her wedding ring and placed it on the bathroom shelf before she left. Adrian had reverted to his old self. And it had all happened so suddenly. Maybe it will pass, she thought.

But when she got back, he was still sitting at the breakfast bar in the kitchen, tapping away like a dervish at the laptop.

She went to bed and read a book. She dozed off and when she woke at one o'clock Adrian was still working.

He was there at eight when she got up. He looked bleary-eyed and feverish. She made him coffee.

"You should try and get some rest," she said. "You'll feel better."

"Don't disturb me."

"I suppose there's no point asking you to come for a walk?"

"No, there isn't," he snapped.

The whole day stretched before her. What was she going to do? Maybe she could still get a seat on one of those tours

that Penny had been trying to sell? She went down to the
lobby and waited for the first tour bus to arrive. Luckily, it
had an empty seat. She paid for her ticket.

"Where are we going?" she asked the guide.

"Puerto de la Cruz," the guide replied.

Chapter 13

Monica climbed out of the swimming-pool and walked to the sunbed where she had earlier left her towel and bag, conscious of the little puddles of water that followed in her wake. She walked as gracefully as she could under the circumstances, her head erect and her eyes proud. She was aware that she was on parade and people were watching her. But she didn't mind in the least. In fact, she quite liked it. The day people stopped looking at her would be the day she started to worry. Besides, she had just completed thirty lengths of the pool and she felt a quiet glow of satisfaction. At this rate, she would be hitting sixty before the week was out. Coupled with the diet she had set herself, she knew it would be only a matter of time before she got her weight back under control and regained her sylph-like figure.

Not that her figure wasn't still attractive. She reminded herself of the approving glances she could still draw from the men around the hotel. Even now, as she lifted her towel and began to dry herself, she was aware that the eyes of the barman were following her. She knew he was ogling her as she bent and stretched. His name was Jose. She had spoken to him twice. Once to order a Diet Coke with ice and lemon and the second time to ask for the toasted ham sandwich and a glass of wine which comprised her lunch. He was a thin, handsome country boy with sultry good looks. Another woman might find him attractive but he was too young for Monica's taste. And besides, he had no money which ruled him out entirely.

Satisfied that she was now thoroughly dry, Monica neatly folded her towel and put it into her bag, arranged her sunglasses and slipped into her purple sarong. It was made of silk and had been a present from Woody, purchased last year at an expensive fashion shop on a weekend trip to Venice. She had taken her swim and her regulation one hour of sunbathing. Now it was time to go and sit in the hotel lounge and indulge in some mild flirtation with Carlos.

She had become quite friendly with Carlos. She knew that some of the women were watching her with jealousy. Not that she cared. They could think what they liked. Most of them would do the same thing given half a chance. But she knew that Carlos only had eyes for her.

She thought of their little tete a tete the previous day when she had told him about Woody's death. She had thoroughly enjoyed it. Carlos had taken a great interest and he couldn't have been more sympathetic, offering his profound condolences on the death of her husband, gently commiserating on the terrible fate that a man in the fullness of his health should be snatched away from his loved ones, inquiring delicately about their life together. After an appropriate period, during which Monica had sniffed several times into her handkerchief and Carlos had poured several glasses of sherry, she had been happy to regale him with tales of their travels, their sojourns in smart hotels, the important people they had met and the fabulous parties she had given.

She could see that Carlos was impressed. She formed the distinct opinion that he would have been happy to spend the entire afternoon with her, had the receptionist not come with news of an important phone call from Madrid. Carlos had parted from her reluctantly with a promise that they would continue the conversation on another occasion soon.

But now, when Monica entered the cool surroundings of the lounge, she was surprised to find the place deserted. Carlos was nowhere to be seen. And there was no sign of that strange writer person, Adrian, who had assisted her with the crossword puzzle, which was actually a blessing, for Monica had developed an uneasy feeling about him. That red face, the frenetic energy, the dark glasses and straw hat, all pointed in one direction. Monica was convinced he was unhinged. A lot of artistic people were like that. It was something in their temperament. Better to give him a wide berth.

She settled into her favourite chair and pretended to read a magazine while she finessed her plan. Tonight she would visit the Gran Hotel del Rey. There was nothing to gain by wasting time. She had less than a week to find a rich admirer and the Hotel del Rey was the obvious place to go. One thing was for certain. She wasn't going to trip over any millionaire husbands in Hotel Las Flores.

She would go to the hotel around seven, in time for the cocktail hour. She would sit in the bar and wait. Some gallant gentleman would inevitably offer to buy her a drink. If she liked him, she would accept. With a bit of luck, he might even buy her dinner. Gradually, Monica would unfold her sad tale of widowhood. She would adopt her noble, yet tragic pose. It would have a two-fold effect. It would elicit sympathy, but more important, it would let her admirer know she was unattached.

Monica turned the plan over in her head. It seemed perfect. She looked at her watch and realised with a start that an hour had passed and it was now three thirty. She put down her magazine and stood up. Time to get started. She would begin with a session in the sauna room. It would invigorate her and had the added advantage of being free since use of the hotel facilities was included in the price of the package.

She took her bag and followed the sign that pointed to the Leisure Complex. This too was deserted except for a young man in shorts and vest peddling furiously on the exercise bike and a plump woman in a black acrylic leotard panting on the treadmill. Monica decided she'd had enough exercise for one day. She went into the ladies' changing room and slipped out of her sarong, then entered the sauna.

A blast of hot air hit her as she opened the door. She sat down on the hard wooden bench and felt the perspiration begin to ooze like treacle from her pores. After a few minutes, she was completely bathed in sweat. She stuck it for half an hour, then had a quick dip in the ice-cold plunge pool and emerged shivering and spluttering for breath. But it did make her feel fresh and clean and purified like she had been rolled in the snow, which was what she heard the Scandinavians did after a sauna.

For tonight's adventure, it was vital that she look her best. She considered a visit to the beauty parlour but a quick glance at the price list on the board outside quickly changed her mind. A full treatment cost €200. What did you get for that? Botox injections? She would have to make do with a self-administered wash and blow-dry. Luckily, someone had left behind a half empty bottle of shampoo. Monica stepped under the shower and gently massaged the shampoo into her scalp. Then she rinsed her hair, dried herself and put on her sarong once more. She left the Leisure Complex feeling refreshed and took the lift up to her apartment.

She felt exhilarated at the thought of what lay ahead. She sat down in front of the mirror in the bathroom and carefully examined herself. Her hair was soft after the wash, her eyes were bright, her skin fresh and glowing from the sauna. And then there were her teeth. Monica smiled into the mirror and parted her lips. She had always regarded her teeth as one of her better features. Ever since she was a young girl, people had commented on them. She smiled now and her teeth gleamed in the mirror like pieces of polished ivory.

She was pleased with what she saw. She was looking extremely good given that she was only weeks away from her forty-third birthday. And then she remembered the resolution she had made when Woody died, to knock a few years off her age. Now that she was back in the market for a husband, she had to be careful not to be outmanoeuvred by these younger models coming up behind. Could she get away with thirty? She examined herself again and shook her head. Thirty would be pushing it. But thirty-five – she could easily pass for that. She smiled to herself. Thirty-five it is! My new identity. Monica Woodworth, young widow of thirty-five. In prime condition. Only one previous owner.

The feeling of exhilaration had now given way to a mood of quiet confidence. She would slay them tonight when she turned up at the Gran Hotel. She could imagine the heads turning as she strode into the marbled foyer. What would she wear? She searched among the clothes in her wardrobe and selected a little black cocktail dress. It had wispy shoulder straps and reached just above her knees. Not too short to be sleazy but short enough to show off her long brown legs. She remembered the last time she had worn it, to a party to

celebrate the opening night of some musical at the Point
Theatre back in Dublin

The cocktail dress was ideal. To complement it, she
chose a fake gold chain and matching ear-rings and silently
cursed the fact that she had been forced to pawn her real
stuff. But in the dim light of the hotel bar, it would be hard
to tell the difference without the aid of a microscope. She
completed the ensemble with a pair of black high-heeled
mules and a little handbag. She put the finishing touches to
her make-up: a small touch of mascara to draw attention to
her eyes, a line of bright red lipstick to set off her dark hair
and a spray of Chanel to round the whole thing off.

She examined herself once more. Perfect, she thought as
she reached for the bottle of duty-free gin she had bought
at the airport and prepared for the excitement of the
cocktail hour at the Gran Hotel del Rey.

Chapter 14

Edward McGinty saw the young woman watching him as he came into the pub. He had seen her before – the evening he had arrived in fact. He had noticed her on the coach coming in from the airport and thought her very attractive. He had seen her several times since around the hotel and nothing had happened to change his initial opinion. She was one of the best-looking women he had ever seen, with her handsome good looks and fine figure. In normal circumstances, Edward would have been happy to say hello, maybe offer to buy her a drink and begin a conversation. But today his mind was on other things.

He was thinking how strange it was that he should be coming here to the Lucky Leprechaun to have a drink with his father. For most people there would be nothing unusual in this. It was what fathers and sons did all the time, all over the world in every culture and every society. But the relationship between himself and Ned was not a normal one. He knew it caused his mother great distress and he suspected it was the real reason she had suggested this holiday after she won the Lotto. But a gulf had grown between him and his father. It was why he was leaving for New Zealand and why he felt so guilty about upsetting his parents who expected him to stay at home and run the family farm. Edward was aware of all this but at the same time, he felt compelled to go. And to think it had all happened over a football match.

Ever since he was a small child, he had adored his father. His earliest memories were of Ned chopping wood in the yard, a gleaming axe splitting the thick logs as though they were matchsticks. He could remember the rippling muscles along his chest and arms, the glistening sweat on his brow, the warm smell of tobacco off his clothes. To the infant Edward, his father was the strongest man in the world. He was the bravest and the cleverest. He knew everything and could do anything. There was no one like him. As he got older, his admiration for his father continued to grow till it seemed to him that that Ned was like a God.

The fact that he was the only boy in the family meant that father and son were always together. Ned took young Edward with him everywhere: to the town, to the fair, to the mart. He took him with him when he went to get his hair cut in Daly's barbershop in Dunmuckridge and afterwards to Morelli's café for ice cream. They became inseparable. The local wags even coined a name for them. They called them The Lone Ranger and Tonto.

When he was old enough to help on the farm, Ned taught Edward the various jobs that needed to be done. He showed him how to dig ditches and fix fences, how to plant seed and harvest corn. He taught him how to milk the cows and disinfect the cattle.

He showed him how to mend farm machinery so that in time he was as good as any mechanic. And he taught his son things that it had taken him a lifetime to know and which some men never learned: how to judge an animal by the sheen of its coat and the brightness of its eyes, how to predict the weather by the movement of the clouds and the behaviour of the birds.

He would say to Edward over and over till it was drummed into the child's brain: "Farming is a constant battle against the elements. Some men see them as the enemy. But the elements can be your friend too, if you know how to harness them."

Even when Ned had half a dozen men working for him and had practically ceased active farming, he still insisted that Edward take his place in the fields. "You can't learn farming from books," he would say. "You have to get your hands dirty." And the pair of them would roll up their sleeves and pull on their Wellington boots and go and clean out the byre.

The time would come too when he would induct his son into the mysteries of farm finance. Ned showed the young Edward how to keep accounts, how to gauge the amount of fertiliser that had to be bought, how to apply for subsidies and grants from the Department of Agriculture. Above all, he instilled in him the absolute need to balance the books, for Ned was painfully aware that in farming there was always a thin line between success and failure.

Edward proved a willing student, both around the farm and at school. He applied himself and learned quickly. In the various examinations that marked his progression through adolescence, he consistently achieved high grades. Nobody ever said it, but everybody knew. Edward was destined to take over the farm when his father retired. It was like one of those things that his mother believed. It was his Fate, already decided and written in the Book of Life.

Edward grew into manhood tall and strong. He had an easy-going nature that made him popular with the other young people around the town. But inevitably, his good fortune drew envy from certain quarters. He could hardly ignore the whispered comments of the corner boys who hung around the billiard saloon at the bottom of Main Street or the spiteful looks that occasionally greeted him in the local pub. And he knew the basis of the criticism: that he had life too easy, that everything had fallen into his lap. That he had been too damned lucky!

He tried to ignore the remarks. He *was* lucky. He accepted that. But he had also worked hard, both at school and around the farm. What did they want him to do? Apologise for his good fortune?

And then an incident occurred that was to mark a fundamental change in Edward's attitude towards his father. He had become a keen sportsman and every Sunday afternoon, he togged out for the Dunmuckridge football team. At one of these games, Dunmuckridge was playing Carrickbeg Rangers, a team from the neighbouring parish. Dunmuckridge were trailing by a point and looked set to lose when, in the dying moments of the game, Edward got possession of the ball.

He raced towards the Carrickbeg defence. In his ears, he could hear the roar of encouragement from the local supporters. He had a clear shot at goal and it seemed that nothing could stop him, when suddenly he felt a sharp tug at his shirt. Frantically, he turned round to see the face of Christy Duggan leering at him. Duggan was a farm labourer and one of those who hung around the billiard saloon.

"You're only a waster, McGinty!"

Edward struck his opponent's hand away and appealed to the referee. But the referee appeared not to have seen the foul and was waving for play to continue. Unfortunately, the incident had given the Carrickbeg defenders time to regroup and now they were swarming all over the goalmouth. Edward drove the ball towards the net but it was easily deflected and sent back down the field. A few minutes later, the whistle blew for full time.

Later, in the dressing-room, an irate Edward confronted Christy Duggan.

"You fouled me. Only for that, I would have scored."

But Duggan was contemptuous. "Get a life! You're imagining things."

Edward's temper was up now. "Don't talk to me like that," he said and swung a punch that caught Duggan full on the side of the jaw. Duggan was taken by surprise. He stumbled back, blood spurting from his mouth. He lunged at Edward and next moment the two were wrestling on the ground as the other players rushed to separate them.

As they were being pulled apart, Duggan spat in Edward's face. "Everybody knows you were born with a silver spoon in your mouth. Your da is the real man around your place! If it wasn't for him, you'd be nothing!"

Edward tried to attack his tormentor again, but strong arms held him back. Later in Clancy's pub, where the team was having a drink, Tom Mooney, his father's foreman, came and spoke to him.

"Pay no attention to that blackguard," he said. "He's a mean-minded liar, eaten up by spite."

"Thanks, Tom," Edward said and finished his drink.

But later, he wondered why no one else had contradicted Christy Duggan. And later still, he began to wonder if it was Duggan who had spoken the truth and Tom Mooney who had been the liar.

The remark played on Edward's mind. He began to

wonder if people really did see him as Christy Duggan had said: a spoiled brat who was set to inherit a thriving farm because of the hard work of his father. The thought grew into an obsession. He became morose, he saw criticism where none was intended. He wondered if people were talking about him. Innocent remarks became the subject of intense speculation as to their true meaning and intent.

At the same time, his attitude to his father began to change. The man he had once held in such high esteem now appeared ignorant and old-fashioned. He had no dress sense; his opinions and tastes were foolish. He was an embarrassment.

Edward found himself picking arguments with Ned over small, stupid things like the number of sheep they should buy or the kind of fertiliser they should use. Always, his father gave ground and let Edward have his way, even when some of the decisions Edward made turned out not to be the best. And the more Ned retreated, the more Edward provoked dispute.

He stopped appearing in public with his father. He gave up attending the marts and fairs. He stopped going to Mass on Sundays and gave up the weekly outing to the pub on Saturday nights. It was as if he was trying to escape completely from his father and make a public demonstration that he was now independent and able to stand on his own two feet.

But it caused him terrible inner conflict. Deep down, he still loved his parents and he hated what he was doing to them by this obsession. He felt guilty every time he had an argument with his father. Yet no matter how he looked at things, he could see no way out. As long as he stayed on the farm, he would never be free. He would always have this suspicion hanging over him. He would always feel that people were sneering at him because of Ned.

By now, Edward was at college and studying Agricultural

Science. Part of the course related to farming methods in other countries. That was how he came to hear about New Zealand. What he learned about the country appealed to him. The climate was temperate, the people were friendly and it had a thriving agricultural industry. And so the idea began to form in his mind of emigrating there once he had completed his degree. He wrote to the New Zealand embassy in Dublin seeking information about work permits and visas. He explained about his farming background and his agricultural studies. The replies were encouraging.

Immediately, he felt a tremendous sense of relief. By leaving his family and the farm, by cutting himself off entirely, he would be able to escape. He would be making a clear statement for everyone to see that he had finally emerged from under his father's shadow and was making his own way in the world.

And then Mollie won the Lotto. It was the talk of the town. The *Dunmuckridge Clarion* sent a reporter and a photographer to interview her and she appeared in a half-page spread complete with a picture of herself and Ned drinking champagne while seated on a tractor.

It gave the critics more ammunition. It just proved what a lucky bastard Edward really was. Now he would inherit the lottery money as well as the farm. But by now, Edward didn't care. He had made his decision. He knew the money would make little difference to his parents' lives. All they wanted was for him to stay behind and run the farm and maintain it in the family's hands. But he knew it was something he couldn't do.

So, when Mollie proposed this holiday, he was in a mood to compromise. It might be the only holiday they would spend together. For what his parents didn't know was that, just a week ago, his visa and work permit had come through. And with them, a one-year contract to work as an agricultural advisor on a farm near Auckland. He had his ticket bought, and once his exams were completed in six weeks' time, he would be gone.

The women were finishing their drinks and getting ready to leave. As they approached the table where Ned and Edward were sitting, the pretty one looked at Edward and smiled. Instinctively, he smiled back.

"Have a nice day," he said.

"You too," the woman said.

Edward's gaze lingered on the women as they walked through the door and out into the bright afternoon sunshine.

"You know something," Ned said, draining the remains of his pint, "I think you see things differently when you're away from home. You get a new perspective."

His father's remark drew Edward out of his reverie.

"Do you want another one?" he asked, indicating to the empty glass.

But Ned shook is head. "There's a race on television this afternoon. I think I'll just go back to the hotel and watch it."

Chapter 15

Charlie slept soundly for most of the trip to Puerto de la Cruz and only came to when the coach was at the outskirts of the town and the voice of the tour guide woke him from an inky oblivion.

At first, he didn't know where he was. He seemed to have been in so many strange places in the last twenty-four hours that he wouldn't have been surprised to discover he had somehow been transported back to Dublin and was now on the 31 bus to Howth. But the sights that greeted him from the window quickly convinced him. Palm trees swayed. People chatted at pavement cafés in the bright morning sunshine. And in the distance he could see the light sparkling on the bright silver sea. Dublin never looked like this!

The voice of the tour guide came crackling out of the microphone.

"Originally a tiny fishing village, Puerto de la Cruz is now one of the finest holiday resorts in Tenerife and boasts some of the oldest and most elegant buildings on the island."

At that precise moment, the coach hit a pothole in the road and jolted Charlie into an awareness of his physical condition. His head ached, his throat was parched and there was a thin line of perspiration sticking like clingfilm to his forehead. He realised he was distinctly hungover.

He tried to assemble the events of last night and found only disjointed fragments, like pieces of a broken picture. He could remember the Monaco Bar and the seemingly endless supply of vodka and Red Bulls. He could recall flashing lights and loud music and someone passing him a funny cigarette in the men's loo. After that, he could remember little till he woke up this morning.

He was in a strange bed in a strange room and Penny was beside him. She had her arms wrapped tightly around his neck. Charlie realised with a shock that they were both naked!

His first reaction was panic. He had to get out. He slowly raised his arm and tried to focus on his watch. It was almost eight o'clock. What was he going to do? With racing heart, he attempted to untangle himself but Penny only moaned and cuddled closer. Gingerly, Charlie extricated himself from her embrace. He carefully stepped out of the bed and replaced the sheets round her sleeping form. He picked up his scattered clothes from the floor and tip-toed out of the room. He got dressed in the hall, ran down the stairs to the street and managed to hail a passing cab. Back at the hotel, he just had time for a quick shower and a cup of coffee before making it down to the foyer in time to catch the coach.

What he needed now was another cup of coffee and something to eat. He could hear his stomach begin to rumble menacingly from lack of food. As the coach passed further into the town, another thought came thundering into his head. What had happened last night?

160

Did he have sex with Penny? He couldn't remember. Through the fog in his brain, he tried to muster the facts. He had wakened in bed with her. They were both naked. And she was clinging to him like he was the last life raft off the *Titanic.* Of course he had sex with her. What other rational explanation could there be? Which meant . . . Charlie felt an enormous surge of joy as the realisation finally dawned on him. He had accomplished his ambition, his reason for coming here in the first place! He had lost his virginity!

At a stroke, Charlie's hangover seemed to vanish and was immediately replaced by a tremendous feeling of satisfaction. He realised that he hadn't felt this good since Mr Gregg had made him manager of the bookshop. He felt like turning to the man beside him and shaking his hand. But just then, the coach gave another jolt as the driver negotiated a steep bend and came to a halt in a quaint little square. The tour guide was speaking again.

"Ladies and Gentlemen, we have now arrived in Puerto de la Cruz. We have a very interesting itinerary planned that will show you the best attractions of the town, including the cathedral and the town hall. Please stay together. At one o'clock we will have lunch at El Molino restaurant in Plaza del Charco. And then at four o'clock, the coach will depart once more for your hotels. Please now descend from the coach."

Charlie dutifully fell into line as the passengers got off and began to form an orderly queue like a party of children on a school outing. But he was in no mood to go trooping around old churches and ancient monuments. He decided to peel off on his own.

He waited till the party moved off and at a convenient moment slipped away down a side street. Within a few minutes he found an attractive little café and sat down at one of the pavement tables. What would he order? He had something big to celebrate, a milestone in his life. It should really be champagne. But they only sold champagne by the bottle and Charlie realised that a bottle of champagne this early in the day would land him right back where he was last night. Instead he ordered a large brandy and followed it with a coffee and a croissant.

He sat in the sunshine and watched the world stroll by. What a wonderful feeling! It was like joining a club or passing an initiation test. Even though he could remember absolutely nothing about it, Charlie knew that something vital had changed. No longer need he blush and feel shy in the presence of an attractive woman. No longer would he envy other men. No longer would he watch lovers holding hands or dancing cheek to cheek and feel excluded. He could be part of it too!

He ordered another brandy and felt his confidence expand. Wasn't it amazing the way the sun sparkled on the rooftops and brought out the colours of the flowers in the window-boxes? Had the air ever smelt so fresh or the skies look so blue? Did life ever feel so appealing or hold out so much promise?

He eventually finished his brandy, settled the bill and set off to see the town. He followed the crowds down the Calle Blanco as far as the fish market. Everywhere he went, he saw happy contented faces. People smiled at him and Charlie smiled back. Outside a church he tipped a beggar and then realised he had given the man a twenty-euro note. But what did it matter? He was celebrating. Why not share his joy?

When he arrived at the Lago Martinez, he checked his watch and saw that it was twelve forty-five. Soon, the rest of the passengers would be sitting down to lunch, sated with culture after their sightseeing tour. It was time to turn back.

He retraced his footsteps and shortly arrived at the Plaza del Charco. There, beneath the sign of the windmill, was the restaurant, El Molino. The walk and the fresh air had restored his appetite. Charlie confidently pushed open the doors and walked in.

But the restaurant was packed and there was scarcely a seat to be had. Charlie searched the room till his eye lighted on a table at the back where a woman sat alone. Without a moment's hesitation, he strode purposefully across the floor.

"Excuse me," he said. "Is this seat free?"

The woman looked up and smiled. She had high cheekbones and a wide mouth and beautiful blue eyes.

"Yes, it is."

"May I join you?"

"Of course."

Charlie pulled out the chair and sat down. He thrust out his hand.

"I'm Charlie Dobbins."

The woman placed her hand in his. It felt soft and warm.

"Trish Blake," she said. "Pleased to meet you."

Chapter 16

While Trish was settling down to lunch at the El Molino restaurant, Adrian was back in the apartment, struggling with the novel that just wouldn't come right. The high hopes that had encouraged him when they first arrived had quickly evaporated. Working on the novel had turned into a heartbreaking grind. It was like wrestling with an octopus. No sooner had he got one problem solved than another reared up and threatened to strangle the life out of him.

And Trish hadn't been much help with her constant demands to go out to dinner or to lunch or to take a break and eat a sandwich. As if he had time to eat! For a creative artist in his situation, food was just a distraction. He needed to be alone with his muse. He needed peace to work.

The strange behaviour which he had noticed before they came away seemed to have reasserted itself. She was acting oddly again. At night, she kept trying to lure him into bed, even going so far as to dress up in ridiculous frilly underwear and black stockings. So far he had managed to resist. But he found her behaviour a constant irritant, which was why he was secretly pleased when she went off in a huff this morning and left him alone.

Tap, tap, tap. Adrian's fingers fairly flew across the keyboard of the laptop, positioned on a table on the balcony where in the distance he could see the mountains shrouded in a blue haze. *Tap, tap, tap.* Stop. Adrian peered at the screen but could read nothing because of the glare from the sun reflecting into his face.

"Hell's bells," he muttered, through clenched teeth.

He got up and moved his chair and repositioned the laptop so that he was now facing into the sun and the screen was shaded. He tipped his straw hat over his eyes and pushed his sunglasses closer against his nose and began again.

The cruel landlord's lip curled in a vicious sneer as he hurled a curse at the pitiful figure of Michael O'Houlihan and his starving wife and sixteen children as they huddled in a ditch in the pelting rain outside the smoking ruins of their little white-washed cottage which had been their happy home for the past twenty years but had been reduced to a heap of rubble by the ugly Redcoat soldiers who now stood gloating at their vicious handiwork.

"Bad cess to you, Michael O'Houlihan. You owe me two weeks rent and it's the bog road for you now, me bucko! That'll teach you to default on your lawful debts."

"Please, sir," Michael pleaded, "have mercy on me and my starving family. I'll work my fingers to the bone to pay you back the money if only you could find it in your heart to spare me a crust of bread and a sup of milk."

Adrian sat back and scratched his head. There was something not quite right. Too bleak? Would the reader be able to take the pathos of the eviction scene or would the tragedy prove too painful for all but the most hard-bitten cynic? It was a delicate point. This chapter was one of the key sections of the novel and much of the plot hinged on it.

If he got it wrong, it could tilt the balance of the entire book.

He started once more.

"Give over your bleating" the cruel landlord hissed. "Or I'll have you horsewhipped for your trouble. You'll get nothing from me, you blackguard. The last time I loaned you the price of a boiled pig's head, it took you a month to repay me. I know your sort, O'Houlihan. You are a lazy scoundrel who doesn't know the meaning of hard work. Why only last month, I reduced your workload to eighteen hours a day and this is how you thank me."

Nearby, the Redcoat captain sniggered and drew his pistol from his belt with an unmistakable air of menace.

Adrian stopped typing and examined the page again. Still not right. Was it the dialogue? He had always regarded dialogue as one of his strong points. And those people who had read extracts at the writers' group had praised it for its gritty realism.

The pace seemed to be OK, and the atmosphere, and the characters. His characters were another of his strong points. Not for Adrian these milk-and-water creations who were so paralysed with angst and indecision that they could hardly get out of bed in the morning. Adrian's characters were larger than life. They were so real, you half-expected them to jump off the page and take a bite out of you.

He ran his fingers across his stubble chin and let out a long heartfelt sigh. Dammit! There *was* something wrong. He knew it, even if he couldn't put his finger on it. The novel wasn't reading the way it should. It seemed to lack the epic grandeur he was aiming for, the sweep and intensity of Tolstoy or Victor Hugo, the human pathos of Dickens. Some ingredient was missing.

He sat back in his chair and closed his eyes. He could feel the hot sun beating on his face. From the swimming-pool, he could hear laughter. People were down there enjoying themselves while he was stuck here on this bloody balcony wrestling with a novel that just wouldn't come right no matter how hard he tried. Adrian felt so frustrated he could weep.

He had been worrying the book non-stop since they got here. First thing when he woke, he switched on the laptop and began typing. He only stopped to eat and sleep. And sleep was a fitful business. He hadn't been to bed since the first night, despite Trish's coaxing. He preferred to work till he fell down exhausted on the settee, only to wake a few hours later and start all over again.

He hadn't shaved. He hadn't washed. He hadn't listened to the radio. A third World War could have broken out and Adrian wouldn't be aware. Time was ticking away and Adrian knew this was his last chance to get it right before the new school term called him away.

This thought spurred him into action once more. He returned to the laptop with fresh vigour. He pounded the keys as his imagination transported him to a bleak Connemara hillside where a little white-washed cottage was burning and a sadistic Redcoat captain was about to shoot a poor starving peasant. Maybe he should have the cruel landlord rape Michael O'Houlihan's wife while the Redcoats bayoneted the children? Did they have bayonets in 1847? He would check later. In the meantime, Adrian launched himself on an orgy of violence.

All afternoon, he typed. He hacked off arms, slit throats, gouged out eyes, crushed skulls. He disembowelled and decapitated. Adrian gleefully wreaked havoc and destruction across the Connemara landscape. With each line he wrote, the corpses piled higher and the blood flowed till at last the chapter resembled the boning hall of an abattoir.

He sat back and a smile of satisfaction wreathed his face. The novel was finally moving. He had cracked the problem that had plagued him for the past few weeks. All it required was more action and Adrian had provided it. He did a quick count and estimated that in the last four hours he had killed sixty-four people.

Perseverance, he said to himself. Never give up. He was right to keep at his work and not be distracted by Trish. But now it was time for a little reward. He glanced at his watch. It was almost seven o'clock. Where had the time gone?

He would go down to the bar and treat himself to a glass of brandy. Maybe he might even run into Monica and help her with her crossword. Now there was a woman who appreciated him. He recalled the look of admiration that had come into her face when he mentioned the fact that he was a writer. Monica was the type of woman who would understand the trials and the struggles that faced a creative artist like himself. Unlike Trish who was only concerned about getting him to eat and sleep.

Adrian switched off the laptop and closed the case. He brought it in from the balcony and placed it carefully on the sideboard. He went into the bathroom and examined himself in the mirror. Dark pools lurked beneath his eyes from lack of sleep, three days' growth of beard darkened his chin. His hair was ragged and unwashed. Maybe he should strip off and get under the shower, put on a shirt and tie and spruce himself up?

No, he decided. I'm an artist and people expect an artist to have a wild, untamed look. Artists don't conform to other people's rules. Artists set their own standards. And there is a certain whiff of brimstone about the way I look that makes women go weak at the knees.

He checked to make sure he had money and then he let himself out of the apartment, whistling as he made his way towards the lift.

Chapter 17

Charlie sat down at the table, straightened his collar, politely picked up the menu and flicked it open with the casual air of an experienced diner. He was feeling exuberant after the brandies and peckish after his walk. He let his eye travel down the page and immediately got a shock.

Cabra estilo Canario.

Conejo.

Pulpo a la Gallega.

The whole damned thing was in Spanish. Across the table he was aware that Trish was observing him with interest. What should he do? Bluff his way? Pick something at random and hope it didn't poison him? Or should he just come out with his hands up? Charlie looked into Trish's face and made a gesture of helplessness.

"Have you ordered yet? It's just that I haven't got a clue what any of this means."

"What would you like to know?" she said, suddenly leaning forward with a helpful smile.

"This *cabra* stuff? What is it?"

"Goat."

"Goat?"

"It's a local dish. It's cooked in wine and garlic."

"My God," Charlie muttered. "What about *conejo?*"

"Rabbit."

"You're joking?"

"No, I'm not."

"You mean a little bunny rabbit with a fluffy tail?"

Charlie put his hands to his ears and wiggled his fingers while Trish smiled indulgently.

"Not exactly. These rabbits are bred specially for the table. Although they are the same species as the little bunnies you refer to."

"And people eat them?"

"They regard them as a delicacy."

"I'm amazed," Charlie said. "*Pulpo a la Gallega?* No! Let me guess. Hairy spiders in their own juice with a sauce of stewed cactus leaves?"

A frown spread across Trish's face. "Not quite. But you *are* getting warm."

"Grilled vulture meat?"

"No. Nothing like that."

"Tell me, then."

"Octopus. Gallician style."

"I give up," Charlie said. "What are you having?"

"Chicken."

"Do you think you could order some for me?"

"I could try."

She signalled for the waiter and gave her order, then spoke again to Charlie. "What about something to drink?"

"Keep going. You're doing fine."

"Care to share a bottle of wine with me?"

"It's not made from dried banana skins?"

170

"I sincerely hope not."

"OK. So long as it's wet and alcoholic and reasonably palatable."

The waiter left. Charlie broke off a piece of bread and began to nibble. He was feeling good. He had just arrived and here he was, two minutes later, making witty conversation with a pretty woman he had never met before in his life. And by the look on her face, she didn't seem displeased.

"I'm very impressed," he said. "How do you know all this?"

"Simple. I brought my phrasebook. It's a basic requirement when you're visiting a foreign country."

"I thought they might have the menu in English," Charlie said. "Or at least a translation."

"Why should they? You don't expect the menus in Irish restaurants to be in Spanish."

"But this is different."

"No. It's not," Trish said emphatically. "It's considered good manners to at least make an effort. Even a few basic phrases can go a long way."

Charlie tried to appear suitably chastised. He regarded this woman anew. Maybe he had been wrong about her. His initial impression had been of someone warm and friendly. Was she going to turn into one of these politically correct harridans with no sense of humour? Was she about to give him a lecture on cultural imperialism and the depredations of tourism?

"You're perfectly right," he said, feeling like a coward. "But to tell you the truth, this holiday was a bit of a rush job. I didn't even know I was coming to Tenerife till I went into the travel shop."

"I was the same," Trish confessed. "I just wanted a week in the sun."

Charlie glanced at her hands. There was no wedding ring. He thought of asking if she was here on her own but decided not to. She might think he was being too inquisitive. They had only met, after all.

"What do you do for a living?" he heard her ask.

"I'm a bookseller. *Dublinia Books*. I've got several shops back home."

"Really?"

"Do you know them?"

"Of course. That's where I bought my phrasebook."

"Pity I didn't follow your example," Charlie said as the food arrived.

He glanced nervously at his plate. Something that vaguely resembled chicken breast resided in a dark sauce alongside a handful of tiny potatoes that looked like marbles and a few leaves of lettuce. And the whole thing reeked of garlic.

He took the bottle of Rioja she had chosen from the wine list and filled their glasses.

"Here's to your holiday!"

"And yours!"

He was pleasantly surprised to discover that the chicken was delicious, the meat tender and bursting with flavour.

"Taste okay?" Trish asked.

"Marvellous."

"Good." She wiped her mouth with her napkin. "You know, it's something of a coincidence, you being a bookseller."

"Why?"

"Because I know someone who's a writer."

"Oh? Anybody I might know?"

"Not really. He hasn't been published yet."

"What does he write? Fiction? Poetry?"

"He's writing a novel."

"That's a big undertaking," Charlie said. "What's it about?"

"It's a sort of historical novel. About the Great Famine."

Charlie looked impressed. "That *is* ambitious."

"You think so?" Trish asked, brightening up.

"Of course. The Famine's a very delicate subject. Over a million people starved to death and as many more were forced to emigrate. Many of them died of disease on the ships that were taking them to America. This was a very bleak time in Irish history."

"You think maybe it's too sensitive?"

"Not at all. The secret of good writing is to engage the reader. You can write about anything you like so long as you make it fresh and entertaining."

"Oh, it's certainly fresh," Trish said. "The central character is this 160-year-old man who's discovered living in a bog in Connemara. This person has read extracts to his writing group and they think it's very good."

"It definitely sounds – *original,"* Charlie said, chewing on a piece of chicken.

Trish lowered her voice.

"I'll let you into a secret. He's not having much success."

"No?" Charlie asked, sympathetically.

"Afraid not. It's been rejected all over the place. In fact, he can't even get an agent to represent him."

"He shouldn't get too depressed," Charlie said. "That happens all the time. There's a lot of luck involved in publishing. People like to pretend that it's all down to talent. But talent is only part of the story."

"And he's starting to act strangely. I'm afraid if he doesn't get his novel published, he'll get totally depressed. He's obsessed with it. He spends all his spare time cutting it and rewriting bits and sending it off in jiffy bags and waiting in vain for a response."

"Maybe he's sending it to the wrong people," Charlie

said, trying to sound reassuring. "Maybe he should be more focussed."

"Like what?"

"Well, there's no point sending a love story to somebody who only publishes scientific textbooks. Your friend should research the market, see who publishes the type of book he has written and then send them a few chapters with an outline of the plot and a polite letter asking if they'd like to read more. Apart from anything else, it'll save him postage."

"You're so right," Trish said.

Charlie beamed. This was a subject he knew intimately and, in Trish, he had a willing audience.

"Best thing would be to get an agent, though. A lot of publishers won't even look at a book unless it comes from an agent. They get inundated, you see."

"He's got his heart set on it," Trish said, "and he works very hard. If he doesn't get it published, I think it will crush him."

"I'll tell you what," Charlie said, suddenly carried away. "Why don't I take a look at it? I might be able to advise him."

Trish leaned across the table and grabbed Charlie's hand. "Would you really? That would be wonderful. I'd be so grateful."

She looked at him with large, admiring eyes and Charlie was suddenly seized with an impulse to kiss her. He shook his head to make this crazy notion go away. What on earth had come over him? He'd only had one glass of wine and a couple of brandies. Maybe he was still suffering the aftermath of those damned vodka and Red Bulls?

A look of concern had now crept into Trish's face. "Are you all right? You look strange."

"I'm fine," Charlie said. "Just a slight headache."

"Maybe it was the bus journey?"

"Don't worry about it. It'll pass."

"Are you sure? You look pale."

"Tell you what," Charlie said, as another idea popped into his head, "would you mind if we continued this conversation outside? Maybe the fresh air will help."

He left some money on the table for the waiter and together they went out to the bright sunshine.

"It *was* a bit crowded in there," Trish said. "You don't suffer from claustrophobia, do you?"

Charlie gave a weak smile. "I hope not."

"Do you want to sit or would you prefer to walk?"

"We'll walk, shall we?" Charlie said. He glanced quickly at his watch. It was two fifteen. The coach didn't leave till four o'clock.

"Could have been the heat," Trish said. "That's very common."

"It was really nothing at all," Charlie insisted, deciding there was mileage to be had in playing the brave soldier. "I'm fine now."

"Where would you like to go?"

"Let's head down to the seafront."

Trish slipped her arm into his and they set off. Charlie felt wonderful. This is marvellous, he thought. A sympathetic woman, a clear blue sky, a nice lunch and not a care in world. *Why hasn't this happened to me before?*

"What do *you* do for a living?" he asked as they headed down a cobbled street hung with baskets of flowers.

"I work for an auctioneering firm. It's my job to assess the value of properties we're asked to sell."

"That sounds very interesting."

"I love it. I've been doing it now for fifteen years."

Charlie made a quick calculation. Assuming she had to go to college to get some sort of professional qualification, that would put her in her mid-thirties. The same age as himself.

"Mind you, it can be very stressful," Trish continued. "People always believe their properties are worth more than they really are and if they don't get the prices they expect, they think I've been swindling them."

"Bookselling's the same."

Charlie told her how he had begged and borrowed and worked every hour that God sent to build up his business. He told her funny stories about the pompous authors he had met who acted like royalty and were rude to the staff and insisted that everybody jump to attention when they came to book signings in the shops.

"Are you married?" he heard her ask.

"No," Charlie said, sadly.

"But you must have a woman in your life. I would think a handsome man like you would have lots of women."

Charlie felt his heart flutter. Tell me more, he thought, I could listen to this all day.

"I have various women *friends* I see from time to time. But I suppose the right person just hasn't come along yet."

"She will," Trish said and looked at him tenderly as they turned a corner into a little park with roses and fuchsia and pink and red geraniums. "Some morning you'll wake up and the sun will be shining and the birds will be singing and everything will look so fresh and wonderful. You'll ask yourself why you're feeling so good. And suddenly you'll realise you're in love."

When it was time to return, they sat together on the coach and chatted the whole way back to the resort. Charlie had never felt so comfortable with a woman in his whole life. It was as if he had known Trish forever. He didn't want the journey to end.

As the coach finally pulled into the hotel, he turned to her and said: "Are you free to have dinner with me tonight?"

She seemed to blush a little. "I'd love to Charlie. But I can't. My husband will be waiting for me."

Charlie felt his stomach churn. "Your husband?"

"He's the writer I mentioned. He's been working all day on his novel. He's bound to be starving when I get back."

Charlie quickly tried to cover his confusion. "I didn't realise. Please forgive me."

"There's nothing to forgive. It was lovely of you to ask. And I've had the most wonderful time. Maybe I'll see you round the pool and we can have a drink, sometime?"

"Maybe," Charlie said, weakly.

"I'm there nearly every day," she added, pointedly. "And thank you so much for agreeing to read the manuscript."

"My pleasure," Charlie replied, as she walked away from him and into the hotel.

He followed her. As he entered the foyer, he spotted Penny, sitting at her little desk beneath a large poster advertising tickets for some attraction she was promoting and a queue of people already formed before her. I suppose I'd better speak to her, he thought. Apologise for disappearing this morning. He started towards her but as he approached, she looked up. Her face filled with horror as if she was seeing a ghost. Then she rose quickly from her desk and fled off down a corridor.

Charlie gazed after her in amazement.

What's happening, he thought? One minute everything is swinging along beautifully and the next minute, women are deserting me as if I was carrying the Black Death.

Chapter 18

Monica stood in the foyer of the Gran Hotel del Rey and gasped in astonishment at the richness that surrounded her. She had forgotten just how magnificent it really was. All about her were thick-pile carpets, glittering chandeliers, classical statues, tinkling fountains, trailing plants, huge displays of fresh flowers. She felt dizzy at the sight. This place oozed wealth and elegance. She could almost smell the money.

She paused to get her bearings. There was a pianist in a white dinner jacket playing soft background music while couples drifted towards the restaurants and bars. Monica recalled similar occasions with Woody when the toughest challenge of the evening was deciding which wine to have with the lobster. How long ago was that? Two years? Three at most. They used to have a rule to get to the Canaries at least once every winter to recharge the batteries and keep their suntans in prime condition.

She gave a quick glance towards the manager's desk and saw a man in pinstripes and waistcoat who she didn't recognise. Somebody new? There was a time when she knew all the staff here and they knew her. Woody made sure of that by making it his business to grease all their palms. And then it occurred to Monica that she hadn't recognised the commissionaire either and he was somebody she *should* remember for he had opened countless taxi doors for her in the past. Odd, she thought, and then dismissed it from her mind.

Where should she go? The Gran Hotel boasted eight bars and she had been in every single one of them. There were two cocktail bars, three lounge bars, two terrace bars and a disco bar. She ruled out the disco bar immediately. It didn't open till eleven and in any case, it tended to attract the younger set and got so noisy you couldn't hear yourself think. It was too chilly this evening to sit on the terrace in the little dress she was wearing and the lounge bars were usually populated by older married couples.

That left the cocktail bars. There was one on the ground floor beside the ballroom and another, more discreet, which was tucked away behind the main restaurant. Monica remembered it had soft lights and romantic music. That's where she would go. It would be perfect for what she had in mind.

There were only a handful of people in the bar when she arrived; some couples and a few single men. She decided to sit boldly at the counter where she would be seen. It would be easier to fall into conversation there. As she sat down, she recalled with a shudder the frightening prices of drinks in this place. They were the sort of prices that demanded a reference from your bank manager. She did some quick mental arithmetic and decided she had just enough cash for two G and Ts.

Carefully, she lowered herself onto a high stool and placed her handbag delicately on the counter. She crossed her legs and ran her fingers through her hair. It was at times like this she wished she smoked. But she had long ago given up cigarettes. They were bad for your health. Worse, they were bad for your teeth, Monica thought, remembering one of her prime assets.

The barman swooped and she ordered. It was usual practice in the Gran Hotel to put the drinks on your bill to be settled at the end of the stay but she wasn't a guest, so she couldn't do that. Instead, she withdrew a €50 note from her bag and placed it on the counter. With a bit of luck, some nice rich gentleman would come along and pay for her drink.

Monica stared at the rows of shining bottles behind the bar and tried to make her gin and tonic last. She remembered a previous occasion when she had done the very same thing – the night she was supposed to meet Woody in the Horseshoe Bar of the Shelbourne Hotel in Dublin and the bastard turned up late. Probably did it on purpose, she thought ruefully. Since he died, she had found herself recalling numerous small incidents that underlined just what a deceptive reptile he had been from the very start.

Out of the corner of her eye, she noticed several men glancing surreptitiously in her direction, attempting to size her up. She toyed with her glass and took a little sip. There was a nice-looking guy in a blazer, slacks and cravat at the end of the bar who was clearly taking an interest in her. He was fit and tanned and Monica reckoned he was in his mid-forties. There was another man sitting alone in one of the little alcoves across the room. A bit older, Monica thought, but quite presentable with his greying hair and neatly-trimmed moustache.

She tried to observe the scene by staring into the mirror above the bar. It made her feel like a female spy from one of those James Bond movies. Let's hope nobody tries to shoot me, Monica thought as she took another tiny sip of her drink. After a few minutes, two men came in and stood at the end of the counter. Monica saw them nudge each other and give her the once over. One of them, a tall blond man in a lightweight suit, smiled. Monica smiled back and then demurely lowered her head. I've got to play this carefully, she thought. I mustn't appear too forward. Mustn't make it look like I've got a *For Sale* sign stuck on my back.

The men ordered their drinks and sat down at one of the tables. Monica poured tonic into her glass and watched the ice slowly dissolve. A few more people drifted in. She wished again she had a cigarette. It would give her something to do with her hands. Half my allotted allowance gone and nothing to show for it, she thought as she finally drained her glass and placed it firmly on the counter. She checked her watch. Forty-five minutes on one G and T. It must be the slowest drink I've ever consumed.

At that moment, she saw the man with the moustache signal to the barman who looked at Monica and then poured a fresh glass and placed it in front of her. He leaned closer and whispered: "With *Senor* Browne's compliments."

A bite at last! Monica tried to look surprised. She turned in her stool and smiled at *Senor* Browne who smiled back and raised his own glass in salute. Monica responded and lifted the glass to her mouth and felt the fresh bubbles tickle her tongue.

Senor Browne was getting up to join her. But at the same time, the man in the blazer and cravat was moving too. He deftly vacated his seat at the end of the bar and slid onto the empty stool beside Monica. Good Lord, she thought, it's like waiting for a bus. Three-quarters of an hour with no response and now I've got two of them practically fighting over me. *Senor* Browne looked annoyed but reluctantly sat down again and the new man immediately engaged her in conversation.

"Are you alone?" he asked. He had a Spanish accent but his English was good.

"Yes," Monica said. She looked into his face: dark skin, brown eyes. Her first guess had been correct. He was about forty-five and really very handsome. And was that a genuine Rolex on his wrist?

"Do you mind if I join you?"

You already have, Monica thought but kept it to herself. "Not at all," she said.

The man smiled and moved closer. She saw him examining her hand for signs of a wedding ring.

"Have you no husband?"

My God, Monica thought, this guy doesn't hang about. She adopted her forlorn widow pose.

"He died recently," she sighed.

"That's very sad," the man said sympathetically. "So you have come to Tenerife to get away from everything?"

"That's right."

"Do you like it here?"

"Of course," Monica said, fluttering her eyes and showing her shiny teeth. "It's such a beautiful place. So much to do and see."

"And may I enquire where you are from?"

"Ireland."

"Ah. We get a lot of Irish people here. I like them. Do you mind if I ask your name?"

"Monica."

"That is a nice name." The man smiled. "And your surname?"

"Woodworth."

"Are you staying at the Gran Hotel, Mrs Woodworth?"

What a lot of questions, Monica thought, and he hasn't even bothered to introduce himself. Maybe it's the Spanish way to get down to basics without wasting time on small talk.

"No. I'm staying somewhere else. But I've stayed here before when my husband was alive. I thought I'd come back and see the hotel again. Just for old times' sake." She lifted her glass and took a sip. "And what do you do, *Senor* . . .?"

"Peres. I'm the hotel detective."

Monica froze, her glass midway between her mouth and the counter. Was she hearing things or was this some elaborate practical joke? But the man was reaching into his pocket and had taken out a wallet. He flicked it open to reveal a photograph and an official-looking stamp.

"I must ask you to come with me, Mrs Woodworth. I suggest you do it quietly and do not make a fuss. Otherwise, I will be obliged to call for assistance from the security staff to have you removed from the bar."

Monica felt the blood drain from her face. "There must be some mistake," she gasped. "What have I done?"

"Please keep your voice down. I will explain later."

Peres got up and stood like a menacing presence beside her. Monica hesitated, paralysed by shock and indignation.

"I demand to speak to the manager."

Peres didn't flinch He placed a heavy hand on her arm. "I advise you to do as I say."

Reluctantly, Monica got down from her stool. She lifted her handbag and followed him out of the bar, aware that all eyes in the room were now staring after them.

This must be a case of mistaken identity, she decided. He must be confusing me with somebody else. She tried to remember if she had brought her passport and if there was an Irish consulate in Tenerife. I'll sue them for every miserable penny they possess, she thought, as the initial shock turned to anger. Practically arresting me in front of a room full of people, as if I was a common criminal! *Senor* bloody Peres will have a lot of grovelling to do before he hears the end of this little episode.

He led her across the wide expanse of foyer and down a carpeted corridor till he came to a room. He took a key from his pocket and ushered her into a tiny office. There was a desk, a phone and two chairs. Monica felt her heart sink. It looked exactly like an interrogation centre.

"Please sit down," Peres said.

"I prefer to stand," Monica replied, firmly.

"As you wish."

"What do you think you're doing?" she began. "Making a show of me in front of all those people? I'll have you know I've been a respected guest in this hotel for many years. I demand to see the manager, Senor Roper. He'll confirm everything I say."

"Senor Roper is no longer employed here."

"Well, then, Ramon. The head waiter. He'll remember me."

"He's not here either. The hotel is under new management since last summer. All the staff are new."

"Why am I here?" Monica demanded, her voice rising. "You haven't even told me what I'm supposed to have done."

"Have you any identification?" Peres asked, calmly.

"What do you mean identification? I haven't done anything."

"That remains to be seen. You are a trespasser in this hotel. You are not a guest here and you have no legitimate business."

184

"I came for a quiet drink."

"Mrs Woodworth, don't play with me. You know that isn't true." There was a mocking tone in his voice.

"Of course it is."

"No, you came for something else."

The man is a lunatic, Monica decided. Maybe *she* should call security. "I demand an explanation," she said. "You can't treat me like this. I demand to know why you are detaining me here against my will."

"Mrs Woodworth, I must tell you that we value our reputation very highly. And that of our guests."

"Reputation? I don't know what you're talking about."

Peres's cold eyes pierced her. "I think you do. You didn't come here for a quiet drink, as you claim. You came for the purposes of soliciting."

"Soliciting?"

"For prostitution."

Monica gasped. She couldn't believe her ears. She had never been so insulted in her life. "How dare you!"

"I observed you in the bar," Peres continued, unfazed. "I saw you propositioning various gentlemen."

"That's a lie. I propositioned no one."

"I have witnesses. Do you know the penalty for prostitution? You could spend time in prison."

Monica felt faint. This isn't happening to me, she thought. It's all a bad dream and any minute now I'm going to wake up to reality.

"I came for a drink," she repeated feebly. "You can check the hotel records. You'll see I stayed here before." Her voice trailed away.

"Do you have identification?" Peres repeated.

Monica fumbled in her bag till she found her passport.

Peres flicked it open and examined her picture. It was a

younger Monica by ten years, with different hair and thinner face. She prayed that he could still recognise her.

All sorts of wild thoughts tumbled through her brain. What if he hands me over to the police? What if they put me in jail? What if they deport me? What if my name appears in the papers? I'll be destroyed. Deported from Tenerife for soliciting. I'll never live it down. I'll have to emigrate.

"Please," she pleaded, "can't you just forget all this? Can't you just let me go?"

Peres snapped the passport closed. He lifted the phone and spoke to someone in Spanish. After a few minutes, he replaced the phone. He quietly observed Monica with his cold eyes. Then he slowly reached across the desk and returned her passport.

"I've checked what you said. You did stay here."

Monica felt weak with relief. "I told you."

"But that doesn't alter the fact that you came here to solicit."

"No," Monica whispered.

"Oh, for God's sake," Peres said, "we both know it's true. Why do you keep up this silly pretence?" He folded his arms and considered for a moment. Then he appeared to relent. "Mrs Woodworth, I have already told you how much we value our reputation. We do not wish to have a scandal. Under the circumstances, I am prepared to drop the matter. You may go."

Monica felt her heart miss a beat. But Peres hadn't finished speaking.

"However, I do not wish to see you return to the Gran Hotel del Rey. Ever! You may consider yourself persona non grata. I am now going to escort you off the premises. If you turn up here again, the staff will have instructions to remove you."

He opened the door.

Monica's only thought was to get out fast before he changed his mind. He was standing beside the door, waiting for her. She meekly followed him and felt her face burn with shame as once more they traversed the foyer, filled now with small groups of whispering people.

At last, they reached the main entrance. Peres stood aside and let Monica pass into the cool night. He didn't speak or even say goodbye. There was a row of taxis waiting but she ignored them and started to walk. She didn't trust herself not to break down in the back of a cab.

She felt a cool breeze fan her face as she headed for the main gates at the end of the drive. She had never been so humiliated. She had never felt so cheap. She had never felt so resentful. All the money she had spent there in the past and now to be treated like this!

She shuddered as she thought how close she had come to disaster. She prayed that word never leaked out. She thought of that harridan, Colleen McQueen, and how she would use the incident in her column: *LEADING LADY LED AWAY*. It was enough to make Monica's blood run cold.

Twenty minutes later, the lights of Hotel Las Flores came into view. Monica had never thought the place would look so welcoming, so cosy, so safe. She would go straight up to her apartment and pour herself a large gin and tonic and try to banish the horrible events of the night completely from her mind.

As she hobbled through the front door, her heel blistered from walking, the first person she saw was Carlos. He was writing in a ledger at the Reception desk. He looked up and caught her eye and she saw the concern in his face. He immediately stopped what he was doing and came out to meet her.

"*Senora* Woodworth. You look distressed. What is the matter with you?"

"I just need to sit down," Monica heard herself say as the thought flashed through her mind: it's true. God never closes one door but he opens another.

Carlos immediately wrapped his strong arm around Monica's shoulder and led her to a comfortable sofa. He signalled to a waiter who set off at once and returned with a tray and a decanter of sherry that he put down carefully on a little table before hurrying away again.

"Now," Carlos said, skilfully pouring two glasses and giving one to Monica, "drink that. It will make you feel better."

"I'll be fine," Monica said. "You really shouldn't fuss."

"You don't look fine. You look like you have had a nasty shock."

Monica sipped her sherry. It was sweet and she felt it immediately begin to soothe and calm her shattered nerves.

"Tell me what happened. Do I need to call a doctor? Or maybe the police?"

At the mention of the police, Monica felt her blood pressure soar. She put down her glass for fear she might spill it. "Not at all," she said, quickly. "There's no need for the police. Nothing happened."

"So why are you so upset?"

Monica sat silent for a moment. Then she gently removed a tear from the corner of her eye.

"Do you really want to know?"

Carlos moved closer. "Of course. I am the manager of this hotel. You are my guest. Anything that makes you unhappy is my concern."

Monica took out her handkerchief, wiped her eye and gave her nose a little blow. She sniffed and tried to look suitably bereft. "I was dining alone. At a beautiful little restaurant at the harbour. And I looked up at the night sky with its canopy of stars. It looked so romantic that I couldn't help thinking of all the happy times I have spent in Tenerife in the past. With my poor dead husband. And it just made me so sad, I had to leave."

Carlos gently patted her arm. Should I allow him such familiarities, so soon, Monica thought? I hardly know him. But it *was* comforting after the nightmare of the Gran Hotel.

"I understand completely," Carlos was saying in his soothing voice. "You are suffering from the broken heart."

It's amazing, Monica thought. He's a foreigner. But he has put it so poetically. "Yes. That's it."

"It is always the same after a great love," Carlos continued. "Even after the loved one has passed on, the events of their life remain behind."

"How true," Monica sighed, thinking of the debts that bastard Woody had left in his wake.

"When did your beloved husband die?"

"Just three months ago."

"Was he young? Like you?"

Monica couldn't help but notice the lovely compliment he had just paid her. "A little bit older."

"And you must have adored him?" Monica almost choked as she took another sip of sherry.

"Yes, I did. I worshipped the very ground he walked upon."

"Tell me, *Senora* Woodworth, did he die suddenly?"

"Oh, he did. Very suddenly. There was absolutely no warning. It took everyone by surprise."

"What was it?"

"A massive heart attack."

"I guessed it," Carlos said with satisfaction. "It must have been a terrible blow."

"It was. I still haven't come to terms with it. Sometimes

189

I expect the phone to ring and hear his voice. Sometimes I think I hear his footsteps in the hall. Some mornings I wake in bed and expect to see his face on the pillow."

"It will take time," Carlos said sympathetically. "Are you all alone? Do you have any children?"

"No."

"That is so sad. My heart bleeds for you."

"Thank you," Monica said and decided to sniff again.

"Do you mind if I ask? What did your husband do?"

"He was a businessman."

"What sort of a businessman?"

Monica tried to remember what it was exactly that Woody did. She recalled her conversation with Mr Flynn of Grabbit and Leggit. Something to do with roubles. "He was an investor."

"Ah!" Carlos exclaimed. "He put together deals."

"Exactly," Monica said, longing to get away from a subject she suspected was faintly unsavoury.

"I know his work. In our business, I have often come across men like your late husband. When we are buying a new hotel, we sometimes need people who will invest their funds with us. Your late husband was such a man?"

"That's right."

"These men are vital," Carlos announced, gravely. "They play a very important role. But they must be shrewd. Your husband was a very intelligent businessman?"

"I know he made a lot of money," Monica said.

"And who runs the business now?"

"No one. The business died with him. There was no one to take his place."

Carlos shook his head. "It is too sad. All too sad. And now you are alone."

"I do have many friends," Monica said quickly, in case he thought she was some kind of recluse. "And I live a very busy life. I organise parties for charity."

"Are they large parties?"

"Oh yes. Sometimes I would have two hundred guests. Last year alone, I raised over a million euros."

Carlos looked impressed. "But that must involve much work, *Senora*."

"It does. But I have assistance. And besides, I enjoy it. But you have a busy life, too. You have this hotel to run."

"Yes, it is busy," Carlos conceded. "And my father works me very hard."

Monica's ears pricked up. "Your father?"

"*Senor* Luis Hernandez. He is the owner of Hotel Las Flores. He lives in Madrid. My father owns five more hotels. This is the first one in the Canary Islands. My father is a very shrewd businessman. Just like your poor husband. He believes there is a lot of money to be made from tourism. It is a growing industry."

"And who runs the other ones?"

"My father. He has managers, of course. But he is the overall boss. He has appointed me to run Hotel Las Flores. If I make a success of it, he plans to open more."

"What do the other members of your family do?"

"There are no other members. Except for my mother. I am an only child."

"It is a heavy burden for your father."

"Yes. And he is getting old. I expect that soon he will retire. If I have proved myself, he will hand the business over to me. So you can understand it is important that I make a big success of this hotel."

Very interesting, Monica thought. She did a quick

calculation. Six hotels. Ageing father. Only son. No wife. This sounded too good to be true.

"But you *are* making a fabulous success," she gushed. "Everybody says so. I have stayed in some of the finest hotels in the world and believe me, Hotel Las Flores is easily the most comfortable."

"You think so?"

"Certainly. People feel at home here. You have managed to combine service with informality and that is not an easy feat."

"I try my best," Carlos admitted, modestly. "But there is strong competition. There is the Gran Hotel del Rey, for instance. Every year it is awarded five stars while we can only manage three."

At the very mention of the Gran Hotel, Monica felt her blood chill. "Don't talk to me about that place!" she said with passion.

Carlos arched his eyebrows. "You know it?"

"Of course. I stayed there with my husband and we had a dreadful experience. It's stuffy and over-priced. And so uptight you'd be afraid to breathe in case you offended someone."

"Uptight? I do not understand that word. What does it mean?"

"It means it's run like a concentration camp. That's what it means!"

"Really?" Carlos said. "I didn't realise."

"Oh yes. When people come on holidays they want to relax. They don't expect to be supervised by security guards and detectives. They want to enjoy themselves."

"You are so right."

"As for the way they treat single women in that dump.

It's disgusting. If you don't have a companion, they immediately assume you're up to no good. Don't you have anti-discrimination laws in Spain?"

"Of course, we do."

"Well, the Gran Hotel doesn't seem to have heard about them. They seem to think the world is composed entirely of married couples. A single woman shows up and immediately, the security staff think she's going to make off with the cutlery. It's an outrage. It's like something out of the Dark Ages. I'm surprised they haven't been closed down by now."

Carlos was staring at her in amazement.

Slow down, Monica thought. Mustn't get carried away or it might only raise suspicion. "Don't compare yourself with the Gran Hotel," she sniffed. "Hotel Las Flores is a far superior establishment. When I return to Dublin I intend to recommend it to all my friends."

Carlos beamed with delight. "That is very kind of you to say."

"It's only the truth."

"Let us drink to that." He lifted the decanter and refilled the glasses.

This is wonderful, Monica thought. It's so good to be treated like a lady again. It's so nice to be appreciated and given the respect I deserve. She lifted her glass and took another tiny sip. "This sherry is very good."

"It is a special reserve. I only serve it on certain occasions. Like now, when I entertain a beautiful, intelligent woman."

Monica let her eyelids droop. "Thank you, Carlos. That is very kind of you."

"You see, I am so busy here that I get little opportunity to talk to someone special, a woman who has seen the world and is so sophisticated."

"But I would have thought a handsome man like you would have lots of opportunities."

Carlos smiled. "Now it is my turn to thank you."

"I see the way women look at you."

He made a dismissive gesture with his hand. "Pah! They are only silly young girls. They are merely seeking a holiday romance. I am talking about a mature woman."

I'm not sure I like that word mature, Monica thought. It's got negative connotations.

"I am talking about a woman that I can confide in, a woman who has experience, a woman who can listen and give advice. A woman who is not only beautiful but has judgement and taste. You are such a woman, *Senora* Woodworth."

"Please just call me Monica."

He laid his manly hand on hers. "Monica," he whispered.

She felt her heart flutter. Oh, this is bliss, she thought.

Carlos's hand was gently caressing hers.

"I have enjoyed our little talk," he said.

"And so have I."

"But now, I must return to work. We have fifty new guests arriving tomorrow and I must make the arrangements. Are you recovered now?"

"I think so."

"I have a small favour to beg of you."

"What is it?" Monica said, softly.

"Would you think me ill-mannered if I was to ask you to dine with me some evening?"

"Not at all. I'd be delighted."

His face seemed to light up with pleasure. "I will make the arrangements and then I will confirm with you. Oh,

Monica. You have made me so happy. Tonight, I will not sleep because I will be thinking of you."

He raised her hand to his lips and gently kissed her fingers.

Monica felt so light-headed, she thought she was going to faint.

Chapter 19

Edward had grown quite fond of the Lucky Leprechaun. He didn't much care for sunbathing, unlike his sister Mary who could cheerfully spend the whole day lying out by the swimming-pool, slowly turning brown. He grew bored watching television, even though his father had discovered a sports channel which showed soccer and horseracing and sat glued to it for most of the afternoon. Edward's interests were simple. He liked to swim and he liked to walk. And increasingly in the last few days, his walks had taken him down the hill to the harbour and the cosy atmosphere of the pub.

He found it a shady place to shelter from the torrid heat of the day and catch up on the news from home from the many Irish visitors who passed through its doors. The drink was cheap and the food was good and he liked to eat his meals there. And of course there was always a chance of meeting that attractive young woman again. And next time, he might get to know her a bit better.

But now his attention was focussed on his parents as he

sat with his sister at a little table and discussed what they could do about them.

"You know, it's crazy," Edward said. "This is the first family holiday we've ever had and we end up coming to a place where Mum can't stand the heat and Dad won't eat the food. It could only happen to the McGintys."

"Ah, but you have to remember that Mum wasn't thinking of herself when she organised this trip," Mary said. "She was thinking of us. In fact, she was thinking specifically of you, Edward."

It was true. If his mother had been thinking of herself she would probably have arranged for a nice safe holiday in Ballybunion, County Kerry, where everything would be familiar right down to the boiled eggs for breakfast. And they would have been Irish eggs laid by Irish hens which would have kept Ned happy. But his mother was the least selfish person Edward had ever known. She was always thinking of other people. Even with the lottery money she had won, her chief concern was how she could spend it to some useful purpose.

"How is she anyway?" he asked.

"She's not exactly enjoying herself," Mary said. "I looked in on her before I left. She was sitting on the balcony under her umbrella, complaining about the heat."

"She could have done that at home. She didn't have to come to Tenerife just to feel uncomfortable."

"And then she has to cook dinner this evening over that cramped little stove. They're having bacon and cabbage. *Irish* bacon that she brought the whole way from Dunmuckridge in her suitcase."

Edward shook his head. "This is madness. I blame Dad. He can be so bloody stubborn at times."

"I think it runs in the family," Mary said, pointedly.

Edward chose to ignore the remark. "I think we have to do something," he said.

"Like what?"

"Get Mum out of the apartment for one thing. She can't stay cooped up there all day long. She has to go out and meet people."

"I've tried that," Mary said with a sigh. "She won't come to the pool because she says it isn't modest to parade in a swimsuit in public. Wherever she got that notion from. I suggested the beach where there would be a breeze and she said she would only get sand in her toes. What am I supposed to do?"

"What about the hotel lounge? It's cool there. And it's quiet. She'd be able to read. We could buy her one of those books of horoscopes and she'd be happy as Larry."

"I suggested that too. But she said people would only come up to her and speak in Spanish and then she'd get embarrassed."

"But they all speak English."

"*We* know that, Edward. But they're a different generation. If they weren't my parents, I'd say they were definitely eccentric. Do you know what Mum said to me today? She said I shouldn't go swimming – I should take it easy."

"What?"

"I know, it's weird."

"But what did she mean?"

Mary shrugged.

"How am I supposed to know? She's been dropping lots of little remarks recently. Telling me I should rest up and 'take good care of myself'. Do I look all right to you?"

"You look fine."

"I wonder if the heat's beginning to get to her?" Mary pondered. "Maybe it's affecting her brain. That can happen to people, you know."

"I've heard enough," Edward said emphatically. "We have to take action. We have to start with Dad. He's the main culprit. All this nonsense about Spanish food. Most of it's from the EU anyway. The damned potatoes could be Irish, for all he knows."

He looked around for Tom Casey and waved him over to their table.

"I've got a request," he said when Casey arrived. "You've met my father."

"A decent man," Casey said. "A bit stuck in his ways."

"You can say that again. You know he's got this fad about Spanish cooking? Thinks people are trying to poison him?"

"Well, he doesn't make any secret of it," Casey said. "Although he seems quite at home with the beer now."

"That's my point. I think if we could just persuade him to eat something here, he'd soon get over that prejudice too." He turned to Mary. "What would you say is his favourite meal?"

"Steak and onions," Mary said. "Without a doubt."

"What if we were to present him with a fat sirloin steak?" Edward said to Casey. "Nicely cooked, medium rare, the way he likes it?"

"That shouldn't be any problem," Tom Casey said. "I'll talk to Brian. We can manage that."

"You'd need to be extra careful," Edward said. "He's very fussy."

"Just leave everything to me," Tom Casey said. "When I put this steak down in front of him, it'll be so tempting he won't be able to resist. When do you want it for?"

"Tomorrow lunchtime."

"Fine."

Edward ordered more drinks and sat back with a smile of satisfaction.

"Well, that's a start," he said to Mary.

But she had lowered her eyes. "You know there is something *you* could do, Edward."

"I know what you're going to say."

"If you would just agree to stay at home and look after the farm, it would make this a truly memorable holiday."

"I don't want to talk about it," Edward said.

"It's not a lot to ask. Most sons would jump at the chance."

"Subject is closed," Edward said firmly.

The drinks came and he looked around the bar. It was beginning to fill up. No sign of the pretty woman, Edward thought. I wonder where she is?

At that very moment, the woman he was looking for was in the casualty department of the local hospital having a plaster cast put on her leg.

The day had started fine. Bobby had wakened shortly after eleven feeling slightly fuzzy following a late night in the Leprechaun where she had won a bottle of tequila after taking part in a quiz. The crunch question that had swung it for her was to name the local unit of currency in Turkey which she had correctly identified as the lira only because she had recently read about it in a holiday brochure.

And of course, having won the prize, the decent thing was to share it with the other participants at their table. As a result, it was after three when they finally got back to Hotel Las Flores and had to be let in by the night porter. But the hangover wasn't severe and was soon dispelled by a quick swim in the pool and a coffee and croissant at the café bar.

"What shall we do today?" Angie said, stretching her long legs in the sun.

"We could go shopping?" Bobby said. She had seen some nice dresses at a pretty boutique in Parque Santiago and was determined to buy some of them before her credit-card limit ran out.

"I don't feel like traipsing around shops," Angie said. "Not on a nice day like this."

"But every day's a nice day. That's the whole point of Tenerife."

"Why don't we do something energetic for a change? All we seem to do is laze around in bars or at the pool. Why don't we get some exercise?"

Bobby wasn't sure she wanted exercise but she was in a mood to be agreeable. "What have you got in mind?"

"There's supposed to be a nice little bay out by La Caleta we could walk to. And it's got nice fish restaurants. Maybe we could eat there?"

"Okay," Bobby said. "If that's what you want."

They left the café and went up to their room to change into shorts and tee shirts and runners. It was after midday when they set off. The sun was high in the sky and it was already very hot. They followed the path along the coast where they could see people lying in the sun or splashing about in the sea. Before long, Bobby was out of breath.

"I'm not sure this is a good idea," she panted. "Maybe we should turn back?"

"That's just because you're out of condition. C'mon, we haven't far to go." Angie pointed to a cluster of white houses in the distance which seemed to cling like limpets to the cliff face. "Look, you can see it. You'll be able to rest when you get there. Think of the nice cool drink that awaits you."

Bobby thought of the nice cool drink she could have at any of the bars and restaurants they were passing by. They didn't have to go the whole way to La Caleta. But she kept her thoughts to herself and trudged on.

They arrived shortly before two o'clock and plumped

down at a table in the first restaurant they came to. Bobby was exhausted. The combination of heat and exercise had completely drained her of energy.

"How are we going to get back?" she complained. "There's no way I could possibly walk."

"We can get the bus," Angie said.

Bobby demolished a pint of ice-cold Dorada and ordered another while she studied the menu.

They ate prawns and salad and washed it down with a carafe of white wine. When the meal was finished and the bill had been paid Bobby stood up to go to the ladies' and felt her legs go wobbly.

"You're going to have to carry me to the bus," she wailed. "There's no way I could make it under my own steam."

"Don't be such a ninny," Angie retorted. "We've only walked about four miles. Anybody would think you'd run a marathon."

"Four miles? It felt more like forty."

But once she was standing for a while she felt the strength return to her legs. She made it to the bathroom and then they set off for the bus-stop. It was about half a mile away along a dirt track that led uphill to the main road. They came eventually to a small dip in the path which meant climbing over some rocks and it was here that the accident occurred.

Angie went first. She stood at the top and reached down to give Bobby support. But at the critical moment when she started to climb, Bobby felt her foot slip. Her shoe touched shingle and immediately it gave way under her. She went crashing down onto the rocks. A vicious bolt of pain shot through her leg and then everything went dark.

Half an hour later she was in an ambulance. Angie was

sitting beside her looking frightened and stroking her forehead with a damp handkerchief.

"How does it feel?" Angie asked.

"Terrible," Bobby muttered. "I hope I haven't broken anything." There was an ugly bruise on her leg and blood on her shorts and socks.

"It's all my fault. I shouldn't have forced you to walk so far."

"Don't blame yourself," Bobby said through gritted teeth. "It was just a silly accident. At least I'm still alive."

"My God, don't talk like that. I'll never forgive myself if it's something serious."

The ambulance screeched to a halt outside the hospital entrance and the siren went dead. Two orderlies carefully placed Bobby on a stretcher and she was whisked off to casualty while Angie was asked to wait in the reception area.

Once in casualty, a doctor quickly examined her. He didn't say anything as he gently probed the leg for indications of broken bones. He gave her an injection to kill the pain and then she was taken to the X-ray department.

Twenty minutes later, the doctor came to see her again. He held up the X-ray negatives to the light and pointed to a dark area. "The good news is there is nothing broken." He smiled kindly as he spoke. "However, the bad news is you have torn a ligament. I'm afraid you will be out of action for some time." He looked at the notes that the nurse had taken when Bobby was first admitted. "I see that you are on holiday. Well, I'm afraid there will be no more swimming for a while. Or dancing." He smiled again, playfully this time. "Your leg will be put in plaster but it is only for a few days. In the meantime you will have to give it easy."

"Take it easy," Bobby corrected him. Her head felt light and giddy from the injection.

"Of course. Take it easy. You must come back to the hospital before you go home and I will write you a note for your own doctor in Ireland."

"OK," Bobby said.

"You have been a very brave woman, Miss Bannon. You know, you never cried once."

"Did you expect me to cry?"

"Frankly Yes. You must have been in great pain."

"Thank you," Bobby said, feeling proud of herself.

After half an hour, she came hobbling back into reception, assisted by the nurse. Her leg was now in plaster and she was leaning on a crutch.

"Well?" Angie asked, her face creased with concern.

Bobby was still feeling giddy. "All I need is a parrot for my shoulder and I could pass myself off as Mrs Silver."

"Who?"

"Long John Silver's wife," Bobby said with a grin.

Chapter 20

Adrian and Trish were eating breakfast on the balcony of their apartment. It was one of the few meals they had shared together since they arrived. Trish had returned from her trip to Puerto de la Cruz the previous evening to find her husband working on his laptop in ebullient mood. He even gave her a quick kiss on the cheek as she came through the door, which had taken her completely by surprise.

"You're in fine form," she said, grateful that he appeared to have overcome his surly mood.

"I've solved the problem," Adrian replied gleefully. "I've got the novel moving again. It was just a matter of injecting some action. Since you left this morning, I've killed sixty-four people."

"My God, you sound as if you enjoyed it."

Adrian giggled. "I did. It gave me tremendous satisfaction. I should have thought of it sooner. People love bloodshed and gore. That's why plays like *Hamlet* are such a great success."

"Well, I'm really pleased for you," Trish said." And I have some good news too. I went on a coach tour and I met the most charming man. His name is Charlie Dobbins. He owns the *Dublinia* bookshops."

"Never heard of him," Adrian replied.

"And guess what? He offered to read the book for you. He said he might be able to advise you. Isn't that the most wonderful news?"

Adrian paused, his fingers poised above the keyboard. "I beg your pardon? Did I hear you correctly? You asked a *bookseller* to read *The Green Gannet?*"

"I didn't ask. He volunteered."

"*A bookseller?*"

"But he's in the business, darling. He knows what sells. That's his job."

"But just because he sells books, doesn't mean he knows anything about *literature*. A greengrocer knows how to sell cabbages. It doesn't make him an expert on agriculture. I'm surprised at you, Trish. I really am, discussing my novel with a complete stranger, and a bookseller to boot."

Trish quickly realised she had better tread warily if she wasn't to set her husband off again. "But I'm so proud of you. It's not every woman is married to a writer. And I thought I was being helpful. You know some professional advice might be just what you need."

Adrian's face had grown pale and stern. "When I want advice, I'll ask for it, thank you very much." He turned back to the laptop.

She stroked his neck. "Why don't you take a break? Why don't we go out and eat a nice dinner somewhere and drink some wine? You owe it to yourself. You've been working so hard."

He was tempted. The thought of food and wine was very appealing. The idea of turning off the laptop and walking away from *The Green Gannet* for twelve hours sounded very attractive indeed. But he was at another crucial scene and he knew he couldn't relax till he got it right. He wavered for a split second and then he said: "I can't. I'm at a very important juncture. I've got to keep going."

Trish looked disappointed. She went into the bathroom and he heard the shower running. Twenty minutes later, she emerged dressed in a nice light dress with a low-cut bodice which showed off her breasts.

"Eating again on my own, Adrian. You know this will start the tongues wagging."

She was out the door and gone before he had a chance to reply.

Afterwards, he felt a tinge of regret for his brusque behaviour. Perhaps he shouldn't have been quite so abrupt. Trish probably did think she was being helpful talking to this bookseller person about his novel. And it was nice to know that she felt proud of him. He would accept her apology when she returned and warn her to be more careful in future.

And then he began to think that maybe he shouldn't have been so dismissive of the offer. After all, what harm would it do to have another pair of eyes look over his work? And even if this Dobbins fellow didn't know anything about writing himself, he might know someone who did. That's the way the world worked. Adrian knew it perfectly.

He thought of the literary cliques back home and the way they reviewed each other's books, interviewed each other for radio programmes and wrote profiles of each other for the newspapers. It was a kind of literary freemasonry. And he was outside that loop. He had deliberately excluded himself. He recalled the invitation he had received to attend the launch party for a novel by Sebastian Pennyfeather, a new young writer who was attracting attention for his satirical critiques of modern Irish manners.

Adrian never knew why he was invited in the first place but he suspected it had something to do with the writers' group. He had taken great pleasure in scribbling across the invitation before sending it back: *Adrian Blake regrets that he will be unable to attend, as he is busily engaged in writing his new novel.*

His response was intended to imply that he regarded events like book launches as mere froth for lightweight dilettantes and something that a serious writer like himself could not possibly entertain. It was meant to put down a marker to the literary establishment that a new force was abroad who had nothing but disdain for their cheap tricks and no need of their friendship or support. It had given him a certain satisfaction at the time. He remembered the thrill as he dropped the reply into the post box. But no more invitations followed.

Maybe he would let Mr Dobbins look at one or two chapters and see what his reaction was. If he showed any appreciation of the great undertaking that *The Green Gannet* represented, he might let him look at the whole novel. Adrian was convinced that the book had received a frosty reception so far because no one had taken it seriously. What was required was a word in the right ear. Someone in authority in one of the publishing houses who would give it the attention it warranted. The person to do that might well be Mr Dobbins.

The following morning he was in brighter mood.

"I've changed my mind," he said across the breakfast table as the sun glinted off the cutlery.

"About what, darling?"

"About letting Mr Dobbins read some of the novel. I suppose it can't do any harm."

"Oh, that's marvellous," Trish trilled. "I'm sure he'll be delighted."

"And I've been thinking. Tonight we should go out and have a really good bash somewhere. You're right. I've been working too hard. Time to relax a little."

"Why, Adrian!" Trish's face looked perfectly radiant.

"Things are coming along nicely. You know I killed another twenty people when you were out last night?"

Trish smiled. "You're beginning to sound like Hannibal Lecter."

"At least I don't eat them," Adrian laughed.

"So, what time will we say?"

"Eight o'clock?"

"Sounds fine. What are you planning to do today?"

"Murder some more of my characters, I suppose. And you?"

"I think I'll just laze by the pool."

"I might come down and join you later," Adrian said, wiping a smear of butter from his chin and draining the remains of his coffee.

He worked steadily all morning and didn't stop for lunch. Now that he had unlocked the problem, he found the novel was flowing along like a great tide. He was confident he would get it finished before they returned to Dublin and this time it would surely find a publisher. Indeed, if this Mr Dobbins could be enlisted to help, he might even find himself in the middle of a bidding war with several publishers fighting over the manuscript of *The Green Gannet*.

The thought gave Adrian great satisfaction. It wasn't just the money, although a bidding war would surely drive up the advance. It was the recognition and the publicity it would bring. Adrian had become so used to failure and rejection that his heart longed for acceptance. He craved to be recognised for the true creative artist he believed himself to be. It would make up for all the long lonely weeks and months he had slaved over his word processor, the words dripping like drops of blood upon the page. It would make all the effort worthwhile.

At four o'clock, he stopped. He hit the word-count button on the laptop and was delighted to see that he had squeezed out 8000 words since this morning. He had done enough. It was time to join Trish at the bar for a couple of drinks before they went off for a nice dinner somewhere. He had been neglecting her recently with all his concentration focussed on the novel. He would have to make it up to her.

He let himself out of the apartment and went down to the lounge. It was shaded and cool. An elderly gentleman was snoozing in a comfortable armchair. Two middle-aged women were sharing a pot of tea. Somebody else was reading a book. There was no sign of Monica. And there was no sign of her yesterday when he had gone looking for her. Adrian suspected that something was up. That damned Carlos was paying too much attention to her. The last time he saw her, they had been drinking sherry together. Ah well. She would soon get fed up with his mangled English and be glad of some civilised conversation. That would be his opportunity. Adrian passed through the lounge and went out to the pool area, adjusting his dark glasses against the dazzling sunlight. He paused to look around.

And here a sight awaited him that took the very breath right out of his lungs. He couldn't believe what he was seeing. A man was kissing Trish beside the bar!

Chapter 21

Charlie woke in a confused state. On the one hand, he was still feeling euphoric after his experience with Trish in Puerto de la Cruz. The memories of that wonderful afternoon were still fresh in his mind: the way they had chatted together as they wandered along the little narrow streets, the way they had confided in each other like old friends, how she had complimented and encouraged him and made him feel good about himself. Charlie had never experienced an afternoon like that in his life. But, it had all come to nothing in the end. He had been brought down with a bump when he discovered she was married. Just my bloody luck, he thought. I finally meet a nice woman I can feel comfortable with and it turns out she's already spoken for.

If only she had been wearing a wedding ring, he would have noticed and might have been more restrained. It would have sent him a signal. But there was no ring, which was strange.

And it wasn't the only strange thing. There was that odd business with Penny last night, taking off like a bat out of hell the minute she spotted him, leaving all those people without tickets for whatever racket she had been promoting. What was that all about? What had he done to upset her?

It had to be related to the night they slept together. Something he had omitted to do or say. Maybe he was supposed to send flowers? Or ring and thank her? Or maybe they had special cards you could buy at the newsagent's for an event like this? A dark thought crossed his mind and caused his confidence to ebb. Maybe his performance hadn't been up to the mark. Maybe he hadn't satisfied her. But then he remembered that he had wakened with her arms clasped tight around him as if he had been sleeping all night with an octopus. Charlie gave up. He would never understand women. Their minds and his ran along parallel tracks that stretched to infinity but would never meet.

He wished Tommy Brick was on hand to advise him. Tommy, who had featured in dozens of bedroom encounters, would know exactly what to do. Charlie toyed with the idea of ringing him on his mobile but he couldn't remember the number. And anyway, it would just make Charlie look like a complete idiot. He decided the only way to sort this out was to confront Penny directly and apologise. But first, he had to find her.

He remembered that she was usually in the hotel lounge each morning at ten to host her Welcome Meeting. But when he arrived at five to ten, he got a surprise. A different rep was sitting behind Penny's little desk. This one was tall and skinny and had a sign which read: *Tracy, Your Friendly Representative.* In her yellow uniform, she looked like a ripe banana.

Charlie marched up to the desk and stood before her.

"I'm looking for Penny," he said.

Tracy immediately lifted her head out of the magazine

she was reading. "Penny's not 'ere today," she said in a friendly cockney accent.

"I can see that," Charlie said. "I was wondering where she is."

"Not ding dong bell, I'm afraid. Taken the day off, she 'as."

"Not ding dong bell?" Charlie asked. "What does that mean?"

"She's not well. Spending the day in the garden shed."

I can see I'm going to need an interpreter, Charlie thought, as he took a deep breath and started again. "She's *where?*"

"In bed," Tracy emphasised and gave him a look that suggested that was where he should be too, in a home for the sadly bewildered.

"Oh," Charlie said, catching on at last. "I hope it's nothing serious."

"Just a touch of BSE," Tracy said, dismissively and returned to her magazine.

Charlie felt the blood drain from his face. BSE? My God! No wonder she hadn't turned up for work. She should be in intensive care. And then another thought struck him and he felt his knees go weak. Could you pass it on through sexual activity?

"How on earth did she get it?" he asked. "Was it something she ate?"

"Naah! Something she drank, more like."

"*What?*" Charlie immediately thought of the vodka and Red Bulls they had been downing in the Monaco Bar. Had some virus got into the bottles? "I didn't know you could get Mad Cow Disease from drinking?"

"It's not Mad Cow Disease," Tracy laughed. "Although she *is* a mad cow, come to think about it. It's BSE. Bloody

Silly Egbert. She got pissed again last night. That's two nights on the trot. Couldn't get up this morning."

Charlie felt a wave of relief wash over him. "You think she's going to be okay?"

"Course she will. Good sleep and she'll be right as rain. Told her to go easy on the sauce, I did. But would she listen? Not on your fork and knife!"

"Thank you," Charlie said and wandered away thinking what a close shave he had just had.

He wondered if he should call at Penny's apartment. Bring her a basket of fruit or something. And then he realised he didn't know where she lived. He had arrived at her apartment spaced out and in the dark. And he had left in a hurry early the following morning. All he could remember was that it was somewhere in Los Cristianos. He decided to wait till Penny reappeared and then apologise. In the meantime, he would go for a walk and get some breakfast.

His journey led him to the harbour and the Lucky Leprechaun. He had passed it by a few times but had never gone in. He stopped to read the menu and his eye was drawn to an item described as *Ma Casey's Monster Irish Breakfast*. He read the ingredients: two eggs, tomato, bacon, sausage, fried soda bread, black pudding, white pudding, mushrooms, fried potatoes, beans, toast and tea. My God, he thought, there must be enough cholesterol in one of those breakfasts to grease the wheels of a Panhard tank. He looked in the door and saw people happily munching away at the plates piled high with food. Ma Casey certainly knows how to feed the customers, he thought. They seem to be enjoying it. And the smell is certainly attractive.

He hesitated. He hadn't eaten a breakfast like that since he was a youngster living with his mother on the north-side of Dublin. What the hell? One breakfast isn't going to kill me, he thought. I'll skip lunch. He walked inside and sat down at the first vacant table.

A man with curly hair appeared, to take his order.

"Ma Casey on duty?" Charlie inquired.

"He's in the kitchen," the man said.

"You mean Ma Casey is really a man?"

"That's right. My brother Brian. He's the chef. Ma Casey is just a name we use."

"I see," Charlie said, deciding that this was going to be one of those bewildering days. "That Monster Irish breakfast? Is it possible to have a smaller version? Like maybe, a midget Irish breakfast?"

"Sure. What would you like?"

"How about bacon, egg and tomato? And maybe one sausage? A small one?"

"No fried bread?"

"I don't think so," Charlie said. "Too heavy."

"It's very good bread. Flown in fresh from Dublin every morning. You won't taste bread like it anywhere in Tenerife."

Charlie relented. "OK. I'll give it a try. One slice. Lightly-fried."

"Pudding?"

"No, thanks."

"It's from Clonakilty in County Cork. It's the very best. People go mad for it."

"OK," Charlie said. "A tiny piece of pudding."

"Black or white?"

"Black."

"The white is good too."

Charlie took a deep breath. "All right. Give me both."

"Fried potatoes?"

Charlie leaned back in his chair. "Tell me something. Did you ever work in the used car business?"

"Never."

"Pyramid selling?"

"Why do you ask?"

"Because you sound like you could sell ice cubes to the Eskimos."

Tom Casey laughed.

"Forget everything," Charlie said. "And give me the Monster Breakfast. I might as well be hanged for a sheep as a lamb."

An hour later, he was draining the last drop of tea from the pot and licking his lips. He had enjoyed the breakfast immensely.

"That was delicious," he said when Tom Casey came with the bill. "I can feel my arteries clogging up already."

"No complaints?"

"Not this time. My compliments to your mother."

"My mother?"

"Sorry. I meant your brother."

A thin smile broke on Casey's lips as Charlie paid the bill and sailed out into the bright sunshine.

The journey back to the hotel was mainly uphill. Charlie could feel the breakfast straining like a bag of cement against his waist. When he arrived at Hotel Las Flores, he decided he needed a cold drink to refresh himself. He made his way through the lobby and out to the pool. But as he approached the bar, he heard someone call his name. He turned quickly and was surprised to see Trish hurrying towards him. She was wearing a swimsuit and had her hair tucked into a baseball cap.

He felt his heart swell with pleasure. "Well, fancy meeting you," he said. "What a pleasant surprise!"

"I just saw you come in. Where have you been?"

"Down at the harbour having breakfast. And now I'm going to have a cold drink. Would you care to join me?"

"I'd love to. I'll have a beer."

Charlie ordered and Trish sat down on one of the stools at the counter.

"So, what have *you* been doing?" Charlie asked.

"Not much. Just lazing by the pool."

"Well, it must be doing you good. You look radiant."

Her eyes lit up. "You say the nicest things, Charlie."

"It's true. You've got a lovely tan and your hair is shining and your skin is so clear. You look dazzling."

Trish looked embarrassed. "Thanks again for a lovely afternoon," she said. "I had a wonderful time."

"It was my pleasure. I enjoyed it too. In fact, I've never had an afternoon like it."

"Really?"

"Yes," Charlie confessed. "It was bliss. I only wish we could do it again sometime. But of course we can't."

She seemed to hesitate. "I told my husband you had offered to read his manuscript. And he's delighted."

"That's good. I know it can be tough being a writer. It's such a lonely business. I'd be glad to help in any way I can."

Trish toyed with her glass. "I've been thinking about you, Charlie. Why did you never get married?"

"I already told you. I haven't met the right woman."

"Have you been hurt in love?"

Charlie blushed. "Whatever gave you that idea?"

"Just the way you behave. You're a very handsome man. You're witty and charming. Over thirty I'd guess. And still single. It's unusual."

"I've been too busy working."

"Maybe you should take more time out to meet people."

"You think so?"

She gazed deep into his eyes. "Yes. I'm sure lots of women would find you very attractive."

Some impulse took hold of Charlie. He leaned close and took her hand.

"And you're attractive too, Trish. In fact, you're beautiful. I think you're the most beautiful woman I've ever met."

He was shocked at his own boldness. The remark had slipped out before he realised.

But Trish just laughed and playfully pushed him away. "You're such a charmer, Charlie."

And then her face froze and the laughter died on her lips. She was staring at something past his left shoulder.

"Just behave naturally," she whispered. "My husband is coming towards us."

Chapter 22

For his scheme to overcome his father's resistance to Spanish food, Edward enlisted the support of Mollie. She was a willing conspirator. She was already growing tired of cooking three meals a day over the cramped little stove in the apartment which was only designed for preparing snacks. The heat in the room was bad enough without the additional burden of sweating over sizzling pans of rashers and sausages. So when Edward told her what he had in mind, she immediately agreed to go along with it. Little did she know that she was next on the list for reorientation.

The following morning, after a long lie-in, Ned was presented with plain toast for breakfast so that he would be in good appetite for lunch.

Then, Mollie proposed that they go for a walk along the beach.

"Mother of God, what's got into you, woman?" Ned demanded to know. "One minute we can't get you out of the apartment and the next you want to go parading all over the town."

"We need some exercise," Mollie insisted. "You're stuck in front of that television all afternoon. The fresh air will do us good."

Still complaining, Ned was led down the hill and on to the beach.

Eventually they reached the harbour and the Lucky Leprechaun came into view.

"Let's sit down and rest a bit," Mollie suggested as they approached the pub. Ned readily agreed. The walk had given him a thirst. But the minute they walked in the door they found Edward and Mary already waiting.

"Well, isn't this a bit of surprise?" Mollie said, trying hard to keep a straight face. "Fancy finding you pair here!"

"We're just about to have lunch," Mary said. "Why don't you join us?"

"I wouldn't mind at all," Mollie said. "I was just thinking that a nice fresh salad would be the very thing to perk me up."

"What about you, Dad?" Mary said. "Can we tempt you?"

"Ah, no," Ned said quickly, "I'm not hungry. I'll just have a pint of that Dorada beer."

"The food is very good," Edward said. "I can vouch for it."

Ned seemed to waver but only for a moment. "I'll stick to the pint, if it's all the same."

Tom Casey approached to take their order and soon three plates appeared; lamb chops for Edward, chicken for Mary and a platter of salad for Mollie.

Ned glanced enviously at the plates piled with food: fluffy potatoes, glistening chunky vegetables, succulent meat and salad. A delicious aroma rose up from the table. His nostrils twitched and he quickly ran his tongue across his lips.

"Is it nice?" he inquired as they picked up their knives and forks and started to eat.

"Delicious," Edward replied, slicing off a piece of tender meat and holding it out for Ned's inspection. "As good as anything you would get at home."

"Better," Mary said, spearing a moist piece of chicken.

"And look at this lovely salad," Mollie said, pointing to her plate which was heaped with fresh vegetables.

"Why don't you be a devil and try something?" Mary encouraged him. "You don't know what you're missing."

Ned was just about to reply when Tom Casey swooped again. And this time he deposited a gleaming platter on the table in front of Ned. On it rested a large slice of seared steak, lush garden peas, floury potatoes and fried onions. The aroma was delicious.

Ned's eyes almost popped out of his head.

"What's this?" he said, staring at the plate in disbelief.

"What does it look like?" Edward said.

"It looks like sirloin steak."

"Congratulations. You're in sparkling form today. I want you on my next table-quiz team."

Ned stared at the plate in horror as if he half expected the steak to rise up and attack him.

"But who is it for?"

"You."

"Me? I never ordered anything."

"We ordered for you."

"But you don't expect me to – eat it?"

"Of course not," Mary said. "We expect you to sit there and watch it in case it attempts to escape."

"It's cooked exactly as you like it," Tom Casey added. "Medium rare."

Ned looked at their expectant faces.

"You've ambushed me," he said, finally. "My own flesh and blood. I only came in for a beer. I didn't say anything about sirloin steaks."

"Well, it's time you were a bit more adventurous," Mary said. "Besides, it's not fair on Mum having to cook for you every day in that hot kitchen."

"I never hear her complaining."

"That's only because she has you spoiled. From now, on we're eating out."

"But I can't eat it. It's *Spanish!*"

"Argentinian actually," Tom Casey put in.

"It's all the same. It's foreign!"

"Oh, for God's sake," Mollie interjected. "Don't be making a show of yourself! The man has spent all morning preparing it. You're not going to insult him now, are you?"

Ned's face had turned pale. "What will happen if I get sick?

"You're covered by insurance."

He tentatively picked up his knife and fork. "There's no garlic or any of that stuff?"

"No," Tom Casey said.

Ned's hands shook as he gingerly cut off a little portion of meat. "May God forgive you if I get food poisoning!"

"Food poisoning, my big toe," Mollie said. "You're more likely to get food poisoning from those ould rashers I brought in the suitcase. Sure, they're gone mouldy by now what with the heat!"

"But at least they're Irish rashers."

"But we serve Irish rashers here," said Tom Casey. "And sausages. And Clonakilty black and white pudding. And soda bread. In our Ma Casey's Monster Irish Breakfast."

The McGinty family stared at him in indignant amazement.

Ned voiced their collective outrage. "Now why the *hell* didn't you tell us that before?"

"Well, anyway, eat your steak now," said Mollie hastily, sensing that things might well get out of hand.

Ned opened his mouth to protest.

"Eat it," Mollie commanded, surprised at her own vehemence.

With one last glare at Tom Casey, Ned timidly raised the meat to his nose and sniffed. Then he put it in his mouth and began to chew while everyone watched expectantly. He cut another slice and chewed that too, more quickly this time.

"Well?" Edward said, exchanging a glance with his sister. "How does it taste?"

Ned grunted, sliced a potato in two and forked up a mouthful. Then he attacked the onions and peas. In a few minutes, half the steak had disappeared,

"Tomorrow's special is pork," Tom Casey announced. "I can strongly recommend it."

Ned warily raised his head from the plate.

"You're going to eat that pork," Mollie said, before he could speak. "And I don't want to hear another word out of you. You've been behaving like a lunatic and I've been encouraging you. But things are going to change. From now on, we're eating our meals here and that's that."

Edward carefully put down his knife and fork and looked at his mother. "Well, now, that's not the only thing that's going to change."

It was Mollie's turn to look surprised. "How do you mean?"

"You will have to get a bit more adventurous too."

"Me? Adventurous? What does that mean? I'm the one who brought you all here!" Mollie said indignantly.

"You'll have to get out more. You didn't come all the way to Tenerife just to stay cooped up in your apartment all day long."

"But I'm happy in my apartment. I like it there."

"When you get home and people ask about your holiday, what are you going to say?" Mary put in. "That you spent all the time sitting on your balcony under an umbrella? People would laugh."

"They can laugh all they like," Molly said huffily. "How I spend my holiday is none of their damned business."

"You have to get out and see some of the resort."

Mollie sniffed. "I see enough from my balcony."

"There's a market in Puerto Santiago tomorrow," Edward said, softly. "You can get a bus to it."

Mollie was beginning to get flustered. "I don't like crowds. And I'd never stand the heat."

"The buses are air-conditioned," Mary said. "And we'll bring your umbrella to keep off the sun."

"You mean we'd all go together?"

"Of course," Edward said. "That's what you want, isn't it? Isn't that why you suggested this holiday? So that we could all be together?"

"I suppose I did," Mollie admitted. "But I didn't mean for us to be traipsing around crowded markets."

"Well, then, it's agreed. I'll check the times at the bus depot."

A sudden thought seemed to occur to Mollie. She turned to Mary and fixed her with a beady eye.

"And what about *you*?"

"What about me?" Mary asked, with surprise.

"Will *you* be able to walk around in the morning heat?"

"Of course I will. Why wouldn't I?"

"Because in certain situations, it's advisable for a woman to rest up and take things easy. Any doctor would tell you that."

Mary looked bewildered. "I don't know what you're talking about, Mum."

"I think you do."

There was a silence round the table.

Then Edward coughed. "Does anybody feel like dessert?"

In the confusion, no one noticed that Ned had pushed his plate away. It was wiped clean. Not a single scrap of food remained on the sparkling surface. He was sitting contented with a smile on his face like the cat that got the cream.

Chapter 23

"Look at this," Bobby said excitedly, holding out her mobile phone for Angie's inspection.

It was a fresh text message from Alex Piper that had just popped up on the screen. In it, he said he was going crazy worrying about her and if she didn't respond to his calls, he was coming out to Tenerife on the next available flight to see her personally.

"My God," Angie said. "Is he serious?"

"I think so. His messages have been getting more desperate. In the last one, he said he was going to jump off Liberty Hall without a parachute. I think he's really suffering."

"I think it's romantic," Angie said. "The thought that a man would come the whole way out here just to see you. It's very touching."

"But I don't want him coming out. I came here to escape him."

"Are you sure about that? It sounds to me like he's learnt his lesson."

"I'm positive."

"Maybe it's time to relent a little bit. He sounds suitably chastised. Did you tell him about your accident?"

"I told him nothing. That's the whole point. I've been refusing to answer his damned messages. That's what's driving him crazy."

"So what are you going to do?"

Bobby stuck her thumb in her mouth. "I don't know. What if I was to reply and tell him the island is quarantined because of an outbreak of Green Monkey Disease?"

"I'm not sure that would work," Angie said knitting her brow. "He could easily check if it was true."

"I could say that a war has broken out and the North Koreans are threatening to invade."

"He wouldn't fall for that. North Korea's on the other side of the world."

"What's the nearest country?"

"Morocco?"

"They'd never invade, would they?"

Angie shook her head. "I don't think so."

"So what am I going to do?"

Angie screwed up her face in concentration. "I think he has you snookered. You're going to have to reply. Why don't you text him back and say you're considering your options and you'll respond to him as soon you get back to Dublin?"

"You think he might buy that?"

"Possibly. Although he sounds quite determined."

"If he comes here I'll have him arrested for harassment," Bobby said.

"Now, now let's just calm down," Angie said. "Who knows, you might even change your mind and take him back again? It would be a terrible shame to waste that beautiful wedding dress. And all those lovely presents. And I was so looking forward to being a bridesmaid."

A defiant set had come into Bobby's face. "Never!" she said through gritted teeth.

They were sitting on the balcony of their apartment, looking out over the rooftops of the town and the sea glinting in the distance. It was another beautiful day. In fact, they hadn't seen a single cloud since they had arrived at Hotel Las Flores.

Bobby had her leg resting on a chair and a cold drink and a book within easy reach on a little table beside her. If it wasn't for her leg and Pig-face Piper sending her threatening text messages, everything would be bliss. The pain had receded to be replaced by a slight tingling ache. She hadn't needed to take any of the pain-killers the hospital had prescribed for her and she had managed to get a reasonably comfortable night's sleep. Indeed, only for the fact that the white plaster-cast weighed on her leg like a ball and chain, she felt sure she would be fit enough to resume her normal activities. But the doctor had insisted that she rest. He had spoken firmly as if he expected her to obey, so that's what Bobby was going to do.

"That Charlie man is down there," Angie said. She had got up to stand at the rail and look down at the swimming-pool. "He's at the bar. Deep in conversation with that woman who's married to the writer."

"Really?" Bobby said with mild interest. "No sign of her husband?"

"Not that I can see."

"Probably up in his room hammering away at his book. He should watch that."

"You mean his wife?"

"Yes. She's a good-looking woman. He should take more care of her. Have you noticed that he never seems to be around?"

"I saw him in the lounge the other day. He was helping that Monica woman with her crossword puzzle."

"Indeed?" Bobby said and raised an eyebrow. "Does Carlos know about that?"

They laughed. They prided themselves on knowing all the little goings-on of the other guests at the hotel like they were private detectives.

"You still fancy him?" Bobby asked with a wicked glint in her eye.

"Well, I wouldn't kick him out of bed," Angie said.

"He is quite handsome," Bobby conceded, "but I don't think he's my type. I think he's got ideas about himself. He's always fluttering his eyes and gazing in that moonstruck way at the ladies. You notice he never pays the same attention to the men?"

"Just as well. Some of them might take exception."

Bobby stretched her arms and yawned. "I'm getting bored sitting here. Why don't we go down to the Leprechaun?"

"You think that's a good idea?

"Why not? I'll only have a beer."

"The doctor said you were to rest."

"But he didn't say I was only to rest at the hotel, now did he? C'mon. We'll get a taxi and I can lean on your arm. It'll be a bit of fun."

They got changed and made their way down in the lift to the foyer, Bobby leaning on her aluminium crutch while Angie supported her with her arm. Their appearance caused quite a stir and Bobby found herself enjoying being the centre of so much attention. She hobbled out to the street where one of the hotel attendants quickly summoned a taxi. Ten minutes later, they were disembarking again outside the Lucky Leprechaun.

Bobby leaned on Angie's arm and started towards the door but just as she reached it, it opened and four people came out. Bobby immediately recognised Edward McGinty and his family.

"Hi," she said, putting on her suffering face.

But she had caught him by surprise. He muttered a hurried "Hello" and was gone.

They continued inside and found a seat midway between the door, the bar and the toilets so that Bobby wouldn't have far to travel whatever her needs were. Angie ordered two pints and they were just about to start drinking when the door suddenly opened again and Edward was back.

"I'm terribly sorry," he said. "I hope I didn't sound rude just now, but I didn't recognise you till you had gone and I saw you had your leg in plaster and I thought I'd better come back and commiserate with you." He stuck out his hand. "I'm Edward McGinty, by the way."

Bobby placed her hand in his and looked into his eyes. There was something there. Something that stirred her imagination. "Bobby Bannon," she said. "Now tell me, Edward, before we begin. Are you fond of animals?"

They stayed chatting all afternoon. Angie gave up halfway through and made her own way back to the hotel after extracting a firm undertaking from Edward that he would ensure Bobby returned safely.

Bobby told him about the accident and her job and her dog and two cats which were in kennels back in Dublin. She didn't mention the reason for the holiday which she felt was best left to another conversation.

Edward told her that his parents ran a farm and how he planned to make farming his career, so they had something in common in their shared interest in animals. He told her that he had just had lunch with his parents and had finally persuaded his father to eat Spanish food, which Bobby thought was hilarious.

The conversation went back and forth till the sun began to go down and the shadows lengthen. Bobby allowed him to buy her a gin and tonic but drew the line at one small one, since the doctor had warned her to take it easy. She kept looking into Edward's eyes and finding that strange, exciting quality in there that so inflamed her. It was nine o'clock when they finally left.

Bobby leaned back in the taxi with a sigh. She had really enjoyed herself. Edward had been like a tonic with his witty remarks and his cheerful demeanour. He was just what she needed to lift her spirits after the grim experience with Pig-face Piper. When he finally deposited her outside her apartment door, she found herself wishing he could stay.

"Would you like to have a drink some other time?" he asked.

"I wouldn't mind," Bobby said.

"How about tomorrow evening? We could go back to the Leprechaun. Or somewhere else if you prefer."

"The Leprechaun would be fine."

"Okay. How about nine o'clock?"

"That's perfect," Bobby replied and wondered if he would try to kiss her.

But Edward just smiled and said goodbye and walked off down the corridor.

Bobby let herself into the apartment to find Angie waiting up for her. "I've just spent the evening with the most exciting man," she said. "I can't begin to tell you –"

But Angie cut her short. "Guess who just rang when you were out?"

"Who?"

"Alex Piper."

231

"You're joking."

"No, I'm not."

"How did he get this number? You said nobody would ever find us here."

"I don't know," Angie said. "But he did. And it gets worse. He's flying in to see you tomorrow."

Chapter 24

Monica stepped gingerly onto the weighing scales in the ladies' changing rooms at Hotel Las Flores. She had completed her early morning walk and her swim (up now to forty lengths). She had put in ninety minutes in the sun (forty-five minutes front and back) which had been increased from one hour and now it was time to check the results of all this activity. She watched as the little wheel spun round and then came quivering to a halt. Nine stone, three pounds! Immediately, she felt her spirits lift. All that exercise and starvation had been worth it. She had lost half a stone in little over a week. It just went to prove what she had always known – a little self-will and discipline could move mountains. Another small effort and she would be back to where she was before that awful business over Woody had caused her figure to balloon. And in the meantime, she could let her hair down a little at this dinner that Carlos had invited her to.

Although he still hadn't got round to issuing a formal invitation and Monica was beginning to wonder if she should be worried. She had seen him once or twice flitting around the hotel and all he had done was smile and wave. But he hadn't spoken. Monica hoped he hadn't changed his mind. For she had her heart set on Carlos.

All her life, she had depended on men. First it had been her father who had been an old-fashioned disciplinarian with fixed ideas about women's education. As a girl growing up, Monica had been a bright student. She had done well at school and had hopes of continuing to university and a career in management. She thought she had talent in this area. She was a good organiser and was always picked as captain of the sports teams at school. She was the one the other girls turned to whenever they wanted something arranged.

But when it came to her final year at secondary school and the girls had to opt for a university course, her father had pooh-poohed the idea.

"Why waste four years of your life on something that will be of no earthly use to you?" he said.

Monica wanted to tell him that it would be useful, that the world of work was opening up to women and the old outmoded male barriers were crumbling but she was afraid of her father who ruled the household and never brooked any opposition. So instead of going to university, Monica was packed off to a secretarial college where she spent three months learning shorthand and typing and office organisation before securing a job with Grabbit and Leggit.

There she made good progress and soon was promoted to be personal assistant to Mr Flynn who was the junior partner. This was a very responsible job. Her duties included keeping Mr Flynn's diary up to date, organising his appointments and arranging his business schedule. Monica looked up to Mr Flynn and was completely in awe of him. He came to replace her father as a male authority figure in her life. She was only twenty-two and very impressionable and Mr Flynn was a middle-aged man with wide experience of the business world. Whatever he said was law and it never crossed Monica's mind to question him. But he was a good boss and she enjoyed her work. She was quite proud of her position and tended to lord it over the other secretaries in the firm even if she didn't find the tasks very onerous. She felt she was capable of much more. And then Woody had appeared out of nowhere that wet afternoon twenty years ago and changed her life completely.

Woody provided for all of Monica's material needs. She never had to worry about money or bills. If she wanted something she just ordered it and charged it to his account. She rarely asked him how he made his money and, the few times she did, Woody just smiled and told her it was too complicated for her to bother her head over. So she gave up asking. She left everything to her husband and retreated into her own world of dinner parties and charity balls and never paid the slightest heed to household finances. She trusted Woody completely and never guessed that one day the gravy train would run out of steam.

So it was natural in her new straitened situation, that she should focus her attention on another man. In Monica's eyes this was the way for a woman to succeed. Particularly a woman like her who had natural talents like good looks and a fine figure that men found attractive. And Carlos fitted the bill perfectly. She ran her mind once more over the conversation they had the other evening. Carlos had divulged that he was the only child and sole heir to a hotel empire that stretched from Spain to the Canary Islands. And he was unmarried. What was more, he was plainly interested in her. It was all too good to be true.

But she knew she had to play her cards carefully. She

must let him make all the running. She knew that men enjoyed the thrill of the chase and the conquest. If it came too easily, they lost interest. It was something in their genes, something she had never fully understood but men always liked to believe they were in control. It was a woman's job to encourage that belief.

For a brief moment, she allowed her imagination to leap forward to the golden possibilities that might come her way if everything went to plan. She could see herself established in a fine villa somewhere in the best part of Madrid with servants and cooks and everything at her command. Maybe she would be able to establish a court like the one she had reigned over in Dublin. She would gather around her a group of like-minded ladies and they would organise charity events and gala balls. She trembled with excitement as she thought of the envy it would inspire in that vixen Colleen McQueen: *SOCIETY QUEEN EXTENDS REIGN TO SPAIN.*

But first she had to find Carlos and get this damned dinner organised. She had already made one sortie into the lounge this morning and he wasn't there. She didn't want to hang around in case it became too obvious that she was looking for him. It was important that *he* should come looking for *her*. And, of course, there was always the danger of running across that demented writer, Adrian, who would insist on helping her with the crossword puzzle even if she didn't have a newspaper.

Monica decided that she would go straight up to her room and have one glass of gin while she considered the best thing to do. She had lost half a stone so it would be something of a celebration.

She pulled her white sports shirt tight around her chest so that it lent emphasis to her perfectly rounded breasts and stepped back into her shorts that showed her long tanned legs to maximum advantage. Then she fixed the immaculate white sweatband in her hair and glanced at herself in the mirror. She thought she resembled a slightly older version of that tennis star, Anna Kournikova. They both looked sexual in an athletic sort of way. They both gave off the same highly charged sensuality.

Satisfied with her appearance, Monica sallied forth from the Leisure Complex and headed across the foyer of the hotel. And here, she almost stopped dead in her tracks. Not only was Carlos on duty at the reception desk but he was smiling and, yes, he was beckoning her to come and talk.

Slowly, she made her way across to him.

"Good afternoon, Monica. How are you today?"

"I'm fine," Monica replied, smiling pleasantly into his handsome face.

Carlos glanced quickly around the foyer and lowered his voice. "That dinner appointment I discussed with you?"

"Yes?" Monica said, barely able to keep her voice from shaking.

"I was wondering. Are you free tomorrow night?"

Even though she was dying to say yes, she forced herself to hesitate. She could hardly say she needed to consult her appointments diary. She was on holidays for God's sake and, anyway, these days her appointments diary was filled with blank pages.

"I think so," she heard herself say.

Carlos's dark eyes beamed with pleasure. "I finish work at eight o'clock. I was thinking of going to a little place in the mountains. The food is very good and it has spectacular views. Would that be suitable?"

"It sounds lovely," Monica said.

Carlos's face was wreathed in a satisfied grin. "I will ring the patron at once to let him know we are coming. Would it suit if I picked you up outside the hotel at ten minutes past eight?"

What a perfect gentleman, Monica thought, always deferring to me before he makes a decision. "I think that would be fine."

Carlos clapped his hands. "So. It is all arranged."

"Yes," Monica said.

Carlos glanced around once more then leaned close and whispered, "Oh Monica, I am so happy. I can't wait."

Monica smiled to show off her nice white teeth. "My pleasure."

She walked slowly back across the foyer to the lifts. She used all her willpower to maintain her poise, conscious that his eyes were following her. But once inside her room, she threw herself down on the bed and let out a whoop. She couldn't believe this was happening. Handsome, rich, heir to a hotel fortune and so obviously attracted to her it was beginning to be embarrassing.

Monica hugged the pillow. How was she going to keep herself sane till tomorrow night?

Chapter 25

As Adrian approached the pool bar he saw that the man wasn't kissing Trish after all, just whispering in her ear. But as far as he was concerned, the bastard was still taking bloody liberties with his wife. He would certainly give the blighter a piece of his mind.

But as he drew near, Trish suddenly surprised him. Sensing trouble, she stepped forward and flung her arms around his neck and hung on like a drowning woman.

"Why, darling! What an absolutely lovely surprise!"

"Bloody hell," Adrian muttered, struggling to untangle himself. "What have you been drinking?"

"Just beer. It's wonderful to see you!" Trish carolled and continued to cling to Adrian like a barnacle to a rock.

"Really?"

"Of course. I've missed you terribly. And now you're here, it's just marvellous."

Adrian blinked. This wasn't what he had been expecting at all. He had approached the bar prepared for a good old row but the fervour of her greeting had taken the wind completely out of his sails and now he wasn't sure how to proceed. What was the proper etiquette in a situation like this? Bugger practically making love to his wife. And in public! Should he make a fuss? Or would that simply make him appear ridiculous? For once, Adrian was flummoxed.

After a struggle, he managed to disentangle himself and straightened his glasses. "Just nipped out for a breath of air," he said.

"Well, I'm delighted," Trish laughed. "Are you going to have a drink?"

"Don't mind if I do," Adrian said stiffly, deciding that the best thing was polite formality.

"Beer OK?"

"Beer's fine."

Trish gave the order to the barman.

"By the way, Adrian," she said, "this is Charlie Dobbins. The man I told you about. You know, the man who owns the bookshops?"

Adrian shot daggers at Charlie who had been standing at the bar trying to look innocent. So this was the man who had offered to read *The Green Gannet* and give him professional advice. He was surprised to see he had a bright, honest face, the sort of face he imagined Michael O'Houlihan, the hero of his novel, might have.

"Pleased to meet you," Charlie said.

Adrian grunted.

"I was just sunbathing by the pool when Charlie came along," Trish added.

"Well for you," Adrian growled. "I've been wrestling all morning with the novel. Some of us have work to do."

"Trish has been telling me all about you," Charlie put in. "She's been raving about your novel, *The Green Gander.* I must say, it sounds wonderful."

"*Gannet,*" Adrian corrected him. "It's called *The Green Gannet.*"

"Sorry," Charlie apologised. "They sound the same."

"Gander is a male goose. Gannet is a seabird. There's a big distinction."

"Of course. How is it coming along?"

"It's not finished yet," Adrian said, coolly. "I've still got some work to do."

"Well, I must say I admire your stamina. Is it a long novel?"

"Three hundred and fifty thousand words."

"My God," Charlie said, genuinely surprised. "That *is* a big book. That must be nearly as big as *David Copperfield.*"

"Bigger," Adrian said, tersely. He was trying to weigh up this Charlie Dobbins person and wasn't quite sure what to make of him.

"Really?"

"Yes. I've done a word count. *The Green Gannet* is bigger. In fact, it might well turn out closer to 400,000 words. The more I revise it, the bigger it gets."

"Amazing," Charlie said.

"Beer," Trish interrupted and handed Adrian the cold glass the barman had just left down. "You know, it's really great to see you taking a break, Adrian. You've been working far too hard. I said that, Charlie, didn't I?"

"Yes, you did," Charlie confirmed.

Adrian observed his wife. She was definitely acting strange. He still wasn't convinced there wasn't something funny going on here between the pair of them.

"You need to get out more," Trish continued. "Bent over that laptop all day long. You know, Charlie, he works so hard, he doesn't even sleep, for God's sake."

Adrian tilted his straw hat and took a sip of his beer. He

liked it when Trish went on like this, singing his praises in front of strangers.

"In fact, I doubt if there's another writer with Adrian's dedication. He's been totally single-minded, totally focussed. You hear authors boasting about the 3,000 words they punch out every day. Well, let me tell you, Adrian writes double that."

"Treble, actually," Adrian said, allowing a modest smile. "In fact there have been days when I've knocked out 15,000 words. My personal record is 22,000 words in a single day."

"I'm gobsmacked," Charlie said. "Even a machine couldn't do that."

"It's nothing really," Adrian continued, with a dismissive wave of his hand. "Once my imagination is fired up, the words just come pouring onto the page. It's like a volcano erupting."

"Well, that's an amazing gift. There are writers who spend their entire careers on a tiny handful of projects. Their output is painfully slow. Look at James Joyce, for instance. He spent seven years writing *Ulysses*."

"Ah, yes," Adrian said, "but poor old Joyce had financial problems. He wasted a lot of his creative energy simply trying to keep body and soul together. Who knows what he might have produced if he'd been sure of three square meals a day?"

"You have a point," Charlie conceded.

"Of course, I do. If Joyce didn't have to worry where the next week's rent was coming from, he would probably have produced a book a year. There could have been a whole series of *Ulysses* novels. I can just see them. *Ulysses Two, Ulysses Three. Return of Leopold Bloom. Son of Leopold Bloom*. It's just a matter of rearranging the plot. It could have been a real money-spinner for him."

Adrian took another drink of beer. He was starting to enjoy this conversation. This Charlie person was showing him the kind of respect he deserved. Perhaps he had been a little rash? Perhaps he had misjudged him?

"When do you expect to finish the book?" Charlie asked.

"Fairly soon. As a matter of fact, I've just managed to crack a particular problem. There was something bothering me for some time and I couldn't lay my finger on it. And then I suddenly realised what it was."

"What?"

"There wasn't enough action. I needed more dead bodies so I just killed off a load of people. Must say I enjoyed it enormously. There was blood everywhere."

Charlie gasped.

"Isn't that marvellous?" Trish said. "But, Adrian, I told you Charlie has offered to read it."

"Yes. Should have it completed by the end of the week. The final draft. Ready to greet a bright new dawn."

"How would you describe the novel?" Charlie asked. "Historical fiction, romantic saga?"

There was silence. Adrian's face grew dark.

Trish and Charlie exchanged a nervous glance.

"Thriller?" Charlie prompted. "Would you describe your book as a thriller?"

Adrian put down his glass and drew in his stomach. He stared menacingly at Charlie. "Is this an attempt at humour, Mr Dobbins?"

"Hhhumour?" Charlie stammered.

"Are you trying to insult me?"

"No. Not at all."

"Mr Dobbins, let me tell you something. *The Green Gannet* represents a defining moment in Irish literature. In years to come, the critics will divide the genre into two

243

periods: pre and post *Gannet*. Do you begin to comprehend?"

"Yyyes," Charlie muttered, not understanding a single word.

"So please refrain from parading your ignorance by ever again referring to it as a *thriller. The Green Gannet* is *literature!*" By now, Adrian's face was pressed up against Charlie's. His eyes bulged and a vein on his temple had started to throb.

"Yes," Charlie said and finished his beer. "It sounds very interesting. I can't wait to read it."

"Please," Trish pleaded. "Let's not get over-excited. Anybody want another drink?"

"Not for me," Charlie said, deciding it was time to get out of there before this Adrian went completely bonkers. He glanced quickly at his watch. "In fact, I've just remembered I have to meet someone." He nodded politely and made his way gingerly past Adrian as if he expected him at any moment to sink his teeth into his leg. "Delighted to have met you, Mr Blake. And you, Trish. Keep up the good work, everybody. Goodbye."

Adrian watched him make his way quickly across the pool area and disappear through the door into the hotel. He was feeling rather pleased with himself. "Fellow's a bloody charlatan. Hasn't got a clue what he's talking about. I warned you, Trish. I did tell you. Just because he's a bookseller doesn't mean he knows the first damned thing about creative writing."

"He was only trying to be helpful," Trish said, sadly. "You didn't have to be so rude."

"Rude?" Adrian laughed. "You heard what he said. Asked me if I was writing a thriller. Me? A *thriller?*"

"Well, he hasn't seen it. And you didn't describe it to him. So how was he supposed to know?"

"My dear Trish, anyone with an ounce of intellect would

see that a man of my position is hardly likely to spend hours of his life, locked away in a room, without contact with another human being, just to write a *thriller*!" He waved to the barman for more drinks. "Anyway. it wasn't me he was interested in. It was you."

"I beg your pardon?"

"I could see the way he was sniffing around you. My God, you can't leave a woman out of your sight for fifteen minutes but every damned tomcat in the area is prowling around trying to get a leg over."

Trish's face turned pale. "I think that's very unkind."

"It's the truth."

"It is *not*. He was just being nice to me. I met him on the bus tour and we shared lunch together. Then today, I happened to bump into him at the pool and he asked me to have a drink. There's nothing sinister in that. If there was, I'd be the first to know."

Adrian snorted. "Anyway, I don't think I'll be needing the help of Mr Dobbins, thank you very much. I've made the breakthrough I require. Believe me, when the publishers see the new revised version of *Gannet,* they'll be killing one another to sign me up. All that hard work is about to pay off." He looked at his wife. "Are you hungry?"

"Peckish. Why?"

"I'm ravenous. That dinner we talked about? Let's go now."

"It's rather early. Are you sure?"

"Positive. I've finished for the day."

"I'll have to get changed first."

"That's all right. I'll just sit here and wait."

Trish gathered her towel and slid off the bar stool. "Fifteen minutes. OK?"

"Take your time," Adrian shouted after her.

He finished his beer and decided to order a whisky. A large one. He'd earned it. He swirled the whisky in the glass and listened to the ice crack. The attention that Dobbins fellow had been paying to Trish had started him thinking. When was the last time they had made love? He tried to remember. Must have been at least six months ago. He had been damned careless. While he was locked away all day with the novel, he had left her to the tender mercy of sharks like Dobbins who prowled the resort in search of prey. He could easily have driven her into their arms.

He shook his head. Mustn't get my metaphors mixed up. Sharks don't have arms. They have fins. And they don't prowl. Into the fins of one of those sharks? No. It didn't sound right. He took another drink and made up his mind. The book was practically finished. Only another few days and it would be ready to burst like a meteor on an unsuspecting world. Adrian felt a warm feeling envelop him as the whisky began to take hold. He was on the threshold of achieving his ambition. He was on the verge of becoming a literary superstar. He would celebrate tonight. And he would make love to Trish and put her out of her celibate misery.

He looked up and saw her coming back across the pool area. She looked terrific. She had put on a little vest and a short skirt and had tied back her hair. My God, Adrian thought, I could ravish her right here on the bar counter. Wouldn't that give them something to talk about?

"You look stunning," he said.

"Thank you."

"One more for the road?"

"Maybe we should wait till we get to the restaurant."

"Whatever you say, darling."

They walked through the lobby and out to the street.

Adrian was proud of the envious glances that followed their progress. He saw the look of admiration from the smarmy Carlos. I *am* a lucky devil, he sighed. And to think, it was right under my nose all the time and I didn't appreciate it.

They found a small restaurant beside the water. It was almost empty when they arrived. They ordered sardines to start, with veal and spaghetti and mixed salad to follow and a nicely chilled bottle of white wine.

"This is perfect," Adrian said. "A delicious meal, a breathtaking setting and a beautiful woman."

He raised his glass. "What more could any man want?"

"What's suddenly got into you?" Trish laughed.

"I've just realised how fortunate I am. I've been a fool for neglecting you."

"But it's perfectly understandable. You had your novel to write. And now it's almost ready."

"Ah, Yes. And I can't wait to have my revenge on all those arrogant nonentities who hadn't the intelligence to recognise my talent when it was presented to them."

She reached out and stroked his arm. "You shouldn't feel that way, dear."

"But I do. I can't help it. Tell you the truth, I enjoy it. I can't wait to see the looks on their miserable faces. I can't wait to watch their puny careers reduced to toast when word gets out that they had *The Green Gannet* on a plate and they hadn't the intelligence to appreciate it."

Trish took his hand. "You should put all that behind you now and look to the future. When you're successful, that should be enough."

"But don't you understand? I want more than success. I want blood!"

When they had finished eating, they took a taxi back to the hotel. Once inside the apartment, Adrian pounced on her. His hands were everywhere, groping and pulling at her breasts, her thighs, her hips. She felt like she was being taken by a wild animal. He led her to the bed and undressed her.

"I can't wait to make love to you," he moaned. "I'm hungry for you. I want to possess you."

It was typical Adrian lovemaking. No subtlety. No finesse. He had hardly started when it was over and he was lying exhausted on the pillow, his face flushed and the sweat glistening on his unwashed chest.

Trish stared at the white ceiling and listened to the sound of her heart beating. At last! She had got what she had come all this way to achieve. She had finally got Adrian to make love to her. She could now successfully pass off the baby she was carrying as her husband's child. She should be happy.

Why was it, then, that she felt so sad?

Chapter 26

Charlie hurried away from the bar as fast his legs could carry him, glancing back occasionally to make sure that Adrian hadn't decided to come after him. 'My God,' he thought when he reached the relative safety of the hotel foyer, 'that was a bloody close shave. I've met many writers in my time who were complete egomaniacs but that's the first time I've come across one who was a psychopath as well. I thought for a ghastly moment he was going to hit me and then what would have happened? I would have been forced to defend myself and no doubt the security staff would have been called and it would all have ended up in a dreadful mess. Poor Trish would have been mortified with embarrassment.'

There was no doubt in his mind. Adrian was mad. After meeting him, he was totally convinced. He was stark, raving bonkers and probably dangerous too. And that book he was writing sounded like the novel from hell. *The Green Garbage* indeed. What a ridiculous title. All that talk of blood and dead bodies. No wonder nobody wanted to publish it. And to think I offered to read the bloody thing!

Charlie didn't stop when he got to the foyer. He was anxious to put as much distance as possible between himself and Adrian. He went straight through the foyer and out the front door and didn't stop walking till he was halfway to Los Cristianos. There he came across a row of taxis. He hopped into the first one and slammed the door shut.

"Where to?" the driver asked.

"I don't know."

The driver turned to examine his passenger. No doubt about it. They were getting stranger. It was the sun. These foreigners couldn't handle the sun.

"Would you like to give me a clue, *Senor*?"

"Oh, take me anywhere," Charlie said, absently. "Los Cristianos will do fine."

There was a coughing noise, the engine purred into life and they set off. Charlie leaned back in his seat and gave a weary sigh. What was happening? After a brilliant start to the holiday, everything was suddenly turning pear-shaped.

He let his mind wander back to the earlier events at the pool bar. It had been wonderful until Adrian appeared. It had been just like the afternoon he had spent together with Trish in Puerto de la Cruz. He had felt totally relaxed in her company. She had a quality that he had never found in any other woman, an ability to put him at ease and draw him out of himself. She had looked so good with the sun shining on her hair and that bright sparkle in her eyes that he had wanted to kiss her. It was just like that time in the El Molino restaurant. And he was right on the verge of doing so when that madman had come on the scene. Another minute and he would have taken Trish in his arms and embraced her.

Charlie was amazed at his own audacity. Never in his entire life had he done anything like that. Yet it thrilled him just to think about it. What would it have been like to kiss

Trish? How would her lips have tasted? Would they have been soft and yielding? Would they have been hot and passionate? Would she have responded and returned his kiss? He would never know because her mad husband had arrived at the crucial moment and ruined everything.

Charlie felt a slight unease about what had just occurred. Maybe he should have been a bit firmer with Adrian? Maybe he should have been more forceful instead of allowing himself to be bullied like that? Yet Adrian was Trish's husband after all and he had found them in a compromising situation, even if nothing had actually happened. He was entitled to feel annoyed. But he had treated her so dismissively and Charlie had stood there and said nothing. Worse, he had fled the scene like a scalded cat.

What must she think of me, thought Charlie. At a time when I should have defended her, I scuttled away and left her to the mercy of her lunatic husband. I abandoned her to a deranged maniac with delusions of literary grandeur. He began to feel angry with himself. He felt like a cad. Why hadn't he stood up to Adrian and given him a piece of his mind and to hell with the consequences? Why hadn't he put him in his place?

And why had he let Adrian prattle on with all that literary nonsense? This was an area that Charlie knew something about, yet Adrian had treated him like an imbecile. Why had he stood there and meekly listened to him? *Return of Leopold Bloom* indeed! And that childish boasting about how many words he could write each day, as if he was a butcher churning out strings of sausages. Charlie had never heard anything so ridiculous. But instead of confronting him, he had shown weakness and now Adrian would think he was afraid of him. Worse, Trish would think it too and any respect she might have had for him would vanish.

Charlie sat in the back of the cab and felt miserable. It was Jacinta Brennan all over again. He recalled the humiliations he had suffered at her hands and the way she had repaid his attention with casual cruelty. That experience had scarred him. It had made him afraid of women and awkward in their company. And he had carried the wounds all his life. Until now.

Maybe if he had been bolder, Jacinta Brennan might have had more respect for him. But his shyness had only spurred her on to greater contempt. Was he about to repeat that same mistake with Trish?

The taxi was speeding along the highway into Los Cristianos. As they approached the outskirts of the town, Charlie decided to get out and stroll. He paid the driver and the taxi drove away. There was a gentle breeze which made it pleasant to walk. He decided to head down to the seafront. As he went, he began to make up his mind. He *would* do something. He would confront that lunatic Adrian at the first opportunity and let him know exactly what he thought of him and his stupid book.

As for Trish, there was no point wondering what she felt. There was no point going home filled with regrets about what might have been. If he didn't make his feelings clear to her now, he would never know. She spent her mornings at the pool while Adrian worked on his book in their apartment. Tomorrow morning he would talk to her and tell her exactly how he felt about her. The worst that could happen was that she would tell him it was all a mistake and he had misread the situation. But at least he would know.

Having made his decision, Charlie felt his confidence return and a jaunty swing enter his step. He thought how much he had changed since coming on this holiday. Only last week, he would have run a mile from a situation like this. He would have cringed with embarrassment at the very thought of opening his heart to a woman. And it was all down to the night he spent with Penny, who was probably tucked up in bed this very moment trying to survive a thundering hangover. If he could only remember where she lived, he would buy some nice flowers and take them to her right away and apologise for whatever he had done to upset her.

He was nearing the sea. He could smell the salt air. He entered a maze of tiny streets and before he realised, he was outside the Monaco Bar. Now he remembered. This was the place where he had met Penny and they had got wasted on vodka and Red Bull. Charlie wondered what it looked like in daylight. He decided to go in.

The pub had the same gloomy interior he remembered from his first visit. He paid for a beer and looked around the darkened bar. It was empty except for a figure hunched at a table near the back. He peered closer and suddenly gave a little start.

It was Penny!

At once, he slipped off his stool and boldly marched up to her. She glanced up and a look of uncertainty came into her eyes as she recognised him.

"I heard you were sick," he said.

Penny squirmed. "I am sick. I had to take the day off work."

"Tracy told me."

"I'm feeling better now. It was just a hangover."

"Too many vodkas?" Charlie said, trying to put her at ease.

"Something like that."

"I'm glad," Charlie said. "Look, there's something I want to say. I'd like to apologise for whatever I did to offend you the other evening."

"You didn't do anything," Penny said.

"I thought I might have upset you in some way. The trouble is, I was out of my tree and I can't remember a single thing about it."

"You didn't do anything," she repeated. "Honest."

"Anyway, I wanted to thank you. You did me a big favour, you know."

"Favour? How do you mean?"

Charlie smiled. "It would take too long to explain."

Penny looked confused.

"Actually, I'm really sorry I can't remember anything," continued Charlie. "I'm sure it was the experience of a lifetime."

Penny stared. "You mean, you *really* can't remember what happened?"

"Not a thing." Charlie paused. "Why? What do I not remember?"

"What happened at my flat? You don't remember?"

"No."

Penny tried to look away, but Charlie held her gaze. "Tell me what happened, Penny. I have to know."

She lowered her eyes. "I was sick all over the bathroom floor. So I locked the door and spent ages cleaning it up. I was so embarrassed."

"And?"

"By the time I got back to bed, you were fast asleep."

"Asleep? You mean —?"

"Nothing happened between us, Charlie. Did you think something had?"

Chapter 27

Mollie was not the least bit happy with the way things were turning out. Since Ned had eaten that grilled steak in the Lucky Leprechaun and, contrary to his expectations, hadn't been struck down with dysentery or food poisoning, the children had turned their attention on her. Mary was constantly badgering her to go the beach or the swimming-pool, anywhere in fact to get her out of the apartment. Mollie had finally given in and compromised. She had agreed to sit in the lounge, having extracted a solemn undertaking that no one would approach her and try to engage her in Spanish conversation. And that's where she was sitting now, with a pot of tea on a little table beside her, having just returned from an exhausting day in Puerto Santiago.

When she was younger a day like today wouldn't have taken a feather out of Mollie. She remembered days when she was a girl and she would have been up before daylight to milk the cows or collect the eggs or go with her father to the fair. And they might not be home again till nightfall after Mollie had dragged her father out of Murphy's pub where he wanted to sit and drink pints of porter with his cronies. Indeed it was on just such a day that she had first set eyes on Ned. She remembered how handsome he was and how strong, the way he had wrestled that young bullock to the ground the time it escaped. She smiled at the memory. They were so much younger then and had so much energy. And had far fewer problems on their minds to wear them out and worry them.

For despite the fact that every instinct she trusted told her she should be feeling good, Mollie couldn't shake off this terrible feeling of unease. She knew it was foolish. She had her health, she had a loving family, she had no financial concerns. Indeed, after winning the Lotto, she had more money than she knew what to do with. And even the relationship between Edward and his father, which had caused her so much heartache, now seemed to have improved dramatically. She saw them talking and laughing together. They watched football on the television. They played pool in the games room of the hotel. Their relationship was almost back to where it was in the old days before all this tension began. By any measure, the holiday was turning into a brilliant success.

Mollie knew she should be content. But she was worried about Mary. That horoscope she had read had to mean something. And she feared the worst.

Today's trip to Puerto Santiago had been arranged solely for her benefit. Mollie knew that perfectly. It was another attempt to get her out of the apartment so that she would have something to tell the neighbours when she got home. As if she cared what the neighbours thought. But even though she didn't much like the idea, she had agreed to go along with the others just to get them off her back.

The day had begun at seven. She had hopped out of bed and into the shower and then made tea and toast. She had promised the children she wouldn't cook any more meals for Ned but she felt that tea and toast didn't really count.

It was great that Ned had given way on the matter of Spanish food. In fact, even before Edward had persuaded him to eat Spanish meat, Ned had been broadening his horizons: the milk he put on his cereal was Spanish, the bread was Spanish, the jam was Spanish and the water he boiled for his tea was Spanish. He even drank Spanish beer in preference to Guinness. There were very few barriers left to come down and, as far as Mollie could see, Ned hadn't suffered in the least.

Edward had arranged for a taxi to pick them up, so they all piled in and drove the short distance to the bus station, as the sun climbed higher in the blue morning sky. They had to wait for ten minutes before the bus came chugging into the station in a cloud of diesel fumes. Mollie listened proudly as Edward organised the tickets in the halting Spanish he had gleaned from his phrase book. They climbed aboard and got seats at the front beside the driver, Ned insisting loudly that these were the best seats on the bus and gave an uninterrupted view of the countryside.

They settled back and finally the bus set off. It travelled along a motorway for part of the journey and then it began to climb up into the mountains and the town they had left behind grew smaller and smaller till eventually they could see right along the coastline as far as Los Cristianos.

"Isn't this grand?" Ned said, stretching his legs and gazing from the window at the passing scene.

Mollie wasn't so sure. She didn't like these winding mountain roads. She kept worrying that the driver would get distracted and they'd all go over a cliff. She could see the newspaper headlines: *ENTIRE FAMILY WIPED OUT IN HOLIDAY HORROR, TRAGIC MOTHER WAS LOTTO WINNER.* Who would take care of the farm if they were all killed? Worse, who would get their bodies back to Dunmuckridge for the funeral? It didn't bear thinking about.

But Ned was enjoying himself enormously. He kept pointing out things. They passed yawning gorges and dried-up river beds and each time they went round a bend in the road, Ned's eyes lit up like a schoolboy on a funfair ride.

At last, they came down from the mountain and onto a flat road that ran along the coast. Mollie gave a sigh of relief. They were able to see yachts bobbing like corks out on the ocean and people jet-skiing from the back of boats. They passed through pretty country towns decked out with bunting for some religious festival and then, half an hour later, the bus drew into Puerto Santiago.

"Where do we go now?" Mollie asked, as they all piled off.

Edward opened the map he had got from the tourist office. "According to this, the market's supposed to be held in the square in front of the church. Which should be down this street," he said, pointing, and they all went trooping off behind him.

As they approached the market, a noise rose on the air like a swarm of bees. They rounded a corner and went straight into a crowd of people, an array of coloured awnings, a babble of voices and, hanging over the whole scene, the tempting smell of cooking food.

"My God," Mollie said, "I don't think I'll be able for this."

"You'll be grand," Ned said, bending his head like an athlete and pushing forward. "Just hold on to me and you won't get lost."

He started into the middle of the crowd and the others followed. There were stalls selling fruit and vegetables, cheeses, sausages, craft work, carved ornaments, tablecloths and pottery. Eventually Edward stopped in front of a man selling watches.

But before he could respond, Ned grabbed him by the sleeve and drew him aside.

"You're not buying a watch off that fella, are you?"

"I was just going to ask the price."

"Don't even think about it. I heard about a man once bought one of those watches and when he got it home, the damned thing had stopped. He opened the back of it and what do you think he found?"

"Tell me."

"There was no works in it! Only an empty shell."

Edward laughed. "I'll remember your advice."

So he didn't buy a watch. Instead, he purchased a pair of leather shoes from another stall. Mary bought a silk scarf and a tie for Peter Reilly and Mollie bought some tee shirts and souvenirs for the dresser at home. Only Ned refused to part with his money, convinced that all the traders in the market had combined in a massive conspiracy to swindle him out of his cash.

"What's next on the agenda?" Ned asked as they emerged from the crowd.

"I thought we might take a stroll over to Los Gigantes," Edward said, opening the tourist map again and starting to read: "*Los Gigantes, or the Giants, is the local name given to a wonder of nature – cliffs which tower 700 feet above the sea. Ideal for those special photographs to remind you of your wonderful holiday.*"

"Do we have to go?" Mollie complained. "This heat is killing me."

"Yes," Ned said emphatically. "You're on your holidays. You have to enjoy yourself!"

It was almost three o'clock when they arrived for lunch at The Lucky Leprechaun. Tom Casey was waiting.

"You guys look like you could use a drink."

"You're a mind-reader," Ned replied. "I'll have a nice cold pint of Dorada, please. I've a thirst on me that some people would pay good money for."

"Make that two," Mary said.

"Three," Edward added.

Mollie said she would have cola with lots of ice.

Casey went off to the bar and returned with the drinks.

"Where have you been?" he asked. "You all look bushed."

"We've been to Puerto Santiago," Mollie replied. "To the market. And you're dead right. We *are* bushed. I never encountered such crowds or such heat in my born days. But my family dragged me along because they said I had to enjoy myself on my holidays." She shot a caustic glance at Edward and Mary.

"Get any bargains?"

"Not a one," Ned put in. "Edward nearly bought a watch but I warned him off. I know what those watches are like. The hands go backwards."

Casey laughed. "You must be hungry? I've got those pork chops I told you about."

"I could eat a horse, never mind a pork chop," Edward said.

"Me too," Mary added.

"And me," Mollie said.

Everyone looked at Ned, waiting for him to speak. But he sat with his head bowed.

"Have you anything else? Anything that isn't . . . Spanish?"

"Afraid not," Tom Clancy said. "Not at this time of day."

"Oh for God's sake," Mollie said, sticking her elbow into his ribs, "didn't you eat a Spanish steak yesterday and it didn't do you the least bit of harm?"

"Not so far. But sometimes these things can have a delayed reaction."

"Mother of God," Mollie said, "it's like trying to feed a baby." She turned to Tom Casey. "Make that four pork chops. I'll see that he eats it."

Ned did eat the chop and the roast potatoes and cabbage and gravy that came with it. When he was finished, he sat back contently and patted his stomach. "That's the best meal I've had since I've been here," he said. He glanced quickly at his wife. "Barring the food Mollie cooked of course."

"So you admit you were wrong?" Mollie said.

"I didn't actually say that. However, I'm a fair man. I'm prepared to revise my opinion."

Across the table, Mary caught Edward's eye and smiled.

After lunch, Edward decided to go for a stroll while the others returned to the hotel. Ned said he wanted to take a nap so Mary persuaded her mother to sit in the lounge while she went for a spot of sunbathing by the pool. Mollie listened to the soothing music issuing from the sound system as she poured a cup of tea and added milk from the little porcelain jug which the waitress had brought. She felt the uneasy feeling creep up on her again.

Was Mary pregnant or not? And if she was, why didn't she confide in her? Mollie decided that this was the thing that was bothering her the most. Her mind returned to the horoscope and its clear message: *Prepare for a happy addition to the family.* What could that mean only that a baby was on the way? And who else could be pregnant, but Mary? And yet she hadn't done the most natural thing in the world. She hadn't confided in her own mother.

It wasn't as if Mollie hadn't given her plenty of opportunities. She had dropped hints and made remarks that no-one with half a brain could have failed to pick up. And still Mary had said nothing. What was wrong with the girl? Was she afraid? Was she worried about their reaction? Did she believe, God forbid, that they would disown her? That thought hurt Mollie more than anything else. Did Mary not know that no matter what happened, no matter what calamity might befall her, they would always love her and never turn their backs on her?

She sipped her tea. It was good tea. Nice and refreshing. But it wasn't as good as the tea she made at home. The trouble was, the Spanish didn't know how to make tea. They didn't drink it themselves and they had no tradition. They didn't heat the teapot and they didn't boil the water properly. But still, she was grateful for small mercies.

She made up her mind. The first opportunity she got, she would sit down with Mary in some quiet place and ask her straight out. She knew this had to be a delicate operation so she would be gentle and considerate; she wouldn't be judgmental; she wouldn't argue or scold. She would just tell Mary how much they loved her and how happy they would be if she had a baby. Although Mollie couldn't vouch for Ned's reaction, she felt sure she would be able to handle him.

Once she had made her decision, she felt better. Always best to get these things out in the open. Nothing good ever came from bottling them up. If Mary was pregnant, they would discuss what had to be done. She was assuming the father was Peter Reilly. The pair of them had been walking out now for the past eighteen months, although there had been no talk of marriage. She would have to go and see Mrs Reilly and have a chat. It wouldn't be pleasant, but it would have to be done.

Mollie put down her teacup and glanced around the quiet lounge. It was empty except for one lady sitting by herself near the window, her head buried in a newspaper. At that precise moment, the woman looked up and smiled.

Mollie recognised her at once. She had seen her in here before in conversation with that manager fella, Carlos.

Mollie returned the woman's smile. She was dark and glamorous. Mollie couldn't remember if she had seen her with anyone besides Carlos and some intuition told her the woman was alone. Immediately, she felt a touch of pity for her. The poor creature must be lonely. It must be sad to have to come away on your holidays all by yourself.

As Mollie watched, the woman got up from her seat and began to walk across the room towards her.

"Hello," she said, in a cheery voice. "Enjoying a quiet cup of tea?"

"Yes," Mollie said. "I don't like the sun and it's nice and cool in here."

"Well, you're quite right," the woman said. "Too much sun isn't good for your skin. And your skin looks so fresh and healthy. You don't want to spoil it."

"Do you think so?" Mollie said, feeling pleased.

"Oh, I do. Your skin has a natural freshness. You should take care of it."

"Thank you," Mollie said, thinking the woman might want some company. "My name is Mollie McGinty."

"Monica Woodward."

They shook hands.

"Would you like to join me for some tea? I could ask the waitress to bring another cup?"

But Monica shook her head. "That's very kind but I'm just leaving. I thought you might want this. I've finished reading it." She handed Mollie a folded newspaper.

"Thank you very much," Mollie said.

"My pleasure," Monica replied and sailed majestically out of the room.

Mollie watched her go. She's got style – she's very elegant.

I'll bet a woman like that has got loads of men chasing after her.

She opened the paper. It was one of those tabloids, folded at a half-completed crossword puzzle and filled with stupid tittle-tattle that passed for news: another soccer star in love with a pop singer, another member of the Royal Family getting divorced. Mollie wondered why they couldn't have stories about real people.

As if they had a life of their own, her fingers turned instinctively to the horoscope. And here, Mollie felt her heart give a leap. Under the Taurus sign, she read: *Be patient. Tiny beginnings lead to great events.*

Mollie put the paper down and felt her body tremble. *Tiny beginnings?* Merciful Hour! What could be more obvious?

She no longer had any doubts. Mary was definitely pregnant.

Chapter 28

What a funny woman, Monica thought, as she left Mollie and made her way out of the lounge and up to her room. And such unsuitable clothes; stockings and shoes and a cardigan in this weather. I don't think I've seen her since the evening we arrived. I certainly haven't seen her in the bar or at the pool. What does she do with herself all day? And she looked as if something was bothering her. Maybe I should have accepted her offer of a cup of tea. We could have had a chat. Ah well, perhaps the next time.

But Monica quickly forgot Mollie once she was inside her room. She had more pressing matters on her mind. Tonight was her dinner date with Carlos. The first thing she did when she had locked the door was to go the cupboard, take out the bottle of gin and pour a large measure. Then she sat down on the bed and took a deep breath. This dinner represented a challenge and a turning point. Her very future could depend on it. It was vital that she get everything right. I must remain calm, she said to herself. Above all, I mustn't let him think I'm grateful or overly keen. I must take it all in my stride. I must create the impression that *I'm* the one who's doing *him* a favour. If he gets even a hint that I'm pursuing him, he'll bolt like a frightened horse.

But despite her resolution, she felt herself tremble with excitement. She had arrived at a defining moment in her career. If things went well tonight, she could be on the threshold of a wonderful new life, even more exhilarating than the life she had known with Woody. It was the opportunity she had been hoping for but never thought would actually come to pass. No matter what happened, she mustn't let it slip away.

What age is he? she thought. Late twenties? Early thirties? Certainly a man in prime condition. She searched for a metaphor to describe the smouldering Carlos and the word *toro* popped into her head. That's it! A young bull with all the fiery temperament of this dark and passionate land. The poetry tripped effortlessly off her tongue. And he is captivated by me! Practically down on his knees begging me to go to dinner with him. If I couldn't see this glass of gin in my hand I'd swear this whole thing was just a magnificent dream.

At the thought of the gin, Monica polished off the glass and poured herself another. It was a bit early to be drinking gin but this could be viewed as a medical emergency. She had read in some health magazine that too much excitement was bad for the complexion – something about the blood vessels expanding. She sipped her drink and thought again of the magnificent Carlos. What a specimen of manhood – younger and more handsome and doubtless possessed of far more passion than Woody could ever muster. Monica felt her knees go weak at the thought.

Eventually, she finished her drink, stood up and looked at herself in the mirror. She was pleased with what she saw.

The diet and the exercise had done their work. She had practically recovered the lithe figure that she was so proud of. She examined her face and neck. Skin beginning to tighten a little, one or two tiny wrinkles – although you would really need a microscope to see them. The careful application of some moisturising cream and the deft use of a little make-up should disguise them perfectly. And her selective sunbathing regime meant she was had developed a nice, even tan. She studied her eyes. They were bright and clear. She looked at her nose, her ears, her chin but when she came to her hair, her heart sank like a stone. Her hair was a disaster. It was lank and lifeless. Too much sun, too much chlorine in the water of the swimming-pool. And too long. It needed to be cut.

Monica swore under her breath. She could have kicked herself. Why hadn't she gone to the hairdresser before she came away? But it had been such a spur-of-the-moment decision that she scarcely had time to pack. If only she had enough money to get a proper styling job in the beauty parlour downstairs. But at €100, it was completely out of the question. And of course, the hairdresser would expect a tip.

It couldn't be done. The cost would completely wreck her budget. She went to the safe in the closet where she kept her cash and counted out the notes. One hundred and eighty euro. She emptied her purse. Some smaller notes and coins made a grand total of €225 euro. If she splashed out on a hair style, she would have about €115 left to see her through the rest of the holiday. It would mean a diet of bread and fruit. It would mean no drinks at the bar. No taxis. No little treats. It would mean strict rationing and careful control. But she would just about manage.

It took Monica thirty seconds to decide. This prize was

too great to leave anything to chance. If she was going to snare the sultry Carlos, she would have to go for broke. If it meant starving herself till she got back to Dublin, then so be it. Look on the bright side, she thought. The dieting will do you good.

She lifted the phone by the bed and asked to be put through to the beauty parlour.

"Hello," she said. "My name is Monica Woodworth. Room 306."

"Yes, *Senora*?"

"I'd like to have my hair cut."

"Certainly, *Senora*. Let me check the appointments list."

Something in the woman's voice caused a wave of panic. What if they're booked out? What will I do? Where will I go? But the hairdresser was immediately back on the phone reassuring her.

"Is four o'clock suitable?"

"Four o'clock is good."

"Thank you, *Senora*."

Monica put down the phone. She felt a strange exhilaration pulsing along her veins. Goodness me, she thought. If I didn't know better, I might almost believe I was in love.

She suddenly realised that she hadn't eaten anything since breakfast. Best to have something in my stomach, she thought, so that I don't gorge like a barbarian at this dinner tonight and let myself down. She went to the cupboard again and took out a tin of sardines, a hunk of bread and a tomato. She uncorked the bottle of wine she had bought in the supermarket. She read the price tag still stuck on the neck. €1.50. Monica did a quick calculation and worked out that the wine was costing 25 cents a glass. Enjoy it, she said to herself. It might be your last.

As she ate, she thought of other holidays, languorous days

spent cruising the Mediterranean with Woody, nights spent partying till the golden sun came peeping over the horizon. If I play my cards right, I can have it all back again. I can preside over glittering dinner parties and lunches. I can be restored to my rightful position as Queen of Society. Oh, how she would savour the triumph! Oh, how she would punish her enemies and confound her critics, particularly that harpy, Colleen McQueen! She couldn't wait to see the look on her face when the news broke: *SOCIETY HOSTESS TO WED SPANISH MILLIONAIRE*. Starving herself for a few days was a small price to pay for such exquisite revenge.

When she had finished eating, it was time for her hairdressing appointment. Monica skipped along the corridor to the lift and went down to the beauty parlour. They were waiting for her. Monica was impressed with their professionalism. And they all spoke good English. She remembered, with horror, another experience in Portugal when the hairdresser didn't know what she was saying and had practically scalped her before Monica managed to make her understand that all she wanted was highlights put in.

For ninety minutes, she stared into the mirror as the scissors flew, till at last the hairdresser stood back to admire her handiwork. Monica's hair had been transformed. It was now smooth and silky. It shone with vitality. Each wave and curl had been sculpted into a perfect crown that set off her face and her cheekbones and made her look ten years younger. Gratefully, Monica paid over the money and added another ten euro for a tip.

Back in her room, she poured herself another large gin while she ran the bath and sorted through her wardrobe. There really wasn't much to choose from. A couple of dresses from Mary Grant, a grey trouser suit from Paul Costello, some blouses, a change of shoes. She took out her best outfit:

the little black cocktail dress. And then, with a shudder, she recalled that it was the same dress she had worn on the night of the disastrous expedition to the Gran Hotel del Rey. And Carlos had met her on her return, had brought her into the lounge and got her a glass of sherry. She couldn't wear it. He was bound to remember.

She took out another dress. This one was powder blue. She held it against herself. It reached just above the knee and had a little hem of frilly lace. Monica liked this dress. It emphasised her figure. It was the sort of dress you would wear at a party where there would be lots of dancing, but was it suitable for a dinner date? She put it back and reached for the trouser suit.

This presented a different Monica: a more serious person, a woman with poise and elegance, a woman of the world, a woman with hidden depths of wisdom and experience. Which image did she want to present tonight? The flighty, gay Monica or the mature, sensible woman who still maintained an aura of dark sensuality?

The sensible Monica won. She laid the suit on the bed. She would wear it with a white blouse and low heels and plain jewellery. She would carry her chunky black handbag. And the image would also be in keeping with her role as the recently bereaved wife.

She lay back in the bathtub and luxuriated in the warm water while she slowly soaped her legs and arms. Then she dried herself and began the preparations for her make-up. She used cleansing oil to wipe down her face and then applied a thin layer of sunshimmer, making sure to cover up the wrinkles she had discovered earlier. She took out her mascara and carefully touched up her eyes, just enough to highlight them. She took her red lipstick and drew a long sensuous line around her mouth.

When she was satisfied, she reached for the bottle of *Chanel* and applied a touch to her neck and wrists and finally her breasts. It was a subtle scent. Not too overpowering but with a definite hint of hidden passion. She chose a flimsy underwear set that Woody had bought her: lacy black bra and matching panties. Not that she intended to undress for him. Not on their very first date. But experience had taught Monica that it was always best to be prepared.

At five to eight, she took the remains of her gin and sat on the balcony and watched the lights of the town twinkle in the darkness. She would force herself to wait. Ever since that embarrassing occasion when Woody had left her sitting alone at the Horseshoe Bar, Monica had a dread of being early. It betrayed too much keenness. She waited till the hands of her watch showed eight fifteen – five minutes late. Then she rose and, with one last glance in the mirror, left the apartment and took the lift down to the ground floor.

She strode confidently through the foyer and out into the warm night air. She could feel the excitement return. It was like starting out on a magnificent journey filled with wonderful promise. But when she got out to the street, she felt her confidence drain away.

There was no sign of Carlos.

Chapter 29

The news that Alex Piper was coming hot-foot from Dublin on the first available flight to Tenerife sent Bobby into a spin. On one hand she was flattered. Angie was right. There was something gallant and romantic about a man being prepared to travel thousands of miles to reclaim his betrothed, even if the bastard had stood her up practically on the steps of the altar. But it was obvious that he had changed his mind and now realised the great prize he had sacrificed by his foolish action. Angie had been right about this too. In fact, bloody Angie seemed to be right about just about everything that was recently happening in Bobby's life and she was beginning to resent it.

But what was she going to do?

"You could agree to see him. I can't see any harm in it." Angie said after she had made Bobby a hot cup of chocolate and made sure she was sitting comfortably with her leg resting on a chair.

"I don't want to see him. When are you going to get that fact into your head?"

Angie sighed. "Look, I know this has been a terrible shock to you and I'm not for one minute trying to minimise the gravity of what he did. But it's not the end of the world. People postpone their wedding plans all the time."

"Not with me they don't."

"He just said he needed time to reconsider. And now he's done that. You know, worse things could happen to a girl. I have a friend at work who found her new husband in bed with the bridesmaid. At the wedding reception! Think how she must have felt."

"Well, I just hope she had a carving knife handy," Bobby said. "Anyone did that to me, I'd make damned sure they weren't able to do it again. Ever!"

Angie tried her soothing voice. "I think you should agree to meet Alex. Sit down and have a chat with him. At least hear what he has to say. It's clear to me he still loves you. You can easily rearrange the wedding date. I'd be delighted to help you with the new arrangements."

"I will *not* meet him," Bobby insisted, wishing her leg wasn't in plaster so she could stamp it on the floor for emphasis.

"You know this is just your pride speaking. You've been hurt and that's understandable. But you shouldn't let your pride overrule your head. Alex Piper is an excellent prospect. You'd be crazy to throw him over."

"If I agree to see him, it's like giving in. He'll know he can do this sort of thing any time he wants and get away with it."

But Angie was vigorously shaking her head. "I don't think so. I think you've sent him a clear message that you won't be messed about. I don't think Alex Piper will ever do anything like this again."

"I need to sleep on it," Bobby said, finishing her chocolate and hobbling off to the bathroom.

273

But sleep didn't make things any clearer. In normal circumstances, Bobby might have been prepared to relent under Angie's prompting and give Alex Piper one more chance. But something had happened in the meantime. She had met Edward McGinty.

As she lay in bed, Bobby thought of the afternoon she had just spent with Edward in the bar of the Lucky Leprechaun. It had been one of the most exhilarating times she could remember even though they had done nothing more exciting than sit chatting and getting to know each other. There was a quality about Edward that she couldn't quite identify but she knew she loved being in his company and couldn't wait to be with him again. And she knew something else: Edward was a man who understood his own mind. He wasn't a ditherer like Alex Piper. If Edward decided to do something, he would go through with it.

The following morning after breakfast, she sat down on the balcony and sent Alex Piper a text message. It was the first contact she had made with him since that terrible phone call from Barcelona cancelling the wedding plans. She knew that even doing this much was a concession but it was an emergency. At all costs, she had to stop him coming to Tenerife.

Don't set foot on this island, she wrote. *Armed police with instructions to arrest you the minute you land. Bobby.*

She sent it off and took a sip of coffee. That should settle it, she thought. When he gets that message, he'll quickly change his mind. The thought of finding himself in the hands of the Spanish police will soon bring him to his senses.

But shortly after, a fresh message popped up on her phone.

Don't care. Am already at the airport. I have to see you. Love Alex.

Bobby immediately fired off a further text.

Bubonic plague has broken out. Airport closed. Don't come. Bobby.

By now, she was starting to get worried. Alex Piper was showing reserves of determination she didn't know he possessed. Sure enough, within minutes a fresh text arrived.

Will go through fire and brimstone to get to you. I'm on my way. Love you. Alex.

Panic-stricken, Bobby rang the airport to check when the next flight from Dublin was due. She was told it was expected in five hours' time.

She turned to Angie. "What am I going to do? He's already on his way. He'll be here in five hours."

Angie shrugged. "You'll just have to make yourself scarce."

"But I thought I was making myself scarce. That was the whole idea of coming here in the first place."

"Then you'll have to bite the bullet and meet him."

Bobby spent the rest of the afternoon pondering what to do. It was imperative that Alex Piper should not get to her. But it was going to be difficult. He knew they were staying at Hotel Las Flores and he even knew the room number for he had spoken to Angie last night on the hotel phone. How he got the information was a mystery, for only a handful of people knew but they obviously had a mole in the camp.

She thought briefly of trying to change hotels but dismissed it immediately. It would be impossible at such short notice and anyway Alex Piper was in such a determined mood that he would probably scour the entire island till he found her. Maybe she could send a hoax bomb alert to the airport and have all the planes diverted? But the very idea scared the living daylights out of her. The authorities took a very dim view of anything like that and the penalties were very severe. She could end up in the women's prison getting a permanent sun tan.

At nine o'clock she had her appointment with Edward at the Lucky Leprechaun. She had been looking forward to it all day. Should she cancel? Hell no, she thought. I'm not letting Pig-Face Piper ruin my social life as well as everything else. He's done enough damage already. She had a bath, which was difficult with her leg in plaster, and then she got dressed. At half past eight, she made her way down to the foyer to get a taxi. As she passed by Reception, she stopped to have a word with the young *senorita* on duty.

"I have a request to make," Bobby said. "It is very important."

"Si, Senora."

"A young man from Ireland may come inquiring about me."

The receptionist was listening politely.

"If he turns up at the hotel, you must tell him I'm not staying here."

The young woman looked taken aback.

"He's a little deranged," Bobby elaborated.

Now she *really* had her attention.

"Should I call the *policia?*"

Bobby thought about this for a moment. It wasn't a bad idea but it could lead to complications. "I don't think that will be necessary. He's not dangerous."

"How will I know him?"

"He looks quite normal," Bobby said. "He will probably be dressed well. And he is under the illusion that I am going to marry him."

"Madre de Dio!" the young woman exclaimed.

"All you have to do is tell him I'm not staying here. Oh, and don't tell him my friend Miss Clarke is here either."

The young woman was frantically writing all this down.

"If you are firm with him, he will probably go away."

"Yes, *Senora*."

"He is a poor demented man. He is not right in the head."

"I understand, *Senora*. I will tell him."

"Muchas gracias," Bobby said and hobbled outside to get a taxi.

Edward's walk took him along the coast in the general direction of La Caleta. It was pleasant here, not quite so developed as other parts of the resort, still wild and rugged in parts. He remembered Bobby telling him it was somewhere near here that she had her accident. The thought of Bobby cheered him up although he was feeling good already after the lunch at the Lucky Leprechaun and the earlier trip with the family to Puerto Santiago.

It was amazing the way the relationship with his father had improved now that they were free from the goldfish bowl that was Dunmuckridge. Here in Tenerife, Edward had escaped from the malicious gossip and the prying eyes of his small home town. There was no one here to judge him and nothing to prove.

There was no one to make slighting remarks and no one to compare father and son and measure one against the other. As a result, the natural bond between them which had brought Edward so much pleasure as a child, was able to reassert itself. And he could see that Ned was happy too, although he said little and never referred to their breach.

Yes, everything seemed to be working out well. It was an inspired decision by his mother to bring them all away like this on a holiday. Yet, she was the only one who seemed unhappy. There was something eating at her. Mary had referred to it recently and Edward had noticed it too. Something to do with Mary. She had started dropping little hints about her health, making pointed comments as if she knew something the rest of them didn't. Edward shook his head. His mother could be strange at times – all this reliance on Fate and the stars. It was probably just a phase she was going through. No doubt it would pass.

His thoughts returned to Bobby. He had spent a wonderful afternoon with her. He was glad he had taken his courage in his hands and spoken to her for she had turned out to be fantastic company. She had told him all about herself: her childhood, her education and the death of her parents. It had made Edward even more conscious of his own good luck in having a loving family, while poor Bobby had none. Except of course, her animals. She seemed to dote on her cats and dog.

But she had borne her misfortune bravely. She had got on with her life, had built a good career and owned her own home and Edward admired her for that. She was independent. And she was bright and cheerful. Yet, even with Bobby, Edward thought he had detected some underlying concern. Something was bothering her too. No doubt, in time, she would tell him.

In the meantime, he had this evening to look forward to. There was a quiz tonight at the Leprechaun to be followed by Irish ballads. It promised to be a good night. He turned back and returned to the hotel. The sun was beginning to go down but the air was still hot and sticky. Edward went straight to his room and had a long shower, then shaved and dressed in a casual shirt and slacks.

He checked himself in the mirror. The sun had done its

work and he noticed the nice healthy tan that was developing around his face and neck. He was looking good. He set off down the hill towards the harbour. Bang on nine o'clock, he was outside the Lucky Leprechaun.

He pushed open the door of the pub and was amazed to find Bobby in a heated argument with a man he had never seen before.

Chapter 30

Monica stood for a moment in dismay. Carlos was nowhere to be seen. She blinked in the dim light from the street lamps and cast her eyes around in desperation. There were plenty of people about; the street was crowded with evening strollers who came out when the sun went down. From the restaurant on the corner, she could hear the gay chatter of the diners carried across on the soft evening breeze. But where was Carlos? Surely, he couldn't have forgotten their appointment? He had been adamant this morning.

She felt a sick feeling in the pit of her stomach. Had she got the time wrong? Ten past eight outside the hotel foyer, he had said. It was now twenty past eight. What could have happened? Had some urgent business problem called him away? God forbid, had he changed his mind? She looked wildly about. A feeling of panic began to grip her as she began to see her dreams drift away.

And then she heard a car horn. Across the street and a little way down, an open-roofed BMW sports car was parked in a lay-by and a dark-haired man with wraparound sun-glasses was sounding the horn and waving to her. She looked closer and saw it was him.

She felt relief wash over her like a tidal wave. But it was quickly followed by a feeling of foolishness. What a figure I must have cut, standing here flapping like an idiot, she thought. Now, he will have seen how scared I was that he wouldn't come. And at once, she felt angry with herself for betraying her feelings and not remaining cool and composed as she had planned. It had totally wiped out any advantage she might have gained by being late.

She waited for a break in the traffic and made her way across the road with all the dignity she could salvage. As she approached, Carlos pushed open the door of the car and she slid into the passenger seat beside him. At once, he began to apologise.

"My dearest Monica, I think I must have misled you. I should have given you precise directions. I should have said I would be parked here. Please forgive me."

"It's nothing," Monica laughed, nervously.

"I thought we should be discreet."

"Of course. Think nothing about it."

"Right outside the hotel, everyone could observe us. And you know how they can talk. But now you are here and everything is all right. May I compliment you on how well you look? You are . . . what is the word? Enchanted."

"I think you mean enchanting."

"Yes. That is correct. You cast a spell over every man who comes your way."

How touching, Monica thought. He certainly has a way with words.

"May I present you with a little gift? It is only some chocolates. I take it you like chocolates?"

"In small doses," Monica said with a brittle laugh. She still hadn't fully recovered from her earlier shock.

Carlos reached under the seat and brought out an enormous box, wrapped with a pink ribbon.

"Oh Carlos," she said, "this is far too much!"

"No, please. You must take it. There is also a little note."

He smiled shyly and Monica slid the card out from its pink envelope. It had a drawing of entwined flowers and the inscription: *For my beautiful friend, Monica. For making my day so happy. Carlos.*

"Why, that's lovely," Monica sighed.

Carlos shrugged.

"It is merely a token of my gratitude for your agreeing to dine with me tonight. You cannot appreciate how much pleasure it has given me." He placed the chocolates on Monica's lap and started the engine. "And so, now we are off. Are you hungry?"

"Let's say, I'm peckish."

"Peckish? What does that mean?"

"It means I'm hungry."

"You will enjoy this dinner," Carlos said, as he skilfully reversed the car and started up the street with a roar of the exhaust. "This restaurant is called *El Guanche*. It is the name of the people who originally lived here in the Canary Islands. And the food is traditional Canarian cooking."

"I'm sure it will be wonderful," Monica said.

"Oh, yes. And the patron is my friend Antonio Ramos. I think tonight he will cook a good dinner for us. I already told him I was bringing a very special lady friend." He glanced at her. "You don't mind me describing you like that?"

"Not at all. If it's true."

"Of course, it is true. You *are* special to me, Monica. From the first moment I saw you, I felt my heart sing like a bird."

They had left the town and were now ascending into the mountains. There was a scent of wild flowers on the night air. Monica looked down into the valley at the lights of the houses twinkling below. She leaned back in the seat and felt the cool breeze whistling past her face. This is too good to be true, she thought. Carlos is so thoughtful. He says the sweetest things. And such a perfect host. Imagine giving me that enormous box of chocolates. I'll have to ration myself. Otherwise I'm in danger of eating the whole box in one go and completely wrecking my diet.

She heard his voice above the roar of the car.

"A shilling for your thoughts."

Monica smiled. "Not a shilling. A penny."

"All right, then. A penny. What are you thinking?"

"I'm thinking how much I'm enjoying my holiday. And how lovely this place is. And how sad I will be when I have to leave."

"Maybe you would like to stay?"

Monica's ears pricked up. Was she hearing things? "But I have to go home at the end of the week."

"If there was a way to stay longer, would you do it?"

Her heart skipped a beat. Unless she was completely misreading him, this was getting extremely close to a proposal and they were only on their very first date. "That would depend."

Carlos glanced at her and there was an enigmatic smile playing round the corners of his mouth.

"I would like you to stay. And there may be a way. Perhaps we can discuss it later."

Discuss it now, Monica thought. Why wait? But he was already turning off the road and driving down a narrow lane that suddenly brought them into a cobbled courtyard set with wooden tables and hung with fairy lanterns.

Carlos pulled the car to a halt outside a stone building with open windows. Inside, Monica could see more lights and hear the fiery rhythm of flamenco music from a sound system. Carlos turned off the engine and pushed open the door.

"Now, we have arrived."

A small, plump man in a white apron came hurrying down the steps to greet them. The two men embraced and then Carlos broke free and took Monica's hand.

"Antonio, this is the special lady I told you about. I would like to introduce you to my friend, *Senora* Monica Woodworth. Monica, this is Antonio Ramos."

Antonio took her hands and gazed into her eyes. "*Senora*. I am so honoured."

"I am too," Monica said.

Antonio raised her hands to his lips in a soft kiss. "It is my privilege to meet you. Come inside. We must drink some sherry."

He waited for Monica to walk before him and then ushered her politely inside the restaurant. The walls were constructed of exposed stone and there was a lot of dark, heavy Spanish furniture. There were copper kettles and pots hung on hooks behind a dark wooden counter. The only light came from oil lamps. Monica was immediately reminded of a castle she had once visited in Kerry.

"This is very quaint," she said.

"It was an old farmhouse," Antonio explained. "When I bought it five years ago it was falling down. I had the idea of opening a Canarian restaurant, so I rebuilt it."

"How is business?"

"It is very good. We get local people and discerning tourists. But it is not to everyone's taste." He grinned. "We do not serve the *hamburguesa*." He produced a gleaming decanter and poured out the sherry. "May I propose a toast? To Senora Monica!"

They touched glasses and sipped their drinks.

"Carlos has told me much about you," Antonio said. "He tells me you are a widow. I am so sorry to hear that your husband died. Was he a young man?"

"He was forty-three," Monica said, knocking several years off Woody's age so that it would reflect positively on her own.

"So his death was unexpected?"

"It was very sudden," Monica said. "He died of a massive heart attack while on business in London."

"This is very sad," Antonio said and lowered his eyes in sympathy. "But life must go on. Are you enjoying your holiday?"

"Oh, yes. Carlos has been very kind to me."

She glanced at Carlos who smiled shyly.

"I told Monica you would cook a special dinner for us tonight, Antonio."

"It will be my pleasure." He refilled the sherry glasses. "Where would you like to eat? Inside or out?"

Monica looked to Carlos for guidance.

"Outside would be better," he said. "It is cool and we can see the lights of the town and the moon shining on the sea."

"That would be lovely," Monica said.

They finished their sherry and Antonio led them to a table already set for two people. There was a chequered tablecloth and a little vase of wild violets. A few minutes later, he came bustling out with baskets of freshly-baked bread and little dishes of olives and cheese and cooked meats. A young boy followed with jugs of red and white wine.

Carlos was right. They could see down across the valley with the lights strung out like a necklace of stars. Further out was the dark mass of the sea with a big yellow moon sailing majestically across an empty sky. How romantic, Monica thought. And in daytime it must have breathtaking views.

Carlos had lifted both jugs of wine. "Which one would you like? Red or white?"

"Which do you recommend?"

"I think the white to begin. And then, when we are served the meat, we can drink red. Shall I pour for you?"

"Thank you."

What perfect manners, Monica thought. These Spanish men certainly know how to make a lady feel important.

The wine was cool and crisp and there was a hint of lemon in its soft bouquet. They nibbled bread and cheese and stared down the valley at the lights.

"Is Antonio expecting other guests?" Monica asked.

"Not tonight. Tonight, the restaurant is closed."

"You mean . . .?"

"Yes. We have the place entirely to ourselves. He is cooking specially for us."

Before she could say anything more, Antonio and the boy were back with plates of crispy fried fish and little bowls of potatoes and dishes of sauce.

"*Cherne*," Antonio announced. "And *papas arrugados*."

"*Cherne* is a kind of bass fish," Carlos explained. "And *papas arrugados* are Canarian potatoes boiled in salt. Here you have two sauces: *mojo rojo* and *mojo verde*. The verde is made from oil, vinegar, garlic, cumin and coriander. The *rojo* is hotter. It has paprika added."

Monica sliced into the fish. It was white and flaky and delicious to the taste.

"It's beautiful," she said.

"May I suggest you try the *mojo verde* with the potatoes?"

Monica spooned some sauce from the dish and dipped a potato into it.

"Mmmmmm," she said.

"You like it?"

"It's marvellous."

"Good. I am pleased."

"I think it was very kind of Antonio to open the restaurant especially for us," Monica said.

"But he is my good friend. It is a favour. He understands I would do the same thing for him."

"Is he married?"

"Yes. The boy is his son. His name is Francisco."

Carlos refilled the glasses. "I think if I was married I would like to have lots of children. Why did you not have children, Monica?"

How could she tell him the truth? *We didn't have time. We were too busy enjoying ourselves.* "It just didn't happen."

"Perhaps your husband – what was his name?"

"Woody."

"Perhaps Woody was not a passionate man?"

"Oh, no," Monica said. "It was nothing like that. He was very passionate."

He reached out and touched her arm and she was drawn to look into his dark, brooding eyes.

"Would you like to have a child?"

"I don't know," Monica said quickly. "It would mean a lot of adjustment to my life. It is something I haven't thought about very much."

His eyes held hers. It was as if he was trying to look into her heart. "A child is a precious gift. It creates a bond between a man and a woman. You should remember that, Monica."

At that moment, Francisco came back to clear away the

empty plates and Antonio followed with a pot and more dishes. He took the lid off the pot with a flourish and the most delicious aroma drifted out.

"*Puchero*," he said.

"It smells wonderful. What is it?"

"It is a stew," Carlos explained. "Pork, rabbit, peas and vegetables. I think you will like it."

He dipped a spoon into the pot and held it out for her to taste.

"Oh yes," she said. "It tastes superb. You're a marvellous chef, Antonio."

"It is nothing. The ingredients are simple."

"Don't be so modest," Monica scolded. "You're a very good chef and you should take credit for it."

"Thank you," Antonio said. "I am most gratified."

He proceeded to ladle portions of stew onto their plates and then poured more wine into fresh glasses, red this time.

As she ate, Monica felt the band of her trousers strain against her waist. I should really slow down, she thought. But I'm enjoying this food so much. In fact, it's the first decent meal I've had since I came here. And if I don't eat, Antonio might take it as a sign of disapproval. She finished the food on her plate but declined a second helping when Carlos tried to tempt her.

The *puchero* was followed by a dessert of cake with a sauce of almonds and honey and then coffee. Antonio came and sat with them in the balmy night air. He brought a brandy bottle and insisted that they drink another toast.

"To Carlos and Monica!"

They laughed and drained their glasses and then Carlos proposed a toast to Antonio.

"Yes," Monica said. "To the best chef in Tenerife! You know, Antonio, I really want to thank you for a wonderful meal. And for opening specially for us, when you should have been enjoying your evening off."

"It was my pleasure. When I cook for my friends, I do not regard it as work."

It was after one when they left the restaurant. Monica was feeling tipsy from the brandies and the wine, but Carlos seemed to be perfectly sober. He negotiated the winding road down from the mountain with ease. The clock on the dashboard said 1.45 a.m. as he parked the car in the hotel garage.

"Thank you for a truly wonderful evening, Carlos."

"But, my dearest Monica, the night is not finished yet. You will have one more nightcap in my suite? Yes?"

Through the fog in her brain, Monica knew this was the moment of truth. Did she continue to keep him at bay or did she surrender? If she went to his suite, it would surely not stop at a nightcap.

"Yes," she said.

Carlos's face spread in a warm smile. He locked the car and led her through a back entrance to the hotel. A few seconds later, he was opening the door of his suite.

It was magnificent. The walls were painted white, the ceiling pale blue. Sunken lamps cast a subdued light. There was a black leather settee and rugs on the polished wooden floors. On the table in the lounge, a big vase of lilies filled the room with their scent.

Through the open door of the bedroom, Monica could see a king-size bed.

Carlos locked the door and turned to her. He took her in his arms and held her close.

"My dearest Monica. This is the moment I have waited for."

His lips closed on hers and she felt herself melt.

Chapter 31

Once Alex Piper realised that Bobby was gone and was not responding to his messages, his first reaction had been to feel hard-done-by. Why was she behaving like this? It was so over-the-top. After all, he hadn't said he wouldn't marry her. All he had asked for was a little time to think things over. He had said he wanted a *postponement* which was a perfectly natural request and certainly not a justification for the histrionic behaviour that Bobby was now indulging in.

He decided to do nothing for the next few days to give her time to cool down. Eventually, she would contact him from whatever bolthole she had fled to. But when nothing happened, he realised that perhaps things were more serious than he thought. So he set about trying to find her.

He started with his sister, Orla, who was one of Bobby's friends and was scheduled to be a bridesmaid at the wedding.

"Where is she?" he asked.

"I don't know."

"You must know. I've got to find her. She's not answering my messages."

"I'm not surprised," Orla said. "The way you treated that poor girl. I'd have done exactly the same thing myself."

"But all I asked for was a little time. You ever hear the phrase 'Marry in haste, repent at leisure'?"

"You behaved totally selfishly. The shame and embarrassment you caused her!"

"But that's why I need to find her. I want to apologise."

Orla hesitated. She'd got a text message that morning from Angie and knew exactly where they were.

"She's in the Canaries," Orla said. "I don't know any more than that."

"The Canary Islands?"

"That's right. You know, where people go on their holidays?"

With this flimsy information, Alex recruited Freddie Dunne and together they began ringing round the travel agents. They pretended to be relatives with an urgent personal message to deliver. After about a dozen calls, they hit lucky.

"We've got two young women with those names staying in Tenerife," the pleasant young woman on the telephone said.

"Can you tell me where exactly?" Alex asked using his best accent. "This message I have to deliver is of the utmost importance."

"Hotel Las Flores," the young woman replied. "Would you like me to give you the number?"

"If you wouldn't mind," Alex said, scrambling in his pocket for a pen.

He rang immediately and got confirmation that Bobby and Angie were indeed staying at the hotel but when he asked to be put through to their room, he ran into an obstacle. The receptionist put him on hold and came back to say that no one was answering. She asked if he would like to leave a message. Alex knew that leaving messages would be no earthly use. He had already sent her dozens of messages and she'd refused to answer a single one. He said he would ring back later and put the phone down.

Another plan was beginning to form in his mind. He would go out to Tenerife in person and confront her. That way he'd be able to convince her of the sincerity of his repentance and get her to give up her foolish behaviour. He started ringing the travel agents again looking for a flight to Tenerife.

This wasn't as easy as it sounded. Most of the agents dealt in holiday packages and they were all fully booked. It took him nearly three hours to find an agent who had a flight-only ticket to Tenerife leaving the following day. Alex booked it by credit card and went off with Freddie Dunne to have a drink.

"All this fuss over nothing," he said, genuinely perplexed at the way things had turned out. "You'd think I'd murdered one of her animals or something, the way she's behaving."

Freddie Dunne was vigorously nodding in agreement.

"Women," he said, disgustedly. "We'll never understand them."

Alex decided to get quietly drunk but before he did, he thought he would ring the number he'd been given once more. This time, he got Angie.

"Tell her I'm coming out tomorrow to speak to her. We have to get this thing sorted out once and for all."

Satisfied, he switched off the phone and ordered another pint.

The airport was packed and the flight was a nightmare. It was delayed for two hours, which taken together with the two hours he had been told to allow for check-in, meant he was sitting in the cramped departure lounge for over four hours. It also meant he wouldn't be landing in Tenerife till after seven thirty with nowhere to stay.

But Alex was in no mood to entertain doubts about the wisdom of his decision. He had to find Bobby and talk some sense into her. She had to be persuaded to give up this nonsense and come back to Dublin where they would sit down like two civilised people and reschedule this whole wedding business. It shouldn't be too difficult. All the big items like invitation lists and wedding presents had already been taken care of. All they had to do was fix a new date and send out fresh invitations. It would take a week at the most.

The plane touched down at seven forty-five and twenty minutes later Alex had cleared Customs and Immigration and was walking out into the torrid heat of the Tenerife evening. He looked about him cautiously. No armed guards around and no obvious signs of bubonic plague. It was all a bluff by Bobby, as he suspected. He struggled with his case to the taxi rank and asked a driver to take him immediately to Hotel Las Flores.

But here he ran into another problem. After looking at him nervously for several minutes and checking the register, the young lady at the reception desk announced that there was no one called Bobby Bannon staying at the hotel.

Alex felt his spirits sink. "But there must be. I have it from the travel agent. I rang here myself yesterday and confirmed it. And I actually *spoke* to her companion Angie Clarke. Try the register again."

The young woman gave him a strange look and turned the pages once more. Alex stood at the desk and felt the perspiration begin to stream down his face and soak his armpits. His shirt was already sticking to his back like cling-film. He realised that he must look odd with his red face and dishevelled appearance and the excited nature of his demands. So he tried to speak reasonably.

"It's very important that I find her," he said. "I'm her fiancé."

He held up his finger but this only seemed to make the woman more agitated. Now she looked positively afraid of him. He quickly withdrew his finger, realising that she probably thought he was making a rude gesture. How can I convince her, he thought?

"We're going to get married," he smiled and made a motion like rocking a baby to try to get the woman to understand. But it was no good. She kept turning pages while alternately watching him anxiously out of the corner of her eye. A thought struck him. "Were they here yesterday? Last night? They may have checked out today."

"No one here called Bannon," she said finally and closed the register with a loud snap. "Or Clarke. I cannot help you. You must try another hotel."

Alex picked up his suitcase disconsolately and set off into the humid night air. He must have got the name of the hotel wrong.

Half an hour later, he had tried six more hotels, but the response was always the same. No one called Bannon. No one called Clarke. Alex realised it was like looking for a needle in a haystack. He could spend the next week checking hotels in Tenerife and never find them. But they were here. He had spoken to Angie just last night.

There was something fishy going on back at Hotel Las Flores. The woman on Reception was covering up. Maybe he should go back and interrogate her once more.

And then he had a brainwave. At the last hotel, as he was

about to leave, he turned to the man at Reception and asked: "Is there an Irish bar near here?"

"Oh yes, *Senor*," the man confirmed. "The Lucky Leprechaun. It's a very good bar. All the Irish people go there."

"Muchas gracias," Alex said as he shook the man's hand and gave him a €20 note.

The pub was filling up when the taxi disgorged him outside at five minutes to nine. A poster on the door told him there was a Pub Quiz tonight followed by Irish ballads at ten o'clock. He pushed open the doors and strode in, hauling his case behind him.

And there she was, sitting at a table near the widow. And my God, she'd had an accident. Her leg was in plaster.

Alex dropped his suitcase on the floor and rushed over to her. She saw him coming and tried to get up but her plaster cast prevented her.

"What do you want?" she said, scowling at him.

"I want to talk. I want you to come home with me and reschedule the wedding."

"I don't want to talk. And I don't want to go home. And I definitely don't want to reschedule the wedding. I came here to get away from you."

"But we have to talk. Everything will be fine when you calm down."

"How many times do I have to tell you?" she said, her voice rising. "I don't want to talk. I don't want to see you. Now please leave me alone."

At that precise moment, the doors opened again and Edward McGinty walked in.

Chapter 32

Edward stood in the doorway and observed the scene before him. Who was this strange man and why was he arguing with Bobby? He caught a snatch of their conversation.

"I don't care if you've come the whole way out here to find me. Please leave me alone."

"But I love you," the man said. "That's what I've come to tell you. And I'm sorry for what I've done."

"It's too late."

"Just see a little sense and come home with me. We can talk this over like two rational people."

"I am not coming home. I'm staying where I am. Now please go away."

The man went to take her arm but Bobby angrily brushed him aside. "C'mon."

"No," Bobby insisted. "I'm staying here."

The man tried to grab her arm again and Bobby pushed him away.

Edward didn't wait. It was time to intervene. He made his way to the table and stood before the man.

"What's going on?" he demanded.

The man immediately stopped struggling with Bobby and turned to him. Up close, Edward could see the wild state he was in, his hair disordered and the sweat pouring down his face.

"Who the hell are you?" the man barked.

"My name is Edward McGinty and I'm a friend of Bobby's. Now, who are you and why are you assaulting her?"

"I'm her fiancé. We're supposed to be getting married."

Edward froze. Was it true? Was this why she had seemed uneasy when he talked to her yesterday? He turned to Bobby. "What have you got to say?"

She lowered her eyes. "It's true," she said.

Alex Piper looked triumphant. "There you are. Now I've come to take her back."

Edward felt his stomach wrench. "I'm sorry," he said. He turned to go.

"Wait," Bobby said.

Edward stopped.

"We *were* engaged. And then Alex postponed the wedding and I felt so humiliated that I just couldn't face anybody. So I came here to get away." She looked at Alex who was smiling now. "I was mad as hell at you for humiliating me. I could have murdered you. Now I can see it was just my wounded pride."

"I always said you'd get over it," Alex said.

"But things have changed."

Alex's face dropped.

"Now I realise what I felt for you wasn't love at all. It was just infatuation."

"Don't listen to her," Alex said to Edward. "She's upset! She doesn't know what she's saying."

"I know exactly what I'm saying. And I've decided I don't want to marry you. It's got nothing to do with the postponed wedding. And all to do with meeting Edward."

Alex grabbed her once more. "You're coming home with me. This very minute!"

"Let me go!" Bobby shouted. She looked at Edward. "Help me! Make him let me go."

Edward didn't hesitate. He quickly reached out and took hold of Alex's arm.

"You heard her," he said. "Let her go."

"Push off," Alex said. "This is none of your business."

"I'm making it my business. She's just said she wants you to leave. Now why don't you listen to her?"

Alex quickly shook off Edward's arm. He was taller than Edward and looked menacingly into his face. His angry eyes stared wild and fierce. "You're asking for trouble."

"Just leave," Edward said and pushed him in the chest.

"Will I hell! I didn't come the whole way out here to be ordered about by someone like you!"

He swung a blow at Edward. But Edward nimbly ducked and the blow just grazed his chin. He countered with a jab to Alex's gut and a quick punch to his kidneys. The bigger man let out a gasp and slumped in a heap on the floor.

The commotion had already attracted attention. All over the pub, people were standing up to see what was going on. Edward felt a hand on his shoulder and turned to find Tom Casey standing behind him.

"Having trouble?"

"He was interfering with Bobby," Edward said. "I had to restrain him."

"Well, we'd better get him out of here," Casey said. He summoned a waiter and together they dragged the prone body of Alex Piper to the front door and dumped him unceremoniously onto the street.

"It's the heat," Casey said, brushing his hands on his

trousers when he returned. "Some people just aren't able to handle it."

"Your poor chin," Bobby said, dabbing at Edward's face with a damp handkerchief once he had sat down and the scene had returned to normal. "Is it painful?"

"I've got worse playing football."

"That brute Piper, attacking you like that!"

"Well, I did push him first," Edward said.

"But you were defending me. To think I once considered marrying him. I shudder to think how lucky I am." She cuddled closer to Edward and gazed at him with wide admiring eyes. "But you made short work of him. And you know he plays rugby for St Margaret's? Oh Edward, I'm so proud of you!"

"Would you like to tell me what it was all about?" Edward said, taking a long drink of beer.

"I thought I loved him," Bobby said. "He can be very charming. But just as we were about to get married, he rang me from Barcelona and called the whole thing off."

"Are you sure you're over him?" Edward asked.

Bobby looked into his eyes. "Totally. I've found the man I want."

When it was time for the quiz Bobby and Edward formed a team with the people sitting next to them but got knocked out in the last round by a question about the capital city of Lithuania. Bobby thought it was Riga and the other people though it was Kiev but it turned out to be Vilnius.

After the quiz, the ballad group came on and in no time everyone was joining in the choruses and singing along. It was after two when they finally left the Lucky Leprechaun and made their way back to the hotel.

Bobby stopped outside her apartment door. Inside, Angie would be fast asleep. What a story she would have to tell her in the morning! But before she could think any more, Edward had taken her in his arms and was kissing her. She surrendered to the warm sensuous embrace.

At last, he released her.

"See you tomorrow?" he asked.

"You bet," Bobby said.

Chapter 33

After his recent euphoria, Charlie had suddenly been brought down to earth with a bump. His encounter with Penny had revealed that he was still in the state in which he had arrived in Tenerife, the state in which God had sent him into the world. He was still a virgin. His confidence had been built on sand.

He went straight back to the hotel and threw himself down on the bed. It was only nine o'clock but he hadn't the energy or the inclination to go out for dinner. He couldn't face anyone. He needed time to come to terms with the news. Eventually, he drifted off to sleep but it was the sleep of man who was distressed. He tossed and turned and was visited by horrible nightmares in which Penny pursued him, laughing and jeering, through the narrow, white-washed streets of Los Cristianos. When she finally caught up with him, her gloating face turned into that of Adrian Blake, babbling madly about the Famine and death and bloodshed. Only one person showed any pity for him and that was Trish, but when he reached out to touch her, she was no longer there.

He woke before dawn. The sheets were soaked in sweat and depression hung over him like a black cloud. Ringing in his ears was the last sentence that Penny had spoken to him: *Nothing happened between us.* He was right back where he had started. Now, he wished that he had never listened to Jimmy Brick and come to Tenerife in the first place. He wished he had stayed at home and got on with the business of running his shops instead of pretending to be a playboy. He wished he could catch the first plane out of here and high-tail it back to Dublin.

But even that option was closed. There was only a handful of regular flights from the island; the bulk of the traffic was charters. It could mean hanging about the airport, maybe for days, in the hope of a cancellation. Charlie realised with a sinking heart that he was trapped; he had no choice but to stay where he was for the remainder of the holiday and face the music.

Oh, the embarrassment of it all! Here he was at thirty-four, and there were boys half his age who had twice as much experience with women. And to think he had been parading around the resort for the past few days like some Casanova when the reality was he couldn't even manage to make love to a woman when it was offered to him on a plate. He felt like a reject, a failure. The thought made him cringe. He wished he could die. He wished there was some dark cave he could crawl into and just vanish.

He lay in bed till the first streaks of dawn began to dapple the window panes then slowly he dragged himself up and pulled back the curtains. Outside, it was still quite dark. The sky matched his mood. He plugged in the kettle and while he waited for it to boil, went into the bathroom and got washed and dressed. Then, he sat on the balcony with his coffee cup and watched the sun brighten the sky.

He saw the early fishing boats puffing out from the harbour, the gulls and guillemots wheeling and diving in their wake. He watched the sun grow stronger and reflect off the ocean in brilliant spangles of light. It was a scene to gladden any heart but it did nothing for Charlie except to confirm him in his misery.

He thought of his resolution only yesterday to find Trish and declare his love for her. How hollow that resolution seemed now. He would never find the courage to look at her again, never mind speak to her. All his confidence had evaporated like mist off a mountainside. He cursed the fact that he had gone into the Monaco Bar. Why hadn't he left well enough alone? If he hadn't gone in there, he wouldn't have met Penny and he would still be in blissful ignorance instead of having this dreadful depression wrapped around his neck like a dead albatross.

This brought a new thought into his head. Why don't I just pretend that I never had that conversation with Penny? After all, what difference does it make? I'm the same person I was before I met her. If I was confident then, why can't I be confident now? Charlie tried to reason with himself. The only person who knows what happened is Penny and she is too ashamed to say anything. Why can't I just carry on, as if nothing had happened? Nobody has to know.

But even as he tried to convince himself, he realised it was no use. He could feel the familiar sinking feeling gather in the pit of his stomach. *I know*, he thought and that's what makes the difference. I know the truth. I know I'm a virgin. And if I tried to pose as something else, I would just feel like a fraud and a cheat. It's impossible. I could never carry it off.

He sat on the balcony and watched the resort stir into life, people getting ready to enjoy another bright day. A sad melancholy took hold of him. Would he never pick up the courage to find a woman to love? Would he always be like this, timid and afraid? He thought of the future that lay ahead, a succession of empty days and lonely nights stretching away into old age. There would be no laughter, no woman's smile, no babble of children. My meals will be eaten alone, he thought; my bed will be cold, my only companion a cat or a dog; my only diversion, those rare occasions when an acquaintance takes pity and invites me over for dinner.

The prospect filled Charlie with a terrible sadness. He stood up and tried to steady himself. He had come here to Hotel Las Flores with such high hopes and now they had turned to ashes.

There was only one thing to do. For the remainder of the holiday, he would have to lie low. He would get up early and disappear. He would travel the island from top to bottom. He would return late at night just to sleep. He would do everything he could to avoid the two women he least wanted to meet – Penny and Trish. And he would start now.

But first, he had to eat. He would find a place to have breakfast, some quiet bar off the beaten track where no-one would recognise him, and then he would get a taxi to the bus station and take the first available coach.

He locked up the apartment and started along the corridor towards the lift. And with each step he took, he felt his heart grow heavier.

Chapter 34

If Charlie was depressed, Adrian was in tip-top form. His book was almost finished and he was delighted with the way it had finally turned out. And last night, he had made love to Trish. He couldn't remember the last time he'd done it, it was so long ago, but he had made a mental note to do it again and soon. The attention he had been paying to *The Green Gannet* had led him to neglect her, which was a dangerous thing to do with a good-looking woman like Trish. He had seen it happen before, some other bugger nipping in when the husband's back was turned and making off with the wife.

Not that Trish was the sort of woman who would fall for that palaver. She was the sensible type who knew what side her bread was buttered on. And being married to a man who would shortly be rich and famous was not a prize she would give up lightly. Trish would stay loyal, no doubt about it. She would enjoy the razzmatazz that would shortly accompany his triumph when *Gannet* took the world by storm: the travel, the publicity, the best hotels, the fine restaurants. And of course the money! Adrian had absolutely no doubts. The book was going to make him rich. But first, he had some final details to take care of.

He strode to the edge of the balcony, gripped the rail firmly with both hands and in quick succession performed a dozen perfectly executed press-ups. Then he threw out his chest and filled his lungs with air. It smelt fresh and sweet, a slight saltiness mingled with the scent of bougainvillea. Amazing that he hadn't noticed it before. But then he had been too damned busy with his novel to notice many things: how alive everything seemed, how the birds sang in the branches of the mimosa tree outside the apartment window, how the mist clung to the tops of the mountains across the bay.

It was just after breakfast. Earlier, Adrian had decided to start the morning with a brisk walk down to the beach and a vigorous swim in the sea. He hadn't been in the sea since he arrived and he found it bracing and the exercise stimulating. On his way back, he called into the local shop to pick up some provisions. At the checkout desk, there was a rack of newspapers. He realised he hadn't read a paper in almost a week. He had been so immersed in his novel that he hadn't even listened to the radio. Adrian added the *Daily Telegraph* to the items in his basket and made his way back to the hotel.

When he returned, Trish was already cooking breakfast and there was an enticing smell of ham and eggs wafting through the apartment. That was another thing he had neglected – food. But not any more. It was one thing to starve in a garret when you were a struggling writer but now that he was on the verge of stardom, Adrian was determined to eat and drink his fill. He had made a good start last night with that meal with Trish and planned to continue. He needed nourishment for the brain cells, if for nothing else.

Trish had set the breakfast table on the balcony and all the cups and saucers were neatly laid out and glasses of freshly squeezed orange juice waiting. He gave her a gentle peck on the cheek. He would have to make some gesture to her when the novel was published, maybe include her in the list of acknowledgments. It was the least he could do, even if she had been more of a hindrance than a help, if the truth be told, constantly interrupting him when he was wrestling with some knotty creative problem. Still, she had meant well.

"Sleep all right?" he inquired as sat down at the table and polished off the first glass of orange juice that came to hand.

"Perfectly," Trish replied. "And you did too. I woke at seven and you were out to the world. I'm really glad, Adrian. You haven't been sleeping at all well recently."

He gave her a tolerant smile. "But I had weighty matters on my mind." He wondered how much sleep Shakespeare got when he was writing *Hamlet*.

"Anyway," Trish continued as she watched him tear into the ham and eggs, "I'm delighted. And I'm also pleased to see you've got your appetite back. I was really beginning to get worried about you."

Adrian laughed. "You married an artist, my dear. Not an accounts clerk. Artists lead disordered lives. It's the nature of the beast."

"Nevertheless, you get so enthusiastic that sometimes you get carried away. You don't want to burn yourself out, now, do you?"

Adrian gave a guffaw and filled his cup with coffee. "No danger of that. I already have my next novel planned. This one will be a futuristic allegory with touches of magic realism. It will be set a hundred years from now and will involve a poor boy growing up in a Dublin tenement. I see it as a cross between *1984* and *Oliver Twist*."

Trish opened her mouth to reply but no words came out.

A gentle breeze cooled Adrian's face. A blissful feeling stole over him. This was as near to perfection as it could get. Down at the pool, the first of the sunbathers were laying claim to the deckchairs and sunbeds. The sound of a radio drifted from an open window. He finished eating, stuck his sunglasses on the end of his nose and stretched his long legs. Trish got up and began to clear away the breakfast things. "I think I'll go for a stroll. Before it gets too hot. Would you care to join me?"

But Adrian shook his head. "I've already had my exercise while you were still taking your beauty sleep. I think I'll just sit here and enjoy the sunshine before I start the final revision. I'm almost there, Trish. At long last, the end is in sight."

"What will we do about lunch?"

He waved his hand dismissively. "I'll think of something. Don't worry your pretty little head. I'll take care of it."

"Suit yourself," Trish said and put the last of the dishes in the sink to soak.

He heard her potter about the kitchen and then the sound of the apartment door closing. Adrian shook his head. *Where would she be without me? Women really are such simple creatures. But then, they don't have to deal with the big traumas of life. All they need is a strong man to make the choices for them.*

But it was no use complaining. Trish had her qualities. In her confused way, she had even tried to help him with the novel. She had roped in that idiot bookseller person, Charlie Whatsisface, to read the manuscript. The memory brought a smile to Adrian's lips. *He asked me if I was writing a thriller! He laughed out loud. A thriller! Me! Adrian Blake! There was no doubt about it. Charlie was a rank amateur.*

And Trish had been taken in by him. What a simple soul she was.

Of course, he had seen through this Charlie fellow right away. A couple of pointed questions to sound out his knowledge and then a few well-aimed sallies and he had demolished Mr Charlie Dobbins and left him gasping like a hooked mackerel. And what had Mr Dobbins done? He hadn't even tried to defend himself. Instead, he had run away without a fight. Adrian felt proud of the way he had routed him. It reminded him of his days in the debating hall. No question about it. His old weapons of sarcasm and wit hadn't deserted him after all these years.

He poured the last of the coffee from the percolator and shook open the newspaper he had bought earlier. He would have a quick perusal of the news before settling down to work. The lead story concerned the economy. *INTEREST RATES SET TO FALL*. Should reduce our mortgage, Adrian thought. A political scandal in Italy. Nothing new in that. Overeating likely to cause blood pressure. Tell me something I don't know. He turned the page and his attention was immediately drawn to a photograph in the top right-hand corner.

A face smiled out at him. It was a face that Adrian recognised instantly; a thin face with neatly groomed hair above a knotted cravat, posing artfully for the photographer. He knew who it was before he read the caption. Sheldon O'Neill, it said. But it was the headline that caused Adrian's heart to skip a beat. It was splashed in bold type across four columns.

US WRITER SIGNS $5 MILLION DEAL FOR BOOK ABOUT THE IRISH FAMINE.

Adrian's eye quickly travelled to the report underneath and with every line he read, he felt his life begin to fall apart.

Chapter 35

For her morning walk, Trish decided to head down to the sea. She strolled aimlessly along the promenade, past the little cafés where the smell of freshly-baked bread came wafting out on the cool morning air and down the steps to the beach. By the sea wall, the roses and clematis were in bloom, their bright flowers opening to the warming sun. At the edge of the sand, the sea stretched like a plate of glass as far as the eye could see. The sky was a vast expanse of blue, empty of clouds. The scene was so peaceful and still. She should have been deliriously happy. But she was not.

She was pregnant. At thirty-seven, when she was beginning to doubt if she would ever have a child, she had finally conceived. True, the baby was not her husband's but, here too, Trish had been successful with her plan. The purpose of this holiday had been to lure him into bed and last night she had achieved her objective. In a few weeks' time, when she announced her pregnancy, he would be none the wiser. She had felt no guilt about deceiving him in this way. In her mind, it was all for the best. He would accept the child as his own and everything would be fine. But in her heart, Trish knew this wasn't true. For the problem had moved on. It was no longer the baby. The problem now was Adrian himself.

She wondered when exactly her marriage had started to go wrong. Her thoughts travelled back to the first time they met. Surely she had loved Adrian then, in those days when they were both young and the world had seemed such a simple, uncomplicated place? She was a first year Arts student and he was auditor of the college Debating Society. It was November and the debating hall was packed with eager students wrapped up in their scarves and anoraks against the evening chill. They were debating something to do with apartheid in South Africa and Adrian had given a brilliant performance, demolishing his opponents with the clarity of his logic and the sharpness of his wit.

Trish remembered watching him from the front row. It was like a piece of theatre. Adrian was so handsome and in control. He wore his hair long in those days and the dark locks tumbling round his face made him look like Che Guevara in the poster she had pinned to her wall. The other speakers had been in awe of him, tip-toeing around the subject for fear of bringing the weight of his devastating argument crashing about their ears. Afterwards, there was a sherry reception and in the crowd, she found herself standing next to him.

"You were marvellous," she said, shyly. "I thought your performance was brilliant."

Adrian smiled at her compliment but his reply was contemptuous. "I had no competition. It's easy to appear good when your opponents are so poor."

Even then, at that early stage, had she not noticed a hint of the arrogance that was later to turn him into a monster?

They fell into conversation and he asked to meet her again. A few nights later, he took her to a poetry reading in a smoky basement of a house off Baggot Street. It was packed with intense young people like themselves. Later, they went to a pub and drank beer and talked about Dylan Thomas.

They started to go out together. Trish had never had a boyfriend. She was happy to be seen in Adrian's company. It was as if some of his radiance reflected onto her. But there was never any doubt who was the guiding spirit. From the beginning, Adrian made all the decisions. She never argued. She never even considered that he might be wrong. It was as if Adrian had succeeded in totally eliminating her personality and subsuming it into his own. When, eventually, he suggested they get married, there was only one response she could make. Trish was delighted to agree.

Her parents paid for the wedding but it wasn't the fairy-tale affair she might have dreamed of when she was younger. It was held in a shabby hotel with thirty guests drawn equally from both their families. They ate roast beef and sherry trifle, drank bottles of Piat D'Or and at five the young couple left in a taxi to catch a plane to Majorca. They spent ten wonderful days cycling the hills and drinking in little out-of-the-way bars and then it was back to Dublin to begin their married life.

Those early days were very happy. They had both graduated and were earning their first incomes, Trish as a trainee estate agent with Stokes and Stokes Auctioneers and Valuers and Adrian as an English teacher at St Ignatius's Comprehensive College. After a year living in a rented flat in Ranelagh, they were able to put down a deposit on a three-bed semi-detached house in Sandymount. They fell in with a crowd from college, giving dinner parties in each other's homes. Saturday nights would find Adrian, wineglass in hand, monopolising the conversation at the dinner table just as he did in the old days in the debating hall.

Was it round about this time that Trish began to have her first doubts? While Adrian dominated the male circle in the dining-room, she would gather with the other young wives in the kitchen. They would compare notes. Trish would hear tales of wild love-making, of exciting positions and erotic games. Were they making it up? Did they read about it in books? She kept quiet and listened. Her own lovemaking with Adrian was nothing like this. He was her first and only lover, so she had nothing to measure him against. She had only the wild-eyed stories from the tipsy wives draining the last of the wine bottles at the kitchen sink.

Nevertheless, she began to look at her husband with new eyes. Wasn't it true that he had become somewhat dowdy? He wore corduroy pants so old they had been rubbed smooth at the knees and now gleamed in the light. He wore tweed jackets and check shirts. And he never left them off, so that when styles moved on, Adrian began to look like a sailor marooned on a desert island.

He grew careless about his personal appearance. He still allowed his hair to grow long; but where once it had been fashionable, now it just looked untidy. He got egg-stains on his tie and dandruff on his collar. Sometimes, he forgot to shave and his grizzled face reminded her of the down-and-out men she saw drinking cheap wine around the back of the supermarket.

She made gentle suggestions but Adrian, who had never taken advice from anyone, simply ignored her. She even bought him new clothes from time to time as presents but they would be put away in the wardrobe and rarely worn. She gave up trying to improve him and instead began to find excuses for not inviting him to company functions where the guests would invariably turn up impeccably dressed.

This was to become another source of discontent. For as Trish's career prospered and she grew in confidence and experience and earned promotion, Adrian remained stuck in his teaching job at St Ignatius's. His applications for junior lecturing positions at universities and colleges ended in failure. He rarely got beyond a first interview. Eventually, even these small achievements dried up and his letters of application were politely declined. In a few years, Trish was earning twice as much as her husband.

The experience made him bitter. He grew to hate his job. He despised the students and the other teachers. He despised the rigid routine. He despised the very school building. He came to regard his failure to progress as a massive injustice perpetrated on him by an ignorant world. And he grew jealous of Trish. He envied her lunches with clients in fancy restaurants, the occasional travel, the flexible hours she worked, the salary she earned. His envy turned to carping contempt. He began to make disparaging remarks, calling her a huckster and a philistine grubbing in the murky world of commerce.

But she continued to love him. Or so she thought. For as time went by, Trish found herself thinking about the handsome young men she would meet at work, young men in smart suits and fresh shirts with clean-cut features and nice-smelling aftershave. In her mind, she would picture them naked and wonder what they would be like in bed. For a long time it remained just fantasy. But then the day came when she decided it was time to find out.

She chose the night of the office Christmas party. The firm had just completed a successful year and decided to celebrate in a smart restaurant in Ballsbridge. There was a lot of drinking; cocktails to start and then wine during the meal. But Trish wasn't drunk. She could never say afterwards that she didn't know exactly what she was doing.

Conor Dowling was the young man she had selected as her partner in adultery. He was twenty-six, confident verging on cocky, a recent recruit who was anxious to prove he was the man who could close the most sales, for the highest prices in the fastest time. He stood over six feet tall and trained twice a week with Monkstown Harriers. He was loud and brash, a young man in a hurry. And he was putty in Trish's hands.

She waited till the party was almost over before she made her move. There were only a handful of people left, the bill had been paid and some of the younger staff were talking about going on to a club in Temple Bar. But Trish had other ideas for Conor Dowling. She sat down beside him and twisted her fingers through his tie till their faces were almost touching.

"You're a gentleman," she whispered. "Be a darling and organise a cab for me. I'm too bushed to go dancing." She gave him her most seductive smile. "I think it's time for bed."

She saw his alcohol-befuddled brain struggle with this new situation and then a light come into his eyes.

"Certainly, Trish. Where you wanna go?"

"Sandymount."

He marched unsteadily to the desk and spoke to the head waiter. A few minutes later, he was back. "On its way. I spoke to them personally." He leaned closer. "Do you mind if we share? I think I'll turn in myself."

"Not at all. Where do you live?"

"Bath Avenue."

Trish knew this already. It was just a couple of streets away from her own address. It was one of the reasons she had settled on Conor.

The taxi came and they got in together. She snuggled close to him so that he could catch the scent of her perfume. Their knees touched and her hand dropped casually onto his thigh. She felt his breath hot on her cheek.

After that, it was child's play. When the taxi arrived at his apartment, he invited her in for coffee. She 'reluctantly' accepted. They climbed the stairs and she waited while he fumbled with the key. Once inside, all pretence of coffee was forgotten. They fell into each other's arms, their hands frantically exploring each other, their mouths wet with kisses. Trish kicked off her shoes and unbuckled his belt. She slipped out of her dress and in a moment, they were both naked on the bed.

What could she say about the sex? It was tender. It was unhurried. It was intense. Even though he was tipsy, Conor proved to be an experienced lover so that when the moment came, she found herself swept away with passionate abandon. She wrapped her legs tight around his waist and gave a little cry of pleasure.

It was a revelation to Trish that lovemaking could be like this. It was completely different to anything she had experienced with Adrian. Conor Dowling had displayed an expertise, a skill and a passion she had never met in her husband.

So this was what she had been missing. The stories she had heard in the kitchen had been true. Sex could be wildly pleasurable. And she knew that Conor had also enjoyed the encounter, for when she met him unexpectedly in the lift a few days later, he shyly asked her if she would like to go for a drink some evening after work. She made an excuse. She wasn't ready yet for a full-blown affair. She was still loyal to Adrian. She still hoped that things would get better. But she stored the memory away and from time to time she brought it out to remind herself that this was what was waiting for her should she ever make the break.

But Adrian didn't improve. In fact, he just got worse. He became confirmed in his bitterness. His suspicion about the world became an obsession. Still Trish hung on. She pinned her faith on a child. If she had a baby, things would change. Adrian would mellow. A baby would bring them closer together. It would save her marriage. It was the conventional wisdom. But even here, Adrian failed. As the months turned into years, no baby came. And then Adrian decided to become a writer.

For a while, things did improve. Adrian was swept along with a new energy and enthusiasm. The adulation he received at the writers' group nourished his ego. He grew determined to make it as a successful novelist. It would be his passport out of the teaching job he had come to hate. It would be his revenge on all those people who had failed to recognise his talent or accord him the respect he believed he deserved.

He devoted all his spare time to his novel. He worked long and hard. He would come home from the writers' group smiling and refreshed from the kind words of praise he had received. Trish was delighted. She wanted her husband to succeed. She wanted him to be happy. Despite some reservations, she too became convinced that this project would unlock the door to a new life for both of them.

Gradually, the book began to take over his life. He neglected to eat or sleep properly. From early in the morning, Trish would hear him tap, tap, tapping on his word processor. He would continue late into the night. He gave her pages to read and she was shocked to find the writing turgid and dull, the characters limp, the dialogue wooden, the plot as predictable as an AA roadmap. Adrian, who could talk up a storm about the giants of English literature, who could discourse for hours about Dickens and Hardy and Jane Austen, appeared to have learnt none of their skills in communicating with readers.

But she kept these doubts to herself. Maybe she was wrong. Literary trends were always changing. What struck her as trite might well turn out to be the height of fashion. Maybe Adrian's friends in the writers' group were right and this book was going to be a masterpiece.

Eventually it was finished and sent out to publishers and agents. But further setbacks lay in store as the slow, corrosive process of rejection set in. The large jiffy bags would come back with boring regularity, the short typed rejection slip pinned to the top. His obsession turned into paranoia. There was a conspiracy to do him down. His enemies were everywhere and they were out to get him. His talent wasn't recognised. But he took comfort in the experience of the great writers who had to struggle against similar adversity.

For Trish, this period was particularly difficult. Adrian became increasingly volatile. For a lot of the time, he ignored her completely except for those rare occasions when he wanted clothes washed or food prepared. He moved out of the marital bedroom and installed a camp bed in his study so that he could work on his book when inspiration struck, which now meant all hours of the day and night.

She began to have brief encounters with men. It happened from boredom and sexual frustration. Trish convinced herself that these liaisons were good for her morale and her feeling of self-worth. Then she had her affair with Henry Doran and everything changed. She found herself pregnant with the child she had long desired. And last night, she had seduced Adrian into her bed for the first time in months and thereby secured her alibi.

She should have been happy but she had a terrible

feeling that it was all too late. The man she married had turned into a demon. Could she continue to live with someone whose moods swung as regularly as a pendulum? Who was so volatile and unpredictable that she never knew how he was going to react? She thought of this morning and the condescending manner in which he had addressed her, as if she was just a stupid woman who could do nothing for herself. And that was Adrian in one of his *good* moods.

Maybe the time had finally come to leave him? She would tell him the truth about the baby. She would find a small flat somewhere. It wouldn't be easy but somehow she would manage. And she would be free. She would be able to start again and build a new life for herself and her child.

Suddenly, Trish was startled by the dangerous direction her thoughts were taking. She found a bench and sat down while she struggled to take stock of the situation. Hadn't she married Adrian for better or worse? She felt a pang of guilt. If she left him now, she would be letting him down just when he was most vulnerable and needed her support. Didn't fifteen years of marriage count for something? And maybe if his book was successful, he would change. People did change. It happened all the time. Why not Adrian? Shouldn't she give him one more chance?

She felt torn, not knowing which way to turn. In desperation, she searched in her pocket and found a coin. Heads, I stay with Adrian, she decided. Tails, I leave him. She flipped the coin and watched it flash in the light of the sun before it fell clattering to the ground. She quickly bent to look.

It had come up heads.

Chapter 36

Monica came awake and sat up in the strange bed. What time was it? Immediately she glanced at her watch. It was twenty past ten. How had she slept so long? The sun was already flooding through the curtains of the room and beside her in the massive bed lay the still-slumbering figure of Carlos.

She sighed in admiration as she looked once more at this fine display of manhood: the tightly-muscled body, the smooth skin, the naked chest with its mat of thick black hair curling like a snake towards his stomach. And it was hers, all hers. Monica closed her eyes and the events of last night came flooding back. It had been a very long time since she could remember a night like it.

After he had closed the door, he had taken her in his arms and kissed her. Any lingering resolution she had left just crumbled away. She hungrily kissed him back as she felt his hot mouth pressing greedily against her own. Next moment, without taking his mouth from hers, he began fumbling with the buttons of her blouse. He quickly pushed it down towards her waist. Next came her bra. With an expert twist, he had undone the hooks and stripped the garment away. Her breasts stood exposed in the pale light.

She didn't want him to stop. She willed him to go on as his fingers found her waistband. He undid the zip and her trousers fell in a crumpled heap to the floor. She kicked them free and stood naked except for her sheer black panties. Carlos pulled her closer till she felt him pressing hard against her. All caution was gone now. She drew his head down and sighed as a wave of pleasure engulfed her.

Carlos bent and gathered her up in his arms and carried her into the bedroom. He laid her gently on the bed. Then, he discarded his shirt, trousers and underwear till he too was naked. He held her shoulders and gazed into her eyes.

"My dearest Monica," he said and kissed her once more and she heard herself moan with pleasure.

It was the best sex Monica had ever experienced, far better than anything she had known with Woody or any other lover. Carlos was strong as a horse, yet gentle and considerate. He quickly adjusted to her rhythm, pushing the pleasure higher and higher, postponing the moment of climax till it could be put off no longer. When at last it was over they lay in the twisted sheets, their bodies bathed in sweat. Carlos took her in his arms and planted a soft kiss on her forehead.

"That was wonderful," he sighed.

He woke her shortly after four. She was lying with her back to him and he was behind. She was aware of the tingling pleasure beginning again and gradually building in intensity. His hands were circling her breasts, his mouth hot against her ear. Monica bit the pillow as the pleasure grew and swelled till it exploded in a long ecstasy of joy. He laid his head against hers and she could hear his heart pumping like a piston inside his breast. Exhausted, they both fell once more into a deep sleep.

Now, she examined the body of her sleeping lover. It was the body of an athlete. Although Carlos was heavily built, there was no superfluous flesh. There wasn't an ounce of extra weight or an inch of additional fat. She looked at the long curling lashes on his dark eyelids, the broad manly face, the little dimple on his chin that she hadn't noticed before, the thick hair that twisted from his chest to his neck. He looks like a young god, Monica thought. And such a lover! I have never met any man before who could make love like he does. And he has chosen me!

She marvelled at how suddenly her luck had turned. A few short days ago, she had arrived at Hotel Las Flores practically penniless after her no-good husband had blown away his money and then died. She knew she was long past the first flush of youth. She knew she was not as attractive as she once was. Every day, there were younger women coming along to compete for the limited number of eligible men. And yet despite these drawbacks, she had landed a magnificent prize, sole heir to a hotel empire, a handsome, vivacious stud with the impeccable manners of a gentleman. And totally devoted to her!

He stirred and opened one eye. Then he smiled and she felt her heart soar with happiness. He reached for her, pulled her down and planted a warm kiss on her mouth. She thought he was going to make love to her again. She hoped he would. Despite the night of passion, Monica was hungry for more.

But instead, Carlos checked the time and quickly threw back the sheets. "My God, it is late!" He stepped out of bed, then asked, "How do you feel?"

"Marvellous."

"Me too. It was a wonderful night, Monica. A night I will never forget. But now, I must get ready for work. We have more guests arriving at twelve o'clock. Would you like me to order some breakfast?"

"Yes," she said. "That would be nice."

He lifted the phone and she heard him speaking in Spanish.

"Please use the bathroom first," he then said. "I can wait till you are ready."

Monica would have preferred to lie on in bed. Now that she had captured him, she wanted to spend more time with this wonderful creature. Reluctantly, she climbed out of bed, gathered her clothes and handbag, and made her way to the bathroom. She closed the door and ran the shower. I am on holiday, she reminded herself, but he has the hotel to manage. I can't expect him to lavish all his time on me.

She stood under the warm shower and gently soaped her body. Only a few short hours ago, it was his hands caressing this skin, his fingers running along these thighs. Monica shuddered at the memory. But it was just the beginning. She would have to learn to be patient. Unless she was gravely mistaken, she would have many more nights of passion with the marvellous Carlos.

She dressed and rapidly attended to her make-up. When she returned, Carlos had put on a dressing-gown and opened the windows onto the balcony. He had set out a little table with a white tablecloth, cups and plates, a basket of warm croissants, little pots of marmalade and a jug of strong black coffee.

"Come and join me," he said and prepared a chair for her.

She sat across the table from him. His hair was tossed and he needed to shave. But to Monica he was still the same wonderful man she had dined with last evening, who had entertained her, who had been so kind to her and who had spent the night making passionate love to her.

The balcony had a magnificent view over the harbour. Monica could see the masts of the boats and hear the cries of the wheeling birds. She looked at the sea, still as glass, the blue sky, the morning sun dancing on the water. It looked so peaceful. Wouldn't it be wonderful, she thought, to wake each morning to such a view; to sit here on this balcony and have breakfast with this gorgeous creature? If I could achieve that, she thought, I would want nothing more in my life. I would die happy.

She poured a cup of steaming coffee and smeared marmalade on a croissant.

"Did you sleep well?" Carlos asked. "Was the bed comfortable?" There was a playful smile in his eyes.

"The bed was very comfortable but something kept interfering with me."

"Oh dear! That must have been the fairies. Did you know we have fairies here in Spain? Just like in Ireland?"

"Some fairy," Monica laughed. "More like a hobgoblin if you ask me."

"I'll have it seen to at once. We can't have our guests disturbed like that."

"Who said anything about being disturbed?"

"So you enjoyed this distraction?"

"Of course. I loved it!"

"Well then, since you are our guest and you are happy, then I am happy. But Monica, I must ask you not to mention this. If the other lady guests get to hear about the hobgoblin, they might wish him to visit them too. And I might not be able to oblige."

Monica laughed. "No one will know. It will remain our secret."

He reached across the table and took her hand and gently raised it to his lips. "You know what I am thinking, Monica? I am thinking how happy I am to have found you and how sad I will be when you return to Ireland."

"I can always come back again," Monica said quickly. "It's not as if I lived in Australia. It's only four hours by plane. And we can talk on the phone."

"But it's not the same as having you with me."

He sipped his coffee and stared out over the courtyard. A brooding, unsettled look had come into his eyes.

"What's the problem, Carlos? You look unhappy."

He shook his head. "It is nothing."

"No. I can see it in your face."

He tossed his napkin on the table. "You want to know the truth, Monica? Sometimes, I get fed up with my life. It is so restrictive. Always the same routine, always the same problems to resolve. When I go down to my office this morning, there will be a list of things to do. My father will ring from Madrid with demands. There will be complaints from guests. Someone will not turn up for work and I will have to get another person to cover. It is always the same and it never stops."

"But you are making such a success of it. Everyone speaks so highly of you. Everyone comments on how well you manage the hotel."

He lowered his eyes and stared into his coffee cup. "My father doesn't think so."

"Oh Carlos, I'm sure he does."

"No. He criticises me all the time."

"But that is probably just his way of testing you. He probably comes down harder with you because you are his son."

"He is always comparing Hotel Las Flores with the Gran

Hotel del Rey. He thinks we do not get the proper type of guest, the type of person who will spend more money. He is envious because they have five stars and we have only three."

Monica was anxious now. She wanted to soothe him. So far, Carlos had succeeded in concealing the demands his job placed on him. He was always cheerful but now she realised the pressure he must work under.

"But I told you there is no comparison. The Gran Hotel has more facilities. But it doesn't make it a better hotel."

Carlos shrugged. "They get the stars. And the stars mean they can charge higher prices. And that means larger profits. That is how my father looks at it. He is a businessman. He looks at the bottom line."

"I'll write to your father," Monica said sternly. "I'll tell him I have stayed in both hotels. I'll tell him my experience. Why, I'll even get up a petition of guests to testify how well you run the Hotel Las Flores!"

Carlos looked aghast. "You must do nothing of the kind. My father would immediately suspect that I have been talking to you."

"But it's so unfair!"

"Yes, it's unfair. But that is life." He toyed with his coffee cup and stared out over the rooftops of the town. "Monica. Can I confide in you?"

"Certainly."

"I am going to tell you something that no-one else knows. I am trusting you not to mention this to another living person."

"What?" Monica said, eagerly.

"I am thinking of leaving Hotel Las Flores."

Monica's jaw dropped. This was a bombshell. She had no idea he was so unhappy.

"But you can't do that," she said quickly. "Your father would be outraged."

"Listen to me. I have discovered a small hotel in Los Abrigos. Only fifty bedrooms and it is right on the edge of the ocean. Los Abrigos is a coming resort. In a few years' time, it will be discovered and everyone will want to go there. I can buy this hotel at a bargain price if I move now."

"You would still have all the same difficulties you have here."

"But don't you see? I would be my own boss, no need to be always jumping to my father's tune. However, there is one problem."

"Tell me," Monica said.

"You remember last night when I asked if you would be interested in staying in Tenerife if there was a way to do it? And you said it would depend."

"Yes," Monica said, breathless. Was he going to propose right now? And how should she respond? Should she accept straight off or ask for time to think about it?

"I have a proposal to put to you."

Monica tried to still the thumping in her breast. Keep calm, she told herself. Don't react. For God's sake, don't show him how keen you are.

"You told me that back in Dublin you work at organising parties?"

"That's right," Monica said.

"Sometimes as many as two hundred guests?"

"Yes."

"How would you like to be my partner in this new hotel? You could help me to run it. You could organise the dining facilities and the entertainment."

Monica felt vaguely disappointed. This wasn't quite what she was expecting. But it sounded fantastic, nevertheless.

Partner? Maybe he saw marriage a little bit further down the road once the venture was established. What should she do? What should she say?

"That's a very attractive proposal, Carlos. I would certainly be interested. But I would need some time to get organised."

His face broke in a wide smile. "I knew it. I knew you would agree. Oh, Monica, you have made me so happy!" He stood up and took her in his arms and kissed her. "We will make a perfect partnership. We will work so well together. And once my father sees the success I make of the new hotel, he will be totally convinced."

Monica could see the possibilities: organising the dining facilities and the entertainment, drawing up menus, directing staff. It would be just like organising her parties before Woody died. She could do it with her eyes closed.

Carlos was talking on in an excited voice. "We can start immediately. I will speak to the bank this morning. I can buy the hotel with all the fittings and furnishings for €600,000. It is an absolute bargain. It is easily worth twice as much. Would you like to come with me this afternoon to see it?"

"I'd love to," Monica said.

"I will make the arrangements. I will ring my lawyer and tell him to draw up the contracts. How soon can you let me have your share of the purchase?"

"My share of the purchase?" Monica echoed.

"Yes, €300,000."

Monica blinked. Was she hearing things? "€300,000?"

"Yes. It is exactly half. We will own the hotel between us. It will be perfectly legal. You do trust me, don't you?"

Her head began to swim. This was ridiculous. He was asking for €300,000 when all she had in the world was €6,435. It was a ghastly misunderstanding. When he said partner, Carlos had evidently meant business partner.

"It's not that I don't trust you," she began.

"Well then, what is the difficulty?"

"I can't do it," Monica stammered.

"Why not? When you see the place, you will fall in love with it."

Monica took a deep breath. "Because I don't have that sort of money."

Carlos was staring across the table at her. "But I thought you said your husband was a rich investor?"

"So he was."

"And when he died . . .?"

"He left me penniless. He had spent all the money. He left me nothing but debts. The banks seized my house and my car. They sold my furniture. The truth is, I have barely enough to live on."

She looked at him. The excitement had drained from his face.

"What?"

"I have no money," Monica said.

In his face, there was now a dark anger. "You have deceived me," he said, coldly.

"Oh, no!"

"Yes! You led me to believe you were a wealthy widow. And all along you had no money!"

"That's not true. I never mentioned money."

"You are a deceptive, scheming woman!"

Monica couldn't believe she was hearing this. She couldn't believe the transformation that had suddenly come over him. "No, Carlos. I am still prepared to help you run the hotel. I would even work for nothing."

"Don't be ridiculous," he laughed.

"Why not?"

"I could never work with you!"

"Please, Carlos," she pleaded. "This is all a mistake."

He stood up. His face was black as thunder. "I think you should go now. I have wasted enough time with you. I have to get ready for work."

He strode past her and she heard the bathroom door closing with a heavy thud. Monica felt the tears well in her eyes. In a matter of minutes, her dreams had crumbled into dust.

She grabbed her handbag and ran out of the apartment, as fast as her legs could carry her.

Chapter 37

Adrian's hands trembled as he anxiously devoured the newspaper report.

Irish-American writer, Mr Sheldon O'Neill, has concluded what insiders say is the biggest financial deal in publishing history. Mr O'Neill, a native of Boston, Massachusetts, has signed a contract which guarantees him a total of $5 million for the rights to his blockbuster novel, The Hungry Years. *Informed sources say that film rights for the book, which are under negotiation, could net the wealthy author a further $5 million.*

Mr O'Neill's new novel is the torrid story of the Irish Famine told by a 160-year-old man who is discovered living in a bog in the wilds of Connemara. The author says he got the inspiration for the book during a visit to Ireland last year.

Adrian felt the blood drain from his face. He saw the words blur and swim before his eyes as the paper slipped from his grasp and fluttered to the ground. For a few moments, he sat in a daze, as if someone had hit him over the head with a hammer. Then he leapt to his feet.

"God damn him! The bastard has robbed my book!"

His first impulse was to kick his foot through the plate glass of the balcony window, but some instinct warned him that such action would be quickly followed by an angry demand to leave the hotel and a bill for damages. Instead he smashed his fist into the hard brickwork of the wall.

He regretted it at once. Pain went shooting up his arm as if his hand had been caught in a mangle. Small beads of blood began to trickle from his bruised knuckles. He sank back into his chair and a strangulated moan, like that of a dying sheep, issued from his lips.

It was like all his worst nightmares rolled into one. It was like he had wakened up in hell. He picked up the paper and read the report again to make sure there was no mistake. But there it was in black and white. Sheldon O'Neill had stolen his book and sold it for five million dollars, the biggest deal in publishing history. Adrian felt like weeping.

He had sent the cur an outline of *The Green Gannet* for his comments and O'Neill had replied with encouragement. And what was the advice he had given? Adrian could remember it vividly. *Take it slowly. No need to rush. Take your time.* It was all so obvious now. Of course Sheldon O'Neill wanted him to take it slowly. Of course he didn't want him to rush. It was so that the bastard would have plenty of time to copy his idea and produce his own book. And now he had done it and sold it for five million dollars.

Adrian felt his shock give way to anger. He thought of that dinner with O'Neill in Guilbaud's restaurant when he had boasted of his literary conquests. Now he wished he had shoved the lobster down his throat, claws and all. Now he wished he had strangled him with the wild salmon. He had been too trusting, too naïve. It had always been his principal fault. Everybody knew that Adrian was the most trusting man who ever walked, the sort of man who would take off his shirt and give it to a beggar in the street. But he had never dreamed in a million years that the fast-talking shyster, O'Neill, was going to abuse that trust and steal his novel from him.

Was there anything he could do? Was there anyone he could complain to? Surely people couldn't just walk off with your book like that and get away with it. Maybe he could write to O'Neill's publishers and threaten to sue for plagiarism? But who was going to believe him? Sheldon O'Neill was an established author. Adrian was an unknown. It was like David and Goliath. And how could you sue somebody for plagiarising a novel that had never been published?

Adrian was beside himself with rage. If Sheldon O'Neill was here now, he would tear the bastard limb from limb. He would tie him up, pour honey over his arse and let the ants devour him. It would give him the greatest satisfaction. He wouldn't care if they locked him up forever and threw away the key. It would be worth it.

As his anger swelled, it was stoked by a fresh realisation. Now, *The Green Gannet* would never be published. The book that he had spent months slaving and sweating over would never see the light of day. If he tried to have it published, *he* would be the one accused of plagiarism. Adrian cringed at the injustice; all that work and all that energy had been a waste of time. He might as well have spent his time studying flower arranging!

His fury rose to fever pitch as new grievances occurred to him. Now there would be no adulation, no newspaper interviews, no book signings, no radio and television appearances, no publicity tours. He thought of the revenge he had planned on his detractors and how he had hoped to snub them once *Gannet* had been published to universal acclaim. None of that would come to pass. They would be the ones who would sneer now when they learnt of his predicament.

He thought of the wonderful life he had planned; the money; the villa in the sun; *the escape from St Ignatius's!* As a result of O'Neill's treachery, none of this would ever happen. His dreams had been shattered. He was doomed to end his days a broken man, struggling to teach English Literature to a pack of mentally challenged ingrates who wouldn't know a simile from a hole in the road.

It was all too much to bear. He needed a stiff drink, something to settle his shattered nerves. He rooted about in the cupboard till he found the bottle of whisky he had bought at the airport and poured himself a tumbler. He drained it in one swallow, then took the bottle with him to the balcony and poured another. He sat blinking in the sunlight as a maudlin self-pity descended on him. He had tried so hard and this had been his reward. He was a victim, a decent man who had given his all and had been cruelly betrayed. What had he ever done to deserve a fate like this?

Inevitably, Adrian's thoughts searched for someone to blame. O'Neill, of course, was the arch villain. But he was far away and out of reach. He needed someone nearer to home, someone within striking distance; someone close. He reached for the whisky bottle and poured another drink.

Trish! She was to blame. After all, if it hadn't been for her, he would never have met Sheldon O'Neill and none of this would have happened. She had introduced them. She was the one O'Neill invited to dinner after she found him that house in Wicklow. Adrian had only tagged along.

It was typical of Trish and her fluffy-headed incompetence to be taken in by a charlatan like O'Neill. It was Charlie Dobbins all over again; only a hundred times worse. Trish just couldn't resist poking her nose into his business and dredging up all sorts of scoundrels who were only waiting an opportunity to take advantage of his good nature.

He thought of the ways she had interfered at home when he was trying to focus on some knotty dramatic problem, insisting that he eat when she said so and go to bed when she demanded until in the end she had driven him from the bed altogether. How often had she interrupted his train of thought at a critical juncture to inquire if he would like a nice cup of tea, or if the room was warm enough, or if she should open the window to let in fresh air?

It was clear now that Trish had been a totally negative influence, dragging him down, holding him back. If it hadn't been for her, he would have finished the novel long ago and it would now be in the bookstores, well beyond the grubby clutches of Sheldon Bloody O'Neill.

He finished his glass and his fevered brain filled with wilder conspiracies. He wouldn't be at all surprised if Trish and O'Neill had been in this together from the very start, if it wasn't some elaborate plot they had hatched between them to rob him of the literary glory that was rightfully his. It wasn't so unusual. Wives were often envious of their husbands' success. Why should Trish be any different?

All around him, Adrian saw enemies, critics, malcontents, all consumed with jealousy, all waiting their chance to bring him down. There was no one he could trust any more, not even his own wife. The whole world was joined in a gigantic plot against him. It was too much. He hadn't got any more energy. He felt a weariness descend on him. He was tired. He had been working too hard. He closed his eyes against the strong heat of the sun and immediately fell asleep.

He was wakened by the sound of the apartment door opening. Trish was standing in the room and she was smiling at him.

"I'm back, dear! How is the work coming along?"

Adrian sat up with a start as Trish's smile gave way to a look of concern.

"What happened to you?"

"Whatyoumean?"

She picked up the bottle. "For God's sake, Adrian! It's only eleven o'clock and you're drunk already!"

He tried to stand up and collapsed back into the chair. "It's all your fault," he slurred.

"What are you talking about?"

"This!" With trembling hands, he held up the copy of the *Daily Telegraph*.

Trish quickly read the report. Then she stared at Adrian. "Oh my God! I don't believe this. He's stolen your book."

"Yesh, he has. And it's all your bloody fault!"

A look of shock came into her face. "My fault?"

"You introduced him," Adrian said, making another effort to get out of the chair.

"But I'd no idea he'd do anything like this!"

"Well, he has. And if it hadn't been for you, it would never have happened. You've been a millstone round my neck ever since I met you. If it hadn't been for you, I'd be a world-renowned writer by now."

Trish gasped. "That's an awful thing to say."

"It's the bloody truth."

"I've always encouraged and supported you. I've gone out of my way to help you."

"Help me?" Adrian's mouth twisted in a sneer. "Well, you can see where your damned help has got me now."

Trish looked at her husband as he sat in a drunken heap on the balcony. She struggled to contain herself. "Adrian, you are saying things now because you're hurt, and because you're drunk. I think you'll regret them when you sober up."

He laughed. "The only thing I'll regret is ever meeting you."

Trish winced as if he had struck her a blow.

"You've been jealous of me all my career. Why, I wouldn't be surprised if you and Sheldon O'Neill had been in this together."

Her face burned crimson. "That's done it. I won't stay here a minute longer to listen to your drunken ravings."

"Okay. Just take yourself off. See if I miss you."

Trish turned on her heel and made for the door.

"I took pity on you," Adrian shouted at her departing back. "When I met you, you were just a timid little mouse who couldn't make a decision to save your life. I made you what you are. Without me, you'd be nothing!"

He heard the door slam shut. That shook her, he thought. Glad to get that off my chest. Should have told her years ago.

He looked at the tumbler. It was empty again.

He reached for the bottle and poured another drink.

Chapter 38

"Now," Mollie said, leading Mary to a nice soft sofa in the hotel lounge and making sure she was comfortable. "What would you like to drink?"

"Tea," Mary said.

"A wise decision," Mollie said in that strange insinuating voice she had recently adopted. "You have to take care of yourself."

"But I always take care of myself. You should know that."

"Special care," Mollie said and smiled knowingly.

Mary's eyes widened. What on earth was she talking about? And what was she up to, hijacking me from my sunbathing routine by the pool and dragging me in here and treating me like I'm an invalid?

"I'm going to have tea myself," Mollie continued. "I find it very soothing. Especially when I'm under stress as I have been recently."

"Stress? What kind of stress?"

"We'll come to that later. Now would you like a nice slice of cake to go with your tea?"

Mary shook her head. "I'm fine."

"Are you sure?"

"Certain."

"It's just that some women develop a sweet tooth."

While Mary looked at her strangely, Mollie got hold of a waiter and gave her instructions. When he was gone, she sat back with a sigh in the deep armchair she had commandeered.

"You know, I've really come to enjoy this lounge. It's so quiet and peaceful. And it's a lot more comfortable than that balcony I was sitting on. I must say it was a brainwave to think of it."

Mary smiled. "Thank you, Mum."

"And another thing. You'd be amazed at what you'd notice going on." Mollie lowered her voice. "Have you seen that glamorous lady who is in here sometimes? Her name is Monica Woodworth?"

"The name rings a bell," Mary said. "And you know, I think I've seen her face before."

"She's a very nice lady. We had a chat together the other day. And she gave me a newspaper. Well, I think that Carlos fella is interested in her."

"Really?"

"Oh, yes. I see him fussing around and offering her glasses of sherry. And he took her to dinner last night."

Mary laughed.

"How do you know all this?"

"Because I saw him give her a lift in his car. A nice sporty model. They didn't think anyone could see them, but I did. I was sitting right here and I saw them through the window."

Mollie sat back with a satisfied grin.

"You're turning into a real Miss Marple," Mary said.

"Well, I just hope he treats her right. She's a nice lady and I get the strong impression she's lonely."

The tea arrived and Mollie poured two cups.

"Why have you brought me here?" Mary said sipping her tea. "Was it just to have a gossip?"

"Partly," Mollie replied. "Mothers and daughters should be able to confide in each other. They shouldn't keep secrets, you know, particularly if there's something bothering them."

"I agree."

Mollie leaned forward and examined her quizzically. "You do?"

"Yes."

"Well, I'm glad to hear that. Because I would like to think if there was something bothering you, I'd be the first person you would come to."

"Oh Mum, of course I would. You know that."

"Well," Mollie said, putting down her teacup, "that paper that Monica gave me. The first thing I turned to was the horoscope."

"Any surprises?"

"Yes, there was something that surprised me. Let me read it to you."

Mollie took the horoscope from her handbag. "*Be patient. Tiny beginnings lead to great events.*"

Mary looked puzzled. "So? What's that supposed to mean?"

"I'm not finished. There was another one a few days ago. It said: *Prepare for a happy addition to the family.*"

"Is somebody joining us that I don't know about?" joked Mary.

"You tell me," Mollie said.

Mary was becoming exasperated. "Me? For God's sake, Mum, what are you driving at?"

"The Stars never lie," Mollie said firmly. "In my experience if they say something is going to happen, then as sure as God made little apples, it will happen."

340

"But *what* is going to happen?"

Mollie put the horoscope down. "Oh, let's stop beating about the bush. There's nothing you have done that I haven't done. And I've done it before you. None of these things are a mystery to me."

Mary stared. "Well, whatever they are, they're a mystery to me."

"I've seen a lot of the world and there is very little can shock me," Mollie continued.

"Yes," Mary said.

"So you needn't be afraid. Your father and I will both support you."

"Support me with what?"

"With the baby, of course."

There was a shocked silence while the realisation dawned on Mary. Now it all began to make sense: all those little remarks she had been making recently about her health and not drinking and talking it easy in her condition.

"You think I'm pregnant?"

"Well, aren't you? You can tell me. I am your mother after all."

Mary began to smile and the smile slowly spread all over her face till it turned into a laugh. It was all so ridiculous, this crazy figment of her mother's imagination. "Of course I'm not pregnant. And if I was, you'd be the first to know."

Mollie's mouth fell open. "You're sure?"

"I'm totally sure. I'd think I would know if I was pregnant, Mum."

"But the horoscope?"

"Never mind the horoscope. I'm telling you here and now that I'm not pregnant."

Mollie blushed. "Well, I'm glad about that," she stammered. "It's not that I would have minded so much, it's just that I thought you were afraid to tell me. And that's what hurt me." She was now totally flustered and confused. "I'm sorry for doubting you, and for offending you. Please forgive me."

Mary quickly leaned across and wrapped her arms around her mother in a warm embrace.

"Oh, Mum, of course you haven't offended me. And of course I forgive you. It was just a silly mistake. So put it right out of your mind and don't give it another minute's thought. OK?"

She kissed her mother's cheek and stood up. "Now that you've got that off your chest, I'm going back out to the pool to resume my sunbathing."

Mollie watched her walk across the foyer and through the door to the pool. Well, that's a relief, she thought. What a bloody fool I've been. She poured some more tea and then a thought struck her. If Mary wasn't pregnant, what did the horoscope mean?

But before she could ponder this any further, she was distracted by a most distressing sight. Monica had just gone hurrying past the lounge and it looked as if she was weeping.

Chapter 39

Trish charged out of the lift and went storming through the foyer of the hotel. At reception, the girl looked up in surprise as she went dashing past. Wasn't that the Irish lady who had just come in a few minutes ago and now here she was rushing out again? And, my God, she looks angry. She looks like she is going to kill someone. Oh well, she thought, and continued writing. As long as she doesn't do it on hotel property, it is none of my business.

Trish *was* ready to kill. She couldn't remember when she had felt so angry. She was so upset that she didn't know where she was going. All she knew was that she had to get as far as possible from her drunken lunatic husband. She stopped when she got outside and looked around for a taxi but the rank was empty. She would have to walk. It would do her good. She started for the beach along the route she had already traversed just half an hour before.

She noticed that her hands were shaking with rage and her heart was pumping. Try to calm down, she said to herself, try to relax. But at least the path she was taking was quiet and deserted. Just as well, for in my present state I don't want to meet anyone from the hotel. I need time to collect my thoughts and decide what to do next.

After a while, she came to a bench. She sat down and looked out at the ocean, the waves gently rising and falling on the sand. The sound and the sight had a soothing effect. She closed her eyes and thought of the events that had just taken place. She had never been so insulted in her entire life. Adrian had told her she was a millstone, that she had dragged him down. That only for her, he would have been a successful writer by now. He had even suggested that she had been in league with Sheldon O'Neill to steal his damned book. She couldn't believe the things he had said.

It told her exactly what her husband thought of her and confirmed everything she had known for a long time but had excused or covered over. Adrian considered her his inferior. What was that phrase he often used? *"Don't worry your pretty little head."* It revealed how he really saw her – as a pretty female companion but basically a nincompoop.

It stoked her anger. She was the person who had made a go of her career. She was the successful partner. She was the one who paid most of the bills. And in addition, she did the housework and the cleaning. She cooked his meals. She mollycoddled him and wiped his brow while he spent all his time on that stupid book that she had long ago concluded would never find a publisher. And this was what he thought of her. Oh, the ingratitude!

The idea that she was in league with Sheldon O'Neill was lunacy. She had only met the man a couple of times while she tried to find him a house. The only social occasion she had spent in his company was at that famous dinner at Guilbaud's when she had introduced him to Adrian. But it proved one thing beyond any doubt. Adrian was definitely deranged.

She had observed the symptoms developing over the past few months: the erratic behaviour, the delusions of grandeur, the refusal to face reality. And now he had flipped into full-blown paranoia.

Trish paused in her thoughts. To be fair to Adrian, he had just received a devastating blow. He had spent all that time on his novel only to have his ideas stolen by someone he trusted, a confidant he had gone to, seeking advice. It would be enough to crush the most rational person. No wonder he was bitter. And he was drunk. He didn't realise what he was saying.

But did that excuse him? His parting words were still ringing in her ears. *"I took pity on you. I made you what you are."* That's what Adrian really thought. That's what he had always thought. This was the cruellest cut of all. He took pity on *me?* Trish had carried him and nursed him, practically since the day they were married. She had endured his sulks and his tantrums. She had consoled him through the long series of rejections and setbacks as he tried to get his wretched book published. What other woman would have put up with him the way she had?

But that had always been Adrian's way. She could see it all so clearly now. Selfishness had been his controlling vice ever since she had met him. Selfishness and arrogance. He had always regarded himself as superior to everyone around him, had always believed he was cleverer than everyone else, had always considered that he was right and they were wrong. And she had encouraged him. She had kept herself in the background, lest by accident she might overshadow him. She had never complained, never asserted herself. She had allowed Adrian to make all the decisions right down to the colour of the bathroom wall.

Why had she done it? Was it because she loved him? Was

it to keep her marriage together? Was it in the forlorn hope that Adrian might eventually grow out of his selfishness and become a normal human being? But, of course, he hadn't. While other people had matured and developed, he remained stuck in the same selfish groove. Instead of improving, he had simply got worse. And now she realised that he would never change.

Her anger had cooled and she was thinking much more rationally now. Barely an hour ago, she had this very same conversation with herself. She had been on the verge of leaving her husband. Only the flip of a coin had decided her to stay. In the meantime, she had come to see the true nature of the situation. She was going to have the baby she so desperately wanted. She had enough money to look after it. There was no longer any need to stay tied to a man who clearly held her in contempt and who she had long ago ceased to love.

She made up her mind. She would return immediately to the apartment and inform him of her decision. She would pack her bags and move out. All the other messy details could be worked out later. She felt strangely euphoric as she turned back to the hotel, as if a terrible weight had been lifted from her shoulders.

She rounded a bend in the path and ran straight into Charlie Dobbins.

Chapter 40

Monica left Carlos's suite and didn't stop running till she got downstairs to the foyer. She could feel her face flush and the perspiration break on her forehead. She hadn't had a shock like this since the day she got the news that Woody had died. Or, rather, since the day she had learned he had left her destitute. After a romantic dinner and a passionate night, when things couldn't possibly get any better, Carlos had suddenly turned on her. The bastard had been fooling her all along. It wasn't her he had been interested in at all, but the money he thought she had.

When she reached the foyer, she forced herself to slow down. I've got to maintain my composure, she thought, aware she must look distracted. I mustn't allow people to see how upset I am. I must go up to my apartment, she thought, and have a good, long weep. But for now, what is required is some stiff upper-lip.

She gave a weak smile to the reception clerk and began to make her way across the foyer towards the lift. The route took her past the lounge. Please God there's no one there to see me in this dreadful state, she thought. Monica struggled to contain the feelings of hurt and despair that threatened to overwhelm her. Maybe it was all a bad dream? Maybe when she got to her apartment, there would be a phone call from Carlos begging her forgiveness? But she knew it wasn't going to happen. Ever since Woody died, her luck had been running out.

And it seemed to be getting worse. Monica's life now seemed to be careering downhill at an alarming speed. This was the second time in a few days that she had been humiliated. First, she got barred from the Gran Hotel del Rey and now she had been rejected by Carlos. What was happening to her? How had she allowed herself to be taken in like that? She was a forty-three-year-old woman, for God's sake! She wasn't a star-struck youngster with no experience of the world. She had been with lots of men. How had she *not* seen it coming?

Mind you, she had to hand it to him. He had been so smooth and plausible. He had convinced her that she was the only woman in the world for him. And she had been so keen that she was blinded to reality. She thought of the dinner in the moonlight, the sweet, whispered compliments and later the wild lovemaking. He was so polished, he would have swept any woman off her feet. Monica shook her head at the memory, as she waited for the lift. Twelve hours ago, she believed she was on the brink of a wonderful new beginning. And now everything lay in ruins.

Despite her resolve, she felt the tears well up in her eyes. Perhaps this is the way my life is going to be. I'll just have to get used to the idea that I'll never again preside over glittering parties and prestigious lunches. I'll just have to accept that my career as society hostess is well and truly over. Colleen McQueen will be happy. She'll have got her revenge.

I'll be a faded memory. If I'm lucky, I might get invited on the *Late Late Show* from time to time, when they're stuck for a panellist to reminisce about the good old days. And to think I had so much to offer.

Suddenly, she broke down and despite her resolve, she burst out weeping. Must get up to my apartment she told herself. Mustn't let people see me like this.

And just then, she heard a voice call her name. She stopped and wiped her eyes with her handkerchief. Someone came out of the lounge and put their arms around her shoulders.

"There, there," a voice said gently, "everything's going to be all right."

Monica blinked through her tears. It was that strange woman Mollie she had been talking to yesterday. She was taking her by the hand and leading her like a child.

"Just come in here and sit down and rest yourself for a while," Mollie said. "I'll take care of you." She led Monica to the seat that Mary had just vacated and sat her down. "Now what you need is a stiff drink. And I think I'll join you."

She signalled to the waiter and ordered two large brandies.

"Have a good cry," she said to Monica, "and you'll feel better. And if you need another handkerchief, I've got another one."

Monica sank her head in her hands and her body shook as all the grief and pain poured out of her. When she was finished, she wiped her eyes once more.

"I hope I'm not embarrassing you?" she sniffed.

"You're not embarrassing me in the least. Sure there's only me and you in here."

"I'm terribly sorry."

"No need to be sorry. You've had a bad experience, that's all. Are you feeling better?"

Monica nodded.

"Here," Mollie said, handing her one of the brandies the waiter had left. "Get that inside you and you'll feel better again."

Monica took a sip of the brandy and felt it warm her throat

"What's hurting you?" Mollie said "Do you want to tell me?"

But Monica didn't respond.

Mollie leaned closer and whispered. "It's that Carlos fella, isn't it?"

Monica looked up in surprise. "How do you know?"

"Oh, I know lots of things. Do you want to talk about it?"

Monica blew her nose. "He led me on. He was promising me all sorts of wonderful things. But it turned out he was interested in something else. And when he discovered I didn't have it, he turned on me and cast me aside."

Mollie gently patted her arm. "Don't let it upset you. He's no loss. Sure if he was a proper man, he wouldn't behave like that at all."

"You're right," Monica said.

"And your husband is dead?"

Monica looked startled. Mollie was like a clairvoyant. "You really do know lots of things."

Mollie shrugged. "It's just an observation. What did he die of?"

"A heart attack."

"And you have no children?"

"No."

"So now you're all alone?"

"Yes," Monica said and felt the tears start again.

"It doesn't mean you have to be lonely," Mollie said. "There are lots of things you can do. Clubs you can join. Hobbies you can take up. It's not like the old days when your life was over if your husband died. And you're such a good-looking woman. You're still young. And you're very glamorous."

Monica smiled, despite her tears. "I used to be a society hostess. When my husband was alive, we used to give great parties. All sorts of people would come, musicians and actors and politicians. I gave the best parties in Dublin. Everybody wanted to be invited."

"So, there are you are. Why don't you just throw a great big party when you get home?"

"I can't. You see, I've . . ." Monica stopped. What was she doing telling this total stranger all about her life? But there was something about Mollie, some warm comforting quality that made her eager to pour out her heart to her.

"No money?" Mollie prompted.

Monica gasped. How *did* Mollie know all these things? She nodded. "That's right. When my husband died, he left me nothing but debts. The liquidator took everything. My house, my car. I've barely got enough to survive."

"And that's why that blackguard, Carlos, threw you over? He thought you had money?"

"Yes."

"I never liked him," Mollie said, sharply. "There's something creepy about him. I could tell from the very beginning and I'm seldom wrong about people."

"I don't even have a job," Monica confessed. "I'm living in a tiny flat and I'm terrified that my cash will dry up and I'll be thrown out on the street. And then what will I do?"

"Have you no friends could help you?"

351

Monica sighed. "No."

"All these people who came to your parties? Would none of them lend you a hand now that you're down on your luck?"

Monica slowly shook her head.

Mollie sat back in her chair.

"Well, I just don't know what to say. I've always heard that the people up in Dublin were odd. But if a neighbour in Dunmuckridge had a sick cow, everybody would rally round to help them."

"The people I mixed with weren't typical Dubliners," Monica said apologetically. "They weren't the real, you know . . . old stock."

"You can say that again. They sound like a crowd of sleveens. What sort of job are you looking for, anyway?"

"Anything I can get. You see, apart from secretarial work, I haven't any skills."

"Nonsense," Mollie snorted. "Didn't you just tell me you gave all these parties? Doesn't that require skill? Getting the right people together? Organising the food?"

"I –"

"Taking care of the music and the drinks? Making sure everybody is entertained? I would have thought that called for a very high degree of skill. There's not many people could take on something like that and make a success of it." Mollie spoke firmly. "You'll have to stop running yourself down. You'll have to think positive. And you'll have to stop relying on men. Learn to stand on your two feet. Do you believe in the Stars?"

"You mean the horoscopes?"

"Exactly! Did you know your future is written in the stars? God keeps a book and it contains all the things that will ever happen to you in your lifetime."

"I didn't know that," Monica said.

"Oh it's true. I'm a great believer in the Stars. The Stars have never let me down. Here." She pulled a tabloid newspaper from her bag. "What's your birthday?"

"June 28th."

"That's Cancer. Let's see what the Stars have in store for you."

She flipped through the pages till she came to the horoscope and then her face expanded in a happy smile. "Look at that. What did I tell you?"

She handed the paper to Monica.

Be glad. Your life is about to change.

Monica looked at Mollie. "Do you think it's true?"

"Of course it's true. In my experience, the Stars never lie. Now I have to leave you. I promised my husband I'd go for a walk."

"Do you have to go?" Monica said quickly. "It's been so good talking to you. You've been like a tonic to me."

Mollie smiled. "What a nice thing to say. You know, if people would only be a little kinder to each other, the world would be a much better place." She stood up. "I'll be here again in the morning. Why don't you join me and we'll have a nice cup of tea and a chat?"

"I'd love to," Monica said.

She watched Mollie pass out of the lounge and into the foyer. She lifted the paper again and read: *Your life is about to change.*

I wonder if there is any truth in that stuff, she thought.

Chapter 41

"Why, Charlie," Trish said, once she had recovered from her surprise. "Fancy bumping into you?"

Charlie gulped. He felt his face go red. This was incredible. There were only two people in the whole world that he didn't want to meet and one of them was Trish. He had deliberately gone out of his way *not* to meet her. Yet here she was standing in front of him. He felt like turning on his heels and running away, except his legs had suddenly turned to rubber.

"Hello," he said, shyly.

She turned a big, warm smile on him. "I was just taking a stroll. It's so peaceful down here."

"Yes," Charlie said, "so it is."

He realised that his mouth had gone dry and his tongue seemed to have grown to twice its normal size. But he needed to say something or else she would think he was a complete idiot.

"It's going to be hot," he managed to blurt out. "The weather. It's going to be another hot day."

The moment he spoke, he realised how pathetic it sounded. It was like saying it was cold at the North Pole. But Trish didn't seem to notice. In fact, she looked pleased to see him which was odd given the debacle of their last meeting.

"What are *you* doing here?" she asked.

"I'm on my way to have breakfast."

"Well, then, I'll join you for a cup of coffee. If you don't mind?"

Immediately, Charlie was seized with terror. Meeting her was bad enough. But now she was inviting herself to breakfast! How was he going to get through a whole conversation with her? What was he going to say?

"Of course, I mind. I mean, of course I *don't* mind. Having coffee with you would be very – nice."

She gave him a strange look.

"Over there," Charlie said, quickly. "There's a spare table."

They sat down and Charlie ordered croissants. His appetite had vanished and his stomach seemed to be stuffed with cotton wool. There was an embarrassing silence before he said: "Are you enjoying your holiday?"

Good God, he thought. This is dire. This is the most dismal attempt at a conversation I have ever heard in my entire life. A parrot could hold a better conversation that this.

Trish's brow furrowed and a frown appeared. "Not really," she said.

So she *was* angry with him for running away from the argument with Adrian. He knew it.

"Is it because of me?"

"You?"

"Yes. Is it because of me that you're not enjoying your holiday?"

She looked at him quizzically. "Are you all right, Charlie?"

"Certainly. I'm absolutely wonderful," he said. "Why wouldn't I be?"

"Why do you ask if you're the reason why I'm not enjoying my holiday?"

"Because of my behaviour yesterday when we were at the pool. I think I was a bit forward. I didn't mean to embarrass you."

Trish relaxed and suddenly began to laugh. "Oh, Charlie. You're so funny. You told me I was beautiful. That's the nicest thing I've heard for a very long time. Why should I be embarrassed by a lovely compliment like that?"

"You mean you're not upset?"

"Not in the least."

"And then, when your husband came along . . ."

She seemed to tense. "Let's not talk about that."

"But I want to get it off my chest. I felt guilty about chatting with you. And he seemed angry. And I didn't want to create a scene, so I just took myself off. But afterwards, I thought I should have stood my ground. I felt bad about leaving you behind with him. I felt . . . like a coward."

"You did exactly the right thing," Trish said. "My husband is a pompous fool and a bully. Nothing would have been gained by arguing with him."

"You mean that?"

"Yes. You behaved perfectly correctly."

"So you're not angry with me?"

"For God's sake, Charlie! The person I'm angry with is Adrian."

All at once, Charlie felt his appetite return. He took a croissant and smeared it generously with jam.

"You know, he adopted a very superior attitude to me as if I didn't know anything about books. And I've read thousands of books. To be honest, Trish, I thought he was talking nonsense."

"Who are you telling? I've had to put up with him for years. But I don't think he'll be pontificating about literature for a long time to come. You see, his novel is never going to be published."

"Why not?"

"Somebody else has got there before him."

She told him about Sheldon O'Neill and how he had stolen Adrian's idea and sold his book for five million dollars.

"My God," Charlie said, "that's awful. All that work for nothing. How did he react?"

"Badly. He's blaming me."

"But why should he blame you?"

"Because that's his nature. He can't accept that he might be at fault. He always has to blame somebody else. And I suppose I'm the nearest one. Mind you, I *am* largely responsible for the way he has turned out. I've spoiled him, really. I've always given in to him."

Charlie was dumbfounded. Here was Trish openly criticising her husband. He took another bite out of his croissant while he thought of something to say.

"Anyway, it doesn't matter any more. I'm leaving him."

Charlie almost choked. "*Whaaat?*"

"I'm leaving him."

"You're not joking, Trish? There are some things you shouldn't really joke about."

"No, Charlie. This is no joke. More like a nightmare and I've only awakened."

"But why, after all these years?"

"Because I've finally accepted the truth. Adrian isn't going to change. He'll always be a selfish monster. And I deserve a better life." She toyed with her coffee cup while Charlie stared at her open-mouthed. "He said some very cruel things this morning. Accused me of being in league with Sheldon O'Neill to steal his book. Called me a millstone round his neck. Said he took pity on me and made me what I am." She took a sip of coffee. "He was drunk. But he spoke the truth. That's the way he really feels. He showed the true extent of his contempt for me."

"Maybe he'll apologise when he cools down."

"It doesn't matter. My mind's made up."

Charlie shook his head. "I don't know what to say."

"There's very little *to* say. I suppose it's sad in a way. We've been married for fifteen years. But I can't help feeling happy that I've finally made this decision. I'm free, Charlie. At last, I'm my own woman."

Charlie felt a strange emotion take hold of him. "What will you do?"

"Move out. He can have the house. It's got too many bad memories for me. We'll let the lawyers work out the details."

"But where will you stay?"

"I don't know yet. I only made the decision to leave him ten minutes ago."

Before he realised what he was doing, Charlie heard himself say: "You could always come and stay with me." He looked into her face. At first there was no reaction. He wondered if he had blundered again. And then he saw a light shine in the corner of her eyes. "I've got loads of room," he went on. "I've a big place in Sutton. Four bedrooms. Two en-suite. Twenty-five minutes from town. You'd be very welcome. And you can stay as long as you like."

"Oh, Charlie! You're the most generous man. But I couldn't possibly take up your offer."

"Why not? I'd love to have you. I'd be absolutely delighted."

She lowered her eyes. "Because I'm going to have a baby."

Charlie gasped. This was unbelievable. It was like riding a roller-coaster. Events were moving much too fast. "That complicates matters, all right. What will Adrian say?"

"He doesn't know."

"B-b-buu —"

"It's not his child."

Charlie swallowed hard.

"It's a long story," Trish said. "I wanted a child and Adrian was so tied up in his bloody book that our sex life was a distant memory. So I had an affair and got pregnant. That's why we're here in Tenerife. You don't want to know all the gory details."

"How will you manage with a baby on your own? Won't it make things more difficult?"

"I suppose it will. But I'll cross that bridge when I come to it. At the moment, I'm just happy that I've finally decided to leave him."

Charlie fiddled with his coffee cup. "You could bring the baby, if you like. I wouldn't mind. I wouldn't mind at all."

He saw her mouth pucker. "Do you mean it?"

"Yes." Instinctively he knew he must seize the moment. He reached out and took her hand. "Come and live with me, Trish. Nothing would make me happier. The truth is, I've wanted you since the first day I met you. But, if you only want a place to —"

She laid a finger on his lips. "And I've wanted *you*. Oh, Charlie!"

"Will you come?"

"Yes."

The next thing he knew his arms were around her and they were kissing wildly. He heard a cup crash to the ground. He was aware that people were staring. But Charlie didn't care. He was ecstatic with joy.

He heard her murmur in his ear. "I'm so happy. Charlie, I think you're the most wonderful man I have ever met in my entire life and I thank God I've found you."

"Well, that's nice to know," Charlie said and kissed her again.

Chapter 42

Adrian came to on the balcony shortly before twelve o'clock, with the boiling sun burning his face and a thundering headache rampaging like a herd of elephants through his brain. He sat up in confusion. Where am I? What have I been doing? With great effort, he managed to focus on the whisky bottle where it glinted in the harsh noonday light. It was half-empty.

My God, he thought, surely I didn't drink all that? And then it all came back to him in a blinding flash. He had been drinking because Sheldon O'Neill had stolen his novel and now he had the mother of all hangovers. All the pain and disappointment came flooding back. He needed another drink to steady his nerves. He reached for the bottle and poured another glass and downed it in a gulp.

That's better, he thought. Now I can focus a little clearer. Didn't I have a row with Trish? Through the fog in his brain, Adrian groped for those bits of the morning that had been obliterated by alcohol. They had argued over something. What was it? And then the fog cleared a little and he remembered. He had blamed her for what had happened.

Damned right, he thought. If it hadn't been for Trish, Sheldon O'Neill would never have heard of *The Green Gannet*. He winced again at the memory of all that wasted effort, all those long hours toiling over his word processor, feverishly producing intricate plots and fantastic characters. Now it was just so many sheets of scrap-paper. If it hadn't been for Trish poking her nose in, he wouldn't be here. He'd be in Hollywood or somewhere, drinking cocktails with movie moguls and talking film deals with people like Steven Spielberg.

Doubtless she'd be back any moment now, begging for forgiveness. Well, he'd have to think about that. Adrian was in no mood for forgiveness. The memory of his betrayal was too painful. But that was Trish all over. She hadn't the talent to write her own book, so she had to meddle in his. If it hadn't been for her constant interference, he could easily have increased his output to 25,000 words a day and finished the novel six months ago. It would be walking out of the shops by now.

He downed another whisky and the hangover seemed to vanish. Miraculous, he thought. Bloody marvellous! I'll have another one to celebrate. As he sat there, his thinking began to take a new turn. So, I've just had a reverse. But it's not the end of the world. Why, look at some of the great figures of literature: slaving in dark garrets, racked with consumption, in hock to moneylenders and pawnbrokers, the cries of their starving children ringing in their ears. Did they let the situation depress them? Did they lie down and die? No, they did not. It just spurred them on to greater effort. It just encouraged them to create some of the greatest masterpieces the world has ever known.

That's it, Adrian decided. That's what I'll do. As soon as I get back to Dublin, I'll start all over again. And this time, I'll keep it to myself. No reading chapters to the writers' group. No talking about the plot. No discussing the characters over dinner with Trish. This time, *nobody* will know what I'm writing till it's finished and it bursts, in all its glory, on an awestruck world.

The thought cheered him. He drained his glass and poured another. If he got up at five in the morning he could have three hours work done before it was time to go to school. In the evening, he could easily punch in another eight hours before 1am. That would leave four hours for sleep. More than enough.

With a bit of application and discipline, he could crank up his word count to 30,000 words a day. He did a quick calculation. That would make roughly 200,000 words a week. In two weeks, he would have completed 400,000 words. Give another few days for revision, and he would have a blockbuster novel written in under three weeks. A smile of satisfaction spread across his grizzled cheeks. By God, he would do it! He would pick himself up and start again. He would show Sheldon O'Neill and all the rest of those miserable cockroaches that they were dealing with a professional artist who would not only overcome adversity, but would thrive on it as well!

What would he write about? With a dazzling burst of inspiration, the new novel appeared, fully formed, in his brain. It was so simple. He would write about what had just happened to him! All the best fiction was based on personal experience. He would write about a poverty-stricken writer whose work is stolen by a big-name author through the duplicity of his wife. But the writer refuses to give up. He perseveres and eventually wins the Nobel Prize for

Literature. His wife sees the error of her ways and begs forgiveness. The world falls at his feet. He is universally acclaimed as a creative genius. The big-name author is unmasked as the fraud he really is.

It was brilliant. It had all the elements: tension, drama, treachery, sex *and* a happy ending. Immediately, the title flashed into his head. *The Hairy-Handed Plagiarist*. It was short and direct yet had an exotic ring. The characters were already in place. He would make little effort to disguise O'Neill. Those who knew him would recall the thick mat of black hair that covered the back of his fingers and know at once that the title referred to him.

Adrian was swept away on a wave of enthusiasm. He opened the laptop and began pounding at the keyboard. The opening sentence of his new novel flowed effortlessly onto the screen.

It was midnight and in his lonely attic, the impoverished school teacher, Archibald Moriarty, a handsome, dark-haired man of strong build, with bright, piercing eyes set in a face which betrayed goodness, kindness, honesty, decency, courage, integrity, not to mention unflinching principle, undying loyalty and unbending character, sighed as he heard the chimes from the nearby church announce the witching hour by way of the bells ringing in the weather-beaten steeple which sat majestically atop the ivy-clad dome of the venerable and ancient edifice, while downstairs, his wife, Penelope, a slim beauty of maturing years, was waiting for him to decide whether she should pour herself another glass of wine or turn the television off and go at last to the comfort of her solitary cot.

He read the sentence back to himself. It was perfect! It immediately set the scene, introduced the main characters and grabbed the reader's attention. Adrian knew this was important. All the manuals he had read in preparation for embarking on his literary career had stressed the necessity of getting the reader engaged from the outset. He congratulated himself. Despite the setback he had encountered, it was obvious he still possessed the gift for writing good, clean, fluid English.

He was excited now. His head filled with marvellous characters and twists of plot. Snatches of conversation and wonderful turns of phrase leapt unbidden into his fevered brain. He reached for the bottle to pour another drink and discovered it was empty. Dammit! He would have to nip down to the bar for another.

He stood up and staggered to the bathroom. In the mirror, his haggard face and bloodshot eyes stared back at him. 'By God, but I'm a handsome devil,' he thought. 'No wonder the ladies fall for me. No wonder they can't wait to get me into their beds.' He made his way along the corridor to the lift and down to the foyer. And here his progress was interrupted.

Who was seated in the lounge but the tragic Monica! Adrian tried to focus. What an amazing thing. There were two of them. Monica and her identical twin sister! They were even wearing the same clothes. He couldn't remember if Monica had ever mentioned her sister. Anyway, he would go over right away and introduce himself. Tell them his good news. Entertain them with some humorous anecdotes. Charm them with his brilliant repartee.

Pulling in his stomach and pushing out his chest, he entered the lounge and began his slow, unsteady progress towards her.

Monica looked up in consternation when she saw Adrian weaving unsteadily in her direction. Mollie had just left her and she was about to go up to her apartment. And here was that awful writer person coming towards her. And he looked like he had been sleeping under a hedge. As he got closer, Monica realised he was drunk.

Adrian plumped down in the seat beside her and smiled crookedly. "Where did she go?"

"Who?" Monica said.

"Your twin sister. She was here just a moment ago."

"I don't know what you're talking about," Monica said, tartly. "I haven't got a sister."

"But I just saw her. Good-looking bit. Nice tits. Just like you."

Monica winced.

Adrian crossed his legs and accidentally kicked her on the shin. "I was just about to have a drink," he said. "Care to join me?"

"It's too early," Monica said, hurrying to get up. "Anyway, I'm going."

Adrian squinted at his watch. "It's three o'clock."

"You've got the hands mixed up," Monica said. "It's a quarter past twelve."

She stood up.

Adrian stood up too. He smiled at her and winked lasciviously.

"Let's not beat about the bush. Care to come up to my room? My wife's away so the coast is clear."

Monica gasped.

"I can promise you a session like you've never had before. You'll be worn out before I'm finished with you."

Monica's hand was out like a flash and cracking across Adrian's face.

"How dare you, you drunken animal!"

"What do you mean?" Adrian said, his cheek reddening. "I was trying to do you a favour."

Next minute a couple of hotel porters had him by the shoulders and were dragging him away.

"Unhand me, you greasy savages!" Adrian roared.

"You are drunk, *Senor*. You have just insulted the lady."

A crowd had gathered and was staring at the spectacle.

"Drunk? Do you know who you are dealing with? I'm Adrian Blake. The greatest living novelist the world has ever known!"

"You must calm down, *Senor*. You are creating a disturbance."

The porters carried the struggling Adrian out to the foyer and dumped him on a sofa just as Trish and Charlie came walking in.

Adrian took one look at Trish and moaned, "Trish. Thank God you're here. Tell them this is all a ghastly mistake."

She stared in shock. Immediately, she bent over his prone body and sniffed. "I don't believe it," she said. "You're maggoty drunk. You're even worse than this morning."

"I am not drunk," Adrian insisted.

"You should be in bed."

With Charlie's help, she managed to get Adrian off the sofa and out to the lift. Once inside the apartment, they laid him on the bed. Trish got out a couple of suitcases and began to fill them with clothes.

"What's going on?" Adrian slurred. "And what's he doing here?"

He pointed at Charlie.

"I'm leaving you."

"You're *what*?"

"I'm leaving you. I'm moving out."

Adrian blinked. "Don't be ridiculous."

"You told me this morning I couldn't make a decision to save my life. Well, now I'm making one."

"But you can't leave me. This is preposterous!"

Trish stopped what she was doing and turned to him. "I've put up with your arrogant behaviour for fifteen years.

But this morning I finally realised I could take no more. I'm going to live with Charlie."

"You're leaving me for him?"

Charlie smiled.

"Why not? You know, Adrian, I feel sorry for you. You're really a buffoon. All that stuff you were spouting about writers. It was all nonsense. And to think they let you loose on a class of innocent children."

Adrian's lip was trembling and he was close to tears. He appealed to Trish. "Please don't leave me. What will I do without you?"

"You should have thought about that earlier."

She stuffed the last of her clothes into the second case and zipped it up. "Goodbye, Adrian. I'll be staying in Charlie's apartment for the rest of the holiday. When I get back to Dublin, I'll arrange to have my stuff taken out of the house. You'll be hearing from my solicitor."

Adrian moaned and fell back on the bed.

The door slammed shut and they were gone.

Chapter 43

Since the incident with Alex Piper, Edward and Bobby had become inseparable. They spent all their waking hours together much to the distress of Angie who felt neglected and left out as a result. She was the one who had organised this trip and now she was being forced to spend much of the time on her own. But she comforted herself with the thought that this was only a brief holiday romance and when they returned to Ireland she would have her best friend's company once more. After her recent experience, she doubted if Bobby was in the mood to rush into another relationship so soon.

Bobby was sitting now on the terrace of a little whitewashed restaurant in La Caleta finishing lunch. It was the same place she had eaten the day she injured her leg. But this time the scene was different. The sun was high in the sky. There was a haze on the sea and a gentle breeze ruffled the leaves of the flowers in the window boxes. And she was with Edward, drinking wine. It was perfect.

"Have you heard any more from him?" Edward asked.

"Pig-face Piper?"

"Yes. Did he get back home safely?"

"After a lot of trouble. He had to sleep on a bench at the airport for two days till he got a spare seat on a flight."

"I feel guilty about hitting him," Edward said.

"Don't. You were defending me. Anyway, he isn't worthy of your concern. You know the bastard is threatening to sue me if I don't return the engagement ring?"

Edward looked surprised. "You're not telling me you kept it?"

"Of course I did. It's my property. Besides, it's worth €5,000. I had it valued."

"But the engagement is off. Surely you should return the ring?"

There was a twinkle in Bobby's eye. "Of course I'm going to return it. I don't want anything that reminds me of that conceited brat. But I want him to sweat a bit. I want him to think long and hard before he contemplates engagement to some other poor unfortunate woman." She looked at the gentle waves lapping the edge of the shore. "Isn't this just wonderful?" she sighed. "I wish it would never end."

Edward smiled. "Everything comes to an end. We have to go home tomorrow."

"I know. And I'm dreading it. Still, the good news is the hospital will be taking off my plaster later today. I'll be able to walk like a real person again."

"And we have the Leprechaun farewell party to look forward to. Tom Casey said he would organise something special."

"Is that when we break the news to them?"

Edward thought for a moment before replying.

"Yes," he said. "That would be the ideal time."

"So it's all agreed then?" Mollie said.

Monica nodded. "Provided you're happy."

"Oh, I'm perfectly happy. I think it will work wonderfully. I'm very excited about it."

"So am I," Monica said. "In fact, I can't wait."

They were seated in the lounge of the hotel where they had been engaged for the past two hours in deep discussion. Mollie had warned Ned and Mary not to disturb them because she had something serious to talk about.

"I heard all about your experience yesterday," Mollie said. "Everybody was talking about it. The young *senorita* at Reception said she heard it was an escaped lunatic from Ireland. She said he'd been here before looking for somebody else."

"He was a lunatic all right," Monica said, "but he had just escaped from his apartment. It was that Adrian person. You know, the writer? He was drunk as a skunk."

"I'm not surprised. I never liked the look of him. Anyway, you've got over the shock?"

"Just about."

"Well then," Mollie said, "why don't we have a glass of something? What would you say to champagne?"

"I'd say yes," Monica laughed.

"You know, I rarely drink at home," Mollie said, "but I'm enjoying myself so much. This holiday has really turned out well. Much better than I thought."

A waiter was summoned, the bottle uncorked and the two women tipped their glasses.

"What will we drink to?" Mollie asked.

Monica considered. "The Stars?"

"What a brilliant idea," Mollie said. "Let's drink to the Stars!"

Meanwhile, Charlie and Trish were having a late breakfast on Charlie's balcony.

"He's gone," Trish said. "Checked out early this morning. Took a taxi to the airport. I asked at Reception."

"Well, thank heaven for that."

Trish sighed. "I can't believe I finally did it. I'm free. Isn't it wonderful?"

"I'm biased," Charlie said. "If you hadn't done it, we wouldn't be sitting here."

"I don't know why I put up with it for so long. I must have been crazy. But now it's all over and I feel like a new woman." She took a sip of coffee. "Do you think you'll get used to having a strange person living in your house?"

"You're not strange, Trish. I feel like I've known you all my life."

"And later, when the baby comes along?"

"I'm going to love it. I'll have my own little family. You don't know how lonely I've been."

"I think I'll love it too. It's going to be nice living with a normal person again."

She reached out and twined her fingers in his. "This is our last day. What do you want to do?"

Charlie shrugged. "Whatever you like."

Trish tickled his chin. "I know. Why don't we just go back to bed?"

For the farewell party, Tom Casey had decorated the pub with streamers and balloons and strung a huge banner across the stage, which read: BON VOYAGE FROM THE STAFF OF THE LUCKY LEPRECHAUN TENERIFE. Everyone who came in was given a paper hat to wear.

When Bobby and Edward turned up at nine with Angie, they found Mollie already established at a large table in the middle of the room with Mary, Ned and Monica sitting beside her.

"Sit down. Sit down," Mollie commanded in a cheery voice. "Have you met my friend?"

She introduced Monica and they all shook hands.

"Now what would you like to drink?" she asked. "I'm buying tonight."

Soon everyone was chatting amiably. Monica complimented the girls on their outfits. Bobby told them about the horror of having her plaster removed at the hospital, while Ned started a conversation with Edward about a football match he had seen on television earlier. The pub was filling up and waiters began to circulate with plates of chicken and jugs of sangria.

"You realise that's Spanish chicken you're eating?" Edward said as his father tucked into a plump breast.

Ned scowled at him. "It doesn't matter. I'm so hungry I'd eat the leg of this table. And that's Spanish too."

In the midst of all the clamour, Mollie saw the door open and Charlie Dobbins come in with Trish. They looked around uncertainly for somewhere to sit.

"Over here!" Mollie said. "Come and join us."

She got everyone to move closer to make room and Charlie and Trish squeezed in. Fresh introductions were made and the talk resumed.

"Looks like it's going to be a good night," Charlie said, glancing round the room and accepting Ned's offer of a glass of sangria.

"It's only beginning," Ned said. "Wait till the dancing starts."

Soon the whole table was engaged in conversation. Monica and Trish were discussing house prices while Ned was telling Charlie he should open a bookshop in Dunmuckridge. He said everyone in the town was a voracious reader as Mary nodded vigorously in agreement. At the head of the table Mollie looked serene in a new summer dress with a spray of fresh flowers at her breast.

The time seemed to pass very quickly. It was almost eleven when Bobby heard someone call for order. She broke off her conversation to see Mollie standing up and tapping a spoon against her glass. Beside her, Monica was suddenly looking very serious.

"Can I have your attention, please?"

The table fell silent as all eyes turned on her.

"I have an important announcement to make. You've all met my friend, Monica Woodworth."

Monica smiled.

"What you may not know is that Monica is a very successful society hostess. But unfortunately, her husband died recently and by the time those thieving lawyers had gone through poor Mr Woodworth's estate, there wasn't a brass farthing left."

Angie squeezed Bobby's arm and whispered: "I told you I'd seen her before."

"There's something else some of you don't know. I recently won a tidy bit of money on the national lottery. And to tell you the truth, I didn't know what to do with it. Well, Monica and I have put our heads together and we've come to a decision. We're going into business together. When we get back to Dublin we're setting up a company in –" There were a few muted gasps from around the table. Mollie turned to Monica. "In – what's it called again?"

"Events management."

"Events management," Mollie repeated. "Our company will organise parties and receptions and product launches.

We'll do everything from weddings to retirement parties. We'll organise charity balls and fund-raisers. Monica has great skills in that department. Who was it you had to speak at your last charity lunch, Monica?"

Monica smiled modestly. "Bono."

"You see. Monica has a talent in this area. She knows all these important people. And I thought it was a terrible pity that just because her husband died, she couldn't continue. So I'm going to invest some of my lottery winnings in our new company. It will be called McGinty and Woodworth Happenings."

She sat down and poured a glass of sangria as the table burst into applause. People came to kiss and hug Monica and Mollie.

"That's marvellous," said Trish. "I've no doubt your company will be a huge success."

Mary leaned over and planted a big kiss on her mother's cheek. "It's brilliant," she said. "I'm so proud of you."

Mollie blushed. "I just hope I'll be able for all these celebrities. You know me. I wouldn't say boo to a goose."

"You'd have fooled me," Ned said.

Everybody laughed and Charlie began to fill people's glasses with sangria.

"A toast," he said. "To McGinty and Woodworth Happenings!"

When the toast was drunk, Edward slowly got to his feet. He waited till the excitement had died before starting to speak.

"I've got an announcement too," he said.

People stopped talking.

"I finish my studies in six weeks' time and then I'm emigrating to New Zealand."

The table had fallen silent. All eyes were on Edward.

375

"Since coming to Tenerife, I've been very lucky. I've met a wonderful girl." He reached out and took Bobby's hand. "Bobby has agreed to come with me. I have my visas in order and a contract to work as an agricultural advisor on a farm near Auckland."

Mary glanced across the table and saw the big tears well up in her mother's eyes. She looked totally devastated. Beside her, Ned sat stony-faced.

"But . . ." Edward continued.

Everybody held their breath as they waited for his next words.

"In a year's time, when my contract is completed, I'm coming back to Dunmuckridge to run the family farm and we're going to get married."

"Merciful hour," Mollie croaked.

"By the hokey," Ned gasped.

Mollie grabbed Ned by the shoulders and kissed him. The place erupted in tumult. People were shaking hands with Edward and Bobby and more toasts were being proposed.

Mollie slumped back in her chair, fanning herself with a newspaper. "It was the Stars," she muttered. "The Stars predicted it. Didn't they say there'd be an addition to the family?"

Chapter 44

The gold-embossed invitation card stated simply: *Mollie and Monica invite Trish and Charlie to a party to celebrate the launch of their new company, McGinty and Woodworth Happenings.*

"We'll be killing two birds with one stone," Mollie explained on the phone. "It's also a farewell for Edward and Bobby. They're off to New Zealand next week. You will come, won't you?"

"Of course," Trish replied. "Wouldn't miss it."

"It's really all Monica's work," Mollie continued. "She's invited all these celebrities: that actress woman, Sonia Snodgrass, and the rock and roll singer – you know the one with the bald head and the ring in her nose, who looks like the Bride of Frankenstein?"

"Polly Ester?"

"That's her. Funny name, isn't it?"

"I don't think it's her real name," Trish said. "How many people are coming?"

"Two hundred."

"My God! It must be costing you a fortune."

She could hear Mollie laughing on the line.

"Well, that's the really funny part. We're actually going to *make* money out of it. Monica's charging them €1,000 a head and they're breaking down the doors to get invitations. It's all publicity for them, you see. They get their pictures in the papers."

"Ah," Trish said, impressed by Monica's shrewdness.

"Yes," Mollie continued, "and the television cameras will be there. They're a strange crowd of people. VIPs, Monica calls them. I'm afraid she has me lost."

"VIP. It stands for Very Important Person."

"Oh well, then you must attend," Mollie said. "They don't come more important than you and Charlie."

Trish smiled as she put down the phone. Mollie sounded like an excited child preparing for a birthday party and she was happy for her. What she had done for Monica was exceptionally generous. The company deserved to succeed, and so far, the signs were good. The launch was shaping up to be one of the biggest events of the social calendar. News reports were already appearing in the press, no doubt discreetly leaked by the redoubtable Monica.

Colleen McQueen had run an item in her *On the Piste* column: *HOSTESS WITH MOSTEST BACK ON TRACK WITH EVENT IN TENT.* It referred to the fact that Monica's comeback party was being held in a giant marquee in the grounds of Malahide Castle. It went on to list a dazzling array of actors, politicians, media personalities and showbiz people. Trish couldn't remember a more impressive list since Paul McCartney's wedding.

Since moving in with Charlie, her life had been deliriously happy. He had turned out to be everything she could have wanted – warm, generous, witty, caring, considerate. And marvellous in bed! She wondered where he had learnt the skills. He was the complete opposite of Adrian, who she hadn't seen since their return from Tenerife. A school colleague, who she bumped into on the street one day, said he seemed to be getting more distracted. He had grown a beard and had taken to wearing a black cloak and wide-brimmed hat. There were rumours that he had ditched writing and taken up painting and was parading round town as the next Van Gogh.

"Let's hope he doesn't cut anything off," Trish had said before hurrying away.

She had left everything in the hands of her solicitor and banished Adrian from her mind. All her thoughts were now focussed on her pregnancy. Charlie was forever fussing over her and making sure she had loads of rest and ate the right food so she got all the minerals required.

"You're eating for two, remember," he would say as he ladled spoonfuls of spinach onto her dinner plate. "I want to see you finish that. Spinach is bursting with iron."

He insisted on cooking breakfast and bringing her a cup of tea in bed each morning. And he took no decisions without involving her fully and seeking her advice, which Trish found rather flattering. His latest venture was the new shop in Dunmuckridge. It was Charlie's first project outside of Dublin and he was nervous. But he had done all his research and had located the perfect site in an old warehouse in the centre of the town. He planned to renovate it and install a coffee shop as well as a bookstore. He had also recruited an excellent local manager in the shape of Mary McGinty who had been persuaded to leave the library service and join him.

The last few weeks had been hectic. Apart from Trish's own work, planning the bookshop had involved numerous trips with Charlie to Dunmuckridge. It meant they were thrown closer together with the McGintys. Mollie seemed to be totally fulfilled. The new company was consuming a lot of her time, but she was enjoying every minute of it. But Trish knew the real source of Mollie's contentment did not lie in the new company at all. It lay with Edward and the fact that he had met Bobby and was going to marry her and come back to settle down on the family farm.

The night of the launch arrived. Charlie finished work early and was already having a shower when Trish got home. She could hear Frank Sinatra on the stereo as she opened the front door.

Charlie came hurrying down the stairs in his bathrobe.

"Don't do anything," he commanded. "Just kick off your shoes and sit down. I want your advice about what to wear. Now, what would you like to drink? Tea or wine? I've got a bottle of Chardonnay chilling in the ice bucket."

"A cup of tea would be nice. I suppose there'll be loads of wine later."

"Immediatement."

"I didn't know you spoke French, Charlie."

"Un petit peu," he replied, modestly. "Remember what you told me that afternoon in Puerto de la Cruz? How it was bad manners to visit someone's country and not make an effort with the language. I picked up a phrase book today."

"But you're not going to France, are you?"

"You're quite right. I'm not. *We* are."

"What?"

"Paris. I've booked a weekend. Two weeks' time. As soon as the Dunmuckridge shop is opened. By the way, did I tell you that Monica has offered to organise the launch for us? For free?"

"Oh, Charlie. That's marvellous."

Trish stood up and threw her arms around his neck.

"It might be our last opportunity to get away together," Charlie said, pointing at her waistline.

He had organised a taxi. They sat in the back and watched the scenery rush by as they sped across town to Malahide. When they got to the castle, a security man checked their invitations and directed the cab to a carpark. After that, they had to run the gauntlet of flashing cameras and inquisitive reporters.

A tall, skinny woman with horn-rimmed glasses grabbed them as they went past. "Colleen McQueen from the *Daily Bugle*. Can you tell me who you are?"

"Steven Spielberg," Charlie said for a joke.

"My God. You don't look like Spielberg."

"I'm in disguise. To keep the fans at bay."

"Oh, right. And your partner is?"

"Catherine Zeta Jones."

"My God. How do you know Monica?"

"We met on holiday."

Colleen McQueen started scribbling frantically in her notebook: *MOVIE MOGUL AT MONICA'S MALAHIDE MARQUEE MALLARKEY*.

"Be sure to spell my name correctly. It's S–T–E–V–E–N," Charlie said as they pushed past the baying press pack and into the marquee.

It was an amazing sight. The place thronged with people, chatting in little groups beneath brilliant arc lights. Trish recognised several members of the government, a High Court judge, an international rally driver and a famous dress designer. On a stage, a band was belting out jazz tunes while white-gloved waiters circulated through the crowd with trays of champagne. They took two glasses and set about finding Mollie and company.

They came upon them at the back of the marquee, Mollie resplendent in a red dress with glittering black sequins set off with a string of fake pearls, while Ned had squeezed himself into a dinner jacket and trousers. He kept pulling at his collar as if it was bothering him.

"Had to get away from that band," Mollie said. "Couldn't hear myself think, never mind talk. You're looking great."

"Thank you," Trish said. "You too. Where's Monica?"

"She's talking business with some bigwigs from one of the banks. They want us to organise their next annual meeting."

"Where does she get the energy? This party is fantastic."

"And to think the poor woman was nearly destroyed by that blackguard, Carlos."

Trish's ears pricked up. "Carlos? How do you mean?"

"Oh nothing, nothing. Look, there's Angie over there."

Angie came over to join them. Trish barely recognised her. She'd had her hair cut and was wearing a stunning little cocktail dress that showed a lot of leg.

"Isn't this something else?" she said. "She's managed to rope in such big names. You know Steven Spielberg's supposed to be here. And Catherine Zeta Jones. Somebody just told us. They're in disguise."

"Really?

"Yes. You could be talking to them and you wouldn't know."

Trish glanced guiltily at Charlie.

"Imagine," Charlie said.

Edward and Bobby pushed through the throng, Bobby trailing a dog on a lead.

"This is Cleo," she announced to everyone. "She missed me so much when I was away that I can't bear to let her out of my sight. Isn't that right, darling?"

The dog barked excitedly.

"What are you going to do with her when you go to New Zealand?" Trish asked.

"That's all taken care of. Angie will look after her till we get back. Along with my cats."

"Did you know Mum and Dad are going back to Tenerife in a few weeks?" Edward said.

"No, I didn't," Trish said, surprised.

"We'll be house hunting," Ned said, pulling at his collar.

"You mean . . .?"

"We're going to buy a holiday place," Mollie explained. "When Edward and Bobby get back from New Zealand Ned's going to retire and hand everything over to him."

"Isn't it a hoot?" Mary said, joining the group.

"It's not permanent," Mollie added quickly. "Only for the winter. We'll come back to Dunmuckridge for the rest of the year. I wouldn't want to be too far away from everybody."

"What about the company?"

"Monica can run that. Edward's going to link me up with one of them Internet yokes and I can speak to her whenever I want."

"At least I'll be able to get a decent pint of beer, instead of this awful champagne stuff," Ned said, finally breaking the button on his shirt.

"Now, look what you've done," Mollie scolded. "You'll be making a holy show of us in front of all these film stars."

"Film stars, my big toe," Ned growled.

Through the heaving crowd, they saw Monica come into view, wearing a smart navy suit and white blouse. But a transformation seemed to have taken place. This was a different Monica. She looked cool and totally in command.

"You've done a magnificent job," Charlie said. "I'm very impressed with the party."

"That's very kind of you. Thank you very much." She turned to Mollie. "I've just had a brainwave. I think for our next function we should charge the photographers the same as everyone else."

"Aren't the photographers the reason why all these important people want to be here in the first place?" Trish asked.

Monica smiled. "But the photographers need the celebs as much as the celebs need the photographers. They feed off each other. I think we could get away with charging €500 a skull."

Just then her mobile started to ring. "Excuse me." She turned away and spoke in her polite business voice. "Monica Woodworth."

"It's me," she heard someone say.

"You'll have to speak louder. There's a lot of noise here."

"Me, Carlos. I have been trying to reach you all day."

Monica stiffened. "What do you want?"

"First of all, I wish to apologise for my behaviour. I was under the pressure. I beg you to forgive me."

Monica said nothing. "Since you left, I have been speaking with my father. He has decided that he wants to arrange some entertainments for Hotel Las Flores. He thinks the guests would enjoy it. And of course, I immediately thought of you, Monica. You will come back and run it for us? Perhaps we could resume our little friendship? I would like that very much."

"It's too late," Monica said.

She heard a shocked tone enter his voice. "What do you mean?"

"I mean that I'm no longer interested."

Carlos gave a nervous laugh. "You are playing the hard to get, Monica?"

"No, I'm not. I'm deadly serious.

"But you can't do that. You said you would do it for nothing."

"And you said you could never work with me."

He began to plead. "Please, Monica. Let us at least talk."

"The time for talking is past. You had your chance. *Adios, amigo.*"

She switched off the phone.

"Anything important?" asked Mollie, who had been listening with interest.

Monica shook her head. "Just one of those nuisance calls. I think I'll get my number changed. Now, anyone for more champagne?"

THE END

Direct to your home!

If you enjoyed this book why not visit our website:

www.poolbeg.com

and get another book delivered straight to your home or to a friend's home!

www.poolbeg.com

All orders are despatched within 24 hours.